Waiting for the Train
Gervase M. Flick

DEDICATION

We publish this book in honor of my father, whose curiosity and competitive spirit allowed him the experiences of a lifetime. Gerry was an accomplished professional who always appreciated the extracurriculars with colleagues, friends, and lovers. Although he passed too early, may this book preserve the memory of his journey and the fascinating stories he told.

~~~Elizabeth Flick Twardzik~~~

Acknowledgements:

Thanks to Rebecca Wallace for her cover art and Rick Jacobi for tweaking it to fit. Thank you also to Evelina Kocharov Doroshenko for scanning and correcting all 587 hard copy pages.

Most of all, thank you to those special people who aspire to the noble profession that meant so much to Gerry. Physicians and surgeons set their bars high to help us when we are at our lowest. From his lifelong school friends, Harry Thomas and Jim Woodruff, to all those inspired in spite of many years of difficult studying and spending grueling night shifts at hospitals and are perpetually on call, we thank you.

Waiting for the Train

CONTENTS

Chapter 1
Deadly Fear
November 2, 1958

For a petty criminal, 27-year-old Randy Shook had been worrying a lot lately. This evening he worried even more. His stomach cramped as he nervously sat hunched over the cold steering wheel of his pickup truck while he drove west toward the small village of Essex, Missouri. Randy periodically raised his calloused right hand across his furrowed forehead to wipe off the sweat and then used his dirty fingers to comb his unruly hair back into the style he preferred. The anti-acid he had chewed and swallowed started to calm his stomach but it did nothing to alleviate his anxiety.

Randy's constant worries surprised him. He had never been a worrier before last July, even during the long 44 months he served hard time in the Missouri State Penitentiary in Jefferson City. He had been sentenced to prison for a couple of late-night gas station burglaries in St. Louis. A few incidents were all the state of Missouri could prove at Randy's trial, though law enforcement suspected him of a at least a half-a-dozen more. The jury deliberated for less than two hours before bringing in his guilty verdict. Half of the jury's time had been spent eating their last free meal at the expense of the state. Randy's original sentence had been five years, but he served his time with 16 months off considering his supposedly good behavior.

The ex-con stood only 5'9" tall, but he weighed 187 pounds. His build was stocky and not all muscle. He carried a disproportionate amount of his fat flesh falling over the big, brass buckle of his wide, brown leather belt. After only two years out of the pen, Randy had developed a sizable beer belly. His itinerant fingers kept his dirty blond hair combed back in a duck-tail, the fashion of the era for thugs like him, and considerable grease kept the sides fairly straight. His face flushed from recent alcohol consumption and his cheeks showed chronic pockmarks from acne sores. A wide, pink scar nearly four-inches long ran diagonally from the base of his left ear to the upper corner of his thin-lipped mouth showing as the most striking, notable feature of his face. Randy never had much to smile about, but he quit trying the night he realized how deeply the knife wound had permanently damaged the nerves his face which he needed for any expressive muscle movement on the left side of his face.

Randy attempted to go straight by not committing any property crimes for most of the two probationary years since his release from prison. His motivation had more to do with fearing the danger of another arrest and not his newly founded dedication to honesty. Randy found work on his sister's and her husband's small, rocky farm located nine miles east of Essex and a half mile off the black-topped county road running north from Callao. Randy should have been grateful to them for this honest job at fair wages, a clean bed in the old, dry farmhouse, and three square meals a day. Lesser folk might have made him sleep in the barn. Yet he had resentment for his quiet, older sister and her stern, strong husband. They took on the responsibility for Randy while he worked off his probation in their custody. As dedicated Southern Baptists, they were strict about rules. They worked long hours and they expected him to work the same long hours on the farm, six days a week. He hated the hard work. He took only temporary escape in driving in his old, red 1951 Chevy pickup truck and in drinking beer most evenings in noisy town taverns and crowded country bars. By the end of each working day he felt dirty, tired, and totally uninspired.

Randy knew his honest brother-in-law looked down on ex-cons. Randy also realized his sensitive sister had hoped he would move on as soon as the papers releasing him from probation came through in the mail. At this point, his probation had ended four days earlier and his papers should arrive soon, signed and sealed from the State of Missouri Board of Corrections. Randy agreed moving on would be best for all, and he figured on being long gone from his home state by Thanksgiving. He had been told his release papers would be mailed from the capital, Jefferson City, within a couple of weeks, and he planned to go west to Colorado when he received them. He thought Colorado would be far enough away to leave behind his fear, and then he could scheme up a big enough stake to semi-retire and loaf around for a while.

This weekend would be Randy's first chance to go hunting in over five years. He loved to hunt anything living. Hunting would have to keep him occupied while he waited on the farm for the next three weeks. The surrounding countryside was abundantly inhabited with much wild game. Finally free to be in possession of a rifle or a shotgun, but he could never again legally own a hand gun. He had contemplated getting a revolver, but he was too afraid of being caught with it by the police. Missouri law enforced an automatic five-year return to the state penitentiary for an ex-convict in possession of a hand gun.

True to his sister's promise, she had recently retrieved Randy's Remington 12-gauge, pump shotgun from the farmhouse's attic above her bedroom. She had hidden it there when Randy went to prison and vowed not to give it back until he successfully served his probation. He finally finished his sentence after all those months of backbreaking farm and field work. As soon as his probation papers arrived, he would be free of Missouri. Colorado sure looked good from a distance, and he had great expectations for continuing his reckless life style there.

Randy had spent the last three evenings reveling in cleaning and oiling the shotgun in his small back bedroom of the weather-worn home. Cleaning and polishing his gun made him feel more like a man, giving him a sense of power. Tomorrow his shotgun would loudly roar back to life, spilling death for the first time in six years. He could hardly wait. The thought of the shotgun's loud blast, the bright muzzle flash, the pungent smell of gunpowder, and the memory of its strong concussive impact against his shoulder and chest excited him. That same kind of violent excitement had stimulated him to sexual arousal since his first sexual conquest at age 13 - the rape of a 12-year-old girl. He had always considered sex and violence as two sides of the same coin. Yet for all his fears, Randy had felt safer this evening than he had in a long time. He finally had possession of his old Remington. He could again openly display the gun firmly secured to the rear-window gun rack of his faded, red truck. But even with the security of the gun right beside him, he was still a terribly troubled man. The evening's eerie darkness on the rural road further aggravated his fear. He hoped the late harvest moon would soon shed light on his surroundings if only the cool wind coming down from the north would blow away the low-hanging clouds.

Randy wondered why he worried so much lately as he continued driving west. He didn't like the country road from Atlanta to Essex. Much of the land along either side of the rural road was heavily wooded, and farm houses in the area were spaced far apart. Few offered any beacon of welcoming light in the distance. The lonely stretch of narrow, black-topped road was difficult to drive because of its many rolling hills and frequent, abrupt curves. After crossing to the other side of the Chariton River, the road surface changed to crushed gravel, but the road was much straighter and considerably flatter. Randy had never decided which part of the road was worse to navigate. The gravel portion was full of deep ruts and chuckholes enough to rattle any vehicle. His rusty pickup already sounded like it had suffered a lifetime of rough roads and careless driving.

Randy realized those three rapes within the last four months had caused him the most worry, although the last two he committed in Macon bothered him far less than the first. The short, chubby, dark-haired, 22-year-old woman at the bar had been far too drunk that September night to know who had attacked her. Obviously the tall, thin, 21-year-old blond a month later early in October had been too terrified and too embarrassed to tell anyone. Randy was certain of this. He had seen the blond twice since the attack in a crowded country and western bar outside of Moberly and she never said a word to him. The minute she saw Randy watching her, she slipped away in fear with a scared, pale expression on her pretty face. Randy raped for power and violence and his hatred for women - not because of his need for sex.

No, he finally admitted to himself, the beautiful, teenage girl, the high school basketball player he had raped back in July, had him constantly worried. Vivid pictures of that night were part of the permanent gallery exhibited in his twisted mind.

On that hot, dry July evening, he had just finished delivering a truck full of crushed gravel from the farm to the school's outside track and field arena when he found her alone in the Essex High School gym. Classes were out for summer vacation, but the building was open for the community's use of its athletic facilities. The girl dressed in faded green shorts and tight, white t-shirt accentuating her firm youthful figure. She calmly shot baskets after the rest of the girls had finished their summer evening's practice and had all gone home. Randy realized he and the girl were the only two people left in the entire school. He hid in a back hallway for half an hour until she finished shooting baskets and left the gym. After waiting a few more minutes, Randy crashed into the girls locker room, found her naked in the shower, and savagely raped her on the cold, wet cement floor.

After her first single vain act of crying for help and screaming for him to leave her alone she became quiet. Randy slapped her sharply a few times across her fresh, wet face causing her nose and lip to split and bleed. Then he punched her repeatedly, first hard in her lower chest as she held her arms up to protect her face and breasts and then over the sides of her ribs. He thought he may have cracked a couple of them and expected this to subdue the young woman completely. But instead she bent low and tried to run quickly past him to flee through the open locker room door. The suddenness of her move had surprised him. She was fast and almost escaped his outstretched arms. Her bare feet slipped on the wet floor and she fell to her hands and knees. Randy grabbed her left arm, pulled her up, and punched her hard twice more in the upper and lower abdomen. As she suddenly gasped for breath, he forcefully threw her back on the cement floor. Her tanned calves cramped as her closed thighs tensed and tightened in an instinctively protective reflex. Within seconds Randy had his pants down and stood over the naked girl fully enjoying the fear he saw reflected in her innocent face. Then he was on her, roughly biting the soft pink nipples of her firm breasts. In a final frenzy, he started tearing at her with his rough, dirty hands until he forced himself violently into her. Being a virgin, this excited him even more in his vigorous violation of her warm, wet flesh.

He finished brutalizing her and ejaculated quickly, but the young girl's mood already seemed quite different. Randy sensed all the girl's fear dissipated as it suddenly converted into pure, silent hate. The large pupils of her dark-brown eyes dilated widely staring straight through Randy. Her gaze never wavered making him suddenly the one who was afraid. Her look of abject hatred

7

promised vengeance. Even as he left her in the shower trying to stand up and to wrap a towel around her bleeding and battered body, he dared not turn his back on her until he was well out of the warm, damp locker room. He walked quickly down the empty school hallway. Once outside the building, he ran all the way to his pickup truck parked alongside the athletic field. Almost four months later, he still ran from her. He figured as long as he stayed in Northeast Missouri he would be running scared until he could leave for Colorado.

The marks of violence inflicted by a rapist on his victim's body give clues to the attacker's personality. The shorter and more temporary the relationship, the more violence is inflicted upon a woman who is raped. This is especially true when the expectation of the attacker's sexual arousal is not fulfilled by the gratification of acting out his far-flung fantasies. Such fantasies could have been brewing for merely minutes or for many months. Randy lingered around his last two victims long enough after their rapes to spank and beat them black and blue over the backs of their bare upper legs and buttocks. He had always enjoyed spanking and beating women until his own hands hurt.

But this girl was very different. Her fear had suddenly disappeared, replaced with a palpable hatred. Her hatred combined with disgust and total revulsion prophesied painful retribution. Her hatred hung in the damp air of the locker room like predestined doom. Her hatred scared him then and worried him now. He had not been back to Essex since the night of the attack. But tonight would be different. He had his gun to back him up should the need arise.

The only other time he had seen such hatred on a person's face was in the state prison. A convict lifer had suddenly and silently stabbed his 36-year-old cell mate to death with a handmade

8

shiv and then slashed Randy's face wide open. Neither victim nor violator had spoken during the vicious attack.

Randy knew he had to face the truth. He worried constantly and his apprehension increased because he could not forget the young woman's look of pure, fearless hate. He had never expected his sexual assaults to arouse anything more than fear in a victim. Why would some teenage girl react differently? She bewildered him. He needed to make women afraid of him. Their fear gave him the power he needed to rape them. He needed to commit violence against women to keep the feeling of power over them. But this girl's focused hatred confused and scared him.

He still became nervous whenever he thought about the incident, and lately he thought about it every day and every night. He especially thought about it at night as he frequently drove those lonely backwoods roads on a night like this. He kept having the weird sensation of someone following him from a fairly close distance in an unknown vehicle without its headlights out.

Randy's nervous thoughts were suddenly interrupted by a piercing pair of bright headlights immediately behind him. They had come on unexpectedly behind his truck. He had been paying close attention to the road this time both ahead and behind him but the vehicle came up very fast on his tailgate in the dark with no lights until it was less than 40 feet away. Randy finally knew positively someone had been following him and he had not imagined it.

Randy sped up as fast as he dared on the narrow, winding road, but the vehicle behind him kept a constant short space between them. He slowed to about 15 miles per hour, but the vehicle made no move to pass him. He knew he no longer merely was being followed. Someone stalked him. Randy felt a fear deeply into his spine like a hot spike, radiating spastic sensations all the way up his back. Reaching around with his right hand, he tried to take down the 12-gauge shotgun off the rack behind him so he could place it on the wide seat beside him, but could not get it to come free. Loaded but useless, the gun was chained and locked to the gun rack. The padlock key rattled in the back of his glove compartment on the far right side of the dashboard, but he could not stop to reach for it.

Just then the lights of the vehicle following him dimmed as it came up much closer into his bumper just behind his closed tail gate, and then unmistakably rammed into the back of his pickup truck. The driver following him had taken a dislike to Randy's reaching for the shotgun. As he reached for it a second time, this time the jolt from behind was sufficient enough to whiplash his head backward and forward before the vehicle backed off to about 40 feet behind him again. He thought there was no sense reaching for the weapon any more as he had firmly locked it to the rack, and it would not come free without the key.

Now Randy was really scared. Cold sweat poured down his back and his palms were so moist he could barely keep his grip on the truck's steering wheel. He tried speeding up again, but the vehicle just kept the same distance at about 40 feet behind. He tried slowing down a second time, but the same distance still prevailed between them. Not wanting to get trapped on a smaller side road or a private farm road, Randy kept heading west. He did not plan to stop until he reached the village streets of Essex. Another half mile and he would be over the Chariton River Bridge. The road aimed a lot straighter from there into town. He hope maybe he could still make it, and at least he would be able to drive faster on that section of road.

Then it happened. As Randy veered around a particularly sharp curve and down a slight tree-lined incline, he saw the back of a large tow truck right in front of him, apparently stalled in the middle of the road. He could not drive around it. Neither side of

10

the narrow roadway offered sufficient space to squeeze his pickup truck through. Two orange-red lit fire flares and one set of warning lights were set out on the black-top. He had nearly to stand on his brakes with all the force he could muster, and he skid to a stop five feet from the rear bumper of the big tow truck. His engine stalled and shut itself off before Randy could fully disengage the clutch. He reached to the dashboard with his left hand and turned off the ignition.

The vehicle behind him backed off but then moved back up again slowly until its front bumper just nudged the rear bumper of Randy's pickup. Too frightened to move any further, Randy sat frozen, alternating his gaze in staccato motion from the front windshield before him to his rearview mirror above him.

"Get the hell out of your truck before we drag you out," a voice roared from a face hidden behind a stocking mask appearing at his driver's window. His features were flattened, distorted beneath the tightly knit mask. The stocky, muscular man spoke with a loud, authoritative voice. A stranger to Randy, he had never heard his voice before.

"No way," yelled Randy from behind the closed window. Both doors were locked tightly and both windows were rolled up completely. His legs shook so much he could not have stood up even if he were willing to open the door. Even though it was a cool fall evening, sweat dripped down his face and drenched the collar of his clean gray shirt. "What do you want?" he finally managed to ask in a voice barely audible between tightly-clenched teeth. "Why are you doing this? Leave me alone."

Just then the biggest clenched fist he had ever seen encased in a rough leather glove smashed through the passenger window of the cab of Randy's pickup. A massive arm in a denim jacket followed it, quickly reached through the shattered glass and swiftly unlocked the passenger's door of the truck. The owner of the

11

massive fist and arm said nothing as he did his work. This huge arm needed no verbal emphasis to ensure complete compliance with his companion's previously expressed order.

The arm dragged Randy unceremoniously from his vehicle and threw him onto the cold, hard pavement of the road. He hand-cuffed and leg-ironed Randy, gagged him with a cloth, blindfolded him with sticky black electrician's tape, and roughly heaved him into the back flatbed of Randy's own pickup truck. Both abductors wore stocking masks to disguise their identity, but Randy thought he recognized the larger man. Randy had never been this close to the giant before, though he thought he had seen him once before. There was only one man in the county that big. Suddenly Randy could feel the warmth of his own urine and possibly even more running freely down the inside of his pant legs. Finally the smell of his own fear hung in the cool night air. The odor of excitement and excrement mixed when his deodorant finally failed him at this crisis-filled crossroad of his life.

"Get his shotgun from the window. It's locked to the rack. Look for the key in the glove compartment, he fumbled in that direction while we were behind him," said the smaller, stocky man loudly with little effort to mask his voice or its volume.

Within seconds the larger man found the key, unchained the shotgun, grabbed it, and placed it in the cab of the large tow truck. He then took a new box of shotgun shells from the glove compartment of Randy's pickup and stuck the entire box in the pocket of his jean jacket. For so large a man, he moved very fast, his rapid motions uninterrupted by any speech or sound.

Three minutes later, the two men had Randy's pickup truck hooked up to the back of the tow truck. The men worked in silence with the precision of well-planned intent. Soon the two attached vehicles headed west again at a slow but steady speed.

The smaller, stocky man got back into his own Ford pickup. The stranger took off his stocking mask and carefully turned around his small truck. Quickly heading east, he did not stop driving for nearly three miles. Here he came to two wooden barricade horses and two flame-lit road lanterns and a large sign he had previously placed at a junction in the road when he saw Randy's truck pass through the intersection 13 minutes earlier. The black and orange sign read, '*BRIDGE OUT - DETOUR - NORTH MISSOURI HIGHWAY DEPARTMENT.*' Jumping out of his pickup truck after parking it in the weeds beside the road, the man carefully picked up the sign, the barricade horses and the lights, and carefully placed them all in the back of his truck. He took a few extra seconds to extinguish the flames at the top of the lanterns and pour out their remaining kerosene alongside the pavement. Then he returned to the driver's seat, and after a full U-turn, he headed back west as fast as he could safely drive. No other vehicles were in sight.

Half-a-mile west of the abduction point, the bigger man slowed the tow truck to a full stop at a similarly barricaded junction. The large man moved quite quickly once again. In less than a minute, this set of wooden barricades and the big sign leaning against them were all quickly gathered and unceremoniously thrown into the back of Randy's pickup, still attached in tow. Next, the two kerosene lanterns were carefully extinguished, capped and placed in a large tool box attached to the right side of the tow truck. After checking to see all the evidence of the temporary detour had been removed, the driver climbed back into his truck's cab, started the engine, and shifted into first gear, continuing to tow Randy's pickup.

Randy had become much more than merely scared. He was now petrified. Multiple areas of his head and body also hurt severely until unconsciousness gave him temporary relief. He lay with his face flattened onto the hard metal floor of his own truck bed. His head smashed against the bare metal with each solid bump and deep rut in the rough road. His nose seeped blood and his forehead and cheeks swelled from large contusions. He tried to hold his head off the floor in a positive, forced extension, but with his hands tightly cuffed behind him, this effort became difficult and exhausting. When the big man stopped to throw the wooden barricades into Randy's truck, one struck him on his shoulders and neck, while the other ended up lying across both his legs, which were chained together just above his low-laced, leather boots. This made meaningful motion impossible. When the big man threw the heavy metal detour sign into the back of the pickup, its flat surface struck Randy on the back of his head and rendered him unconscious for the rest of the road trip. With each frequent bump and road rut, his face continued to smash against the cold, hard steel of the pickup truck floor bed, but he no longer felt the pain.

Randy awoke suddenly with a splitting headache and the smell of fresh horse manure in his nostrils. He had no idea how long he had been unconscious. He was dazed and confused. In a few seconds he finally realized he was draped upside down over the back of a large, snorting horse, which pawed the hard ground in hopes of finding some overlooked grass. Randy still had handcuffs and leg irons firmly in place. The bent backs of his thighs stretched his hamstrings as tightly as guide wires.

The thick, black blindfold tape, however, had loosened a little due to his sweating and the swelling of his face. Turning his head back and forth allowed him to rub more tape free. He could see the two men conversing in low voices in the bright moonlight. The low-lying clouds had cleared. Now neither abductor wore a mask and Randy knew this was a very bad sign. Obviously now that they had him off the roadway, they no longer cared if he knew what their faces looked like. They stood about 15 feet to his left, outside the rail-fenced paddock of some farm or ranch. The open gate beckoned and the full moon shined high enough in the night sky to shed plenty of light. Both abductors wore holstered revolvers and full cartridge belts. The smaller man also had a sheathed Bowie knife almost a foot long and two canteens attached to a second belt worn just below the ammunition belt.

"I'll tow his truck a ways back towards Cramden Swamp," said the larger man in a deep voice. He leaned over to spit a sizable stream of tobacco juice. "Best they start looking for this punk down in that area."

"Good idea. That's about 19 to 20 miles south of here if I recollect right," answered his shorter companion. "That way any search will be concentrated around there for a while. We wouldn't want anybody finding him too soon."

"Doubt they will where you're taking him," said the larger man.

"What about the broken passenger-side window? Think somebody will question it?"

"No. It won't be a problem. By the time a search party finds his truck it will seem reasonable someone would have first found it locked and have broken into it to steal something. I'll tear out the dashboard radio to make it look good."

"I think that would add a nice touch," replied the smaller stranger.

"Do you need any more help here?" asked the big man. He held the pack horse's lead rope in one huge hand and Randy's shotgun in the other.

"Not really. You've helped me enough in this evening's venture. The final chapter of this punk's criminal life now belongs to me."

"I've already put his box of shells in your saddle bag and his gun is fully loaded. He apparently kept it loaded in the truck even when he was driving."

"Both my horses know the way, so this part will be easy," replied the shorter man as he mounted up. "Hand me his shotgun." He placed the gun in an empty rifle scabbard attached to the right side of his saddle. Then he picked up the reins of his own horse in his left hand. He took the reins of the pack horse on which Randy was draped and tied in his right hand and started the horses slowly heading toward the wooded hills to the north. "Leave now and get rid of his truck," he yelled back over his shoulder. "Oh, by the way, don't forget tomorrow night's basketball game. Essex High will be playing Callao on our girls' home court. We should beat them even easier than we did before."

"Wouldn't miss it for anything," shouted the big man as he closed the paddock gate. "See you there tomorrow."

If only I could talk, thought Randy. He finally realized his abduction had something to do with the beautiful teenage basketball player he had raped in July. It made him feel even more frightened, gutless, and guilty. If only he could talk, he could explain his way out of this. But Randy did not even know who was this man, a complete stranger to him.

Looking back from the quarter horse mare he rode, the stocky man noticed Randy had finally rubbed the blindfold tape free from his swollen, bleeding face. Randy moaned loudly beneath the gag but no words were audible in the cool night air. Only the steady plodding of the two horses' hooves on the hard ground could be heard. The stranger listened for a while with a calm half-smile indicating feelings ranging from satisfaction to boredom.

"It's okay if you want to look around now, Randy. There's a full moon tonight and you can see a lot of nice countryside. We have about a two-hour ride ahead of us before I try out your shotgun. With a little luck you may last until the morning sunrise."

Randy's worst fears were confirmed. His muffled screams of terror were carried on the wind as he finally realized the full intentions of the stranger.

"Enjoy the moonlight and scenery, and stop complaining about circumstances you can't control. Your miserable life is almost over. This is the last evening you'll ever see any of this. You're a dead man come sun-up, and I'm not going to remove the gag just to hear you bitch about it all night."

Chapter 2
Scattered Bones
June 2, 1959

"We sure 'nough got ourselves a right nice mess of rabbits down here on your bottom land, Gus. It's hard for me to believe the huntin' would be one bit better up on that hilly back 40 acres you've got posted. You sure you want to start climbin' up there this late in the afternoon? That is one long, steady pull and these old legs of mine aren't as young as they used to be," Jim Jam said.

"Damn right I do, Jim," Gus promptly replied as he turned to gaze at his tired friend with a look of feigned exasperation. "Scrawny spring rabbits are hardly worth skinning and stewing as it is, but if we don't thin out their numbers a bit now, they will be into my good crops all summer long."

"Yeah, I suppose you're right," the younger man replied.

"You know I am, so stop your complaining. We're going up there now unless you're too tired to keep up with me. None of us are as young as we used to be. But we ought to be able to make our bodies act like they did in years long-gone for at least an afternoon of hunting."

"You really mean to do it, don't you, Gus?" answered Jim in quiet resignation. He took a couple of deep breaths as he hesitated a few seconds before starting forward again.

"Why wouldn't I?" replied Gus who, at age 53, was 11 years older than Jim but in far better shape from the demands of daily physical exertion needed to operate a farm of this appreciable size. "The hills aren't steep enough to sweat over and the land is already drying out fast from last night's thunderstorm. We have a good warm sun on our backs and a gentle cool breeze in our face. What more could any dedicated bunny hunter want?"

"Guess I'm just ungrateful of our luck, Gus."

"Not really Jim. Sometimes I think you just like to complain. It's like you think bitching is an important and necessary part of good hunting."

"Well Gus," replied his tall, lean, middle-aged hunting companion of many seasons, "you've been so frightfully careful about postin' that section of your property and keepin' all hunters out of that parcel of your land for the last few months, I figured you must have found a healthy sized herd of deer up there."

"I did early last fall, Jim. That's why I posted it. Damned if I want a bunch of city folks from St. Louis up on my high ground during hunting season, shootin' everything that moves. They might even shoot each other, or worse yet, one of my wilder whiteface steers."

"Yeah, you're probably right about that, especially since you let your cattle range all over the place in late fall and winter."

"Remember how Carl Winston lost a good Hereford heifer shot to death last fall right in his own back pasture? Some city dummy with a 30-30 Winchester thought the Hereford was a deer, jumped out of his car and nailed the poor animal right from the road. The damn fool probably would have tied it on to his car if he could've lifted it."

Coming to a sharp, three-strand, barbed wire fence, the men stopped their ascent and stopped their talking. The most dangerous part of hunting was crossing fences. Jim took both of their rifles in his hands, checked each one individually to make sure it had its safety on, and then carefully held them with their barrels pointing down toward the ground. His friend and brother-in-law, Gus, stepped forward and meticulously separated the mid and upper strands of sharp steel barbs. Then he stepped through them to the other side. With correctness of motion and conscientious attention to gun safety, Jim handed Gus both rifles. As Gus stepped back carefully from his side of the fence, Jim stooped and made his way between the same two strands of wire. Only then did Gus hand Jim back his gun.

"You know Gus, for as smart as he is, old Carl never would have known who killed his Hereford if the damn fool hunter hadn't been so excited when he jumped from his car. He left the car in gear, and it ran off the road into the deep drainage ditch running alongside the pasture. Since Violet and Carl's farmhouse was the nearest one around, the city boy actually went up to Carl's front door and asked him to please pull his Pontiac out of the ditch with a tractor. City people really have a lot of nerve."

"Knowing Carl like I do, I'll bet that was an expensive tow job," replied Gus. Just then, they flushed a rabbit out of a clump of high weeds to the right of Gus. With one continuous motion, he raised his .22-caliber rifle, quickly sighted down the barrel, and fired once. Gus needed only one shot with the fine, semi-automatic weapon. The rabbit moved so fast even in death, it continued tumbling forward for another three or four feet before stopping. As Gus walked forward to pick up the animal, he heard Jim's gun fire twice off to his left. "Hope you shot two bunnies and not just one you missed the first time," Gus shouted good-naturedly.

"I hit two all right," replied Jim triumphantly with a wide grin on his thin, flushed face, "and I got 'em both." Within 30 seconds, he had retrieved both dead animals and added them to the game bag tied to the back of his belt.

"How much did Carl charge the fellow to tow out his car?" asked Gus. "You seem to know more of the details of the story than I do. I'll bet it was at least 20 bucks."

"It was more than that. He charged $25 for the tow and full price on the Hereford, just as if it were slaughtered, dressed, and wrapped for market." The men said little for a while and each man, with deadly accuracy, shot another rabbit before Jim continued the conversation. "So tell me, Gus, are you saving that posted land for your own private huntin' preserve next fall? I know you're not a selfish man, but are you generous 'nough to let your poor brother-in-law go up there and hunt on it with you? Come every November, your sister and I do get a cravin' for venison."

"I think so," Gus replied in a quieter voice than their previous conversation. "Yeah, I think so," he repeated as if deeply in thought. Gustav had a ruddy complexion, and a muscular build for a 53-year old widower who farmed the extensive, well-kept Missouri farm on which the men were hunting. He owned it all free and clear.

"So, we really are headin' up to your sacred high ground?" asked Jim. He resigned himself to the task but still complained. "Looks to me like there's still plenty of rabbits to shoot down here on this lower patch. Shouldn't we be stayin' on down here takin' care of this problem first?"

"No Jim. I need to thin them throughout the farm. These damn bunnies have become even more than a nuisance. They've finally become a menace. They're doing me in by eating everything in sight. But remember, be sure and don't shoot any spring deer you may see up there or you'll have the state game wardens all over us like fleas on a coon dog. Now let's get moving faster. We only have about two hours of good daylight left before the sun drops behind those western hills."

Leaving their brown burlap bags of killed rabbits loosely tied to a low limb of the lone oak tree standing in the meadow, the two men started the steady climb up into the higher levels of the large farm. Hunting spring rabbits with rifles is not easy. It takes a good eye, a well-sighted weapon, and fast arm and hand coordination. Both men had hunted for years and frequently hunted together. Neither man considered using a shotgun for rabbits. That kind of so-called sport was for city folks, not for real country hunters.

After an hour-and-a-half more and 15 rabbits later, the men had finally cleared a steeply sloping hillside field. Then they started into a well-wooded brush line running straight across the hill. The shadows before them lengthened fast as the sun settled in the west behind them.

"Want to rest for a while?" Jim yelled to Gus who was about 50 yards to his right and slightly ahead of him.

"Not now," answered Gus. "We only have about a half hour of decent light left. Let's make good use of it. Keep to the right side of the big gray rock on your left so we don't lose track of one another. This old wooded area gets pretty dense darn fast in here. We sure don't want to end up shooting at each other."

"No problem," Jim replied as he slowly started into the young growth of pine and birch trees interspersed among the older oak and maple hardwoods. The overhead shadows of their green needled bows and leafy branches dimmed his vision. He stopped and stood still to let his eyes accommodate to the diminished light. He was about 35 feet inside the tree line as he rested. A large rabbit moved

21

suddenly, slightly to his left as it made a quick dash toward a burrow in deeper brush. Immediately Jim raised his gun and fired. But this time the bunny was far too fast for the hunter. Jim's bullet had missed. The animal made it home safely, but scared.

The hunter stood transfixed for a few seconds, still sighting along the warm steel barrel of the rifle. Then he saw the torn, stained clothing, rotting away on what was left of a decomposing body only about 15 feet away from him, but somewhat hidden in the deeper brush. Jim approached it slowly, but could not permit himself to point his gun away until he was only five feet from the corpse.

The form lay on its back with deep, long-vacant, sun-bleached eye sockets staring up towards the sky through the tree tops. A rusty 12-gauge shotgun lay close by the body. Most of the left arm and all of the right hand were missing, having been carried away and eaten by wild animals. Lynx cats and a rare bear had on occasion been sighted in that part of the county. Laced, low leather boots were still loosely attached to the remaining left side of the lower extremities, but the corpse's right leg had been disarticulated at the hip joint. The leg had been pulled from the left of the pelvis and separated from the rest of the skeletal remains by three feet of bare ground.

Jim wanted to scream but was stunned into silence. He felt like he might become sick and did start vomiting. Though he worked at a local rendering plant and was around dead animals all day, he had not seen a dead person outside of an undertaker's parlor since his days as a navy gunner in the Pacific Theater. He had been on a destroyer in battles of the World War II, 15 years earlier. Looking away, he slowly swallowed hard two or three times. He did not want his macho friend to see him vomit. Jim thought Gus wouldn't understand the response to a corpse even though he was a sensitive person and a good friend. Jim also knew Gus would never kid him or mention to anyone that the sight of the body had made Jim sick.

Finally Jim found his voice as he calmed his nausea. "Better come over here now Gustav," he called out forcefully. Then he put his rifle's safety catch on and carefully leaned the gun against the fork of a split trunk birch tree pointing in the opposite direction of the corpse.

"What's up?" his friend questioned as he answered back loudly from no more than 40 yards away through the woods. "Did you just kill a bear with that last shot?"

"Not exactly," replied Jim.

"Well don't shoot this way. Safety your gun for now. I'm coming in on your right."

"Looks like you had some hunter up here poachin' last year regardless of all those damn signs you put up, Gus. I'll bet you never even suspected it. This goes to show how much good postin' one's property does. Some hunters just ignore those notice signs and even ignore the proper season dates."

"Sure looks like this one did," Gus replied. He approached the body and knelt on one knee beside it for a closer look.

"Not much left," Jim exclaimed. He finally drew closer to the skeletal remains. "I wonder who it is?"

"Or more properly who it was," Gus replied.

"Well, we'll sure 'nuff need the Sheriff and the Macon County Coroner on this. Looks to me like a self-inflicted shotgun death. But the authorities will want to make sure. They'll need to know for their records."

"You're right," said Gus. His forehead wrinkled in serious contemplation of the scene.

"Should we call Sergeant Siegfried of the Highway Patrol first? He's probably the closest to here. Not that any delay is goin' to much matter to this guy."

"Good idea," replied Gus after a few seconds thought. "Let him contact the Sheriff. Then they can decide how to handle it between themselves and their departments. Though this happened on my land, I sure don't need to get caught up in any state or county bureaucratic entanglements."

The large blood stain on what was left of the upper portion of the decedent's pants had faded from the climate of intermittent moisture and bright sunlight. But it was obvious to both men the life once traveling within the weather-worn, bony skeleton lying before them on the ground had been terminated by a sudden shotgun blast to his groin and pelvis.

Jim had cold chills running up and down his spine. Judging from the condition of the body and the clothes, it sure looked like the remains of a man who had died after his balls were shot off. He quickly sat down on a nearby rock and bent his head forward to keep from fainting. "Thank God the fresh smell of death and the lingering odor of decomposition and decay had long since evaporated from this gruesome scene," he said to Gus.

"Well," said Gus, "from what is left, I'm not sure if the local authorities will ever know exactly how or why this man died."

"So then what happens?"

"They probably have to call in the coroner from north of here in Adair County. I understand she's a pathologist with the medical school up there."

"You mean the coroner is a woman?"

"Yeah, and they call her a medical examiner. But I do know one thing about these high-ground woods, and I don't need a pathologist to tell me."

"What's that?" Jim asked, though he was not sure he wanted to know. He had seen enough for one day. He would never understand how any woman, even if she were a doctor, could look at corpses like this for a living.

"Lynx cats. They're back in the area again. They're ranging on my farm and this proves it. You can tell it was a lynx by the way the big leg bone is torn away from the rest of the body. That took a big animal of some real strength."

"It could have been a bear. But who cares at this late date? This guy must have been long since dead by then," Jim volunteered. Let the coroner figure it all out. Let's leave here now before it gets dark."

"No, it was definitely not a bear," Gus said. He looked around cautiously and careful not to disturb the scene. "A bear of any appreciable size would have bitten right through the bones. It would have smashed in the entire rib cage and carried off most of the carcass. We wouldn't be seeing this much left of the body. This guy must have been up here awhile, probably since last fall's hunting season."

"I wonder what he was huntin'?" Jim asked. He picked up his rifle and prepared to head down the hill.

"Apparently he was hunting himself," Gus replied as he followed his friend. "Anyway, it sure enough shows one thing...."

"What's that, Gus?"

"Inside each and every one of us there's a skeleton just dying get out."

"I think this one made it out a little earlier than its owner had planned."

Chapter 3
First Patient
December 1, 1961

Doctor Gerry Frank and Doctor Harry Thompson elected to do a rural clinic externship for the final six months of their fourth and final year of medical school. Conducted in 12 clinics of various sizes in individual villages throughout rural Northeastern Missouri, the training provided medical care to residents within the 100 mile radius of the small city campus of a nationally known medical school and its three, affiliated teaching hospitals.

The student doctors, Gerry and Harry, formed a temporary partnership and were assigned to one of the clinic's afternoon sequence of Monday, Wednesday, and Friday. Another pair of externs were assigned to the Tuesday, Thursday, Saturday sequence in the same rural clinic. In the course of their country clinic afternoons, each set of senior medical students had the complete responsibility for the health care needs of the people in the small village and the rural area surrounding it. Mornings and days off from the clinics, the medical students attended lectures and classes at the medical school, and seminars and rounds seeing patients at the school's prestigious teaching hospitals.

Every afternoon at a clinic, three supervising hospital staff physicians would visit four of the village clinics to consult with the novice physicians. The staff doctors generally stayed for an hour to advise on cases when necessary or requested. Other than medical advice offered by those staff members, the student physicians were completely on their own. This new, awesome medical responsibility excited and challenged the unseasoned doctors.

The program purposefully motivated the young medical students through early clinical experiences in actual family and community medical problems towards active careers in general practice. Well known in academic circles, the medical school steered the high number of over 75 percent of its graduates to enter general practice or rural medicine. Most other medical colleges in the 1960s concentrated on producing physicians who would be content only in medical specialties. This extensive, innovative rural clinic program in Missouri was the first of its kind in the United States. Many programs similar in nature would follow in later years.

Dr. Gerry Frank and his partner, Dr. Harry Thompson, were assigned to the rural clinic in the small village of Essex, Missouri. Located 53 miles southwest of the medical school's campus, the overall population of Essex peaked at nearly 550 people within its immediate boundaries. The village's drawing area consisted of an additional population of almost 1,300 more.

As viewed from the old, red-brick buildings lining Main Street, in long-past days the isolated town's permanent population of self sufficient citizens obviously had numbered more than 3,000. Among the still standing, silent buildings included two long-abandoned banks once holding brisk business in the gold and silver rush days. But now the town had no functioning bank of its own. The many paper mortgages on most of the prominent businesses and farms were held by large lending institutions in far away cities. Over half of the red-brick buildings were completely deserted. Parts of the village gave the appearance of a ghost town. A few sturdy oaks, many tall elms, and an occasional red maple tree bordering Main Street seemingly sighed in remembrance of better days as late fall settled in and westerly winds rustled their bare branches. The only leaves still remaining were those scattered on the hard earth and the occasional branch with leaves fully clinging to the oaks.

The small town had been a major livestock shipping depot back in its wild, earlier days. Big cattle drives came north from Texas over the old Chisolm Trail to Sedalia, Missouri, and other towns along the railway line headed east. After the railroads had extended farther west, the importance of these towns declined as major shipping locations and rail heads. Essex had reached its economic and social apex long before 1900 and probably would never scale such heights of importance again. Since that time, the town had settled into the comfortable lifestyle of rural Missouri. Be it ever so humble, it was still home to the people who lived within its boundaries and the area of its influence.

Only two streets were paved in the village and each one was six blocks long, crossing perpendicularly at the center of town. The rest of the major roads were constructed of packed-gray gravel. They were well drained and sufficiently useful most of the year. The barren reddish-brown, dirt side-roads were another story. After heavy spring rains or melting winter snows, they turned to pathways of a thick, sticky mud of gumbo-like consistency.

Main Street, the paved east-west roadway in the center of town, was fairly level and fronted one general store, a yarn and sewing supply shop, two feed stores, a second-hand furniture store, the local pool hall, a one-chair barber shop, two restaurants, two gas stations, the small U.S. Post Office adorned with a large American flag, three bars, three churches, half-a-dozen stray mongrel dogs, the local auctioneer's office, and the rural medical clinic office. These businesses were located in a scattered kaleidoscopic blend with some housed in buildings originally built for other purposes, long since forgotten. Many of the still firm foundations and the outside walls of several buildings were well over 130 years old.

The paved north-south Station Street, ran downhill from a new grammar school and the old high school, both situated overlooking the village on the north end, and it continued through town to the railroad depot located two blocks south of Main Street. There the tracks ran along the fairly flat floor of the valley. Station Street fronted more homes than businesses, but it included a used clothing store, a small beauty shop connected to the owner's home, a combination welding and harness shop, another feed store, a movie theater open only on Saturday nights, and a small combination real estate and insurance office open for business only Tuesday afternoons.

The medical clinic shared the faded, red-brick village hall with the town's volunteer fire department. The fire department's equipment consisted of a single, maroon-red, well-used but still active, 1929 LaSalle fire engine, housed in the eastern third of the building. A community room for town meetings and social functions occupied the middle third of the structure.

The clinic took up the remaining western third of the building and was petitioned to maintain its privacy from the fire department and the community room right next to it. The medical clinic portion of the one-story, corner building consisted of two examining rooms with sinks producing only cold running water and a warm waiting room heated by a pot-bellied, wood-burning stove. The clinic had no indoor flush toilet, and patients were directed to the only close facility - a one-seat, painted green outdoor privy located 45 feet behind the village hall beside a big, healthy, old oak tree.

Gerry Frank and Harry Thompson started their six-month rural clinic rotation in Essex on Friday, the first day of December - a sunny, crisp and cool, late-fall day, and a perfectly beautiful day to start medical careers as country doctors. The countryside was typical of Northeast Missouri. Surrounding Essex were a variety of rolling fields, gentle hills, peaceful pastures, fertile valleys, scattered forests, and slow running streams. The setting was filled with life where death would be difficult for the uninitiated to contemplate.

The first day's schedule included house calls to six outlying farms around the village. Harry appointed himself to this traditional task. He had worked on family farms during much of his youth in West Virginia. He knew how to communicate in farm-talk - from livestock, barn building, crops in the field, and pork bellies and grain futures on the Chicago Commodity Exchange.

Gerry stayed back in the clinic working on storing new medical supplies and going over the written clinical records of the patients scheduled for appointments. He and his partner would be seeing these patients throughout the first week of their medical career.

The long afternoon stretched before him like an interesting and unknown slowly unfolding mystery. Gerry wondered who would be the very first patient of his medical career. He imagined it would be an unfortunate person with a heretofore undiagnosed disease or a well-known world celebrity searching rural America for a caring and industrious doctor. Well, whomever it would be, he was ready. Of course, his first patient did not fall into either of those glamorous categories.

That person would be the unlucky loser of a bloody confrontation between farmer and farm machine. The farmer was 55-year-old Gustav Olsen. The farm machine was Gustav's newly purchased, but used, seven-year-old Massey Ferguson corn picker.

Each year, Gustav planted 58 acres of corn in his choicest bottom land. He took great pride in running a modern, mechanized, and diversified farm, managed as well as any operated in the county. His family farm was financially more than moderately successful. Gustav owed his success to his unrelenting love for the land, his skillful hard work, and the well-maintained machinery he owned and operated. He frequently bought used equipment at local farm auctions during the off season after yearly harvests. With his superior mechanical ability he would then return the worn machinery to like-new working condition before the next year's planting, cultivation, and harvest season. Gustav could never sit idly for very long.

Gustav had purchased the broken Massey-Ferguson corn harvester for a bargain price at Macon's town auction in November. The seven-year-old corn picker sat as a squat 4'9" tall, painted red with rust spots throughout, and weighed about 360 pounds. Gustav stood 5'10" tall, had a ruddy, caucasian complexion, and weighed in at a muscular 188 pounds.

Farmer Olsen would be attempting to replace the broken parts and to rebuild the rugged machine. Initially the job proved to be easier than he had thought it would be when he took the harvester apart and bought the new replacement parts earlier in the week. Gustav had the machine reassembled by mid morning. By late morning, he had it cranked up and running. Unfortunately, the farmer's destiny would be to come in a poor second in a final confrontation. By early afternoon his left forearm, wrist, and hand had become tightly caught between colossal clamping pieces of sharp, moving metal. The outcome of the contest settled fast and was nowhere near close between them. In fluids lost, incredibly more red human blood than black machine oil quickly pooled in a mixture on the hardwood floor of Olsen's large tool shed. Gustav knew instantly the freely flowing blood soaking deeply into the well-worn, wood floor would leave a vicious stain for years to come. However, at the moment, he could not be sure he would be around long enough to see or to appreciate the marks permanently left behind by the blood and the oil.

Gustav immediately managed to cut off the power to the machinery with his free right hand, but he knew the accident meant big trouble for him. At that hour of the day no one else worked on or near his farm to come to his assistance. The only living creatures for approximately two square miles were his animals. No human help would be forthcoming. Olsen, a widower, knew his only child, a college-aged daughter who lived with him on the farm, would not arrive home from school for at least three hours. He realized if he stayed there and waited for her assistance he would bleed to death. His daughter would come home to find her dad's cold corpse. Then there would be no need for her to cook him supper. He felt it strange to be thinking of food at a time like this.

Under conditions of excruciating pain and physical difficulty, Gustav finally extricated the torn tissue and mangled remains of his unfortunate hand and arm from the machinery. His blood splattered nearly everywhere inside the mechanism of the bulky farm implement. However, he put this particular misfortune to good use as the wet blood helped him to extricate his arm by lubricating the tight metal surfaces holding him prisoner. Clearing his injured left arm from the gnashing jaws of the machinery, Gustav worked to stop the hemorrhage. He grabbed a relatively clean, short length of rope from a nail hammered on the shed's inner wall and tied it tightly just below his elbow in a tourniquet with his teeth and his good right hand. Then using the cleanest empty feed bag he could find, he quickly wrapped up the exposed portions of his badly injured and bleeding hand and wrist.

Fast feeling faint, Gustav sat down for a moment's rest at his big work bench in the corner of the tool shed. He bent over far forward to encourage his heart to more easily pump the blood he had left to his brain. This helped, but Gustav still feared he would soon pass out. He knew he needed to replenish his body fluids and he must remain conscious. He remembered the thermos bottle he brought in with him early that morning still contained more than two cups of well-sweetened, warm black coffee. The large blue thermos sat on a waist-high shelf 14 feet on the other side of the room. Gustav forced himself to crawl across the cold wooden floor and finally reached up from his knees to grab the thermos. After sitting back down on the floor with his back against the wall, he drank all the remaining coffee, gradually feeling less faint. After a few more minutes rest, he felt strong enough to try to make it to his truck outside.

Gustav had parked his dark-green Ford pickup close by, next to the farm's big red barn. Luckily, the keys were in the ignition as usual. Gustav carefully climbed into the truck and started it with his remaining good hand. He slowly eased the vehicle out of the hard-dirt farmyard and onto the curved farm road. Next came the fairly straight distance of gravel county road into town. He gradually accelerated the truck as he raced toward the Essex Rural Clinic.

The small medical facility was about five-and-a-half miles away to the northwest of the Olsen farm. In the remaining distance, he traveled over another narrow county road crossing many hills and taking a few right-angle curves. Olsen made the trip in just under eight minutes, the fastest he had ever driven those rural roads in his life. He hoped as he sped toward the village he would never have to take those roads that fast again. More so, he hoped it would not be his last trip to town.

Even with the severe loss of blood diminishing the normal functions of his brain, Gustav still remained alert. He knew he was severely hurt and he realized he had lost a lot of blood before tightly tying the tourniquet around his left forearm. He knew he would be in far worse trouble if none of the new doctors were at the clinic.

On this, the first day of December, the entire population of Essex knew the first days of June and of December were the two days of each year when the small country clinic received its transfer of new doctors for their six-month rotations. Thus, though the paths of extern Gerry Frank and farmer Gustav Olsen had never crossed before, Olsen realized his life, or at least the use of his left hand, depended on the outcome of this fateful meeting with a brand-new physician.

Dr. Frank heard the unmistakable solitary sound of a truck racing loudly up to the small red-brick medical building, the only discernible noise in the village. The vehicle had still sounded in second gear as it emitted the distinctively distressed sounds of forced acceleration all the way from the county road's left turn onto Main Street two blocks away. The screeching brakes abruptly stopped the pickup as it pulled up to the clinic's front office. Gerry wondered if anybody ever moved that fast in this small Missouri village unless there was an emergency.

Gerry hurried from the inner examination room into the outer reception room. Just then, Olsen weakly staggered through the unlocked front entrance clutching his bleeding left arm and injured hand tightly to his chest. His usually rosy, rugged complexion looked ancient and deathly pale. The deep smile lines etched in his weather-beaten face involuntarily contorted in a gruff grimace from his persistent intractable pain. Dark, damp blood soaked his heavy gray-wool work shirt and his faded denim jeans. The blood ran down Olsen's pant legs into his laced black leather boots, soaking his white wool socks. He squished as he walked. Squishing in one's own blood is always disconcerting, even to a brave country man.

With no time for formal or fancy introductions, the young extern did not have to be near the top of his medical school class to realize this patient was seriously hurt.

"What happened?" Dr. Frank asked firmly with concern and worry reflected in his voice. He reached out to steady the injured farmer. For a second Gerry thought the man would crumple into a bloody lump right there on the floor of the reception room. The farmer's gray face showed small, wet beads of perspiration breaking out on his forehead and upper lip.

"Corn picker," grunted Olsen through clenched teeth as he felt increasingly faint from standing. The bleeding farmer leaned against the young physician as they struggled together into the nearest of the two examination rooms, a small white room set up for minor surgery. *Thank God the doctor is here*, kept running through Gustav's mind. *Now everything will be okay. This doctor will save me, for sure. I know he will.*

Dr. Frank helped Olsen onto the long, green leather-covered examination table. He cut off the farmer's soiled work shirt with a pair of shovel nosed, stainless steel bandage scissors. The doctor let Olsen's outer shirt heavy with grease, dirt, and blood slip freely to the floor. The doctor also removed the patient's formerly white t-shirt undergarment, now saturated red with blood, by cutting up the short sleeved left arm and through the blood-stained cloth across the patient's cold, pale shoulder. Blood had seeped through the shirt to the patient's bare skin.

Though still short of breath, the farmer's color began to improve the moment he lay flat on the table. Gerry switched on the small, green, size 'E' oxygen tank stored in the heavy metal stand in a corner close by. He put the oxygen mask loosely over Gustav's nose and mouth and then turned the valve up to five liters per minute. Words were unnecessary as each man instinctively knew what to do. Gustav breathed deeply and slowly into the mask. In less than three minutes his respiration reduced down to a more normal rate of about 16 per minute.

The doctor elected to wait before unwrapping the bloody burlap from around Olsen's left arm and hand, and releasing the tightly tied tourniquet below his elbow until he further elevated the patient's potential for shock. With a blood pressure cuff and stethoscope on the patient's right arm, Dr. Frank determined Olsen had low blood pressure, but it did not reflect shock, although not far from it. The blood pressure gage showed a systolic pressure of 94 over a diastolic pressure of 63. Gustav's pulse was high at 120 beats per minute instead of a more normal 72.

The farmer needed replenishing of fluids fast to expand his vascular space and to prevent shock. Gerry started an intravenous solution of sterile Ringer's Lactate with a large 18-gage needle in a vein of Olsen's right forearm. The novice doctor smoothly hit the large antecubital vein on the first try, then he released the blood pressure cuff and hung up the one-liter bottle on a metal frame. The doctor let the clear, life-sustaining fluid run into the patient's vein as fast as it would go. He would not decrease its rapid rate of diffusion until at least 500 cc's - half the bottle - drained into the farmer's vein. Quickly he secured the needle on a wooden tongue depressor with white adhesive tape and attached it to the patient's forearm skin. Then he firmly immobilized the right arm on a green cloth-covered arm board splint.

Dr. Frank switched the loose gray blood pressure cuff to the patient's injured left arm and placed it snugly above the elbow. There it would serve as a partial tourniquet when he released the rough rope Olsen had tightly applied to himself at his farm. The doctor placed two olive green woolen blankets around the farmer to keep him warm. Only his head and his injured left arm were still exposed. Then Gerry slipped three inch-high shock blocks under the two lower legs of the table so it slanted slightly down towards the patient's head.

Had Olsen been scared, he did not let it show. His Norwegian and Swedish heritage did not permit for a display of fear. He continued to breathe slowly and deeply, not fearfully hyper-ventilating. He never mentioned his obvious persistent pain. His face gradually started to relax from the tight-lipped grimace he had worn when he entered. But this could hardly be confused with an attempt to smile since Gustav still was not out of danger, and he knew it.

Had Dr. Frank been scared, he tried to hide it - and he was very scared. With his first patient a bloody mess with a real potential for bleeding to death right here before his eyes, Gerry was damn scared. He was alone with a critically injured man, with a bloody left upper extremity and probable extensive hand injuries to the degree of which the young physician could only guess.

Gustav was his first, real-live, patient as a solo physician, and Gerry had the immediate and complete responsibility for the life of this person. In the hospital and the medical school clinics there had always been many knowledgeable professors and seasoned staff physicians to back up the students in every routine or emergency case - unlike the case here. Gerry found it a taxing chore to remain rational, cool, calm, and collected. He could feel and hear his own heart pounding loudly in his throat. He wondered if the patient could also hear it. If his own pulse rate were taken then, he knew it would be dangerously high. He quickly sat down on a round metal stool so he would not fall down on the cold, hardwood floor. He also thought there would be less of a chance of the patient hearing his nervous knees rattling together if he were sitting down. He also felt the need to firm up his working base with three, rigid metal legs rather than his own two rubbery ones.

At last he was ready to slowly, steadily unwrap and cut off the blood-saturated, blood-stained burlap. Only five minutes had elapsed since Gustav Olsen had arrived at the small medical clinic. But since then, he and Dr. Frank had spoken only two words each, 'What happened?' and 'Corn picker.'

Gerry realized sincere words of encouragement and competent, assumed authority were now sorely needed in this serious situation. These reassuring words were necessary not only to help Gerry quiet his own fears, but also to instill calmness and confidence in the injured patient. An absence of fright would lessen the man's potential for shock. Gerry wanted to come up with the kind of well-considered words of inspiration by which a young doctor could live. They should be the kind of words that he and his first patient would always remember; words the doctor could tell his future grandchildren when they might ask him, "What did you say to calm your first patient, Grandpa?" They needed to be learned words, words which he could pass on to future physicians should he ever reach the status of academic medicine in the hallowed ivy-covered buildings of prestigious medical colleges.

But hallowed words were not to be. The words that came out were not even close. Dr. Frank gently freed the last of the bloody burlap finally exposing the patient's bleeding hand and distal forearm. As he looked at the mangled arm lying before him, suddenly he heard a strange voice shouting from deep within, "My God man, you need a doctor!" It was more than a shout. It was a scream of primal terror, one that could certainly have been heard out in the small clinic waiting room if anyone else were sitting there. Thankfully, nobody else was there. Gerry hoped he not been loud enough to have been heard outside the building on Main Street in the village.

In that split second as Olsen's warm blood oozed out of his multi-lacerated arm and dripped down onto the cold oak floor, the young physician forgot every bit of medical knowledge he had ever learned. As if awakening from a bad dream, he could not remember where he was. He could not remember who he was. He had forgotten he was a doctor. When would he realize he had almost fours years of medical training to reach this point as a real physician?

Olsen recovered first. He turned his head so quickly the oxygen mask fell on the floor. The brave patient become livelier as the fluids replenished him, and he did not need it any more. Dr. Frank would never forget Olsen's next words, though try as he might to forget his own. "I know I need a doctor, Doc, that's why I came here to see you. And now that I've met you, I know you're the doctor to save my life and my hand." The demanding directness in the farmer's frozen gaze and friendly firmness in his voice immediately stabilized the serious situation. Then Olsen tried hard to smile, but found it still difficult to unclench his teeth. He had held them together tightly for so long the sore muscles to his mandible kept his lower jaw shut snugly.

My God, Gerry thought to himself as he reached to turn off the oxygen tank. *He's right. I am the doctor. I really am. That's what I'm doing here. I can help this man.* Quickly he bowed his head and with eyes closed quietly whispered, "It's working time Lord. Give this humble servant the wisdom and strength to do thy will. Help me help this man." With these few phrases, a tradition started. For many years to come, Dr. Frank would always quietly recite the words of this short physician's prayer before he began surgery or any type of serious invasive procedure on a patient. He would repeat them to himself and he would always remember this day back in the small clinic in rural Missouri.

As Dr. Frank looked up, he heard Olsen's voice as if from a great distance. The farmer lifted his head off the table and fixed Gerry with an expressive glance in which fear and amusement mixed in equal proportions. "It's okay, Doc, it's okay. Don't let this get to you. The whole town knows it's December first, Doc. We all know it's your first day of real doctorin'. Why, I'm probably the first patient you've ever seen on your own."

"That is correct, sir," admitted Gerry. "You really are my first. I won't kid you."

"But young fellow, you gotta' start somewhere and it might as well be with me, trying right now to save my left hand. I think you have already saved my life. Now give it your best. That's all the good Lord or any man can expect of you." So saying, Gustav laid his head quietly back down on the table and closed his eyes. "If I fall asleep, Doc, you just wake me up when you're done," he continued. Gustav certainly knew how to instill confidence in a person. His last sentence was the nicest thing a patient could say to a new doctor under the circumstances. Gerry would never forget Gustav's calm resolve as he placed his future in the young extern's hands.

Olsen and Frank would later become very close friends. They would hunt together, fish together, love the same woman, and on occasion rodeo together. However, in a grand and simple way, Dr. Frank would never feel closer to any man than he did that Missouri afternoon, in his interaction with this brave, seriously injured, Scandinavian-American farmer.

When Gerry had cleaned up all the spent blood from the wounded area, the patient's injuries, though serious, were not nearly as extensive as young Dr. Frank had fitfully first imagined. None of the flexor tendons were seriously injured, although two of the extensor tendons were partially cut. These needed repair. There were also four large, flap-like, full-thickness skin lacerations of the distal aspects of the left forearm, and multiple smaller lacerations to the back of the hand.

By then, Olsen's vital signs of blood pressure and respiration rate were almost completely normal, having recovered from the initial shock of his injury. His blood pressure was up to 115 over 75, though his pulse rate was still fast at 104 beats per minute. To ease the pain, small doses of morphine were slowly injected intravenously directly into the intravenous tubing. Gradually, the patient started to relax and a feeling of euphoria came over him.

"Sure glad you didn't shoot me with that stuff first, Doc, or I might not have cared if my old arm fell off or not. Think the pain kept me going 'til I got here."

The young doctor smiled but did not answer. He realized the injured farmer was right. Pain can save lives at times and can be a great motivator. Pain delivers information to the brain so a person knows something is wrong, needing quick correction.

After copious scrubbing with pHisoHex soap and multiple injections of Xylocaine as a local anesthetic, Gerry started carefully debriding Gustav's mangled, non-viable tissue and meticulously suturing his repairable tissue. To repair the torn subcutaneous tissues below the skin, Gerry used absorbable catgut suture. He used silk suture to repair the lacerated skin. These outer stitches could be removed later. After 110 separate sutures and over three hours of elapsed time, he completed the complex job. Though the patient would carry scars from this trauma to his grave, all the wounds would heal well and without infection. Gustav would keep full use of his hand and it would work well given time. He would farm his fields again.

Olsen had brought with him all the bloody rags. From those and the farmer's saturated clothes, Dr. Frank estimated the blood loss to be probably less than 700 cubic centimeters by volume, but definitely over half a liter. Midway through suturing, the doctor stopped to hang up a second liter of intravenous fluids. This bottle carried an infusion of five-percent dextrose in normal saline. Gerry reset the intravenous tubing's adjustable clamp for a slower delivery of fluid as the patient's blood pressure had increased back to normal. Even before the second liter of fluid was two-thirds empty, Gustav needed to urinate. Shock from fluid loss and trauma no longer presented a problem, at least not for the patient.

Young Dr. Frank's shock and embarrassment was the current problem. But his anxiety proved to be an unnecessary worry.

Olsen would never once hint nor mention to anyone in the village what the young doctor blurted out in the initial excitement of the emergency situation. Instead, Gustav Olsen went far in the other direction. He insisted in front of anyone who would listen that the new young doctor had not only saved his hand, but he had also saved his life against overwhelming odds. Dr. Frank became embarrassed every time he heard the farmer's version of the story, especially since most of the village accepted the story of Gerry's great heroism as the gospel truth. A local legend was born and a professional career was launched on that fateful day.

After a tetanus booster injection, oral and local antibiotics, bandage dressings, splints and a sling, a phone call to the Olsen farm produced Gustav's daughter, Sharon. She hastily arrived at the clinic within 15 minutes of the call. She had not been at the farmhouse when her father was hurt, nor had she ventured into the tool shed since the accident where the blood had stained the floor. She had no knowledge of her father's serious injuries until being informed of them on the phone.

Sharon came to drive her dad home. She promised to make sure he followed the doctor's directions until her dad recovered completely. Though obviously upset, the young woman remained quite calm under the circumstances. Not just her father, Gustav was her best friend. He had raised her as a single parent since her mother died quite suddenly when Sharon was only three-years-old. She would always be her father's pride and joy and he would always be her hero.

Sharon, a 20-year-old beauty of 5'6" and 118 pounds, parted her dark auburn, curly hair neatly on the right and it fell in waves just below her shoulders. Her large, dark-brown eyes were a bit widely spaced but were surrounded by long, lovely lashes. She wore no makeup nor did she appear to need any to cover the clearest, most well-scrubbed complexion Gerry had ever seen. He found her breath-taking with her high, rounded cheekbones and small nose and chin, her face unaccented by any cosmetics.

Meeting like this held great significance in their lives not yet appreciated by neither Sharon nor the young doctor. Gerry would sentimentally reflect on this moment many times in the months to come. He felt instantly familiar with her, as if he had known her before. But he knew that was impossible, because if he had ever met a woman as beautiful before he would have remembered her. At least he thought he would have.

Obvious instant chemistry sparked between the two young people and the true reason for the accident suddenly became quite clear to Sharon's father. Gustav had lived a tough 55 years and had gained the maturity coming only from age and experience. He believed the good Lord always had a reason for everything happening. Sometimes He just took a long time to reveal His point strongly enough for mortals to figure out the purpose of His plan.

Soon Dr. Thompson returned to the clinic after finishing his outlying farms house-call duty. He excitedly inquired for the explanation of the blood stains trailing up the walk, through the waiting area, and into the surgery room. Before much had to be said, Harry quickly sized up the situation. Then he closely and proudly examined his partner's dressings and splints on the rugged individual still seated on the examination table where the surgery had taken place.

Finally remembering proper etiquette, Gerry made polite introductions all around. Harry quickly offered to drive the Olsen's pickup truck back to their farm if Sharon would give him a return ride back into town. He decided it was the least he could do since the two patients waiting in the reception room wanted to see the doctor who had saved Gustav's life and would not be satisfied with anyone else. Word traveled fast in the small village where a party-line phone system helped to carry the news.

Sharon quickly agreed with Harry's plan. The sincerity in her concern toward her injured father filled the small treatment room with the warmth of their mutual feelings for each other. Obvious love and respect was openly displayed between this father and his daughter.

In the formal introductions made after Harry arrived, he and Gerry learned Mr. Olsen was a widower and this daughter his only child. She commuted five days a week to the same college town as the medical school attended by the young doctors. The campus of the state teachers college where she attended was only two miles from the medical school, 51 miles from Essex. The partners realized they, unfortunately, drove one way as she went the other.

The patients waiting in the reception room were both sick with bronchitis, one an acute, recent infection, and one a chronic, longstanding illness. Their evaluation, treatment, and care took about 20 minutes each. It seemed an anticlimactic ending to the day, but Gerry's first real day on the job spanned the true essence of rural medicine. Though sometimes physicians found themselves faced with major life and death situations, more often they were faced with minor, easier to treat cases. In his first day of externship, Dr. Frank had experienced the combination of sudden exciting injury, old lingering sickness, and recent irritating illness.

The slow relentless shadows of a passing afternoon extended into the early darkness of a late fall evening. Lights went on all over town in the remaining open village stores. As he locked up the clinic office and headed over to the Blue Bell Cafe' for supper, Gerry thought about his first exciting day as a country doctor. Bronchitis cases are interesting, but the real excitement was in the drama of blood, trauma, and surgery. A man slowly becomes what he does well. That is why doing things well is so important. The satisfaction provided in performing excellent work is the ultimate ego trip. The surgery he had done pleased Gerry and he felt had

44

done a very good job. He was also glad his first patient had been someone as understanding as Gustav Olsen, this friendly farmer was a man worth knowing. Gerry looked forward to the opportunity in the near future.

In Gerry's glorious moment of reflection, the only thing that could have made him feel at all better at all would be if he had been able to take his patient to the Olsen farm and to have the lovely Sharon then drive him back into town. In matters of women, however, Harry always seemed to jump in first on all the good chances. Gerry's luck came more slowly, but, then again, his luck seemed to last longer. He still thought about Sharon while finishing the main course for supper at the cafe' as Harry returned to join him in time for dessert.

"So how was your day?" Gerry asked while his partner pulled up a chair to sit at the table. "Tell me about the house-call business here in rural Missouri. Anything exciting to report?"

"What's for dessert in the pie department?" Harry asked. He wished to settle the issue before a more serious discussion.

"Try the deep dish apple. I've noticed the locals are all ordering it tonight," Gerry replied.

"My house calls today were all pretty exciting to me, though certainly not the life and death trauma you so successfully dealt with. You did a great piece of work with Mr. Olsen. Maybe you should become a surgeon."

"Thanks. I even surprised myself. Guess it will be quite a while before I realize we really are almost full-fledged physicians. It's kind of scary being out here on our own like this."

"What do you mean?" his partner questioned. He looked up from the menu to the waitress who was setting two pieces of deep dish apple pie on the table without being asked.

"I mean we still have so much to learn," Gerry replied, "and we only have six months left until graduation."

"Does that waitress always bring the food you want without being asked?"

"I'm not sure, but she did seem strongly persuasive that I order the meat loaf tonight. And it was really good," Gerry declared.

Harry started in on his apple pie. "Hey, this pie is pretty hot but really good. Hand me that pitcher of cream to cool it down a little. You're right about there still being a lot we need to learn. But I sure can't think of a better way of learning. Can you?"

"No, but it still doesn't make it any less scary. Now how about recapping the events of your afternoon out and about in the local township? Did you get lost looking for any farms?"

"No, but I ended up seeing seven patients instead of six," Harry answered with enthusiasm.

"Building a bigger practice already? Tell me about it."

"Well, both of the two youngest Morgan children have pneumonia. Then I redressed the feet of a middle-aged, male diabetic who already has a severe decubitus ulcer problem. I saw two older ladies with mild chronic congestive heart failure, an old cowboy with acute gout, and a young farmer with a probable broken left ankle."

"Did you send the fracture case on to the hospital? Those orthopedic residents love to get referrals from the rural clinics."

"Not today. I have him well-splinted and gave him codeine for his pain. Also, tonight I put him on ice packs locally with the leg elevated to try to bring down some of his edema. There were no serious problems with any neurovascular components of the foot. Tomorrow morning his wife will drive him to the hospital for X-rays and casting."

"So, if it were such a good day for the doctors and an inversely bad day for disease, why aren't you eating anything more than just apple pie? A smart physician always keeps to a healthy diet, I'm told," Gerry said. He forked up the last piece of pie from his plate and slipped it in his mouth.

"Because at every farm where I stopped, no matter how humble, the people insisted on giving me food and coffee. The food was generally good and the coffee always strong. I probably won't sleep for two days.

Chapter 4
Changing Voices
December 15 -22, 1961

Another mid-December afternoon of relentless rain and westerly winds had settled in on the small rural village of Essex. Continuous raindrops perpetually pelted all of Northeastern Missouri for two full days and nights. Many of the country dirt and county gravel roads around Essex were nearly impassable. Cold rain water had flowed from the fields and masses of mud pooled deeply in low-lying gullies. A dreary, quick temperature drop from the low forties into the mid thirties nearly caused freezing. This weary weather was worrisome enough to warrant dismal depression even among the usually euphoric villagers. Concern grew as the storm persisted well into the second day and had been predicted to continue for several more. Flooding this last week of autumn was improbable but obviously not impossible if the rain persisted and the temperature stayed slightly above 32 degrees Fahrenheit.

Still a newcomer to the area, Dr. Gerry Frank was a long way from his home in sunny Southern California. The local midwestern weather, the proud country people, and the small rural clinic seemed intricately interwoven into a well-mixed montage shouting to him of culture shock. This brand new country doctor would have found soft snow easier to deal with than all this hard rain and its resulting reddish-brown Missouri mud. He finally understood why the locals felt tied to the land. They were adhered to it by the thick, sticky brown goop. They could not pull themselves away if they had wanted to.

A country doctor's practice is frequently determined by weather conditions. The patient load had been slower than usual on this late fall Friday at the rural clinic. The effect of country weather is contrary to the professional life of a city doctor, whose practice is little influenced by local weather on a day-to-day basis. This difference is not only reflected in the fluctuations of the number of patients presenting but also in the types of illnesses and accident cases seen. Concern over the muddy roads kept the area's potential patients from driving to the cross-road village, except for in genuine emergencies and other serious trips of utmost importance.

With the wet, rainy weather arrived an inverse increase in requests for house calls also presented. Dr. Harry Thompson, Dr, Gerry Frank's partner at the rural clinic, reluctantly volunteered to do the necessary afternoon medical visits to the outlying homes and farms. Harry's two-door, blue '52 Chevy Bel Air had a fairly high road clearance and was better suited for rough-road driving than Gerry's more modern, low-slung, '55 Ford Thunderbird. Gerry's sporty vehicle, though fast and fearsome on smoothly paved highways, had not been designed for the backwoods and byways of rural Missouri. Fair-weather friendly, the sleek black beauty exhibited a decidedly disinclined disposition toward traveling the troublesome back country terrain of mangled muddy roads.

Gerry had only seen five patients at the clinic since 1:00 P.M. on that gloomy afternoon. His next appointment was not scheduled for another half hour, so he decided to leave the small office for a short time to walk down Main Street. A friendly fellow, he wanted to introduce himself to the local shopkeepers and tradespeople who worked and lived close by in the village.

So far, he and Harry had worked at the clinic in Essex for only two weeks. They had met very few of the local citizens except those they had seen as patients. Gerry developed a particular concern and interest in meeting the woman who frequently answered the telephone and managed the counter at

Essex General Store, the largest store in town, which sold a tremendous variety of merchandise. The clerk's low-pitched voice sounded so deep over the phone, at first the young doctor had misunderstood it actually to be a woman's voice. He wondered if her condition indicated some serious medical problem. The mystery stimulated his inquisitive mind as a problem demanding a solution. Gerry hoped her case might indicate a condition he could diagnose and cure. In eager expectation, he briskly walked across the poorly paved street. The miserable wet weather discouraged vehicle traffic and caused large puddles the young doctor carefully dodged in his already muddied cowboy boots.

The jingle of two overhead bells tolled loudly, announcing Dr. Frank as he opened the heavy outer door of the large, warm and cozy store. A pleasant smell permeated the premises as though carefully contrived with a combination of wood smoke, scented soap, fragrant camphor, and pungent clove. Nothing showed the true tone of a small town faster than an inventory of its best general store. A quick look around the narrow cluttered aisles indicated this store carried everything from hardware to clothing. Three large reefer boxes lined the rear wall. Further discovery demonstrated an inventory including well-stocked food staples including all types of dry boxed, fresh packed, and frozen foods. Two old style cast-iron, wood-burning Franklin stoves provided ample heat. Each of their grill-faced fireboxes was ornately trimmed with brightly polished, elaborately engraved nickel. One stove stood at the front, right corner of the store near the wide, wooden counter. A red oak rocking chair sat beckoningly beside it. The other stove warmed the back left corner, surrounded by three unpainted knotty pine chairs. The atmosphere of the store resembled a Hollywood movie set of an old western town. Gerry felt the only thing missing was an open cracker barrel and some dungaree-dressed wood whittlers spinning youthful yarns and tall tales of bygone days. *Perhaps they had been there earlier but had briefly stepped out for a long lunch*, he thought.

"Be with you in just a minute, Doc," boomed the deep but friendly voice of a neatly dressed, nice looking, middle-aged woman working behind the counter. Gerry estimated she was 5'5" tall and probably weighed about 135 pounds. Her glowing green eyes were enhanced by a flushed fair complexion. Time moves fast and first for a woman's face. The worry lines of her life were well-worn and deeply etched around her eyes. Thick chestnut brown hair reflected a healthy sheen, though a few strands of white gave it a grayish cast around the edges. She wore it held high on her head with brown bobby pins. Her choice of hair style gave the illusion she was considerably taller than she was actually. The doctor noted sensible low-heel Oxford shoes below a green, mid-length, warm wool skirt, the hemline showing through the open bottom of the counter. What little he could see of her legs appeared quite shapely, with no evidence of dependent edema.

"No hurry. I'm just kinda' looking around."

"Take your time Doc. There's lots to see."

"You sure do have an interesting place," Gerry said. "I can hardly believe the tremendous variety of things you carry in your store."

"Well, we have to, Doc. We're the only real general store in the area, and its a long drive to Macon or Moberly." The clerk cheerfully resumed packaging hardware for a young woman customer half hidden in a bright yellow sou'wester raincoat with its high hood pulled up over the back of her head. "I guess you've previously met the new young clinic physician here in town, Sharon?" questioned the saleslady. "I hear he's from California and his clinic partner is from West Virginia." She smiled broadly and looked directly at the doctor even as she spoke to the woman standing quietly in front of the counter.

When the young woman finally turned toward him, Gerry recognized Sharon Olsen, the beautiful, auburn-haired daughter of the injured farmer who had been the doctor's first patient on his initial day in the village. Gerry had never before understood farming to be a dangerous occupation. But he had quickly changed his mind the day after seeing the devastating damage a corn picker could instantly inflict on unfortunate human flesh when it got in the way.

Sharon smiled shyly, and though the overhead lighting in the store was poor, the doctor thought he saw her face faintly blush with a pale pink color, lighting up her cheeks. "Yes, Cherry," she replied in a soft but firm voice. "This is the fine Dr. Frank who saved my dad's life."

"Well, I'm not sure I did that, but you are very kind to say so. All I did was to stop his bleeding and sew up some lacerations."

"You need not be modest about it Doctor. My dad told me how serious his injury was. He could have bled to death. We know at least you saved his arm and hand, and we're very grateful to you."

"Isn't your dad due in for a recheck soon?" Gerry asked.

"Yes. Dad is coming to your office again in a couple days to have his last few stitches removed."

"How is he getting along now?"

"We think he has progressed wonderfully. There's no evidence of any infection and he's able to move his fingers better each day."

"That is good news. You have to be very concerned about infection with injuries from farm machinery that's been used out in the dirt."

"We don't call it dirt around her, Doctor," the clerk interrupted laughing. "We call it soil. Our farming fortunes and the local economy depend on it."

"Oh, sorry about that. Guess you're right. I never thought about it much before now," Gerry replied somewhat embarrassed.

"Well, if there is anything my father and I can ever do for you, Dr. Frank, or for your partner Dr. Thompson, please don't hesitate to let us know. The Olsen family is much obliged to you. We always will be," she said while snapping up her raincoat in preparation to leave.

"Thank you. Thank you very much. No new doctor could want a finer first patient than your dad was for me. He is a very brave man."

"I know. He's been my hero all my life," she answered.

"It was a privilege and a pleasure to take care of him, and I look forward to seeing him any time he needs medical attention. Of course, I hope he will never have need for such serious attention again, or for any kind for that matter."

With an answering smile of thanks the young woman carefully gathered up several separate packages the clerk had wrapped for her and quickly excused herself as she departed from the store. The overhead bells at the door rang again as she left. A cool blast of air swept in from outside before she could pull the door closed behind her.

Dr. Frank could not resist taking a last lingering look through the store's misty front window, watching as Sharon walked briskly through the rain to her father's Ford pickup truck parked directly across the street. Even in faded blue jeans, a drenched yellow raincoat and soil-stained brown boots, she was a fine looking lady. The young doctor had to admit to himself he looked forward to seeing a lot more of her. He sincerely hoped another medical emergency such as the her dad's severe forearm and hand accident would not be necessary to provide time to be close to her again.

"Well, if you've met Sharon, Doc, then you've already met the finest and the most fascinating young woman in this part of the county. That's for sure," the woman informed him in her deep voice as she put away the twine and paper from which she had wrapped Sharon's parcels.

"I think you may be right." Gerry had to agree as he had not seen another woman in the area who peaked his interest more.

"Oh, I rightly know I am. Everybody in Essex knows and respects that young woman, but the big news for today is I think she might be more than just a little interested in you, Doc."

"What makes you say that?" Gerry asked as he leaned against the counter with an inquisitive smile on his face.

Well my green eyes aren't as sharp as they used to be, but it sure looked to me like she blushed clear to pink when she saw you here in the store just now. Maybe I am possibly a bit partial since she is my very favorite niece, but that fine young woman would make one of you doctors a wonderful wife. Fact is, she'd be an asset to any man who is smart enough not to try to drag her off to a big city somewhere."

"You mean she doesn't like city life?"

"No, not necessarily, Doc. She's just country through and through. She is everlastingly tied to her family and their farm. Lots of us are like that here. It's not a bad trait. Our inner strength grows deeply from the dark soil of these wide valleys and rolling hills we have farmed for so many generations. My husband Jimmy and I have this store now, but we still farm a few acres on our small place outside of town. You ought to come out and see the place some evening when we have Sharon over for supper."

Gerry hoped the clerk would continue talking so he could surreptitiously study the persistent pattern of her deep voice. But his embarrassment grew as she consistently concentrated the subject of her nubile niece. The conversation become far too personal for him, but he didn't know how to change the subject.

Gerry had acquired a long standing tradition of being very secretive about his private thoughts. He had acknowledged to no one of his strong attraction to Sharon since the first time he saw her on the evening of her father's injury. She had a wholesome country freshness about her. She possessed a well-scrubbed look with curly, shoulder-length dark auburn hair, and a clear, creamy complexion needing no make-up. Hearing Sharon speak again started the fluid flowing fastly inside the young doctor's body. He could feel his blood run its course through his heart when she said his name. *At least she recognized him and remembered his name. That was progress*, he thought.

After seeing Sharon this second time, Gerry remembered the deep disappointment he felt when Mr. Olsen stated Sharon would not be driving him to the medical clinic for the periodic checkups and dressing changes necessitated by his severe hand and arm injury. The farmer had explained to Dr. Frank his daughter commuted five days a week from their family farm to the Northeast Missouri State Teachers College in Kirksville. She drove a considerable distance to the northeast from Essex. Gerry calculated it was about a 102 mile round trip from where she lived on the farm with her dad. He thought she must be serious about her education to drive that route every Monday through Friday.

Sharon's father was typically independent and self sufficient as were most all of the rural people in the county. Mr. Olsen felt he completely capable of driving himself into Essex and back to his farm as needed even with his injuries. The lacerations of his left hand and forearm healed dramatically well. He guided his pickup truck slowly and carefully, steering with his good right hand. He expressed he had no apparent trouble driving the five-and-a-half mile trip each way, every other day.

"Well, I feel kind of embarrassed," said the young doctor slowly with a soft reticence in his voice to the clerk behind the counter "Practically everyone in the village knows me and my partner by name already. But we sure haven't met even half of you folks yet," he continued as he shrugged his shoulders. A shy smile on his face lent a mischievous look to his deep brown eyes.

"Oh, that's alright," boomed the friendly clerk in her persistently deep voice. "Word gets around fast in this small village. Why, everybody here knew who you and your partner were by the second sundown after you both arrived. We even know where you are from and what kind of car you drive. And don't you be surprised if some of us knew of you before you even got here, Doc," she laughed before she continued, "No, seriously, I don't mean to scare you. There's only four of you new doctors for us to learn - you and Dr. Thompson on Monday, Wednesday and Friday, and Doctors Woodward and Miller on Tuesday, Thursday and Saturday. Obviously, there's a lot more of us for you doctors to remember." As she finished speaking she extended her right hand in a firm introduction. "I'm real pleased to meet you. My name, is Cherry; Cherry Jam. Now don't you bother making jokes about my name, Doc, because I've probably heard them all. My husband says there are only five basic 'Jam Jokes' and any other attempts are just variations on the original themes. Of course, if you care to try, I'll be obliged to listen. Maybe you can come up with an sixth one."

"Cherry Jam?" questioned the young doctor. "Now that is an interesting name. Seems like it practically demands a beautiful lady with a mighty sweet personality such as yourself."

"Well thank you Doc. It's right decent of you to say that."

"But tell me, how did you come by such a nice name?"

"Are you really interested in how it happened?" She asked hopefully.

"I sure am. Think I'll make myself comfortable over here in the rocker while I listen to your story." Hoping that his request would compel the clerk to continue talking for a while, Gerry sat down in the old oak rocking chair next to the Franklin stove in the front of the store. He loosened the zipper of his warm outer jacket. Within a few moments, the rhythmic noise of his rocking resounded throughout the store rising from the solid hardwood floor beneath him.

"I like your sentiment, Doc. We're going to get along just fine. I can already tell. You see, my good mother, God rest her soul, ate tart cherries that summer evening long ago just before she went into labor with me. That's where I got my first name."

"But what about your last name? That's the clincher."

"Well, my maiden name was Olsen. It's a comfortable common Scandinavian family name in these parts. However, I have to admit, I did think a long time about what my new full name would be when my sweetheart Jimmy Jam proposed. However, I do love that tall, skinny rascal even to this very day, and I knew by marrying him I wouldn't have to leave my old home town." She sounded like she had repeated the story at least a thousand times and, in the telling, it had become part of the folklore and fabric of her life. "Now, what can I do for you today, Doc?" she said as she stood and leaned forward on her elbows against the top of the wide counter. "I'm here to help."

"I'll be honest with you, Cherry, things are pretty quiet at the clinic today. Ever since I heard your voice on the phone a couple times earlier this week, I've wanted to come over to meet you and to introduce myself. I also wondered if your voice has always been as deep as it is now." A list of possible differential diagnoses ran through the young doctor's mind. He quickly deduced from the feminine appearance and normal weight to height ratio of this nice lady that chronic hormonal problems could be easily ruled out.

"Doc, I'm 38-years-old now and have been working at this here store and yelling into that there telephone for so many years I forget what my real voice was like before it became so low. Come to think of it, it all began about five years ago."

"How do you remember that Cherry? Was it something that happened suddenly?"

"I remember because it was the same time I started doing all these customer's phone orders. Very gradually my voice became deeper and deeper. At first my husband kidded me about it, but he soon stopped when he realized the problem was not going away. I certainly never tried to talk like this. What woman would want to sound this way? It sure doesn't seem very feminine. It just slowly descended upon me."

"How long has it been this deep?" Gerry questioned as he finished unzipping his heavy jacket and, pushed his chair back a foot farther from the high heat of the old stove.

"Its been about this deep for at least three years. I don't think it's changed much since then. Should I be worrying about it?" She asked with a twinge of fear and apprehension. Her formerly friendly and smiling face quickly changed into a furrowed frown. "What should I do? Is there anything you can do to help me?"

"Perhaps Cherry," answered the doctor carefully. "I'm not sure. Why don't you come over to the office later this afternoon around six o'clock when you close the store and let me take a good look down your throat with a small mirrored instrument we have there. We could start a workup to find out what your specific problem is. Even a simple exam could help us a lot."

"Are you sure you have time for it today?"

"Of course, that's not a problem. I'll keep the office open until you arrive. Okay?" The warmth of the stove and the rocking chair was comforting, but it was time to return to work at the clinic. The form-fitting rocker on the solid, sound floor beneath him was addicting, especially in such close proximity to the wood-fired stove. But duty called, and Gerry stood up and stretched as he walked closer to the counter.

"Sure, Doc," said Cherry, lighting up a long fresh cigarette. Only then did the doctor notice a large ceramic ash tray on the counter near the big gold-plated cash register. There were small spent butts of at least 20 cigarettes ground into the ashtray similar to the one she just lit. All of them were smoked to miserly shortness. A half-empty pack of Pall Malls lay next to the full ashtray.

"Are you a pretty heavy smoker, Cherry? I see you smoke a brand of extra long cigarettes."

"Well, I guess you could probably say so, Doc. I smoke nearly two packs a day. This job is a lot of work and the stress makes me nervous. When customers come in to buy their supplies I don't smoke unless they light one. But I really start firing them up during long phone orders from my country customers.

"Why is that?" Gerry asked.

"Well, because they are never content to merely give me their orders. They want to chat and have me fill them in on all the latest gossip coming from here in town. Maybe I would be better off if just kept quiet and put out a newspaper instead."

"You mean they phone for things without wanting to see them first? It sounds like they must trust you to have sound judgment on selections."

"Yes, they like me to pack their purchases prior to when they drop in to pick them up later the same day. It saves them a lot of time and everybody in this old town just about knows everything we carry. Whenever we have a brand new item, we display it up front near the counter here so they can see it right away. I guess I do a particular lot of smoking when I'm busy on the phone." After deeply inhaling another puff she carefully placed the burning cigarette on the edge of the ashtray before exhaling a long breath of light gray smoke.

The doctor purchased a large colorful calendar he thought would be nice to put up on the inside wall of the clinic waiting room. The calendar was published by the Audubon Society and depicted game birds indigenous to the area. Several main water fowl flyways to Canada transacted this section of Missouri. Most of the local farmers owned valuable hunting dogs and were quite involved with bird hunting, both in sport and as a way to supplement their subsistence.

"Are you a bird hunter, Doctor?"

"Not for a long time. In fact the last time I went bird hunting was back in my pre-med undergraduate college days at Colgate University. It's a small college in upstate New York. I used to hunt a fair amount back then. But isn't fowl season over now until autumn next year? I'm afraid I won't be here long enough."

"That's true, but if you decide you'd like to follow a good golden retriever, I know my husband Jim would be pleased to have you join him some late afternoon. He's always out there in the fields and hedgerows, just him and his dog. Though sometimes my brother, Gus Olsen, drafts him to go rabbit hunting."

Dr. Frank thanked her for the invitation and then excused himself to walk back across the muddy street to the red brick clinic for his next appointment. He had about ten minutes to review the patient's past medical records before his scheduled arrival. The record showed the man was a 70-year-old farmer with a persistent condition of shingles. The farmer desired fresh assurance from the new doctor the rash would clear, at least by spring planting time.

Gerry determined from the information already entered on the chart it should be in a stage of remission quite soon.

As soon as the doctor stepped out of the store and walked across the wet sidewalk, Cherry snuffed out the burning cigarette without taking another drag. Her slight apprehension turned to substantial fright. She threw the rest of the red and white unfinished pack into the flaming wood stove. This could finally be the motivation she needed to stop smoking for good. She rarely considered the prospect her habit could be genuinely endangering her life. She now knew time would tell, but would it tell with kindness or with vengeance?

Around six o'clock, Harry finally returned from doing all the afternoon's outlying house calls. He whistled quietly as he walked through the small clinic waiting room to the inner office area. It was already dark outside. Gerry washed up after his last patient, a 44-year-old female diabetic. "I was going to ask you to eat supper with me," said Harry, "but I see you've got one more late appointment. Did you know there is another patient in the waiting room? I saw her come in as I drove up."

"Yes, it's someone I met this afternoon," Gerry replied with a wry smile on his face. "Did you happen to catch that voice?"

"Hey, I sure did and that is either the best looking transvestite I've seen in this part of Missouri or you've got a woman with a really deep voice problem. She seemed friendly and said something to me as I passed through. Her voice shocked me at first."

"How was that?" Gerry asked.

"Because I didn't see anyone around who looked like a man. The voice didn't sound like a lady's."

"Yeah, that's the problem she's coming in about. Do you have any ideas on the subject? I'm open for suggestions on this one."

"Hey, I'm too hungry to have ideas, but I'll be glad to think about it later," Harry offered as he washed his hands at the sink.

"Sounds good," Gerry replied. "Go get something to eat before you starve."

"Well then, meet me at the Blue Bell Cafe' when you finish up here. I'm done for the day for sure. By now back home in West Virginia they'd have eaten supper at least two hours ago." Harry did not bother to wait for an answer and quickly departed leaving his black medical bag on the floor behind the desk. Not one for formality or wasting words, Harry's stomach stretched for something to eat again and he headed out the door. His stomach growled and he could feel and hear it notifying him 20 minutes earlier that supper time had come. He had eaten nothing since an early lunch and now ran hypoglycemically on empty.

Dr. Frank called Cherry into his office and took an extensive medical history of her condition. By her own account, she had a pretty normal childhood and considered herself a healthy person as far back as she could remember. Other than an occasional common cold once or twice a year, she had not suffered serious ear, nose, or throat problems, nor other injuries. The patient's two-pack-a-day cigarette habit was her only past history of possible significance the doctor could elicit. She had steadily maintained this level of addiction for the past three years. Prior to that time, she smoked a single pack a day since she had started smoking in her late teens. She claimed no history of persistent coughing, bloody sputum, chronic bronchitis, nor recent weight loss. If any combination of these symptoms were present, any physician's suspicion of possible malignancy would increase dramatically. As Dr. Frank finished filling in her medical chart from her oral history, he hoped a dreadful cancer was not her problem.

Cherry's preliminary physical exam was negative as to palpable cervical masses and swollen lymph nodes in her neck.

The secondary part of the examination was difficult both for the doctor and the patient. To study the patient's posterior pharynx and larynx it was necessary to use an indirect method by inserting a small mirror into her mouth, attached to a long thin handle much like one used by a dentist. The doctor held the instrument with his right hand far back into the patient's throat. His left hand firmly grasped a fresh tongue depressor to keep her tongue from obscuring his point of view. A chrome, goose-neck lamp shined in from the side with its light reflected off his concave headband mirror deeply into her throat. This enabled him to see an image on the little hand-held mirror from deep in her larynx. He asked her to try to talk, though it was obvious from her gag reflex of her extreme discomfort. At first the shiny mirrored surface kept clouding up with moisture, making it difficult to see anything. Gerry had previously learned the secret of success in this type of examination is to have the metal and glass mirror warmer than the patient's breath. After a little practice with the heat from a hand-sized alcohol lamp, he deftly placed the inquiring implement deeply into the patient's mouth. When the small, round mirror cooled off, it quickly became too foggy to see anything on it, and he then took it out and reheated it. Gerry had to take gentle care because if the mirror were too hot, it could burn the patient's posterior pharynx as he placed it deeply into the back of her throat.

Four successful examinations guided with careful scrutiny later, convinced the doctor the patient's left vocal chord did not move or vibrate as it should during speech. Slowly he stood up straight and quietly placed the used instrument on a nearby counter next to the sink. He said nothing for a moment and Cherry recognized real concern reflected in his eyes and kind face.

"So tell me the truth, Doc. I can take it. You see something you don't like, right?" asked Cherry with worry in her voice. She had grown more nervous and agitated each time the doctor repeated the procedure for better viewing. She had trouble trying to calm down. Throughout the investigation of her throat, she white-knuckled the arms of the examination chair, squeezing tightly with both hands.

"Well, Cherry, I'm not sure. It looks like one of your vocal cords is immobile. Your left one is just not moving at all. That would certainly explain why your voice is so deep all the time."

"But why isn't it moving, Doc? Can you see anything in my throat holding it back? There must be some reason why it stays still that way," she said as her anxiety increased.

"Frankly, it does concern me. I don't see anything from the top that could explain why one chord doesn't move. It's a problem you should have checked out by an experienced ear, nose, and throat specialist. You need to see someone with major expertise in this area. We have a good ENT doctor at the hospital."

"Would he come here to see me?" Cherry asked hopefully.

"No. I think he would probably want to admit you as an inpatient at the hospital for a couple of days first to perform a diagnostic workup. Then when they find out the exact cause of your problem, there could be a possible treatment that might help you a lot."

"Oh my, Dr. Frank, can't you do all the tests and stuff here, in town at the clinic? I'm the main person responsible for running the store. With the holiday season upon us, I don't think I can afford to leave home and abandon my many customers. Do I really have to leave?"

"Yes, I'm afraid so. You see, Cherry, we also need X-rays of your chest and a few other tests performed for which we just don't have the equipment here in Essex. All that would have to be done at the hospital, and it should be done soon."

"Would I only be in the hospital for two days? You know, us country folk like to stay close to home."

"I can't promise it would only be two days. That will depend on what we find. There is a possibility it might take longer."

"So, it could be a big problem with serious significance? It's not something I should delay doing? That's what you're saying?"

"Yes. It really should be taken care of now. I definitely advise immediate and complete competent consultation." The doctor worried but tried not to show it more than necessary. He did not want Cherry overly frightened, but he did want her concerned enough to follow through and do something about a protracted problem over which she had procrastinated for years.

Finally the doctor and Mrs. Cherry Jam agreed early the next week she would check into the medical school teaching hospital 53 miles northeast from her small hometown of Essex. Though it was the largest hospital in that area of the state within a radius of a 100 miles, there still was a sense of warmth and personal concern among its staff not found in most contemporary mega-medical center complexes.

The next week, on Wednesday, December 20th, about 4:00 P.M., Cherry checked in with the hospital admitting office. After giving the clerk the customary information and signing all the necessary forms, the clerk called for an orderly to accompany the patient up to her room in the surgical wing of the building. The orderly then measured the patient's weight and height, her vital signs were taken and recorded, along with further information about any pertinent allergies and current medication, and a plastic identification bracelet was attached to her left wrist. By the time she undressed, put on a short hospital gown, reached her arms around and tied it up the back, and climbed into the high firm bed, Cherry laid down to take a short nap before supper. A technician drawing blood interrupted her nap first, and then a second time a nurse requested a urine sample.

A staff doctor served as the primary care physician for a patient in the hospital. Her staff physician, Doctor Sydney Albin, headed the Ear, Nose and Throat Department. A highly respected surgeon, he had instructed at the medical school for over ten years and had become well known throughout that part of Missouri. Being board certified in his specialty, he was entitled to have resident physicians training under his care and supervision, and had two with him at the time. Their specific ENT postgraduate training spanned three additional years after the completion of their one-year rotating internships.

The young referring rural clinic doctors were encouraged to have as much close observation and contact as possible when their rural clinic patients were hospitalized. Early in the evening, after Mrs. Jam's X-rays and laboratory work were done and the reports posted on her chart, Dr. Frank, together with one of the ENT resident physicians, carefully studied the results. As had been previously anticipated, they now determined the definite need to schedule Cherry for bronchoscopic surgery first thing the following morning. The two doctors also reviewed the nursing notes and attached consultations by an internist and a radiologist. Then they came to an agreement on all the pre-op orders written on her chart and made sure the charge nurse understood the exact steps that must be followed before the patient went to surgery at 7:30 A.M. early the next morning.

Gerry visited the anxious patient late to say goodnight since he would not see her before she would be sedated early the next morning. He reassured her he would be there during her surgical procedure. She squeezed his hand in silent reply. She had full faith in her young doctor and knew he would see to it that everything possible would be done on her behalf. There was little mention of cancer, but everybody concerned hoped her problem was not a complex malignant tumor impeding her vocal chord or lying against its nervous innervation. Were that tragic circumstance the case, it might be impossible to remove all of the tumor and her life expectancy would be measured in months rather than years.

Shortly after 11:00 P.M., Dr. Frank finally finished making the rest of his rounds at the hospital. It suddenly occurred to him how tired he felt as he walked outside the large warm building and headed in the cool evening toward his car. The minute the fresh cold night air hit his face it stimulated him to full wakefulness. Though still worried about Mrs. Jam, the young doctor realized everything possible had been done to prepare for her surgery. Now it was time to relax, get something to eat, and have a good night's sleep.

The evening nursing shift was just changing. As Gerry approached his small black car in the expansive unlit hospital parking lot, he suddenly surprisingly found one of the nurses sitting quietly in the dark on his car's right front fender. The problem with these '55 Ford Thunderbird automobiles was the car was so low to the ground people felt as free to sit on them as they would on a park bench. "Okay, who's sitting on my car this time?" he questioned irritably as the nurse stood up and turned to face him.

"It's me, Gerry, Purity Jones. The 3:00 to 11:00 shift tonight was a killer. I saw your car parked here and I wondered if you'd like to give me a ride to my apartment. I can't wait to get out of this new uniform and into something I can relax in."

The way she said 'relax' made the doctor laugh with acknowledgement. Purity was hyper most of the time and it was practically impossible to imagine her relaxing under any circumstances. "Evening, Purity," replied Gerry, sporting a perturbed smile as he leaned forward to unlock the passenger side door for her to climb into the car. "If you'd stop wearing your nurse's uniforms two sizes too small, you could breathe better on the job and maybe even learn to relax a little bit at work."

"Yeah, I suppose you're right, but it sure does nicely emphasize my boobs and my butt. After all, we single girls have to work with what we have," she said as she pulled her door shut and leaned across the seat to open the other door on the driver's side.

"How's the proposing business going? Any good offers lately or nothing but the usual propositions?" Gerry asked as he sat down behind the steering wheel and started the small car's big motor. They joined in loud laughter in the private joke they had traded back and forth for months.

Registered nurse, Purity Jones worked the evening shift at the hospital. Her collar-length, light brown hair offset her medium height, her deeply set, dark-blue eyes and her large, obviously firm breasts she barely restrained in her size-D bra cups. Some people considered her voluptuous. Others classified her as corn-fed and country. She had long held out as a virgin, and at age 24, she diligently tried to marry a student doctor. She had been working at it continuously for the three years since graduating from nurse's training. She would readily confess to anybody who would listen that marrying a doctor was the only reason she became a registered nurse in the first place. This may have been originally true, but Purity had become a very good and extremely competent and compassionate nurse, and she become an even better one as her experience at the hospital expanded. If another three or four years went by before she married, she could well become one of the hospital's most valued professionals. However, no one could expect she would stay in nursing after she married. She had 'earth mother' written all over her. She wanted a husband and a big family and wanted them soon.

"Just the usual propositions," answered Purity through full, pouting lips. "Though the 77-year-old stroke patient in Room 306 did pat me on the butt tonight when I bent over to give him his medication. I think he showed not only good taste but also real measurable medical progress on his part."

"How do you figure that?" Gerry questioned.

"Well, when the old gentleman was first hospitalized a week ago, he couldn't even move his right arm at all. Now he tries to touch any of my good parts he can get close enough to."

"Bet your progress notes are fun to read."

"I can assure you that they are never boring," Purity replied.

Gerry drove them in the Thunderbird down the quiet street and into the parking lot at Eli's Cafe'. The small restaurant and medical personnel hangout sat only four blocks from the hospital. A pink and white neon sign flickered a warm welcome in a rhythmic staccato beat. The noisy night crowd packed the cafe' with those who had filtered in after a movie at the neighborhood's theater in the next block. The juke box belted out the latest Marty Robbins record and both pinball machines ran full tilt, fed coins by two loud medical students trying desperately to outdo each other's score.

"You know something, Purity? I do thoroughly enjoy life as a country doctor out in Essex, but there is just no cafe' in the village quite like this one. In fact, there may not be another one with food and atmosphere like this anywhere in the country."

"What do you mean Gerry? Are you trying to tell me you actually like this place? That's hard to believe," she continued. "This place is as honky as it gets and you're from California."

"Well, maybe it's more like I rightly miss old Eli's Cooking, especially his delicious homemade pies," he said as a faint mist of past memories clouded his hungry eyes.

They finally found an empty booth all the way in the back of the rectangular-shaped restaurant near the kitchen. Their waitress, a young co-ed from the town's teachers college, still cleared the dirty dishes away from the previous customers as the doctor and the nurse sat down at the table across from each other.

"So what's the big decision for this evening, Doctor?"

"I'm not sure yet," Gerry answered to the young co-ed.

"But you must have the menu memorized by now. After all, for the past four years, Eli has only had seven menus, one for each day of the week," continued the waitress in anticipation of the friends' orders.

"Well, let's see. Tonight, I'm torn between boysenberry pie and apple pie. Think I'll start with the boysenberry first, and make it a la mode please." Gerry thought he might actually have to try both kinds and include a double scoop of vanilla ice cream on the piece of apple pie. His sweet tooth hungered and pie at night helped him sleep soundly.

Soon the coed completely cleared away the dirty dishes and wiped down the still-damp table. Purity took the waitress's offer of a menu but ordered only coffee and a small green salad with oil and vinegar dressing. She had a tendency to watch her weight pretty closely, and so far she had kept it in all the right places. "You know, I think I've been pretty nice to you over the last three years, Gerry. I wonder why you never asked me out on a real date. Do you think I scare the most of the student doctors away with my story about still being a virgin?"

"Purity, I couldn't say for sure, but it probably does discourage a few. But you certainly shouldn't let that bother you," Gerry reassured her. "Not having you as a friend is their loss."

"Did such a blatant declaration inhibit you?" she inquired.

"Not necessarily, Purity. But I don't think your virginity is anybody's business but your own. It just isn't necessary for you to keep running a broadcast of your sexual status to every guy you meet."

"Yes, I suppose you're right," she reluctantly agreed as she undid the top two front buttons of her tight, nurse's uniform blouse.

"What about my good friend and partner, Harry? Maybe I should fix you up with him again. He's available at the moment and he's always enjoyed a real challenge," Gerry offered.

"Thanks, but no thanks. The time you fixed us up before, we went out for a beer and he tried to seduce me in his car on the way to the bar. I just could not believe that man's audacity. I've considerably softened my judgment on him since then, and we've become pretty good friends around the hospital, but unfortunately friends is all we are. With women he's the fastest moving guy I ever did meet."

"Yes, I suppose at times he is, especially when a beautiful and desirable woman like yourself is involved. But maybe you should give him a second chance. After all, that was over a year ago. Now he might even wait until your second date."

"Do you think all those stories he tells about girls back around his home and holler in West Virginia are true?"

"Probably not, Purity. The funny thing is, Harry did really like you. In fact he still does. Just last week he mentioned again what a great help you were on the tonsillectomy case when the young Rogers girl had a post-op bleed. He claims she would have died for sure if you hadn't noticed her deteriorated condition on the ward."

"Well, I still like him a lot too, and he is a fantastic physician, but I'm not about to lose my virginity in some old Chevy in the middle of a parking lot behind a seedy country and western bar.

He could have at least shown at little class and taken me into the bar to buy me a couple beers first before making his big move. I still can't believe what he tried to do," she said shaking her head in wonderment over the bygone incident still fresh in her memory.

"It sure scared him off fast when you started screaming fire. You're a real quick thinker. I heard your yelling emptied the bar in 30 seconds when everybody ran out to see which vehicle was going up in flames. They say you put up a fuss so loud the band even stopped in the middle of an Elvis number."

"Yes. I was pretty loud. But your partner rightfully upset me."

"Some of those folks were also mighty upset with having their entertainment interrupted when they finally figured out it was only Harry on fire. He was lucky they didn't turn a firehose or extinguisher loose on him."

"Do you think I scare all the medical students off by being honest enough to admit that I want to marry a physician and leave this state? I'm not looking for the perfect husband, Doctor. They haven't made one of those yet. I'll settle for one whose faults I can live with."

"Well, I know that's not the kind of thing you should mention on the first date," Gerry counseled. "Wait at least until the third or the fourth."

"The biggest problem is there aren't many students still single by the time they're seniors doing hospital rotation externships. I have to move fast. The only men chasing me now are three married staff doctors. It just doesn't seem right. It's not fair."

"You're right about one thing. Two-thirds of our class were married already by our senior year," Gerry interrupted.

"So what am I saving myself for?" She posed this question to herself as much as she posed to him her challenge. Their food order had been taken several minutes earlier, yet Purity still fidgeted nervously with her menu. As she finished speaking, her voice grew softer and her eyelids half closed in thoughtful contemplation. A very pretty young woman, her open attitude made it more evident.

"Don't worry, you're saving yourself for the right person, Purity, and whether he's a doctor or not doesn't matter at all. In the meantime, you're becoming a damn fine nurse in spite of yourself. This virgin story is something you started perfecting at least three years ago. I remember the first time you told it to me. Now you're stuck with it for a while. It's not a bad ploy, just don't dwell on it all the time."

"Maybe so, because at my age the story is getting a little boring, even to me. I sure hope you're right, and I find someone decent fast. Statistically, considering my age, I'm already halfway to menopause."

"You will find someone. Just don't get so uptight about it. Also, remember that statistically you're also only about ten years post-puberty. It's ridiculous to hear you talk about menopause."

"I must be desperate, because now I'm sorry I ever started talking about my virginity, though it's unfortunately still true. I wish it weren't, especially late at night. I must be the oldest living virgin nurse in this part of the county. Maybe even in the whole state." She sounded sad just contemplating the possibility.

"Be patient. So what if you are? You're one of the smartest and finest looking young women in this city, and if you ever find clothes to fit you, you'll probably stop scaring off all the eligible men around here."

Genuinely voluptuous, Purity was the oldest sibling of a large Missouri farming family growing oats and alfalfa, and raising

Herefords and children on land north of town. She had light-brown hair, cut neatly in a cropped page-boy style. Standing 5'6' tall, her weight hovered around 122 pounds. She had a dreamy figure of many men's fantasies, with measurements of 37-25-35 from top to bottom. Glaring eyes glued to her bust never quite saw her lovely face and the whole charming picture. That was their loss. Her dark blue, deep-set eyes clouded over as she glanced up from the menu.

"Yes, I guess you're right, Gerry. Sometimes I just get so darn discouraged." She paused momentarily as if she weren't sure whether to go on with her thought, then continued, "For instance, I've always liked you and figured someday you might give me some serious romantic thought if I just waited calmly and played it cool. But you never did. We never get past passionless friendship toward frenzied body clutching. Then, tonight I heard from the talkative bronchoscopy patient in Room 210 you're engaged to some farm girl out in Essex."

Since his large piece of boysenberry pie had just arrived, Gerry stopped paying close attention to the content of Purity's continuing conversation. So very hungry, he desperately started to eat his dessert even though the waitress had forgotten to put the ice cream on it.

"Is one of us crazy?" Purity continued. "I grew up on a local farm, Gerry. My folks have a pretty fair piece of good land near Greentop just north of the Schuyler County line. So I know what country life is all about. It took me four long, hard years to work myself through nurse's training, at the same time holding down three part-time jobs. I'm finally a fairly knowledgeable and respected RN at the hospital, and all of the single student doctors in their spare time are out dating the local farm girls. I would have done better had I stayed home with my dad's tractor plowing the north 40, milking the cows, and slopping the hogs."

"Wait a minute. What did you just say? Say that again."

"Say what again?" she replied with her eyebrows raised in question. "You want me to repeat the statement about my dad's tractor, cows, and hogs? Gosh, is it such a profound comment?"

"No what did you just say about an engagement?" inquired Gerry with surprise and astonishment reflected in his voice. It took a while, but it finally dawned on him what Purity had previously said. "What's this nonsense about me being engaged to some girl in Essex? Who told you that?" He became so excited he put his pie-filled fork down and actually stopped eating. The pie had suddenly lost all of its flavor.

Later that night during a nocturnal hunger pang, Gerry realized at about 3:00 A.M he could not remember if he had eventually finished the pie or not. Apparently he had not, because he awoke still hungry. In the kitchen of his apartment he found a supply of peanut butter and crackers, which he hungrily consumed straight out of the jar and the box before he could finally fall asleep again. The engagement story had done more than just excite him - it flabbergasted and stunned him. He could not believe how fast the rumor had started or how far it had spread. Gerry had no idea what to do about it, but he knew he could not let it ruin his night's sleep. He wanted to be fresh in the morning to scrub in on Cherry Jam's surgery. Even though he would only be the third assistant behind the staff physician, the resident, and the intern, his patient wanted him to be there and he gave her his word that he would be present. He hoped to be not only be present but also awake.

On Friday, December 22nd, two days later, the young doctor still periodically immersed himself in the thought of the startling Wednesday evening conversation with Purity. He was back in Essex working his Friday shift at the rural clinic. He could not empty his mind of that conversation. Purity's words, "...engaged to some farm girl...," kept repeating like an irritating jingle, coming back to haunt him.

The bronchoscopic surgery the previous morning on Mrs. Cherry Jam had gone very well. In fact, the patient could not have fared better. The bronchoscopy revealed a small mass just below her paralyzed vocal chord. The staff ENT surgeon easily dissected it free from the area and removed it completely. Biopsy showed the mass was non-malignant and proved to be what is known as a Singer's node, caused by excessive use and irritation of the vocal chords. Dr. Albin's surgical removal of the tumor freed up the unresponsive vocal chord tumor, which then moved and performed normally.

Cherry awakened from the anesthetic of the surgery after close to three hours that morning with a new voice, or, more precisely, with her formerly beautiful soprano pitch restored once again. Ecstatic with joy, she could not believe her good fortune. The nurses warned Cherry she should not talk too much in the beginning. She must take it easy at first and let her throat comfortably heal, but she ignored their advice. On Dr. Albin's orders, the nurses finally removed the telephone from Cherry's room because she had spent most of that Thursday afternoon calling all her friends. Cherry had been at the center of the village's communications network for so many years she could not suddenly break the habit when ordered to do so by a proper authority. Even as the scolding bombarded her from all sides, she persisted in talking to her hospital roommate until the ENT resident doctor on call finally sedated her to full sleep with a combination of Nembutal and Benadryl.

Gerry had just finished with the late afternoon Essex clinic patients. He leaned over his office desk as he wrote up the final patient's medical records. The man was an older diabetic farmer who recently switched from oral medication to injected insulin control. So far the farmer handled the change in treatment quite well, though the doctor assured the patient apple pie for breakfast was not acceptable for a diabetic's diet.

Harry entered the office whistling happily, dressed in his best dark wool pants, newest white shirt, and snappiest tan sports coat. He attempted to tie his favorite black and red striped necktie. After a third frustrating try he finally finished tying it sufficiently correct to gain his own approval.

"Why all fancied up, friend?" asked Gerry. "Your idea of dressing up is usually just matching shoes. Now look at you. What are you after?"

"Hey, don't be getting sarcastic on me just because I'm starting to show some class," Harry replied with a laugh.

"But you never even wear a coat and tie around here to see patients. Are they serving a formal meal or something at the Blue Bell Cafe' tonight? Should I be dressed up too?"

"That's the big problem with you overly dedicated doctors," answered Harry with a wide grin. "You never know what's going on outside the medical office right in your own little village."

"What do you mean by that statement?" Gerry inquired. "What is going on?"

"Hey buddy, tonight's the night of the annual combined Christian Churches' Christmas Social. They're holding it over at the Lutheran Church parish this year. The Lutherans combine with the Southern Baptists, and even Father Schaub and the Catholics are invited. The main event after the Christmas Carols seems to be a homemade pie auction that raises money for our rural clinic.

"That does sound like a neat idea. We certainly could use the money for some new equipment in this place," Gerry responded.

"Yes, we sure could. So the least we can do is attend and show appreciation and gratitude. Besides, every available woman in town prepares her family's traditional special pie recipe for this event. Hey, I wouldn't miss it for anything." Harry smiled as he patted his stomach in anticipation of a good filling feed. He had skipped lunch to work up a really big appetite.

"I'm with you. Wait for me for a few minutes while I clean up a little. How cold is it outside? My last patient said it was supposed to drop below freezing this evening."

Gerry suddenly remembered Christmas was only three days away and he wondered if it would be a white, snowy one. With his heavy work and study schedule, on top of the added serious responsibility of the rural practice, he had completely forgotten about the impending holiday season. Now that Harry mentioned it, he could use a bit of a recreational break. At the same time he knew the social event would provide him with a little more knowledge about the local customs and community population. After all, an important part in the art and science of small town doctoring is in supporting community functions and viewing patients in their natural surroundings as they interact in their interpersonal relationships. The prospect for an amusingly pleasant and educational experience excited him.

Little did Gerry realize then it would prove to be one of the most unique experiences for the young doctor - one which forever would influence his life.

The two new doctors approached the well-lit church's front entrance from Main Street. The outside of the Lutheran Church displayed red and green ornaments twisted around pine bough garlands from roof to sidewalk. Small flecks of snow had already adhered to the branches. From the inside of the church, joyful caroling rang down from the warm choir's loft resonating throughout the cold cemetery occupying the quiet lot across the street. Harry and Gerry pulled open the big double doors and sat down unobtrusively in a back pew until the short evening service ended. Surprisingly interdenominational, the ceremony had each of the two protestant ministers and the local Catholic priest saying a few words, seeming to spontaneously lead their favorite Christmas Carols. Hardly spontaneous, however, the choirs had practiced each of these carols for the past five weeks.

After the short sermons finished, everybody descended into the large recreation hall in the building's basement. Twenty long folding tables were set up in neat parallel rows. Along the entire length of one wall, five of the eight-foot long tables were laden with magnificent food offerings. At the front of the large room, a built-in riser of white oak formed a stage spanning almost the entire width of the 60-foot wide room. It extended into the front of the room for ten feet and stood three-feet high.

Before anyone would have a chance to sample the exquisite country Christmas pot-luck meal, the pie auction had to be concluded. The grand event was just about to start.

The rules of the auction were simple. All single women members of the three churches in town were requested to bake their favorite pie. These were put up for auction to be bid on by the single men of the town. The highest bidder of each pie would not only purchase the pie but also the companionship of its baker as his partner at the supper social gathering. Motivation for the event frequently was that the contests raised a considerable amount of money for each year's intended charitable function. Sometimes, however, the end result of the sale could be quite cruel. Pies baked by less popular ladies never commanded nearly the high bids the more desirable women's cooking produced. Very often the price of the pies had little to do with notoriety of the woman's cooking skills or the pie's potential taste. Sometimes two or three of the young men present conspired to bid a particular pie way past its reasonable worth, knowing the steady boyfriend of the baker would feel tremendous social pressure to buy the pie, no matter what the cost.

In his rural home of West Virginia, similar traditions had long existed, and Harry knew the intricacies and implications of this social convention. Gerry, however, city born, raised in Boston, with the last several years of his life spent in Los Angeles, was completely unfamiliar with these customary country contests. Very soon he would learn more than he ever needed to know about the nuances of small village socials.

The leaders of the three churches knew from long-standing experience to put the pies of the most sought after women on sale first. The pies were always placed in the order the combined church board members dubiously had designated to be 'most eligible'. Generally the crowd became restless if they were required to sit through the bidding on the pies of the lesser belles of the ball. If any subsequent pies were sold at higher prices than the ones previously auctioned, that indicated a definite vote of dissatisfaction against the rigid, predestined order of things. This happened very rarely, but when it did spring up, it served to add additional excitement to the bidding. Only on one occasion in the preceding six years did a wide discrepancy between the projected and actual bids occur. This aberrations had caused the sudden resignation of a majority of the combined board membership on the Sunday after that particular annual Christmas Pie Social.

Mrs. Martin Bishop, the Lutheran Church minister's wife conducted this evening's auction. She was a 5'2" inch, jovial, plump lady of around 160 pounds in her late forties. She conducted the bidding with such obvious relish and conviction Gerry instinctively knew she had won her own husband in a similar rite many years before. In fact, she had probably held him close to the hearth and table with her good cooking and affable personality ever since.

Lena Winters baked the first pie at auction. An imposingly tall, thin, Tri-Delt sorority girl, Lena arrived home for Christmas vacation from her junior year at the University of Missouri in Columbia just in time to make her pie for the auction. She wore her straight, blond hair almost to her waist, and she flashed a mischievous smile back and forth at the two young men who were immediately and intensely involved in the bidding. Her two potential paramours were a Sigma Chi fraternity boy from Missouri State University in Springfield and a senior studying engineering at the Rolla School of Mines. Both of the young men lived in other villages of the surrounding county and were home for the holidays. The spirited suspense in the bidding built to a heated crescendo, and to the surprise of everybody but Lena, the engineer won. The sour red cherry pie turned out to have an insufficient measure of sugar. Comely Lena had a lot to learn about cooking but she could already teach her mother quite a few things about men. Her mother always told her the way to a man's heart was through his stomach. Lena, however, discovered a shortcut during her freshman year attending college and had spent very little time in any kitchen since then.

The second pie auction offered the handiwork of one Karla Landowski. Mrs. Bishop informed the crowd of Karla's sophomore status at Christian College in Columbia, Missouri. Karla appeared also tall and thin like her predecessor, but came as close to homely as anyone would ever want to be. In an intriguing way, however, she effectively flaunted her plainness. She wore her straight black hair pulled back into a severe bun. Thick lenses festooned with pale pink frames, double the average size for glasses, balanced on a rather short indistinct nose. Her upper front teeth protruded from a severe overbite drawing attention to her severe case of acne scarring the lower half of her flushed face.

"What's all the excitement?" Gerry whispered, wondering aloud, as the bidding practically tore out of the gate in its initial intensity. Three extra large-sized local farm boys dashed into the contest. They spiritedly yelled and screamed their offers, all in apparent, but unbelievable sincerity. Within a few short moments the bidding flew way past the normal price of a sorority girl's pie. Obviously, there had to be a reason for the farm boy's sudden frenzied interest. Gerry suffered in confusion.

In answer to Gerry's quietly uttered question, Harry leaned over and told him. "Hey, as with most beauty, it's in the eye of the beholder. If you'd like to behold her attributes at the most advantageous angle, you might try the view from Morgan Hill on Rural Route 149 going south out of town. From there, the country road drops downhill steeply and splits the highly esteemed and openly coveted 330 acres of prime bottom land the young lady's aging daddy owns. Take good notes here, friend. We'll soon see who the real up and coming young adults are in this town."

The inherent socio-economic implications of the auction were fascinating once he understood the subtlety in this annual process of renewal taking place. Gerry had never experienced anything like it before. Through the socially acceptable guise of selling pies for charitable benefit, the small town actually openly evaluated the conscious aspirations and subconscious ambitions of the area's next adult population. Gerry wondered how many of these local folks realized the truth of this situation. He thought very few could probably understand the point in socioeconomic terms, and those people were not talking. For the older observers, the ritual was simply fun and games. In contrast, the contemplative young doctor did not believe the contest was much fun for all of the younger participants. Certainly glad to be merely an observer and not a participant in the event, he enjoyed the experience, even if it meant he would have to eat cake, which was not his favorite dessert. With a sensation of hunger fast expanding in the pit of his stomach, he began to wonder just how long this auction would last. All this excitement over pie made him ready to eat immediately.

Gerry had not noticed Sharon in the crowded room until the auctioneer called her name over the loudspeaker and beckoned her to bring her pie to the front and center stage for the following sale. She had apparently been sitting quietly in the front row of the large room while Gerry sat in the back. She wore a knee-length, forest green, velvet dress trimmed with silver piping down the bodice, sleeves, and collar. A small silver ribbon held her dark auburn hair piled on the top of her head in a neat bun. Her figure and dress emanated an aura of strength, but the fragile hair style indicated deep gentility. Sharon exuded an exotically striking combination. Obviously a favorite of the townsfolk, she received loud appreciative applause when she climbed the five steps to the stage in front of the room.

With one unified motion, every head turned and glared, every pair of eyes in the room burned into the last row of chairs where the two young doctors sat. Gerry could feel his heart suddenly skipped a few beats, and the hot blood coursed through his flushed face. Also surprised by the abrupt undivided attention of all the village folk present, Harry alleviated his embarrassment by calmly tipping his chair back against the cement wall in a purposeful pose of reassuring relaxation.

"Sharon needs no formal introduction to this town," said the speaker, smiling broadly at the happy audience. "We've watched her grow up among us since she was a just a little baby. She led our high school girls basketball team to the state semi-finals in Jefferson city two years ago, and she graduated with academic honors and a full scholarship to the teachers college. Now, I want to hear some loud and real big bids this time, including some offers from our young new doctors sitting back there in the very last row."

A big cheer went up from the crowd accompanied by the raucous clatter of loud clapping. Well over a minute lapsed until the noise quieted down.

Even from a distance the length of the long room, Gerry noticed Sharon looking as embarrassed as he suddenly felt. The subject of pie auctions had not been covered in the sterile environment of medical school. "What are you going to do now?" he harshly whispered to Harry, bending backwards toward him. "They must mean you. You're the one who drove her back alone from her dad's farm the night of the accident. I've never even been alone with her for a minute. What did you two do together in the pickup that night?"

"Hell no, they're not looking at me, buddy," Harry said firmly, shaking his head in the negative. "We did nothing. Hey, they're looking at you, old friend. After all, you're the one who saved her daddy's life. You have some rights in this auction. Put in your bid. Hey, you could end up with a real nice little farm here in Missouri and forget all about returning to your wayward ways in California."

As a rule, all of the evening's bids started at an upset price of two dollars and generally rise in increments of $.25 cents. Bidding for Sharon's mysterious delicacy started briskly, including both doctors and a couple of younger local fellows. Soon the two local boys dropped out when the bid reached four dollars. As the price hit five dollars, Harry politely dropped out. The spirited shouting back and forth between the participants and the stage created a scene of friendly rivalry and good spirit. Finally Gerry triumphantly thought he had won within a price range he could afford. In those days of the early 1960's, gasoline still was priced at $.25 cents a gallon. Five dollars could purchase enough groceries to feed a careful young man for a couple of days or longer. For the doctor, the sum also meant the difference between buying a new medical textbook he needed or going without it.

The minister's wife continued to chuckle, smiling like a Cheshire cat as she sat by up on stage. She could not have been more pleased with the results had she planned the entire chain of events herself. This was the biggest night of her year, her single opportunity to capture the microphone, amplifying her already loud voice. Never had the church's pie auction done so well as with her infectious bubbling enthusiasm. "Going, going, once, going, going twice, going three times...," she declared, "...to our nice young Dr. Frank sitting in the back of the room in the dark gray..."

Then it happened. "SIX DOLLARS!" someone suddenly shouted from the left side of the meeting hall with a harsh male voice. The statement's firm intensity sounded more like a calculated challenge to moral authority than a friendly bid in a church social auction. Instantly the packed room turned from a state of cheerful light laughter to complete stony silence. "I said six dollars," repeated a dark haired, short and slightly stocky young man wearing a dark red sweater. He sat by himself six rows forward and ten seats to the left of the doctors' position. His face appeared rough and pitted from the vantage of the profile view offered to the stunned young doctor. Unable to see his challenger completely as the man sat very still on the other side of the aisle, Gerry's view was partially blocked by a large white column supporting the beamed basement ceiling. With a loud but low and raspy voice, the man shouted out a sound similar to a slow grinding blender-full mix of sludge and rusty nails.

"Who the heck is that?" questioned Gerry in a soft voice to his partner as he leaned towards Harry to try to get a better look at this new bidder. Suddenly a flush of excitement came over the young doctor's face.

A ruddy complected, gray-haired rancher sitting just in front of Gerry, tipped his brown metal chair back and whispered, "It's just that jerk, Dexter Wilkinson, Doc. Don't pay him no mind. He's one of our local punks. Every town has a few. In fact, he's the one who runs the Thursday night poker sessions over at the pool hall." The rancher spoke with such obvious open disgust Gerry instinctively knew he must be telling the truth.

Suddenly Sharon seemed to have a scared look on her pretty face as she stood on the stage and stared out at the crowd. Gerry did not know what to make of it. Why should she be frightened? Repeatedly she cycled her full lower lip past her front upper teeth in nervous anticipation. Before Gerry could think much further, he heard someone loudly yelling with a voice much like his own, "$7.50!" *My God*, he thought, *'that was me. No wonder it sounded so close. What am I doing? I don't have much cash with me.* For a few seconds he felt lost, but then suddenly he remembered with relief Harry had also brought some money. His old buddy and partner certainly would not let him down.

"EIGHT DOLLARS," came the loud answering voice from across the room. There was no pause or hesitation. "EIGHT DOLLARS!" it rang out again, menacingly and deeply. Not smiling, the man in the bright red sweater hardly moved as he spoke and continued to stare straight ahead at the young woman on the stage. His arms were firmly folded across his chest. He seemed to be actually bidding on Sharon rather than on her homemade pie. He may actually have thought he was.

Harry looked sideways at Gerry and shrugged his shoulders. Matters quickly became confusing. This certainly was different than any church social Harry had ever attended back home in West Virginia. Looking in his pocket, he quickly confirmed he only had five dollars with him and a subsequent search of Gerry's wallet produced merely an additional seven. They had a combined total of only $12. They were hardly in a position to be big spenders that evening.

The young doctor yelled, "$8.50!" He was not exactly sure in what type of game he had now inescapably been caught up in. The amount of this last bid represented a lot of money to him. It would definitely be the difference between his being able to purchase the new surgery textbook he wanted to buy this week or having to wait until later next month. The book was important, and he felt he needed it soon. He thought he could possibly borrow a copy from the library in the meantime.

After another quick conference with Harry, they decided in fast agreement Harry would loan Gerry four of his remaining dollars, but only if Gerry promised not to bid over ten dollars total, leaving each of them with a dollar for Sunday services.

He yelled again, "$8.50!" with even more force and certainty in his voice than he had shown with his previous $7.50 bid. There was no turning back.

However, by now noise increased so much in the large hall Gerry had to repeat the bid a third time to be clearly heard over the crowd's loud mingling voices. Everybody talked at once. No one present had ever seen anything quite like this before in the old village. What did it mean? Who knew? The most anybody remembered a pie going for at one of these past church socials was for nine dollars. That had been four years earlier when the rich widow Dailey's mince meat special had been bought by bachelor Carl Winston. Two weeks later they were officially engaged and married in a church wedding a month before starting the serious business of spring plowing and planting. They even went on a big honeymoon, traveling all the way to Chicago by train from St. Louis for five days at the Palmer House Hotel. The widow's farm and fallow fields adjoined to the Winston place on its east side boundary. Now the combined acreage of fully planted pasture constituted one of the best maintained and most efficient farms in that area of the county. That pie was the best investment Carl Winston had ever made.

"Let's have quiet, let's have quiet, please, everybody," yelled out the Lutheran Church minister's wife loudly over the echoing public address system. "We're apparently about to see some history made here tonight in Essex, and I don't want any confusion later over what happened." Even she seemed stressed and suddenly unsure of herself. She no longer laughed and didn't even smile. This auction plowed new territory. Much of the cheerful happy attitude of the crowd slowly ebbed. Tension built. "Dexter," she asked, with as much authority as she could summon in her voice, "do you have a further bid? Make it now if you do."

Dexter seemed strangely struggling within himself. Slowly he tried to produce a small smile, but obviously his prior experience with any expression of friendliness had been severely limited. Quickly his visage changed into a sinister sneer perfectly fitting for his unfriendly face. Now he worried and it started to show. Dexter knew he was getting in over his head. He had never expected the young doctor to go over the six dollar bid. However, he thought, the doctor was new to the small town and probably did not understand the local customs. Bidding over eight dollars on any woman's pie in an Essex auction was tantamount to intentions of engagement. Dexter wanted Sharon. What man would not? However, he knew in his heart his real chances of actually getting her were next to nothing. They were less than zero. In fact, if her dad ever caught him even speaking to her outside of the church, he would probably shoot him. When Dexter first started bidding, he had not considered Sharon's dad might be there somewhere in the crowd. Dexter worried now, and his worry amplified when Gustav stood up to look sternly across the room at him before sitting back down. Dexter realized Olsen to be one tough farmer. Nobody fooled with him or his family; nobody that is, who wanted to stay healthy and alive. The rumor still circulated the decomposed body found on Gustav's farm late one spring day over two-and-a-half years earlier represented more than just an old fall hunting accident. Almost everyone in town felt it somehow represented Olsen's anger. Nobody knew, however, what the dead man had done to deserve such punishment. But it was hard to think of anything that could have justified such a hideous end to a human life.

But as in most lives, there comes a time when even a bully has to take a real risk, and this was Dexter's way of letting the small village know he was big time now. He suddenly saw himself as more than just a local heavy, pool-hall hustler and part time poker player. Dreams took up a lot of space in one's mind and even require more room in smaller people. Or is it just their needs may be greater? Dexter had decided he would finally make a name for himself in town tonight, and the citizens better damned well know it. "NINE DOLLARS," he yelled out in loud defiance. "It's nine dollars, I say, college boy, NINE DOLLARS! Maybe you better sell your stethoscope if you need cash to compete in this auction."

In the interim between the bids, Gerry had been watching Sharon on the front stage. He couldn't decide if she looked frightened or just angry - maybe a combination of both. She stood very still with her hands at her side, her mouth tightly shut, and her eyes switching focus between the two men. He did not know her level of well being enough to judge her mental state as he was too new to the town to realize the full implications of the local customs. Somehow this whole thing had soared completely out of hand. Emotions outraced rational thought. Were there subtle treacheries here to be carefully contemplated and everlastingly avoided? He did not know, but by now he hardly cared. He was committed to the contest.

No medical class or book of science had ever prepared him for this evening. Maybe he did not think with his head, but he knew with matters of women, sometimes you have to lead with your heart. Suddenly he knew where his heart led and he loudly yelled out his final bid, beyond which he knew he could not advance. "TEN DOLLARS!" He had raised the offer a whole dollar at that time, knowing in his mind and wallet it was as far as he could go. He waited. Would Dexter follow or not? The suspense built in a dramatic but unplanned manner.

Everybody in the crowded room turned to look at the man in the bright red wool sweater. Some held their breath and nobody spoke. A few shuffled their feet or moved in their seats for a better view.

For a few seconds, Dexter just sat there looking straight ahead at Sharon on the stage. Then finally he stood up slowly, shrugged his shoulders put on his brown leather jacket and quickly walked out of the nearest side doorway of the hall. Suddenly silence permeated the room until the sound of the door slamming shut on its heavy spring hinges.

Dexter had proven his point. The whole town would be talking about this auction for a very long time. Anyway, since he hoped to entice the young doctors into some of his future poker games, he felt that there was no need or sense in alienating them completely. He figured they would be around for another five months. That should provide ample time for him to get back at both of them. He realized he would have to be better prepared next time.

Suddenly the cacophony in the large basement hall became nearly deafening with sudden boisterous cheering and prolonged loud clapping as Gerry Frank walked up the center aisle and onto the front stage.

He gave his money to Mrs. Bishop, collected his pie, and escorted Sharon to one of the small round tables around the side of the room. The cheering did not stop until they reached their chairs.

Sharon did not speak until after she sat down. "You know, you're some kind of damned fool," she quietly said with a sad sort of disappointment and bitterness to her voice. "That was something a rich showoff would do, and somehow you don't impress me as that. Why did you do it? What were you thinking?"

Her apparent ire surprised Gerry. He thought he had rescued a damsel in distress, but she hardly sounded grateful, confusing him even more because he honestly didn't know why he had done it. "I'm not sure," he replied truthfully in thoughtful reflection. "I just didn't want you to be sharing this special evening with anyone but me." He had suddenly realized and verbalized the truth, and with nothing more to say, he sat down at the small table. Neither of them spoke for a moment. They both looked without hesitation at each other and then realized how much they liked what they saw. Their smiles appeared simultaneously.

"Dexter's a big jerk," said Sharon. "Sure, I'd have had supper with him. That's part of the rules. But then, so what? As soon as we finished the meal, I'd have politely excused myself, found you, and if you weren't busy, I'd have sat down with you. I like you a lot and it's time I let you know it. If Dexter wanted to waste nine dollars on my cherry pie, that's his business, but I sure didn't think you were irresponsible or foolish. Do you realize how much you just spent?"

"Yes," said Gerry after a long pause and now even more completely confused. "I spent ten dollars. It is a lot of money. I'm certainly not rich, but I thought you were worth every cent of it, and besides, I do love cherry pie."

"Who are you kidding?" questioned Sharon in feigned exasperation as she slowly shook her head from side to side.

"No, I mean it. I really do love cherry pie. It's always been my favorite," he continued with enthusiasm after the realizing Sharon had actually said that she liked him a lot.

"Maybe so, but I never even announced what kind of pie mine was. There is no way you could have known it was cherry until you saw it just now. That's the problem with these food auctions to raise money. The men get carried away and soon start thinking they're actually bidding on the women. Standing up on that stage makes you feel like you're in some sort of a slave auction."

"Slave auction?"

"Yes and it's even less funny when you realize there really were such auctions in this town not much more than 100 years ago. In fact, when Dexter's great grandfather was alive in the early 1860s, he still worked slaves on the farm Dexter now owns down on Sully's creek."

"Well, you have you admit tonight at least all the money went to a very good cause. Even as we talk, they have auctioned off another two pies, and most everybody concerned seems pretty happy about it, including the women."

"Yes, you're right about the auction proceeds going for a very good purpose tonight. Believe me, I wouldn't have entered it if the money this year had not been intended for the rural clinic here in the village. Our family really believes in the clinic. Already this month you've dramatically demonstrated just how much we need it for all the medical emergencies. My dad would definitely have at least lost his left hand if you had not been there that afternoon to save him. He even might have bled to death." Suddenly she looked away, and neither of them spoke while three more pies were auctioned. They all went in quick succession with even the lowest now going for seven dollars. Somehow the doctor's high bid had set a new standard in Essex.

"I'm sorry, I don't mean to sound ungrateful," Sharon continued. "You're new to this area, and there is no reason you should know all the unspoken implications to these contests. They are another one of our strange country customs. On the surface it just seems like the eligible men are bidding on the price of a pie, but actually there is a lot more at stake than that." She smiled as she finished talking. Her beautiful smile showed evenly matched white teeth and dimples in both cheeks. Her whole face seemed to glow with thoughts only known from the inside. Her face was difficult to read from the outside.

"You're much different than I first imagined," said Gerry. "I thought you were shy, but you can certainly come on pretty strong. I really like your bluntness. It's very refreshing."

"Thank you for the compliment. I think you're pretty nice yourself," she said.

"Are you serious about everything you just said to me?" In the room the auction finally came to a close, and some of the older people now circulated and started for the food line in the front of the hall. However, Sharon and Gerry were now quite oblivious to everyone else in the room almost as if they were alone. The full festivities of the Christmas season had suddenly descended around them. Sharon reached across the table and put both hands on Gerry's right forearm. "Let's make a promise right now. Let's promise never to kid each other about anything serious under any circumstances. That's all I'm asking for now, and you have over five months to make up your mind about anything else."

"Well, I promise never to kid you under any circumstances as you say, but what do you mean by 'anything else'?"

"What do you think I mean?" she replied in a voice slightly softer but a bit mischievous.

"I don't have any idea," he answered. Sharon was a beautiful girl - obviously intelligent and warmly caring, but Gerry could not believe the sudden serious implications of this talk and where it headed. This hardly qualified for a form of mere casual conversation. He always thought city girls were fast, but this country girl seemed to be trying to move into his life and future in a whirlwind fashion. Where was she coming from? Was she really serious? What should he do? Maybe Harry could give him some advice on rural romance in small country villages.

Gerry had broken up with his last steady girlfriend, Mary Jo, about four months earlier. She had been a loyal lover and favored friend. They broke up over a lack of communication, and Gerry had not quite forgiven himself for his own stupidity. But that was another story.

"I'm not sure I understand," he repeated, now looking straight at Sharon with a quizzical smile on his face. "Tell me more. What exactly are you trying to say? You can tell me. I'm a doctor." His smile broadened as he finished his request. He could hardly wait for her answer.

"There's not much to understand," said Sharon. "It's a small village here as I'm sure you must now realize. Different young rural clinic doctors rotate through Essex every six months. I've been thinking about it ever since I was past puberty, and I've been thinking about it in particular ever since I met you. Now I've decided.

"You have decided what?" he asked.

"That you are the doctor for me. This gives me six months to prove to you I'm all the woman you would ever want. You have six months to decide if I'm the right woman for you. That should be enough time for both of us. Don't you agree? Do you think you will need more?" She smiled as she said this, but she held his forearm in a grip of intensity saying much more than mere words. It spoke deep feelings.

He already knew in his heart he hoped she would not let go. He hoped she would hold on tightly for a very long time. "You're not kidding, are you?" questioned the doctor in a quiet thoughtful reply. "You're really serious, aren't you?" This entire scene seemed like a dream or an unfulfilled fantasy. However, the vanilla smell of her perfume and the warm pressure of her right hand over his bare left wrist permitted no doubt as to the reality of Sharon's declaration.

"Don't tell me you've forgotten already," she replied with smile, slowly shaking her head again in feigned exasperation.

"Forgotten what?" he asked. His curiosity to know right away was complicating his concentration to remember.

"Did you forget the promise we just made two minutes ago? You sure do have a short memory, Doctor, for someone so smart."

"You are a lot to digest all at once. I guess I'm overwhelmed," he replied. He spoke the truth.

"We just promised we would never kid each other about anything serious. I'm as serious as I'll ever be in my life. Therefore, you can rest assured I am not kidding you."

"But somehow it seems so sudden, or am I hopelessly slow?"

"No. It's not as sudden as you might think, though maybe you are a little slow. I've talked about it with my dad, whose life you saved, and with my Aunt Cherry, whose voice you restored. They both think you're the finest physician who ever came to this town, and you've only been here for three weeks so far. I knew that I'd find a way to get to know you from the first time I saw you over two years ago. I knew it then in my heart. I just wasn't sure in my head how it all would happen."

"Over two years ago?" questioned Gerry, trying hard to remember where they possibly could have previously met. "You met me over two years ago? Are you certain? I'd never been to Essex then. I didn't even knew it existed, though I'm glad I do now."

"Yes, it was during a mixer dance at the teachers college in November of '59, my freshman year there. You danced with Judith, my former roommate from Hannibal, a couple of times. The dance had just broken up and the three of us talked a little bit. You were a sophomore and said you had to get back to your apartment to study for a pathology quiz. You seemed like such a serious student. I've had my eye on you ever since." She looked down suddenly as she started to blush. She relaxed her warm hold on his wrist, looked up at him again, and reached up to brush a strand of his thick hair from his forehead. The touch of her hand on his hair felt good to both of them.

"Well, you must have been watching from a great distance. I couldn't possibly be that dumb or nearsighted. You're hardly someone I wouldn't notice." Gently he grasped her right hand and then firmly placed it back on his left wrist.

"No, that's not necessarily true," she said as she tightened her grip. "You obviously had your mind on other things. We also met at two of your medical fraternity house dances last year. I was the date of one of the hospital residents. You were president of the house then, and I remember your date both times was a beautiful tall blond Stephens College girl from Columbia. She had a deep southern accent and was the homecoming dance queen. I think she came from Florida."

"My gosh, you're right," Gerry exclaimed in surprise. "She was my steady girlfriend for over two years. We just broke up this last summer." He said this with some sadness as memories of past pleasures mixed with dreams unfulfilled.

"She seemed very special to you then, and I have to admit I certainly envied her at the time. If I had known you then I'm sure I would have been jealous."

"She was very special. I still miss her at times. She married an engineer in September and moved back to Florida. I received a Christmas card from her last week. We're still good friends but strictly in a platonic way now."

"That's nice to hear for a couple of reasons."

"What do you mean by that?" he questioned. "What are the reasons?"

Sharon smiled sincerely before replying. "It shows you are available, and it shows you value friendship."

"That's true. I'm an available good friend," he said with subtle humor. "So what else is new?"

"So now, next time you meet me, you might remember me?" she answered laughingly. "Now if we don't get a place in those long food lines soon, there's not going to be any of the good stuff left." So saying, she stood up, and they walked together to the end of the shortest line at the long table where the food was served. Sharon held his hand all the way. She suddenly felt more possessive and confident.

Gerry quite carefully and respectfully picked over the food selections until they were opposite the large pans filled with southern fried chicken. Then he nearly made a complete fool of himself piling up the chicken on his plate. He wondered if he could get a doggie bag to take home leftovers if there were any. He and Harry had only two dollars to last the rest of the week and those were destined for the church collection basket Sunday if they did not starve to death beforehand.

Deep in thought, Gerry returned to his and Sharon's small round table by the wall. However, even after considerable concentration, he still could not remember Sharon from any of the three previous times she had mentioned. He certainly felt it a nice compliment that she remembered him. Now, for the first time in the small town of Essex, he found himself really relaxing in spite of the cares and responsibilities of his first medical practice. Country doctoring could be fun and he suspected already that Sharon would make it even more fun.

By the time Gerry and Sharon had finished their main meal and he started on her cherry pie for dessert, it finally struck him what a sincere, open, warm and intelligent young woman Sharon Olsen was. She told him of some of the ancient folklore of the small town and some recent history of herself. She had studied to be a high school teacher of commercial subjects in her junior year at the teachers college. She decided if these teaching positions were scarce after graduation, she could always obtain a good secretarial job with her superior typing and shorthand skills she had perfected by then. She had also elected to take a few courses in biology and botany in keeping with her interest in the family farm. She lived on campus at the college for her first two years but now commuted the distance between home and school since she felt her dad and Aunt Cherry needed her to be closer. She tried to teach them to use a new bookkeeping and inventory system that would help her dad with the farm and her aunt with the store.

"So, I've really been this close to you on three previous occasions in the last three years before I came to Essex without remembering you? I can't believe it," Gerry said, shrugging his shoulders in exaggerated fashion. "Obviously if I'd known of your cooking talents, I wouldn't have let those opportunities pass." Her pie was delicious, and he figured they would probably finish off half of it that evening.

"Actually, we've been this close together on a fourth occasion before you came to Essex," she answered laughingly. "But I'll forgive you for not remembering me from that one also, though I know you noticed me."

"You think I noticed you?" he asked.

"I know you did. You even commented about it," she replied. She did not offer any additional explanation and Gerry saw no reason then to question her further. If he had, their whole relationship might have been very, very different and might have ended right there. It would be a long time before either of them would reflect on this possibility or on the first time she mentioned their fourth meeting.

The evening ended too soon. Time flies fast when you are having fun. Townspeople left and headed home. The cleanup committee had already started clearing the tables and washing the many dishes.

Harry wandered over to their table to help Gerry and Sharon finish the cherry pie. After all, he figured, he also had a fair amount of a financial investment in it. With two additional glasses of milk the pie soon was gone.

"Sure seems like a happy crowd here tonight. What do you think about it, Harry?" asked Gerry. "How does it compare to West Virginia pie auction socials?"

"Well, I did see some disappointed faces on some of the losing bidders, but after all, it certainly is for a good cause," Harry replied. "Counting the price of the admission tickets, I understand the supper raised almost $500 for our medical clinic. We sure can use it on new supplies and updated equipment."

"I saw some shocked expressions on the faces of a few of the successful bidders once they tried to eat the pies they won," laughed Sharon as she stacked up their empty dishes. "I feel really good you two guys actually ate all of mine."

"So then everybody is a winner to some extent," said Gerry. "That makes it really nice. You can't lose when everybody wins."

"Not necessarily," replied Harry. "Have you seen Father Schaub lately? He looked like he was about to cry after the last auction. Tonight a second Catholic girl had her pie bought by a Baptist. Their local church is Southern Baptist, and you know, those men rarely convert in these parts."

"Harry is right," said Sharon. "If poor Father Schaub's flock decreases much further here, they will transfer him back to St. Louis. He loves Essex. He's a country boy at heart."

The subtle social implications of the pie auction amazed Gerry so far beyond his understanding and yet so easy for Harry. As a big city boy, Gerry had already learned a lot from this small town practice, but obviously he had a lot more to learn. He hoped he had time.

"My dad and I would like to have you out to our farm. We want to have both of you as guests for Christmas dinner," Sharon said. "Then you can see how well I cook a turkey with stuffing and the works. You won't even have to bid on it, but you might have to help with the dirty dishes afterwards."

"Golly," said Harry. "I've just now accepted an invitation from the Bloodstones. Seems they have a beautiful, eligible daughter in St. Louis they want me to meet and invited me to drive down with them for Christmas. After seeing her picture in a bathing suit as a lifeguard last summer, I agreed immediately. I know my old friend will accept your invitation, Sharon. Am I right, Gerry?"

"Right as usual," Gerry answered. Harry sure was one smooth-talking son of a gun and the best friend a man could hope to have.

Plans for a fine Christmas weekend were formerly finalized in the old church basement. It had been an educational and interesting evening. Though the young doctor did not realize it yet, by rural Missouri standards, he was practically engaged. Purity's comments on Wednesday evening had proved prophetic.

Sharon found her dad in the crowd leaving the church. He had eaten supper with her Uncle Jim and readily agreed to drive the pickup truck he and Sharon had driven to town back to the farm by himself.

Gerry and Sharon walked quietly hand in hand down Main Street of the small village to his car where he had left it in front of the clinic building. Many of the buildings were festively decorated with colorful Christmas lights shining in the dark. The young people spoke very little. Though the snow had stopped falling, it had already accumulated enough to make the scene as perfect as an old fashioned Christmas card.

The couple took 12 minutes to drive the five-and-a-half miles of narrow country roads to the Olsen farm. It took them a an additional hour finally to get out of the small car before Sharon walked the last 30 feet to her back porch. Gerry waited until she was inside the farmhouse before restarting the powerful engine, and slowly and thoughtfully he drove back to the quiet village. He already missed her. He figured he would sleep over in the clinic for the night and drive back north in the morning to make rounds at the hospital. As he drove he noticed his watch indicated 1:00 A.M., and he knew by then about every sixth driver passing on Route 63 was probably intoxicated. It had started to snow again and the roads would be tough enough to drive without having to dodge any drunks.

Life in Essex might be country, but it was certainly neither slow nor dull

Chapter 5
Snow Fire
December 24-27, 1961

Late in the cold afternoon as the day turned into Christmas
Eve in the rural village of Essex, Missouri, Doctor Gerry Frank
closed up the old, red brick medical clinic on the southeast corner
of Main and Station Streets. The time was well after five o'clock
and it had swiftly grown dark. The clinic had been kept open
Sunday afternoon because it would be closed the following day on
Monday, Christmas Day. Most of the small town's businesses also
stayed open for last minute shopping. Multi-colored Christmas
lights twinkled in decorations outside the buildings. From inside,
white lights shined brightly through semi-frosted windows. The
young doctor had finally finished treating his twelfth and last
patient of the day. He began to like the little country community
and to identify with its self-reliant people. It no longer bothered
him that small town's growth had come to a screeching halt long
ago.

His partner, Doctor Harry Thompson, had left town earlier
that afternoon around 3:30 P.M., driving with the Bloodstone
family the nearly 190 miles southeast to St. Louis in their
powerful, new, big black Cadillac. The Bloodstones ranched
healthy Hereford cattle, and together with Harry, would be
spending Christmas Day in the big city with their daughter and
numerous cousins who resided there. Their large family planned a
celebration upon their arrival. They hoped to arrive by 8:00 P.M.,
but it would depend upon road conditions and traffic.

Gerry worried about the weather and whether or not his
friends could outdistance the oncoming snowstorm blowing in
rapidly from the west. The intensity of the storm had gradually
increased from the moment Harry and Mr. and Mrs. Bloodstone

left town. Large wet, white flakes came down continuously, and already over five inches of fresh snow visibly covered the high dead grasses on the rolling hills surrounding Essex. Snow had fallen four times in the previous three days. The temperature stayed steady just below freezing at 31 degrees Fahrenheit. The soggy snow accumulated fast in and around the small country village.

The young doctor walked carefully across the paved, snow-slippery street and stepped up on the wide, wooden sidewalk running along the front of the faded red brick wall of the general store. He loudly stomped on the damp wood to attempt to kick off the sticky snow from his brown leather cowboy boots before going inside. After four forceful stomps of his feet, most of the snow finally fell free.

The heavy store door opened as stout Father Schaub from the local Catholic Church hurried out carrying a big, red-wrapped Christmas present under his left arm. Pulling the brim of his hat lower with his right hand he headed into the wind. With his head down sheltered against the snow, the priest didn't notice the doctor until the last second, and he narrowly missed suddenly knocking him over in a collision.

"Oh, excuse me Doctor, I guess I'm preoccupied. Good evening to you," greeted the priest.

"No problem, Father, and a very good evening to you, too. It certainly looks like this will be a white Christmas for us."

"You can count on that Doctor, for sure, and now I definitely hope we'll be seeing you at Midnight Mass tonight. It's too stormy to leave the county. Come to church and bring a friend. Arrive early and get a front pew, or you may end up standing in the back of the church with all of the come-lately Protestants."

"Well, I'm not sure about that, Father. I may not be able to make it at all," Gerry answered.

"And why not, pray tell? Your own fine father is a former respected Jesuit and still a member of the church, I've heard. I'm sure he would want you there. By then all the bars in town will be closed anyway. Where else would you be going? It's not just a mortal man's birthday we're celebrating, you know. He is the son of God."

"Well, I'm spending the holiday with Sharon and her family, and she is a Lutheran, as is her whole family."

"Yes. I know them all. Bring them with you."

"But, we may be attending her church this evening. Those Lutherans have been celebrating Christmas lately, too. I'm sure you must have heard about it," the young doctor replied with a smile. "It started long ago with some ex-Catholic named Martin Luther."

"Now don't you be sarcastic and forget, son, Roman Catholics like your dad really began all this Christmas celebration. Those Lutheran Church folks are okay, I will admit to that. I even have some for friends. But for real pious pomp and tangible tradition, you just can't beat a good Catholic Midnight Mass. Don't accept substitutes. Go for the original," with this said, the good priest laughed and touched the brim of his black hat with his free right hand in a parting farewell and hurriedly walked west on the sidewalk towards his distant parish. The priest soon became lost in deep thought as the snow swirled around him from the gusty wind. Since he had learned that Dr. Frank's father, now a well-known radiologist, had been a Jesuit priest for two years before quitting the priesthood to study medicine many years ago, Father Schaub had started a campaign to bring the young Dr. Frank back to the 'one true' church. Certainly his small country parish could use every soul he could save as it slowly but steadily hemorrhaged members and needed a physician to help sustain a viable flock.

Dr. Frank entered the general store to look for Mrs. Cherry Jam, the woman who owned the place. A few customers still lingered in the warm, cozy general store doing their late Christmas shopping, but they were not of immediate concern to the young doctor. Dr. Frank had been the referring physician for her recent hospitalization where surgical removal of a small tumor beneath one of her vocal cords had suddenly and dramatically restored her formerly feminine voice. For the previous five years before the operation, her voice had become increasingly deep and rough. Now Cherry's voice sounded lie a female voice once again. The tumor had turned out to be nonmalignant, and Mrs. Jam had great news for her Christmas present - the gift of life itself. Dr. Frank had brought the best news a physician could bring to any patient.

As Gerry entered the store, he was surprised to see a middle-aged man standing before the cash register. "Good evening, Doc," he said as he walked from behind the wide-wooden counter to shake hands with the doctor. "I'm James Jam. I clerk here occasionally when my wife is busy." He stood tall and straight. At 6'2" with broad shoulders, he showed to be a bit on the lean side at about 165 pounds. He appeared taller as he walked on his toes, moving quickly in fast fluid motions. Though far from handsome and looking every bit of his 44 years, he had a certain planned meticulousness to his presence. An elegantly cut mustache and straight, thick black hair emphasized his steely manner. He dressed in a freshly pressed, green wool shirt, tucked tightly into new gray pants with sharply ironed creases.

"Good Afternoon, sir. I'm Dr. Frank. I'm looking for your wife."

"She's not here. Don't you know?" Mr. Jam continued, "Seems to me, I thought you'd be sending the missus directly home from the hospital today. Instead they tell me she's going to be convalescing for two or three more days over in Moberly town.

Anyway, I don't mean to sound unappreciative. I hear the results of the operation you arranged for her turned out really fine. I certainly do want to thank you for everything you've done for her. We sure are proud to have you for our family doctor."

"Gosh," replied the doctor with a sigh and a questioning frown on his forehead, "we discharged her from the hospital this morning at about nine o'clock. I know that for sure."

"How's that doctor?"

"Because after I saw her on surgical rounds with the ENT resident I wrote the order myself. I thought she would come back home directly to Essex. In fact, I thought she'd be here by now. What's all this about Moberly?"

"That's where she is now, staying with her sister, Helen," replied the clerk as he walked back behind the counter.

"Well, we advised her since the surgery she should not use her voice loudly or talk excessively for the next couple of weeks. I have to admit, though, with all the talking a store clerk has to do, and with so many phone orders she must take, it's probably a very good idea for her to stay completely away from the store for the next few days. I sure hope it won't cause a whole lot of trouble and extra work for you Mr. Jam."

"No, I was just joshing you, Doc. It'll do Cherry a world of good to visit with her sister for a while. That sister will do enough real talking and family gossiping for both of them if I know anything about Helen. Things slow down at the local slaughterhouse and rendering plant anyway during the holidays, so I don't mind filling in for her here at the store for a couple of days. It will keep me busy and out of trouble."

"So, you don't really mind?" inquired the doctor.

"Oh, I'll get by, and I have Rose here to help me if I need it. Don't worry about it at all," he said as he started folding up two new plaid shirts which had been on openly displayed draped over hangers.

"Well, it sure smells a lot nicer here in your store than it does down at the slaughterhouse. How do you stand it there? The odor coming from boiling what's left of those dead animals is sure nothing I could become accustomed to. I even hold my breath when I drive past the place. The town fathers were really smart when they built the plant east of town so the prevailing wind doesn't bring the bad smell back this way."

"Yeah, I know what you mean, Doc. Compared to that place, it's always a real pleasure working inside here at the store. It's just I understand Cherry has a brand new voice now, and I'm very anxious to hear what it sounds like."

"I'll bet you are. It's astonishing how much the surgery changed her voice. Wait until you hear her. I know you'll be really surprised and pleased."

"Yes, she apparently wants to surprise me with it because every time I'd call the hospital to talk to her, I would only get to speak to one of the nurses. They were friendly enough, but I still haven't heard Cherry talk yet since before her surgery. She's the one I want to hear. I can hardly wait."

"Well, you know, we finally had to discontinue her hospital room telephone the day after surgery. She kept calling her friends to show off how she sounded. She talked way too much. Otherwise, we couldn't keep her quiet."

"Yes, the last nurse I spoke to told me told me her phone was turned off so I quit calling. Anyway, she'll be coming home soon. You know, Doc," he said reminiscing, "that fine woman used to have the sweetest voice in this here part of the county. Cherry used to sing every Sunday in our church choir. She had the finest soprano voice that old church ever had or heard."

"She was pretty good?"

"Oh, she was very good, and I'm not just saying this because she's my wife."

"No kidding?"

"Yes sir. Why, on many occasions she even sang solo. You should have heard her do those old hymns. She could make a believer out of the worst sinner. She certainly made a Christian out of me."

"I'll bet she did. Well, maybe we'll hear her sing again soon. She probably shouldn't start singing for a couple more months, though," the doctor advised.

"I wonder if her voice will be anything like it was back then. Her beautiful voice first attracted me to her." The fond memories of those distant Sundays brought a deep smile to his thin face. The corners of his mouth tilted up in a wide grin. "Maybe now she'll stop smoking those damn cigarettes. Her bad habit certainly does her no good. I never did learn why she started."

"Well, the type of problem she had with her voice frequently comes from repeated vocal cord irritation. We usually see it with people making excessive use of their voice. The continual job of answering the phone here and taking long orders, day in and day out, could have taxed her vocal cords enough to cause the trouble. But you're right about the smoking - it's a bad and dangerous habit. It sure does her no good, and I hope she will stop, too. Get on her about it."

"I'm sure going to encourage her to quit. She has come close to burning our place down twice with lit cigarettes she forgot about. Did you ever smoke, Doc? That's one bad habit I never picked up myself."

"Yes, I have to admit I did for almost four years. Smoked about a third of a pack a day. I quit two years ago."

"So what made you stop?" Jim asked, hoping to find a formula he could use to persuade his wife to quit the addictive habit.

"Fear. It's a great motivator. I did an autopsy one night on a 38-year-old male who was a two-pack-a-day smoker. He died of bronchogenic carcinoma. After a long look at his lungs, I never smoked again."

"Well that's one way of bringing some good from another man's poor luck," the clerk replied.

Just then, the heavy front door of the store swung wide open with a gust of cold wind and snow as Sharon Olsen walked in. With the wind opposing her, she leaned hard against the inside of the door to close it. Her face flushed pink from the cold winter weather outside. She quietly laughed but did not speak.

Gerry smiled in response. The young doctor could hardly believe how wholesome and beautiful Sharon was. Seeing her again almost took his breath away. He could not stop thinking about her lately, and he had trouble internalizing the statement she had calmly and bluntly made to him a couple days ago. He learned according to local custom his purchase of her homemade cherry pie at the Christmas church auction social that evening indicated they were 'practically engaged.' He found it fascinating before that memorable evening that he had never even kissed her. In the short time since, he had quickly made up for lost time. Already it seemed natural for her fair face to frequently flicker in the framework of his mind.

As Sharon quickly took off her green wool mittens and shook the unmelted snow from her wet, curly auburn hair, she grasped Gerry's right wrist warmly in both of her hands. She turned to smile at Mr. Jam - a smile of sincere concern and heartfelt relief - the smile of someone who really cared for her uncle.

"I understand you saw my wife since her surgery. How does she seem to you, Sharon? I thought she would be home by now."

"Yes, I saw Cherry in the hospital yesterday, Jim, and she was doing really great. You're not going to believe her new voice. It's so light and lyrical. Maybe now she'll start singing again. We could sure use her in the church choir."

"I'd like to believe that, but first I've got to hear her. She's still not home. Even Doc, here, thought she would be back in Essex by now."

"Well, she wanted me to make certain I gave you this Christmas present from her this evening, in case you can't drive over to Moberly town after you close the store tomorrow. Cherry thought the continuing snowfall would accumulate too fast and be far too deep to drive through by then." Sharon handed Jim a brightly wrapped present - a rectangular box about half the size of a shoe box, carefully covered in silver and red paper and tied with a narrow white ribbon.

"Can I open it now?" Jim asked eagerly as he gently shook the box with a quizzical expression on his face. The gift didn't rattle within the package, but it did seem fairly heavy, more so than one would have thought for the size of the box.

"Certainly not. You should know better than to ask. It's a Christmas present to be opened on Christmas morning and not a minute before. Aunt Cherry made me promise to tell you that. So don't go thinking about any sneak preview, like looking tonight. The ribbon is tied too tightly for you to slip it off and back on again. You will just have to wait until tomorrow, so go home and put it under your Christmas tree until then."

"Sharon, it just won't seem like Christmas without Cherry. It's always been her custom to have the store open for a couple of hours Christmas morning. Sometimes folks will forget to get food they need at the last minute, and it would ruin their whole

Christmas dinner if we weren't open then. I'll try to keep up the tradition - the village has come to expect it. I also promised her I'd rearrange some items inside the hardware area, back yonder, and maybe make it a little easier to find things out in the storage shed. I might even try to bring order to the chaos of everything she's stored down in the fruit cellar underneath the shed."

"That would be a nice surprise for her when she comes back. I know she'd appreciate it. That's one of the things Aunt Cherry keeps meaning to do but never quite finds the time. She mentioned it to me again just before she went to the hospital," Sharon informed the tall, thin man standing before her.

Slowly, a young woman quietly approached the front counter from the back of the store. She appeared to be in her early twenties and spoke very softly with a fragile faint smile on her face. "Hello, Sharon. It's good to see you again, Merry Christmas." Even as she spoke, there was a remote quality to her presence, as if she were afraid a deficiency and an insecurity might become obvious should she speak louder or move more quickly.

Sharon ignored the shy young person completely and appeared to purposely turn her back toward the newcomer. The doctor quickly realized it would have been impossible for Sharon not to have seen the young woman or to have missed her soft-spoken greeting. He wondered about Sharon's obvious intentionally rude behavior. Sharon acted so deliberately out of character he could not understand her abrupt change. She showed a calculated discourtesy with contrived disrespect.

"Oh, Dr. Frank, have you met my sister-in-law, Rose Tice?" asked Jim with signs of considerable strain in his voice. He seemed embarrassed to make the introduction.

"No, I don't think so. I'm pleased to meet you," answered the doctor with a cheerful voice and a sincere smile of welcome.

"Rose is my wife Cherry's kid sister. She has lived here in Essex with us for the last couple of years since her husband, Dan, passed away in a bad auto accident down in St. Louis. Some drunk in a stolen truck hit Dan's Ford coupe head-on.

"Gosh, I'm always sorry to hear of those kinds of traffic tragedies," said the young doctor with obvious feelings of compassion.

"The drunk and Dan were both killed instantly, and if that weren't bad enough, neither vehicle carried insurance. The accident left young Rose not only a widow but also practically penniless."

The doctor noticed Rose looked very much like his patient, Cherry. The main difference being this woman was slightly taller but much younger. She also appeared pale and thin, and her dark brown hair was longer than Cherry's, extending just below her slightly hunched shoulders. Rose had the sad and unnatural look of someone so young who had already been widowed. The doctor could not help but notice the continuing total lack of recognition Sharon showed. Being Cherry's niece, Rose must also be her aunt. He wondered why Sharon exhibited such a persistent lack of response. The two women certainly must know each other and probably had for years.

"I want to thank you, Dr. Frank, for all you did for my sister," Rose said shyly. "As soon as we lock up here at the store for the night, I'll be driving over to Moberly to spend a couple of days with her and Helen. Helen is my married oldest sister who lives there with her family."

"Yep. I'll be here all by myself then," said Jim with obvious dejection.

"Well, we hope he will be joining us in Moberly tomorrow after he closes up the store in the morning." She tried hard to smile as she spoke, but she seemed sadly self-conscious and almost embarrassed. She wore certain aura of tragedy about her like a close-fitting cloak.

"I appreciate your kind thanks and do want you to know it's a real pleasure to meet you," replied the doctor. "I hope you can make it to Moberly safe and sound this evening before we're snowed in here in Essex."

Rose nodded to Gerry and then looked at Sharon once more, but she did not try to speak with her niece again. Quickly she excused herself and quietly walked away towards the back of the large store carrying the two new plaid shirts she picked up from where Jim had folded them. Her shoulders hunched over more as she left, as if reflecting the harsh realities of a young widow's life. She looked truly troubled.

After secret whispers with a conspiratorial sense of excitement between Sharon and Jim, Mr. Jam turned and produced a large cardboard box from behind the wide wooden counter. Sharon smiled brightly as she eagerly accepted the bulky package and thanked Jim profusely. "I wasn't sure you could get it here fast enough," she said with relief in her voice.

"Neither was I," Jim answered, "but they located one in Macon and shipped it up on the produce truck this morning."

Sharon and Gerry soon left the warm general store, and she insisted on carrying the big box herself, saying it was much lighter than it looked and needed no help. The contents of the box were obviously meant to remain a mystery to Gerry. Sharon would not let him lift it so he had no idea of how much it weighed. He wondered if maybe it was a Christmas present for him, but he would have to wait to find out. Even after he asked, she refused to tell him who it was for. When she ignored his second inquiry on the subject he stopped asking further questions. He could take the hint. Just like Jim, he would have to wait until Christmas. This country girl, the young doctor realized more and more, had a very strong will.

Once the young couple were standing in the cold wind and snow outside on the sidewalk, Sharon wisely suggested they leave Gerry's small, low-slung sports car parked at the clinic. "My dad's pickup truck has a higher road clearance, and we will be safer over the rough roads to the farm. If this snow keeps up it could get pretty deep. Your car will be okay if we leave it here and ride together."

"Sounds sensible to me," Gerry answered. "If the snow drifts over my car we can dig it out tomorrow." Just yesterday, Sharon's widowed father had suddenly decided to spend the Christmas holidays in Kansas City with his older aunt and her extended family. He had left early that morning with his young nephew, Rose's son. The boy always enjoyed road trips with his Uncle Gustav in his heavy Chrysler New Yorker. With its finely tuned, powerful engine, it was one of the fastest cars in the county. Gustav and Rose's son had arrived in Kansas City hours ago.

Sharon took responsibility for the familiar chores of looking after the farm animals in her father's absence. She had always enjoyed doing the chores starting from her early childhood. Her ties to the family farm were deeper than she cared to admit, especially to outsiders.

"You know," Gerry said, "when you first invited me out to your farm for Christmas dinner a couple days ago, I thought it was going to be a big family celebration and holiday get-together. I didn't realize it would be just the two of us all alone with all those wild animals out there."

"Are you scared?" asked Sharon, with the sound of mischievous laughter in her pleasant voice, a sound the young doctor loved to hear.

"Should I be?"

"Well, I originally asked your buddy Harry to come with you if he wanted to. You could have insisted on his coming along for protection if you felt you needed it. You had better speak up fast right now because if you don't, you won't have any way back to town."

"What do you mean?"

"I mean I'm keeping my hands on the keys to the pickup once we arrive out there. You'll be my prisoner for as long as I please."

Gerry nodded agreeably, although a bit sheepishly, as he had been intently pondering his fate for the last few hours. He did not mind being teased by her. "I guess I can be had under the right circumstance, and it sure enough looks like this nice white Christmas is exactly the right circumstance. It may just prove to be one of the finest Christmas holidays of my life. What do you think?"

"It will be for me if I can have my way with you," she answered with a slow blush adding more rosiness to her already wind-flushed face. The weather had not turned much colder in the growing darkness of evening though the wind from the west and the intensity of the snowfall gradually increased.

Gerry transferred his small brown Samsonite suitcase from the back of this Thunderbird to the narrow space behind the seat in the truck. They slowly headed east and then turned south out of town. Sharon drove while Gerry tuned in the radio to play Christmas carols from the local broadcasting station. The best signal came from a radio station's transmitting tower located about 28 miles away, near the town of Macon. The music came in loudly and clearly without any appreciable static. The soothing sound immediately uplifted his Christmas spirit.

Sharon drove carefully and Gerry felt fairly safe with her, although a substantial accumulation of snow drifts had already piled up on the gravel county roads. The roads were not plowed, but numerous tracks of other vehicles were barely visible on the white-covered ground. "I couldn't help but notice how you were a little cold to your young aunt back there in the general store," he said. "To be blunt, I felt you were downright rude. I especially wondered why you were like that towards Rose since she seemed to be quite friendly toward you. Want to talk about it?"

"There's not much to talk about. Rose knows where I stand on the family problem involving her. I know where she lies. In fact, that's the big problem. She lies and she lies. First she repeatedly lies in bed with my Uncle Jim and second, she constantly lies to my Aunt Cherry about it."

"Do you mean Rose is having an affair with Jim even though he's married to her sister?" Gerry asked with mild shock in his voice. "My gosh, they all live in the same house. That must be complicated."

"Yes, that's exactly what I mean. After Rose's husband died in the accident, Cherry brought her up here from St. Louis. Brought her and her three-year-old son, Ricky, and took them in without a second thought. Rose didn't have a nickel to her name. After paying for the funeral she was flat broke. The drunk driver who killed her husband drove a stolen truck, and there was no insurance coverage for anything. Now Rose pays her sister back for all of her kindness by carrying on behind Cherry's back in an ongoing affair with her husband. The whole thing is disgraceful."

"So, why does Cherry let Rose stay with them? Why doesn't she make her leave? If that doesn't stop the affair, at least it would put a damper on it."

"Cherry would have thrown Rose out long ago, but she feels sorry for her little boy. He needs a good stable home. Ricky is only five-years-old now. Rose never even finished high school. She got pregnant and dropped out during the end of her junior year so she could get married. She's 22-years-old, can't type, and can barely use the big cash register. There's no way she could support her young son and herself nearly as well as she and Ricky live there together with Jim and Cherry. Besides that, the boy loves living on their small farm. My dad claims little Ricky is a born farmer. Dad is a good uncle and tries to spend a lot of time with the boy. I guess we all feel sorry for the little fatherless fellow."

"Does Rose help out by working in the store? Does she pull her own weight at home, other than with Jim, of course?" Gerry asked, finally warm enough to take off his woolen mittens and stuff them inside the pockets of his coat.

"Oh yes, nobody can accuse her of being lazy. It's not like that at all. Rose tries to help, and she works hard. She cooks most of the meals and keeps house for the four of them. That leaves Cherry available to concentrate on the store while Jim works at the rendering plant most of the year. In fact, Rose is a very good housekeeper and a very hard worker. Their place is always neat and clean. But instead of just keeping house for the family like she promised Cherry she would do, she plays house with Jim whenever Cherry is not around."

"I suppose that's the situation a lot of the time with Cherry working those long hours at the store. Cherry must average at least ten hours a day, six days a week behind the counter."

"That's absolutely right, and it's another reason I've been commuting to college this fall semester. I try to help Cherry out for a couple of hours in the evening at the store so she can get home earlier and spend more time with her husband." Obvious from the intensity and tone of Sharon's voice, she became more upset just talking about this sordid situation. The subject bothered her and she appeared to be on the verge of tears. She became quiet and concentrated on her driving through the thick falling snow as it accumulated on the wet windshield as fast as the slow, squeaky window wipers could remove it in their half-circle sweeps. The noise of the rhythmic motion suddenly seemed louder against the steady background of engine noise.

"You really don't have to tell me all of this," Gerry suggested as he turned down the radio volume. "I mean, it's not any of my business." He reached across the seat and clasped Sharon's right arm to let her know he did empathize with her anxiety over this major family problem. It would be worth talking about it if it would generate a sound solution, rather than to just worry about worrying. Gerry, however, had little hope of helping find a solution to such a personal problem. But if Sharon asked, he would give it serious thought.

She turned towards him quickly and smiled warmly before returning her attention to the long road ahead, "No, that's where you're wrong, Doctor. This is part of your concern. It is something you should know about."

"Why is that?" he asked.

"Because, you have become the family doctor, and it's important you know the family's problems. A little psychiatry is part of your learning and working experience in the rural clinics for these six months. You've already had extensive textbook and technical training at a hospital. Out here in the country throughout your externship, you are on your own to evaluate people in terms of their total environment. That means you must include their work, their home life, and their interpersonal relationships in your evaluation You must even include consideration of the feuds occasionally occurring between family members, between families, and sometimes between extended families or clans, as we call them here in this part of the state."

Gerry looked at Sharon with amazement. He knew she was much more than a college educated farm girl, but her understanding of the many aspects of the medical students' education and the lives of the townspeople included in the

Missouri Rural Clinic Program, was more complete and concise than he would have anticipated. During the three-and-a-half weeks since he had arrived in the country village of Essex, the obvious pride the local people took in their small medical clinic impressed him. The townspeople were responsible for the clinic's upkeep and maintenance, and they kept the faded, old red-brick building meticulously neat and clean.

"Where did you learn all that?" he replied with a big smile on his face. This young woman continually amazed him. She had an inner spirit sparkling with enthusiasm warming the world around her. She made him happy to be a part of that world.

"Well, I may be ignorant and naive about a few things, but I'm not stupid," she laughed in reply. "There is a big difference between ignorance and stupidity."

"No, I didn't mean to imply anything like that. I'm just surprised you know so much about the Rural Health Program. I think it's great you do."

"Oh, I've read a few medical textbooks myself and also some of your medical school bulletins concerning the rural clinics throughout this part of Missouri."

"You must have. I'm really impressed."

"Did you know," she continued, "this was the first Rural Clinic Program established by a medical school anywhere in the United States?"

"Not only did I know it, but that's why I'm here. The experience is great for the student physicians going directly into general practice, and it gives some GP background to those of us who want to take specialized residency training after the required rotating internship. It serves up a little bit of everything so student physicians can find out the areas of interest they like the most so they can decide if they want to specialize later on."

"Did you know this clinic program is considered a very successful model that will probably be duplicated and adopted in the near future by many other medical schools for the training of physicians? Living on our farm we are very fortunate to be so close to one of the 12 Missouri towns participating in this unique venture."

"You're amazing. You sound like the staff doctors and the professors at school when they encourage us to sign up for this six-month externship in rural medicine and general practice. The medical college should have you in the recruitment program for this project."

"Maybe someday I will."

"You should be recruiting now. You would certainly have had no problem recruiting me," he said with a broad smile on his face.

Sharon looked at him briefly and laughed. Then remembering where they were, she quickly refocused her attention back on driving through the rough, snowy road ahead. She accelerated the pickup truck as it finished rounding a snow-banked bend, passed out of the shelter of a sizable steep hill on their right, and forcefully plowed through small drifts extending intermittently for the next half mile. Finally, she continued talking, "You're not the first medical extern I've dated, you know."

"Is that supposed to make me jealous or just more interested? I don't think I could be any more interested than I already am."

"Neither, since I have a real warm feeling you'll be the last. You're what I'd like for Christmas every year. Just stay around and give me yourself. It's your time I'm after."

Gerry had to admit her response elicited a warm feeling deeply within him. Sharon was probably right about the advantages of his learning about family dynamics and pertinent medical information in dealing with these local folks as patients.

Maybe he should know more. "So, getting back to this family triangle, what do you think is the answer to the problem? Is there anything you could do to help? What can anyone do?"

"Oh yes, there definitely is something that can be done," she replied.

"So, what's the plan?" he asked.

"Well, that's the problem. The plan is still under review. A solution is supposed to be worked out carefully in the family war council tonight over in Moberly at Aunt Helen's house. I'm not included. It's being discussed at the generational level of the three sisters. They will talk it out among themselves and decide what to do."

"I'm not sure I like the way you said 'war council'. What do you mean by those words?" Gerry asked.

"Rose is supposed to drive there this evening as soon as she and Jim close the store. He will stay here in town to open the store again in the morning. Rose, Cherry, and Helen will remain at Helen's place for the next two or three days. They have Helen's house to themselves as her husband and three children will be spending Christmas with his parents in Saint Charles. Cherry talked to me about it considerably when I visited her at the hospital yesterday afternoon. Actually, she is the most worried about Helen."

"Sounds to me like Cherry should be more worried about herself. Why all the concern for Helen? I don't understand."

Sharon paused for a few seconds and the frown lines deepened on her face and forehead. She glanced quickly at Gerry before continuing. She obviously worried about how he would accept the details she was about to tell him. She felt a further explanation of family history might help before she reached the bottom line.

The young doctor stared straight ahead. He did not speak and waited for her answer. He did not know where the conversation was heading, but he anticipated he would not like it. He could already feel fear racing deeply through his gut.

"You know, usually our family has one big get-together, and everybody is happy at Christmas time. It's a very joyful and festive occasion for us. Dad and I held last year's celebration at our farm and the year before at Cherry's place. But this year is unique with our extended family split up and spread out over half the state for the holidays. The reason for the separation is so my aunts can straighten out this terrible problem between them with no outside interference. The rest of the family figured they needed this time alone together. A solution must be found quickly as the time for further delay is long gone."

"What's the solution?" asked Gerry with a puzzled expression on his face. "Is there a rational solution to end the heartache and to terminate the problem?"

"Well, that's why I'm afraid," Sharon thoughtfully replied. "It's not an easy decision for any family to make. I know this will sound strange to you as an outsider, unfamiliar with the traditions of our heritage and our hills, but if Rose doesn't agree to immediately stop her affair with Jim, then Helen will kill her."

"She will do what? Who will kill who?" Gerry asked with his voice exploding like a loud whistle.

"Helen will have to kill Rose. It's her duty to the family. As part of our ancient code, this is the tradition of our clan. Some say it goes back centuries to our distant Scandinavian heritage as Vikings, though I'm not sure if it's true. They say it started as a way to convince the brothers who went to sea for long periods their wives and families would be safe from the brothers who stayed home to protect the clan."

Gerry's jaw visibly dropped for a moment. He looked dumbstruck. "What? What are you saying?"

"This was to save the wives from their brothers-in-law. The husband who went to sea for months at a time had to know his wife was safe, unmolested, and faithfully waiting for her sailor's return," she explained.

"Helen can't do that," he yelled. "The sheriff would call it murder. The authorities send people to prison and execute them for murder. Besides, it's her own sister you're talking about."

"Yes, I know that very well. They are both my aunts."

"You are kidding, aren't you? Aren't you?" He tried a sickly little giggle to emphasize his question, but he already knew deep down inside Sharon was deadly serious. In the long, silent pause before Sharon could answer, Gerry felt a cold sweat fast forming, suddenly running freely down the middle of his back between his shoulder blades. Reaching under the dashboard, he turned up the heater in the small truck. He sat stunned in silence, shivering under his heavy coat. Speechless from surprise and fear for this family, he also was shocked for the second time in the same day by the cold callow attitude projected by this woman who fast held his fascination.

"We may be country, Doc, but we've been raised and we live by certain strict codes that have worked well for us folks in these parts for many, many years. In fact, for many centuries and multiple generations, these codes have worked for our ancestors. One of the first tenets is you do not sleep with a relative's spouse. I am not saying you do not occasionally have to tolerate some adultery outside the family along the way, but we will not tolerate sleeping with the husband or the wife of a relative. Bloodlines mean a lot to us, and inter-family adultery is just not approved. It never has been and it never will be. Rose knows the rules of her heritage as well as anyone else. She has nobody to blame for the consequences of her actions but herself."

"You mean Helen is going to tell Rose if she does not stop the affair, then she will kill her? She will actually kill her own sister? Her own kid sister?"

"That's exactly what I mean. It's very sad it has finally come down to this, but there's no alternative."

"She would kill her own sister?" the young doctor repeated again. Suddenly the sound of *Silent Night* on the radio seemed inappropriate, and Gerry quickly switched off the music. For a few seconds he heard only the steady hum of the engine and the slapping of the windshield wipers. The noise seemed to echo the phrase 'kill her', 'kill her', 'kill her'.

"Well, it's actually the responsibility of the oldest brother in a critical situation like this. Obviously that would be my dad, but he flatly refuses to be involved."

"Sounds like your dad is even smarter than I thought he was. I sure do like and admire that man."

"Dad says some of the old ways should pass. He claims this custom we formerly held as a valuable virtue has now become a vicious vice. However, Aunt Helen doesn't agree. So the responsibility reverts to her, since she is the oldest sister and there are no other brothers. Dad is the only boy in the family of four children."

"You really are serious about this. Wow, this is hard to believe. I thought these kind of feudal killings went out of style when the Hatfields and the McCoys stopped shooting at each other and kissed and made up or whatever they did."

Sharon knew she had been right in sensing how difficult this would be for an outsider to understand any of this, especially if the outsider is a highly educated physician. An explainer's lot is never easy. Certainly these folkways of the rural Missouri hills and valleys would probably seem equally unbelievable to someone from big cities like St. Louis or Kansas City, and Gerry came all the way from Boston by way of California. She hoped the conversation would not scare him away or stifle his interest in her. "Yes, I'm afraid I am serious about it. Remember our promise never to kid each other about important matters? What could be more serious than this?" she asked. "I know a lot of medical students have a weird sense of humor, but this is definitely not something I would joke about. I would not want you to think I could."

"No, there certainly is no humor in this situation," the doctor replied. "It's an unfolding tragedy for sure."

"I'm glad you agree. It's my own close kinfolk I'm talking about. I pray for them every night. We are nothing like the Hatfields or the McCoys. That feud between different families started over the theft of a pig. This is a matter of honor to be settled among members of the same family."

"So, just like that, someone will be killed? Someone will have to die?" Gerry asked, still unable to fully believe or accept what he had just heard. *These country people sure do follow some strange customs*, he thought to himself. Rural folk could be really frightening at times. This corner of Northeast Missouri might ultimately prove to be more dangerous than East Los Angeles on a Friday night.

"Well, it really depends on Rose and whether or not she'll agree to stop the affair," Sharon answered. "She controls her own fate and her destiny truly lies in her own hands. Ultimately, she will determine what happens. It's only fair it should be this way."

They finally reached the edge of the Olsen farm, and Sharon turned the truck cautiously to drive down the curved pine-tree lined private road between neatly fenced pastures. The long, narrow road connected the compound of buildings to the local county route. The couple drove the last 200 yards slowly in thoughtful silence. The neat, well-maintained red barn and farm buildings sat in a grove of tall, bare hardwoods at the end of the drive. Sharon tried to keep the pickup truck well within the snow tracks made previously by earlier vehicles. She drove so well she made the job look easy, though it was not easy at all. Then, slowing more, she finally parked the truck in a wide circular driveway curving sharply to the left, a good distance from the barn and its outlying buildings.

They were within 30 feet of the back door and the enclosed porch of a sturdy but comfortable, three-story, white wooden farmhouse, framed on both sides by tall green pine trees. With the snow clinging to its steep roof, window ledges, and trim, the house looked like a Currier and Ives Christmas card. "Welcome to my happy home," she said, as she turned off the ignition.

"Does this place have a specific name? It certainly looks impressive enough like it should."

"Yes. It's called Hidden Hills Farms. That's the name my great-great grandfather gave it a long time ago when he bought his first two adjoining farms here when he returned from the Civil War. He had been wounded in South Carolina after having marched through Georgia with General Sherman." They exited the truck and walked through the soft white snow compacting under their boots as they quickly made their way the last few feet to the enclosed back porch. A cheerfully decorated pine bough Christmas wreath hung on the outside door. The wreath was decorated with a bright red ribbon and small silver bells tinkling in the cool crisp air. Sharon unlocked and opened the heavy solid oak entrance to her home. She stomped the snow off her feet and walked inside.

Gerry slowly followed behind her with his suitcase. Sharon carried the big mysterious package inside to a pleasant, cool kitchen. The sweet scent of pine permeated the air inside from a fresh Christmas tree located in another room close-by. The snow fell heavier as the young doctor closed the thick porch door behind him. He looked outside through the long narrow window next to the door for a few seconds before turning around. He wondered how long the snow would continue to fall because the steady silent white flakes looked like they would never stop. Already the snow started to drift deeply with the increasing wind from the West.

After taking off their heavy boots and hanging up their long, warm coats, Sharon put a speckled gray enamel pot of cold coffee on the large black stove. Quickly, she lit the gas burner beneath the pot as she turned up the blue flame. "Would you settle now for some warmed-up coffee and a fresh fried egg sandwich? Then we'll go back to town for the evening church services and have our real dinner later tonight when we come home. Does that sound okay?" She said as she pulled out one of the heavy matching chairs from under the maple table.

"Sure," said Gerry. He sat at a heavy round wooden kitchen table standing in a corner. "But, gosh, I just can't believe people might still act that way anywhere here in the United States. I just cannot imagine Helen would want to kill her own sister." He was still stunned by the pending danger and having trouble understanding any part of it. The conversation had scared him. He could still feel the damp sweat cooling his back and the cold kitchen made him feel even colder.

Sharon waited a while before answering. She stood at the stove, carefully turned on the oven, and opened its door to warm the room up fast. "It's not that she wants to kill her sister. You must understand what is happening here. Helen is a good honest person without meanness in her mind nor malice in her heart. But now she firmly feels we must adhere to the old code and traditional customs of our clan. The family reputation must be maintained."

"But why are you all so concerned with family reputations?"

"Because, the family gives us standing. It's who we are. It gives us our sense of continuity and our place on the land. The family is our history. Without our clan's reputation, we are nothing. We would be people without an honorable past or a purposeful future."

"What do you mean you are nothing?"

"I mean exactly that. We would soon be even less than nothing. Nothing is at least a neutral value. We would be held in negative numbers," Sharon replied. "We would be disgraced and we might as well not exist. This whole shameful affair has already lasted too long, much too long and it must end soon. Our good family name has suffered. The bloodlines are disgraced. This can not continue. We must recover. What if Rose becomes pregnant? We don't believe in abortion, though I know some people feel it is justifiable in certain circumstances and may some day even become legal."

"Obviously, Jim doesn't realize he's playing with dynamite," said Gerry. "Why doesn't he just stop? Wouldn't that solve everything? He sure doesn't look stupid. In fact, he seems pretty smart. Maybe by now his interest in Rose has already waned and he's carrying on more from habit then from conviction. I'll bet he would not want anyone killed over an affair like this."

"Oh no, he doesn't know we know," said Sharon. "You see, he's an outsider. He's not from this isolated part of the state - he's originally from Jefferson City. His meat company sent up here years ago to help manage the local rendering plant. I guess Jefferson City is more civilized than us, here in the back country of Missouri. It should be. After all, it's the state capitol and a pretty fair-sized city."

"So, what has that to do with anything?" The young doctor demanded in a loud questioning voice.

"It's has a lot to do with everything. People from there would never understand our clan traditions. They don't do things down there the way we do up here. Oh, maybe in the Ozark Mountains but not in the big cities. Jim doesn't even realize Cherry and Helen know anything about the affair. He thinks it's completely secret and only he and Rose know."

"You mean he's oblivious that you all know? Surely he must have some suspicion Cherry and Helen know. Hasn't Rose told him her sisters both know?"

"No. He has no idea they know anything about it. We are all certain of that fact. Even Rose admits it's true. Besides, it's not her place to tell him even if he asked, and he hasn't asked."

"But wouldn't that be a place to start? I mean, shouldn't someone take him aside and clue him in, or punch him out, or do whatever it takes to make him stop?" Gerry quickly lost his appetite. "I'd even be willing to tell him myself if it would help. If it's this serious of a problem, and it certainly sounds as if it is, I'll convince him of the dangers. I sure will - you can bet on it. I'll be able to convince him one way or another."

"You really do not understand, Doc. No. We don't do it that way, and you must not try. If any of us said something to him, then Jim would feel a certain shame and a deep constant guilt for the rest of his natural life. His relationship with Cherry then would never be the same anyway."

"But is their relationship good? I mean, if Jim cheats on Cherry now, how good can their relationship be?"

"Well it's not all that bad, and it can recover when the affair with Rose ends. Jim and Cherry have been through a lot together. They had a terribly tough time when their only child died of the croup as an infant. Those were the days, years ago, before the medical school established a permanent medical clinic here in the village. You must realize how much the medical clinic has meant to this community, how many lives it has saved and changed for the better."

"I think I am beginning to realize it. I sure hope it's true. It looks like it's changing my life and certainly for the better."

"I hope to contribute to the change," she said with a faint smile on her face as she placed the hot coffee pot on a thick, red coaster laying on the table.

"I'm sure you will," he answered as he reached out and pulled her closely to him.

"Now I'm not telling you any of this to have you interfere. You can't interfere. You must not," she cautioned again. "Please promise me you won't."

"You really don't want me to say anything to anybody?"

"That's right. I am only telling you all of this for a better understanding of the family's background and medical history for when you are responsible for them as patients. Anyway, Rose is not stupid. When she's finally forced to understand Helen's determination, Rose will undoubtedly stop the sordid affair." Sharon pulled up another solid maple chair and sat down at the table next to Gerry. She slowly poured two steaming cups of hot coffee. "Better let them cool for a minute or two first. It's way too hot to drink, and I'd hate to have you burn your nice, pink tongue. I may need all your moving parts in good working order before the holidays are over."

"Gosh, the information about this deadly affair sure has put a down-draft damper on my enthusiasm for the holidays. I thought we would be spending our time discussing and doing fun things. Now you have me real worried about something you don't want me to do anything about. That's hardly fair."

"Who said anything is fair about life or fate? No one born alive gets any kind of guarantee. Nobody should expect it."

"I guess you are sure right about that. I should know by now. That's a question I ask every time I see good people needlessly die."

"Look, it's Christmas Eve. Smile a little. We have the whole house here to ourselves for the next few days. Don't worry about Rose. Even if Helen does finally have to kill her, Helen will first have to give her a fortnight notice. So she'll be alive well into January, anyway."

"So, is that supposed to make me feel much better? Do you think I can stop worrying about it now?"

"Sure. A fortnight notice is two weeks. A lot can change in time. Now, lets go on to more pleasant subjects and pastimes. Lets just concentrate on the two of us for a while. We're alone in my home and I plan to play house with my favorite doctor."

"I think I like that idea. Yes, I do. I know I do," he said, finally smiling again.

"You should. You know, even a dedicated doctor has a right to have some fun and free time away from his medical practice. You certainly deserve it," she said as she laughed demurely and blushed a deep pink color. Coyly hiding her embarrassment, she picked up her full coffee cup and started drinking. She drank hers black without cream or sugar. She did not take her eyes off the young doctor as she slowly sipped the hot, dark liquid.

Gerry added cream and sugar to his and let it cool more as he quietly studied the light brown mixture. He did not know what to expect next. In fact, he had not known what would happen next since he first met this fascinating and beautiful young woman. She continually surprised him. Like someone from the pages of classic literature, so old fashioned in some ways, yet she was modern and in the flesh, here and now. He thought about her for the few moments they sat quietly holding hands under the table. His realization gradually grew. Sharon needed him. She made him feel strong and protective, and he needed to be needed by someone who really loved him.

Leaning closer together, they suddenly hugged each other hard and long before they would let go. Then they slowly and silently finished drinking their cooling coffee without further conversation.

Eventually, they heard the wind blowing harder as the snow piled against the west-facing windows. Even from inside they could see the intensity of the snowstorm obviously increasing, turning into a real blizzard.

"Why don't you take your suitcase upstairs and put it in my bedroom. I'll straighten things up here and fix you a sandwich to eat before we leave."

"Which one is your bedroom? Do you think I can find it?"

"It's the one with green wallpaper to the right at the top of the back stairs. There's a good shower in the blue-tiled bathroom at the end of the hallway. If you want to clean up and change before going to church, I'll use the tub in my dad's bathroom."

"How is the hot water situation? Enough for both of us?"

"Enough to get you in all the trouble you can stand," she replied with a laugh.

As he climbed up the narrow, steep, back staircase with his small suitcase, Gerry had many questions to ask, but thought he better flow with it for a while and see in what directions this went. Sharon obviously wanted him to sleep in her bedroom, but where did she plan on sleeping? He wondered what was the local etiquette in this situation? Was there another code he didn't know that might cause his castration? He choked on the thought. Country life had suddenly become complicated for this city boy far from home. Maybe he should have done his six-month externship in a big city hospital on the West Coast. But then he would never

132

have met Sharon or have been making independent general practice decisions this early in his medical career.

Sharon had a large feminine farmhouse bedroom with a four-poster double bed topped by an old-fashioned white lace canopy. The big bed was not built for her to sleep alone, and he hoped soon to fulfill its intended purpose. A yellow and green flowered spread was pulled tightly over two large pillows. The bedspread matched the floor-length curtains flanking the windows of the room. The wide windows had a southerly exposure and extended over a large share of two adjoining walls. The room was meticulously clean and orderly. A tall antique cherry wood dresser stood in one corner. Other furnishings included a triple-mirrored makeup table with matching chair, a big black round-top trunk, and a six-shelved bookcase which covered the entire entrance wall except for the door to the room.

A lot is learned about a person by examining the books they treasure, especially the well-worn ones with repeated reference marks. Gerry spent the next ten minutes looking at the contents of Sharon's large bookcase. His intrigue peaked by the considerable number of volumes Sharon had on agronomy and animal husbandry. She devoted one entire shelf to classic literature and another to the works of Mark Twain. There were neither frivolous modern mystery novels, nor books of romance, and no science fiction. Her library showed him a whole lot about this woman he had yet to learn.

He quickly shaved with his old electric razor and took a relaxing warm shower in the recently renovated bathroom. Finally, he unpacked his small suitcase in Sharon's bedroom and changed into his churchgoing clothes. Afterwards, he slowly walked down the longer and more gradually descending front staircase, through a large formal dining room, and back into the kitchen which had become quite warm and cozy from the heat of the oven.

As he sat at the kitchen table eating his fried egg sandwich and waiting for Sharon to reappear, he glanced through the pages of a book he had brought down from Sharon's bookshelf, Mark Twain's *Tom Sawyer*. He had read it in his youth at grammar school and remembered it as one of his favorite stories. Hannibal, Missouri, where Mark Twain lived, lies to the east of Essex about 75 miles away. Gerry found it interesting Sharon had the entire works of Mark Twain in a matching set. He wondered if she had read them all and planned to ask her when she came down from upstairs where she had gone to shower and to change clothes. He thought some day in the spring when the roads were better, they could drive over to Hannibal together. It gave him a thrill to see the big, broad Mississippi River, bisecting the country in half as it steadily flowed south to the Gulf of Mexico..

Sharon's footsteps were so light in her stocking feet Gerry did not hear her approaching. Her perfume, which smelled like vanilla, preceded her into the room and enveloped him. She gave a warm hug as she silently stepped behind his chair. He asked her if it was vanilla, and she admitted she wore it so she would taste as good as she smelled.

"Maybe that's a good book for you to read now," she said thoughtfully. "Hannibal and the Big River are not too far from here." She leaned her head to the left letting her long mane of auburn hair flow out in cascading waves to the side. Slowly and rhythmically, she brushed it to a gloss with long strokes of a brush which brought out the glints of copper in the individual strands.

"Oh, I already read most of Mark Twain's writings years ago while I was in grammar and high school. I think I started them in the seventh grade and finished them around the eleventh."

"Well, if you read some of them again, now that you're older and live here, you'll understand us strange Missouri folks better. We're not much different than we were back in those days over 100 years ago. In fact some of us are just as close to our land and our animals now as they were back then. This farm has been in our family for almost 100 years. And now there is new acreage with the adjoining additions."

"Gosh, that is a long time," Gerry replied as he reached up and pulled her down to sit in his lap.

"If you'd like, sometime when the snow has cleared, I'll show you the family cemetery plot up on the big hill behind the red barns. There are several generations of Olsens buried back there. I may be there myself some day."

"You folks even have your own cemetery? That has to be the ultimate in self sufficiency."

"We even have our own ghost," she laughed as she pulled on her boots and stood up and stamped firmly for a better fit. "But don't look scared. You need not worry. I doubt he would want to hurt any doctor."

"Why not? It's easy for you to say that. You're probably a relative of his. I'm an outsider."

"Because he only comes out on special moonlit nights in the spring or early fall, and never around Christmas holidays. Maybe he goes south where it's warm for the winter. I'll have to ask my dad. He's well versed in the ways of ghosts, though it's not something we talk much about."

"He'll leave if he's a smart ghost. Even a spook could die of pneumonia in this weather," Gerry answered in the confident voice of a non-believer.

The slow drive back to the Lutheran Church in town proved much more difficult even though only an additional hour and a half had lapsed since the young couple left Essex for the farm. Fluffy white snow flakes came down much thicker, though not nearly as water-soaked and heavy as they were before. The temperature had cooled by five degrees. Luckily, the Ford pickup had circular chains attached to both back tires. Sharon drove carefully with well deserved self confidence. She had driven pickup trucks in all kinds of weather since she was 13-years-old.

The church services were exhilarating and inspiring. The choir members' singing resounded to the rafters and reflected with the congregation's spirited response. Nothing is more beautiful and peaceful than a small, snug church in a snowy rural town on Christmas Eve filled with happy, warm people intent on celebrating their deep feelings of joy and contentment over the birth of the Savior. The familiar services following the choir's performance and the congregation's sincere fellowship lasted close to two hours.

The intensity of the cold snowfall continued uninterrupted throughout the long holiday evening service. Their drive back to the farm was much slower and more difficult than the drive into town. The wind whipped furiously, howling loudly with the blowing snow. Viable visibility decreased fast in the blunt white beams of the pickup's headlights. It was not a nice night to be out for any reason. The large steel chains on the oversized rear tires were a definite necessity. Gerry and Sharon breathed a simultaneous sigh of relief and were very glad when she finally eased the Ford pickup into the circular driveway in front of the large farmhouse. They spoke very little during the difficult drive home. With white knuckles, she clung to the wheel and he clung to the sides of his seat. The bright lights of the kitchen and porch had been purposely left on and were a welcome sight burning through the dark stormy night. The fury of the midwestern snowstorm intensified as the bare hardwood trees near the house swayed loudly back and forth in the wind.

They reached home well after midnight. Sharon cooked a luxurious early morning breakfast of ham, eggs, and toast with orange juice, marmalade, and homemade muffins. In the warm, snug kitchen they ate and they talked. Sharon surprised Gerry that she had read the entire works of Mark Twain and worked through them a second time in a leisurely way. They agreed the story of Huckleberry Finn was Twain's greatest work. They concurred upon many subjects and they took comfort in finding how extraordinarily easy it was for them to discuss anything.

Well past two in the morning they put the leftover food away, washed the dirty dishes, and headed up the stairs. A new chapter was about to start in their young lives. There would be no turning back for either of them.

Sharon walked into her darkened bedroom as Gerry followed. He suddenly remembered she had said it would be his room while a guest in her home. From a soft light shining in from the hallway, he could see her smile as she suddenly stopped and turned around. He followed her so closely they collided together gently. Then she embraced him with reassuring warmth showing him he was in the right room.

"I need that hug," he said with light laughter stemming from self-consciousness.

"I know you do," she replied with confidence. "You seem a little uncertain."

"I think I could use another couple of hugs right now. After the first few they become pretty addicting."

"I hope you'll need more than that. I plan on becoming everything you will ever need in a woman." Putting both of her hands behind his neck, she lifted her face and kissed him with passion.

Suddenly, mixed emotions awoke in him that were nearly overwhelming. He quickly developed a warm tenderness combined with a sense of responsibility for this very special woman. The heart-felt and mind-motivating feelings she evoked in him were much deeper than the level of any of his past encounters.

They were both ready for serious emotional involvement and for sharing their feelings in a physical way. Though Gerry still did not remember ever seeing Sharon until earlier that month, she had contemplated an involvement with him for many previous years. For the past few nights as she had fallen asleep in her room alone, she dreamed of nothing else than this moment.

"Are you sure you're really ready for this?" Gerry asked in a soft low voice as he pressed her tightly against him.

She whispered a muffled 'yes' into his shoulder. She repeated it once more a little louder.

Gerry barely heard her. Quickly he released his arms from around her waist and took a short step backwards to look at her. He raised his hands, placed them on her shoulders, and pulled her close to him again.

He realized already he could not let go of her. As she pressed against him, she felt his hardness through her clothes as he pressed tightly against her pelvis. She also felt a dampness deep between her legs.

"I have never been more ready for anything in my life," she answered as she stood in her stocking feet. She backed away a step and started slowly unbuttoning the many buttons down the front of her red wool sweater. "Could you help me take off the rest of my clothes?"

He finished unfastening the lower five buttons and helped her as she slipped the soft sweater from her shoulders and arms. Reaching down he unbuckled the narrow black belt around the waist of her green plaid skirt and loosened the zipper at her side.

Shyly, she let the skirt fall to the floor and in front of him in her pale pink slip. Raising her arms, she pulled the slip over her head and shook her long hair free. Silently she stood in the middle of the room in her light pink bra and panties. Beneath her panties a black garter belt clearly showed as it extended down her bare white thighs and held up her long nylon stockings.

Gently Gerry turned her around and undid her bra strap from behind. She took it from her shoulders and let it fall to the floor. Still with her back to him, she slowly slipped off her panties and stepped out of them. Only then did she turn back to face him with her long legs slightly spread apart.

The idea raced through his lascivious mind that their relationship was predestined. But could it last? Their backgrounds could not have been more different.

Just before four in the morning they finally fell fast asleep, exhausted and warmly content in each other's arms. Sharon proved to be multi-orgasmic and Gerry knew with great pleasure she had climaxed for the third time before he came for the second. Their passion peaked at roughly the same time as the wind and the snowstorm outside finally let up. Even the elements sometimes must rest.

When Gerry awakened in Sharon's warm double bed late that morning, he realized their consummation the night before had been even greater than the festive anticipation earlier that evening. Light streamed in brightly from the wide windows as the sun made its low ascent in the southeast sky reflecting off the soft white snow blanketing the countryside. He heard the remorseless rhythmic sound of slow dripping as the snowy slush melted and ran off the slanting roof overhang. The noise of the cold dripping water hitting the sun-warmed metal of the roof's gutters awakened him. Being summoned back to consciousness in this manner felt pleasant and peaceful.

Sharon had heard the sound of precipitation in the gutters so many times in the past it did not awaken her at all. She continued to sleep, though her eyelids faintly flickered from distant dreams. She lay facing Gerry on her left side. The top sheet and the heavy blanket back had been thrown back revealing her bare right arm, shoulder, and breast in the bright sunlight of the warm, cozy room.

Gerry looked at her longingly with one eye not buried by the soft pillow. He raised himself up slowly and leaned on his right elbow so he could see her with both eyes to make sure she really laid there next to him. He felt sudden warmth and involuntary tingling in his groin. Even in sleep Sharon, was as beautiful and far more wholesome and appealing than any other woman he had ever known even wide awake and at their very best. He enjoyed waking up with her as much as he loved going to sleep with her. He knew he was a very lucky man.

The day started for the young couple with a beautiful sunlit morning full of life's potential pleasures, making young lovers doubt any remote finality of death's deep darkness. They thought only about each other.

Slowly, Gerry moved over and kissed her pink, naked breast. She responded immediately. Suddenly, Sharon's large brown eyes opened and her pupils quickly constricted in the bright light. She smiled in warm recognition. "Which of your appetites should I satisfy first?" She asked with a wide welcoming grin on her face, "for lust or for breakfast?"

"For lust first, " he chose easily. She threw her arms around him again and snuggled closely with her naked breasts pressed tightly against his warm chest. She still smelled faintly of vanilla, and the natural curls of her long auburn hair fell softly against his face. They said nothing more as they kissed long and hard. Gerry gently felt the low curve of her firm right hip and buttocks. In rapid response to the pleasant pressure of his fingers, Sharon turned over on her back and willingly spread her long, slender legs wide apart.

A good breakfast had always been the young doctor's favorite meal. Now, however, he discovered a new favorite for which his hunger fast and firmly became insatiable. In the tenderness of their intimate touching, he once again felt what he now knew he remembered. It had caused a silent questioning in his mind during their prolonged lovemaking in the past night. He moved his left hand below the covers of the bed so he could feel the unique flesh formation of an obvious silky scar over Sharon's right lower abdominal quadrant. Suddenly, she tensed tightly and involuntarily flinched when he tenderly caressed the area with his left hand. Her restless response seemed more psychological than physical. He wondered at her intense reaction. Obviously his light touch could not have hurt her. Where did this pain come from?

Sharon suddenly did not want to engage Gerry in serious prolonged foreplay as they had thoroughly enjoyed in the previous dark night. Instead, she obviously wanted to consummate their intercourse of carnal connection as promptly as possible. As soon as his penis penetrated deeply within her, she equally responded and within moments she fully orgasmed as intensely the night before. In her post-coital state, however, she reacted differently than she had in the darkness of the previous night. She showed obvious inhibition in the broad bright daylight of mid morning.

Gerry realized she did not want him to see the healed incision marks of her lower abdomen. She tried to keep them hidden from his view. Even as she slowly climbed out of bed to walk to the bathroom, she held a fresh, folded towel next to her lower body. Gerry followed closely behind her.

Their first shower together could have been their last as they experienced their first argument since becoming true lovers. Sharon wanted the water at a temperature Gerry considered scalding. His idea of hot water at best was her idea of lukewarm.

Finally they found a compromise of a temperature midway between which they agreed to be acceptable to both.

Gerry scrubbed Sharon's back first. Then, as she timidly turned to face him, he slowly lathered her high, firm breasts. Her nipples became instantly erect as she leaned back against the smooth, tiled wall. She kept her legs slightly apart as she let the water cascade down over her smooth, naked body. The combination of sensations started to excite her again. As he kneeled in front of Sharon, Gerry slowly soaped her pelvis and thighs in a rhythmic motion. She could feel the slippery wetness of her warm juices inside contrasting with the water's wetness on her skin outside. Reaching between her legs, Gerry lathered her vulva in the front and then farther back, then he spread the cleft of her small, smooth buttocks.

Reaching down under his arms she slowly pulled him to his feet to stand next to her again and they hugged each other tightly. Then, Sharon went down on one knee in front of Gerry to slowly and gently wash and rinse his penis and testicles. Blinking her eyelids free of the falling water she watched with pleasure and wonder as his growing erection rose to her open mouth.

After their long warm shower followed by a brisk refreshing burst of cold rinse water, they dried each other with thick soft towels. Gerry then had his first good soap-free look at Sharon's scar in the bright daylight. She still shyly exposed nakedness in the light as she fully faced him. The young doctor found it difficult to keep from examining the very large and markedly noticeable healed incision.

Finally, in complete surrender to the inevitable, Sharon dropped her towel on the tile floor and stood still. She dreaded this moment.

Then, slowly but firmly, Gerry picked her up off her bare feet and sat her on top of a low chest of drawers in the warm humid bathroom. The large scar on her lower abdomen showed slightly purple from the final cool rinse of shower water. The scar ran least six inches long and a quarter inch wide in a diagonal direction inferiorly and medially down into her abundant auburn pubic hair. Standing between her spread legs, Gerry gently pushed her warm firm body against the blue tiled wall as he knelt and kissed the scar. He ran his smooth wet tongue slowly along the scar from top to bottom. The warm welcome of his open mouth soon brought a noticeable pale pinkness to the raised dark tissue.

Sharon suddenly relaxed, but as Gerry looked up at her face, he could see fresh tears forming in the corners of her deep brown eyes. The tears ran slowly down her flushed cheeks. She very quietly reached out with both hands to pull him closer to her. Carefully caressing his head, she turned it with her hands and held his right cheek hard against her still damp pubic hair. She gently rubbed the left side of his forehead. They said nothing for several moments. By the time she gradually let go, her tears had stopped flowing.

Gerry stood up and Sharon reached out again pulling him firmly between her extended legs. She wrapped her arms tightly around his waist and held her face nestled against his chest. He leaned down and kissed the top of her head as she continued to caress him. They held on to each other in silence for quite a while until they were suddenly startled by the rumbling sound of melting snow sliding down the steep roof overhead and then crashing to the backyard below with an explosive sound.

Gerry finally spoke, "There's no reason why this scar should bother you now, and less reason to think it diminishes your beauty to me." His voice was gentle and soft at first but became more authoritative as he continued. "It's just an old scar of something finished from the past that is sensibly forgotten. Please don't ever cry about it again. I want you to promise me right now. Never again."

"I'm not sure I can make that kind of promise."

"Why not?" he asked.

"Some things are hard to forget and harder to forgive, although I do try. You have to believe me. Just being with you like this has helped me tremendously," she continued. "I'll always remember our being together like this. I'll remember it forever."

"I don't think we should talk about it any more right now," he answered. "Maybe later we can." Nevertheless, he asked the physician's side of his mind, *Why that type of scar?* It was far too long to be an uncomplicated appendectomy incision. Most of the female pelvic surgeries he had seen and assisted on had involved a midline vertical incision or a lower suprapubic horizontal incision. But he was Sharon's lover, not her doctor. He would not ask her what the scar meant or when and why she had the surgery. She would have to volunteer the information if she wanted him to know.

He hoped she would want him to know soon. He knew this would be a true test of her trust in him. A true test of his own trust would be for him not to pull her medical records back at the hospital where undoubtably the surgery had been performed. The medical records could probably tell him more about the surgery than Sharon knew herself. But would that be fair or ethical?

Gerry felt he had seen the scar before - almost as if he had dreamed of the scar before. But when and why? He knew it was impossible for his subconsciousness to project an image into his future. His vague memory played tricks with his mind.

Suddenly Sharon looked up, and Gerry noticed the silent tears running freely and faster down her cheeks. "Hold me tight," she pleaded. "Hold me like you will never let me go."

Firmly and quickly he pulled her warm welcome body close again as she wrapped her still damp legs tightly around his dry thighs. She eagerly gathered herself together within the warmth of his strong arms. Never before had she felt as comfortable and as safe in her own home as she did then. They were good feelings, and she was determined to keep them.

"The scar doesn't hurt anymore, not physically anyway," she said softly, as her voice faintly faded. After a long pause she continued, "I don't want you to think it does. I am glad you want to touch it with your lips and tongue. I need a lot of that. I hoped the scar wouldn't turn you off when you saw how horrible it looks."

"There is nothing horrible about it. Not at all," he repeated loudly for emphasis.

"I do think the pain is all emotional now, but I'm slowly recovering from that. It's been three-and-a-half years since the incident. I guess I should be over it by now. Being with you like this will help me tremendously. Except for my dad when I was a baby, and my doctors recently, you're the first man to see me totally naked."

"We don't have to talk about it if you'd rather not," Gerry said reassuringly, rubbing her back as he held her. He could feel her slowly relax.

Several seconds went by before she finally replied, "No. You deserve to know. I was raped in the summer, three-and-a-half years ago, and if that were not bad enough, I ended up with a massive pelvic infection and an ectopic pregnancy in one of my fallopian tubes."

"So that explains the scar," he stated.

"Yes, I had to have an emergency operation. I lost my tube and ovary on one side. The surgeon had no choice, he had to remove them to save my life. I guess I'm lucky to be alive, but at the time I could not believe all those horrible things were happening to me. For a long time, I felt the pain and shame would never leave me. *Why me, Lord?* I prayed; and being a virgin at the time of the rape didn't help either. Can you imagine that as a first sexual experience?"

"Who or what finally helped you? You are obviously doing pretty well now," he said reassuringly as he continued to rub her back and neck.

"My surgeon helped ease the pain. He even spent considerable time counseling me afterwards. I finally started to feel like a real woman again. Time helped erase the shame. Eventually the times between my periodic depressions grew longer and longer. But without the tremendous emotional support from my wonderful dad and my good Aunt Cherry, I would not have made it through the experience as well as I did. I will always owe them both so much. They never let me down, and I know they never will."

"You're lucky to have such close, caring relatives," Gerry told her. "Not everybody has such a nice family to lean on when they need them."

"Yes, I know," she replied.

"So what happened to the rapist? Did they catch him? Is he in prison?"

"No, my father is not progressive. He doesn't feel all of the old ways should pass and be forgotten. We have not talked about it much, but in my heart I know he settled the issue in his own way. He settled it in the old way."

"What do you mean? What finally happened to the guy?"

"I'm not sure. I never testified at the coroner's inquest. But the man who raped me was killed in a hunting accident the next fall. He had his entire lower pelvis blown away with a full-choke,

12-gauge shotgun. There wasn't much left of his body when Uncle Jim found it in late spring of the following year. They decided it had been laying on the ground for the latter part of the fall, through the winter, and two months into the spring. It was pretty well decomposed."

"Who found it?"

"Oh my dad and Uncle Jim were hunting together one day and found the guy, or what was left of him, in the deep, back woods bordering our north 50 acres. The coroner figured the body lay out there for about seven months. Ironically, no one had ever given the man permission to come on our property for any reason. All of that land is strictly posted against hunting. When he turned up missing, no one ever thought to look up there."

"He must have been either a dedicated hunter or a dumb one."

"Not really. His kin folks said he wasn't known to have hunted in over five years. However, the rusted remains of his own shotgun were found near his body, and it was a 12-gauge gun he had been shot with. Nobody considered it foul play. At least not officially."

"So how did the county coroner list the incident on the death certificate? Did he write it off as an accidental death?" Gerry asked. The physician side of his personality needed to know such details.

"No, they listed the death as a suicide. The circumstances may seem fishy, but I believe he did commit a sort of suicide."

"What do you mean by that?"

"Well I remember my dad telling me after my surgery, *'The man made his own decision to die the minute he touched you.'* Dad always claimed the man was as good as dead from that moment on. He predicted the guy would be dead within six months. Dad

147

foretold the man's fate with such certainty I knew I would never have to worry about him bothering me again once he turned up missing. I knew he was gone for good, and that knowledge helped me get over some of my fear."

"Not a pretty way to go. Most shotgun suicides are to the head or the chest. Why would he shoot himself in the pelvis?"

"Well, maybe he felt guilty about how he had used his genitals against me. Dad figured it must have taken the bastard at least an hour after the shot to bleed out and die. He had plenty of time to contemplate his crimes and yell out to the Lord for forgiveness and mercy."

"Does your dad talk about it anymore?"

"No, nobody does. It's a matter best forgotten. At the time of my surgery, Dad was affected very deeply. All through my severe depression afterwards, he worried I might not survive. Depression itself can be a fatal disease, you know."

"I do know. But you did survive, Sharon, and you're obviously okay now. That's what's important to me. And you even have most all of your moving parts and pieces," he said with a laugh. "After all, when you want to become pregnant, you only need one fallopian tube and one ovary as long as your uterus is still intact."

"Oh, I thought you also needed a willing man with some viable sperm," she replied with a small smile showing beneath the tears. She displayed her subtle sense of humor which had saved her psyche on more than one occasion.

"Yes, of course, but now you have a willing and able man. You were meant to survive and come through all those troubled times, just like you were meant for me." Suddenly he truly realized she was meant for him. Gerry wanted to hold her and be with her forever. He had a profound weakness for her strength combined with her vulnerability. He felt himself falling in love and knew his life would never be the same as before he met Sharon.

Suddenly another muffled clatter of heavy, wet snow fell off the steep, slanting roof and finally fully diverted their attention. "We'd better get dressed and look after the animals. Then we can have the rest of the breakfast we started last night. I promised the new handyman, George, and his wife, I would take care of this afternoon's stock chores if he would do the early morning ones. I'm sure they've already finished their part of the work so they could leave early and have Christmas dinner with their son and his family over in Macon. The county roads are probably plowed by now, so they should be able to make it there okay."

"How is the new handyman and his wife working out around the farm? Will you be able to live on campus next semester?" Gerry asked.

"I'm not sure. They are going to try for three months in the small house by the county road. Dad just hired them last week, but I figure they may move back to Macon in the spring."

Gerry found Sharon very easy to hold on to, but very hard to let go of. He wanted to keep the warmth of her responsive body imprinted on his flesh forever. Disappointed, he let his arms relax from around her and reluctantly watched as her naked body gradually disappeared inside her clothes. Upon his request she did not put on a bra, but did wear an extra warm, soft blue cashmere sweater.

By the time they watered and fed the stock in the big red barn building, they had worked up a ravenous appetite. They were ready for another long, leisurely breakfast.

The weather started to turn considerably colder again and more gray clouds quickly moved in from the west. "Looks like a lot more snow on the way," Gerry said with a glum expression on his face.

"A lot more," Sharon replied gravely. "Looks to me like it will be on us again within an hour the way the fresh wind brings in all those dark clouds."

"This is strange since the day started out with a thaw. Does winter weather always change so fast in these parts?" Gerry asked.

"It does a lot of the time, but don't you worry. When it does, this woman is going to have her man prepared for all kinds of snow and cold weather in the country." As Sharon spoke, she retrieved the Christmas package from the hall closet next to the front door. She proudly handed him the big box she picked up at the general store the day before. Neither of them had minded being too busy wrapped up in each other for her to have found the time to wrap the big package. "Open it up," she ordered as she handed him the big cardboard box.

Surprisingly heavy and to Gerry's delight, the large, flat package contained a dark brown, mid-length, sheepskin lined, beautiful and obviously very expensive leather stock jacket like those worn by the wealthy cattlemen in the area. The jacket fit perfectly, and Sharon could not stop Gerry from wearing it around the house. It took her half an hour to get him out of it and only then with hot hugs and the promise of more pleasure as payment.

In the late afternoon, they went back outside to the barns to check on the livestock again. The new warm jacket worked very well for Gerry and he was glad to be wearing it. The temperature had dropped quickly, and fresh snow came down furiously, this time thick and heavy. Gerry knew if the flurry kept up they would be snowed in for days. A slight smirk registered on his face as he contemplated the idea and looked forward to their possible isolation. The well-heated farmhouse undoubtably had enough food to last for weeks. Suddenly the young doctor hoped the snow would fall for a long, long time, and the silence from the telephone would continue uninterrupted. He benevolently and selfishly hoped for no medical emergencies in town.

Gerry's gift to Sharon a set of ossicles mounted in a small sterling silver locket. Ossicles, the three smallest bones of the body, are found in the inner ear. Medical students pride themselves on their surgical dissection skills if they are able to remove these little bones intact from their cadaver. Gerry had performed this procedure in his freshman year class of gross anatomy and had the bones mounted under the crystal of a small silver locket. He had saved them for years and never gave the locket to anyone as he saved it for a very special person. He now had found that person.

Sharon attached the locket to a long silver link necklace her mother had left her and wore it with pride. The locket lay against her chest, just above the cleavage of her firm, well-proportioned breasts.

The snow continued unabated for the next two days. At times its intensity increased as the temperature outdoors ranged from 26 degrees to 31 degrees Fahrenheit. If the weather had warmed up a just little, all that precipitation would have turned to rain   causing a significant change in many things and quite few people's lives.

The county roads finally became impassible in that area of the state, and the young lovers truly were snowed in at the farm. They became prisoners of the weather, frequently a fate of rural folk. Gerry and Sharon comfortably shared in the private world of their early love and constant companionship, isolated in the warm, well-equipped farmhouse. Off to a comfortable and serious start, their relationship could not have been better in this very happy time for both of them. They could not comprehend a time when any future tragedy would even be faintly foreseeable.

There were few customers at the general store Christmas morning. With the increasing snow accumulating all day, Mr. James Jam knew there would be no traffic moving anywhere in the small village by the next day. He had a lot of trouble driving the three miles home to his farm on Christmas after he closed the store at noon. He debated whether to bother opening for business at all the following morning, and driving to Moberly would surely be impossible.

Cherry took her responsibility for the store very seriously. Jim promised her he would faithfully keep it open at least half of every day she was gone from Essex. Still in Moberly with her sisters, Rose and Helen, Cherry knew because of the severe weather conditions, they could not expect Jim to drive to meet them. Not only were the east bound roads snowed in and closed to all traffic, but also the storm had knocked down telephone and electric lines in several places between the two towns.

The rendering plant shut down most of its ongoing operations every year during the months of December and January, so Jim did not need to go to his regular job. He had carpentry chores to complete on three new horse stalls he had built in his big, white barn. He spent the rest of Christmas Day and most of the following day working in that capacity. He always enjoyed the creative construction of working with wood and had pride in his carpentry and cabinet making skills. The quiet comfort of the warm barn with its familiar scent and the secure sound of the friendly farm animals gave him a chance to think seriously about his life without distracting interruptions. Jim realized he had a big problem. Ignoring it as he had in the past would not help in his quest for a solution.

Specifically, he thought about the troublesome triangle he had created with himself, Rose and Cherry. His mind failed to realize how old was his heart. He remained full of youthful foolishness causing the protracted problems of loving someone half his age. Not only her youthful body had turned him on, but also Rose had projected a spontaneous spirit perking Jim's interest. She had the non-judgmental attitude of a younger woman so flattering to an older man. She still carried the naive innocence most women leave behind after they reach the age of 25. Rose had suffered greatly in the tragedy of early widowhood. This made her extremely needy and highly vulnerable.

Jim could not remember how his passionate love affair with Rose had first begun, as it had just seemed to sneak up on the two of them. Harder for him to understand was how his interest in his wife subsequently had waned. He and Cherry used to sing together in the Lutheran Church choir. In fact, Cherry's fine soprano voice had been the factor first attracting Jim to her. Her wonderfully light and lyrical voice injected a sense of sensuous feeling and music to her conversation.

Not to detract from her looks, however, Cherry stood 5'4" tall, and at age 38, a little overweight at 137 pounds - still within seven or eight pounds of her wedding weight that happy June day long ago. Jim was 23 and Cherry was 18 when they married five days after her high school graduation. For Jim, their wedding day over 20 years earlier had been the proudest day his life and he still felt that way. Sometimes he wished he could go back in time to that happy day. He wanted to start the last half of his life over again with a clean slate. He certainly wanted to try to do better from here forward. Cherry deserved much more than he had provided her and he knew it. She was a good woman.

As a rule, it is hard to pinpoint when things start to go badly between a husband and a wife. Through the many years of their marriage, Jim and Cherry had changed and neglected to keep up with each other. After the tragic loss of their infant son, Jim became bitter and decided their chance for lasting happiness would never again come close to an even-money bet. The best he could hope for was a seven-to-four chance against happiness. Cherry and Jim stayed away from each other - involved in their own, deeply personal grief for so long they were no help consoling each other. Cherry started working longer hours at the store to keep her mind occupied. She would become physically tired to the point of total exhaustion so she could sleep at night. Their sex life became an early casualty of their compounding chaos.

They had also expanded the general store's facilities to keep up with the new business Cherry's extended hours provided. It was at that point Cherry's voice had started deepening. The hoarse quality came on gradually in the beginning. Jim first noticed it when Cherry shouted across open spaces in the store from her permanent position behind the counter. Her husky voice had now lasted for so long Jim could not easily remember its original tone, and it had been years since he had heard it.

Jim heard her surgery at the hospital had been successful, but he still had not personally spoken to his wife since then. He feared asking the doctor exactly how much her voice had improved. He prayed for the return of the sound from years ago - the lovely sound of the woman with whom he had fallen in love.

When first meeting Rose, Jim also noticed Cherry's younger sister had a beautiful voice. Rose's soft soprano voice sparked Jim's early attraction to her when she came to live in Essex on the small farm with Jim and Cherry after the tragic death of her husband in St. Louis. Rose was only 20-years-old at the time.

Rose's voice had a close similarity to the way Cherry's had sounded years before, just like hearing Cherry's lilting speech again. Rose's voice had also been the factor first attracting him to her, probably by the association with her sister. But not until other things mutually tempted him had they started their affair the following summer.

Early one afternoon on a hot, late August day, Jim found Rose swimming naked and alone, in the deep, cool creek running along the deserted western boundary of the family farm. Trees bordered the creek as it crossed the bottom of a sloping hillside meadow, lush with tall green grass. Jim first glimpsed her two wild daisy tattoos through those trees. They were artistically but painfully etched in indelible India ink driven deeply into the tender white skin of her right breast and her left inner thigh. Her wild daisy tattoos provoked his uncontrollable passion and soon became his favorite flowers. But this crop of wildflowers demanded a lot of care. Within two weeks he had stopped in to pluck her daisies nearly every day.

The deep grass of the hillside meadow became their favorite love-making rendezvous spot in the late days of the steamy summer. Real wild daisies grew sparsely among the grasses, but the lovers were too busy to notice.

As Jim daydreamed his way through his chores in the barn, he had no idea Cherry, and much less Helen, knew anything about his infidelity in the ongoing affair. He understood the three sisters were from a close-knit Scandinavian/American family, but it never entered his mind the real reason for their joining together for the holiday at Helen's home in Moberly would prove to be because of his continuing relationship with Rose. Had he known, he would have been stunned. Helen's deadly choice would horrify him. Knowing Helen as he did, he would have realized her to be capable of murder if he only knew of this option being on the table. He still remembered that November day over three years ago, when she and her brother bought 12-gauge shotgun shells from the store. Helen had never been known as a hunter and Gustav's shotgun was a 16-gauge. The matter was not questioned at the time and best forgotten since.

By the next day, the accumulated snow had deepened considerably. Yet Jim dared not leave the general store closed for another day. The new snowfall and heavy ice on the telephone wires had caused the local phone lines to break connections in several places. But electricity in the power lines still connected to his farm. The lights continued burning in the house and the barn. By early morning the snow had finally stopped.

Jim saddled and mounted his favorite reliable quarter horse, Old Betsy. He had ridden Betsy in his rodeo roping days as a young adult. They made a good working team together and had won over 30 trophies.

Cherry kept the trophies prominently displayed on a living room shelf specifically built for that purpose, and she dusted them every week. Sometimes Jim felt she gave the trophies closer attention than she gave to him.

Slowly Jim rode Old Betsy three miles through the drifted snow into the deserted town. The snow-covered countryside looked like an artist's painted landscape for a Christmas card. Snow clung to bare hardwood trees and crowned the green boughs of the coniferous pinewoods. Sharing the view with his favorite mount provided the benefit of the full visual value of such beautiful scenery, though such travel had to be taken at the right tempo. The horse and rider shared a sense of perfection in the tempo of their timing. They had spent countless hours together in days gone by. As he rode slowly into the westerly wind, Jim thought of those happy times. He wondered if Betsy perhaps did also.

When Jim finally reached the general store on Main Street, he quickly realized the small town had no electricity at all. He thought there must be a break in the utility company's power line somewhere between his home and the village. Carefully he tied his horse to the closest hitching post outside the store and retrieved a snow shovel from inside. Next he scraped the heavily drifted snow from the wooden sidewalk around the entrance. Several feet of snow had drifted against the old, red-brick building. The deep white blanket was heavy, wet, and difficult to clear away. With the temperature definitely warming, the snow started to melt.

Jim maintained a small portable generator for the store's emergency power in the one-story wooden shed located 15 feet from the east brick wall of the store. It had not been run in many weeks. The gray weather-beaten shed had been built 60 years before over an eight-foot deep, hand-dug cellar under the foundation. The original building on the site housed a busy saddle and harness shop. Jim and Cherry kept extra food and general store supplies in the old shed and in the cool dark basement beneath it. They referred to the dugout room as the fruit cellar since they had originally used it to store their yearly fruit harvest. Tall wooden shelves covered three of the four stone-lined walls. Heavy lumber leaned against the fourth wall.

After tinkering and trying everything he knew to crank up the generator in the close confines of the shed, Jim still could not get the motor to work. He realized he would quickly need to re-establish the necessary electrical power to the three big reefer boxes in the back of the store and to the smaller one just inside the front of the shed as soon as possible. Otherwise, the large supply of perishable food within them would begin to spoil. The outdoor temperature had already warmed well into the low forties causing the recent snowfall to melt fast all around.

The shed had only one small window but lighting was not a problem as there were plenty of glass kerosene lanterns available in the general store. Jim took three lanterns into the shed, providing ample light while he diligently labored with the stubborn generator. The kerosene lanterns worked well and soon bright flames gave adequate illumination through clear glass sides.

Jim continued to have major problems with the balking generator. The puzzling malfunction proved to be more serious than he had anticipated. As early dusk settled in, and it grew quickly dark outdoors, he finally realized the magnitude of the problem. He hated to admit his failure as an electrician. He hated to admit failure at anything he tried to do.

The temperature rising outside would be more of a serious problem than the approaching darkness. Blowing in from the south, gusty warm winds late in the morning caused the temperature to rise even faster than before. By early evening, the mercury reached high into the forties. As he worked, Jim could hear the water dripping from the melting snow as it ran off the old shed roof onto the surrounding wooden sidewalk. They had over $500 worth of meat and other perishable food stored in those reefer boxes, and Jim realized he must get the auxiliary generator going as soon as possible. Since the telephone lines were down in town he could not call anyone for help.

Suddenly Jim remembered Big Bob Grumley at the local Texaco station owned a similar sized auxiliary generator and a four-wheel drive Jeep they could use to move Bob's generator to the store. Jim knew Bob would let him borrow it and, meanwhile, would help him fix the broken one now taken apart in many pieces spread all over the shed's wooden floor.

Jim unhitched his horse from the front of the store and rode Old Betsy the three blocks east down Main Street to the Texaco station. He found the station closed as were all the other businesses in the small village. No vehicle traffic moved anywhere in sight along deserted Main Street.

Kids slid on sleds down the steep slippery slopes of the old Johansen place just north of town, but no one else ventured outdoors that early evening. By the time Jim dismounted, walked around the closed service station, and looked into the garage windows to see if Bob's Jeep was in there, he turned to find even the children sliding on the hill were gone.

Bob Grumley's home was about three miles north of town. Jim remounted and headed Old Betsy out along the mushy snow-plowed road. Everything around him heated up. Jim knew he had to borrow the generator now. Time would quickly run out on the perishables at the general store.

Just as Jim and Betsy left the village on the road headed north towards the Grumley place, Rose and Cherry arrived on the south side of town in Rose's pick-up truck. She had inherited her husband's well-used, still-working truck and the only valuable property he left when he was tragically killed. Without the red, four-wheel drive vehicle, Rose and Cherry could not possibly have made it through the snowdrifts on the country roads throughout their plodding drive home from Moberly. When they finally pulled up in front of the store, the two sisters could see the light of kerosene lanterns shining from the windows of the store and from the open shed door.

"See, I told you," Rose said with a knowing air as she lightly licked her lower lip with her tongue. "Jim's much more responsible than you give him credit for. He is a good man. Obviously he has already been down here to take care of things. You had no cause for worry." Rose always quickly jumped to defend Jim from potential criticism, especially if the complaint came from his wife. Rose would not let anyone talk badly about Jim in her presence.

"Well, when I realized the phone lines were down, I figured there might be a serious problem with the electrical lines too, and I was afraid we'd lose all the valuable food stuffs stored in the big freezer boxes. We can't afford that. Anyway, I'm glad we're finally home." Cherry was actually not glad at all. The extensive and exhausting discussions over the past few days with her sisters about the affair between Rose and Jim had emotionally and physically drained Cherry and made her more upset about her husband. Anxiety enveloped her when she thought of seeing him again. At that moment, she barely cared if she ever saw him again.

The meeting in Moberly between the three sisters had settled nothing. With the details of the affair open for serious discussion, Rose firmly refused to give up her relationship with Jim. She thought it should be left up to Jim to decide which of the two sisters he wanted the most. Rose claimed if Jim must decide between them, he would most likely choose her. She politely listened to Helen's repeated threats, but Rose simply did not believe Helen would or could do her any bodily harm. Her big sister still loved Rose very much. However certain of that love, Helen gave Rose a fortnight's notice to give up the relationship. If she didn't, Rose would be fair game for punishment in two weeks.

Sex with Jim wasn't Rose's only attraction to him. She appreciated his sense of humor - Jim made her laugh, and she certainly needed laughter in her life since the grief and sadness brought on by her husband's sudden, tragic death. Jim showed Rose a humorous side to situations in their lives she had never before considered amusing. After Dan died, Rose forgot how to smile and Jim had changed all that for her. Rose smiled a lot around Jim.

If she could not have him to herself, she would agree to share him with her sister. She was grateful for any of his attention and affection. After all, he was still her sister's husband, and Cherry could never let Rose forget it. Rose felt if she could not have Jim at all, she decided she may as well be dead, too. There was nothing left to argue about.

Now that the affair was finally out in the open, Rose thought perhaps Cherry would eventually accept sharing her husband with her younger sister. Then, with Rose's son, Ricky, the four of them could be one-big happy family. Already the young boy had virtually two mothers, and he obviously was the better for all the love and attention they both showed him. In Jim's role as Ricky's de-facto father, he did a far better job than the boy's real father ever had. Because of his genuine care for her son and the vast age difference between Jim and Rose, she worshipped Jim blindly in a way young women searching for a father figure tend to love an older man. The younger woman's youthful love is less critical and more forgiving of such men than the love of wives whose age is closer to their own.

When Cherry unlocked the heavy outer door to the closed store and went inside the dry brick building, she immediately realized the electric lights were not working and the auxiliary generator didn't work either. She flipped the switch back and forth several times, but the room remained unlit, and only the kerosene lamp Jim had left on the counter provided any light at all. Instead of the familiar hum of the emergency generator, she detected only a loud, ominous silence.

In several previous blackouts, Cherry had quickly reverted to the small generator in the back shed. She re-locked the store before she and Rose tromped through the deep snow around the brick building and entered the old shed. The obvious lack of power they encountered immediately compounded with a new one problem. They found the generator completely taken apart and in pieces all over the old wooden floor of the shed. Cherry realized Jim apparently had been frustrated by his lack of knowledge of the machinery and left for parts unknown.

The two women could not decide where he must have gone. Rose stumbled in the tangle of machinery on the floor and accidentally kicked a small round generator coil. It rolled with a clang through the open trap door in the floor and quickly bounced down the steep narrow staircase into the deep, dark, dug-out cellar below.

"Apparently Jim's been working on the generator. I sure hope he comes back soon," said Cherry angrily as she glanced at her younger sister.

"I don't think he will be gone long or he wouldn't have left the lantern lights burning here in the shed. You know he's smarter than that," Rose declared protectively.

"Yes, I hope you're right," Cherry replied. "I don't like to think about what will happen if we don't get power to those freezers really soon. We'll be in real trouble once we have to start opening them to get foodstuffs out for customers tomorrow. The meat will probably thaw by then and we will have to give it away rather than have it go to waste. We just can't afford that. I wonder where he went? Do you have any idea where he might be?"

"I don't know either," Rose said with a new self confidence and assurance in herself. She secretly felt flattered she should be considered an authority on the whereabouts of her illicit lover. Yet she countered, "Don't keep looking at me for the answers about your husband." After a slight pause to let her admonishment sink in, Rose continued, "Jim is going to need all the pieces of the generator to put it back together and get it working again. I better find that stray piece before he returns." She carefully descended the steep rickety staircase into the cold dark cellar. She carried one of the burning glass kerosene lamps held high with her left hand.

"Can you see it on the floor down there?" Cherry called into the shadowy basement. "It has to be there somewhere."

"No, I can't find it," Rose yelled back from below. "It's still too dark down here - like a tomb. Bring down another lamp, please. I need more light."

Cherry reached the bottom of the staircase with a lit lantern in her right hand when the heavy, wet, snow-laden roof suddenly caved in. The weather-beaten and well-worn building had been relentlessly rotting for over 60 years and had seen its share of snowy seasons in those many decades. Finally the weight accumulated from the soggy, heavy snow in the last three days proved to be just too much for it. The roof gave up the ghost. The time was 6:12 P.M.

The loud crash of the broken roof timbers could easily be heard in the quiet of the night at least two blocks away. Unfortunately, no one else was anywhere within three blocks to hear the noise. The small business section of the town was completely deserted. For the next few seconds there was total silence. The women stood stunned, momentarily motionless. They would be safe in the cellar should the rest of the roof cave in. The first very faint sound soon following could only be heard by the two women in the confines of the basement. Above them, the third glass lamp had smashed onto the floor when the roof crashed down around them. The lethal kerosene spilled everywhere with a steady drip, drip, drip of highly flammable liquid as it soaked through the wide cracks of dry wooden plank floor into the cellar. But this quiet sound had a deafening impact in the minds of the two women. A finger of fuel quickly ran down the slanted shed floor and rapidly saturated small bales of hay stacked against the shed's inside wall stored there for customers requiring dry feed for their animals. A small flame faithfully followed this stream of fuel.

"I think the shed is on fire above us," shouted Rose as she quickly extinguished the flame in her lamp.

"Let's get out of here, right now." Cherry yelled as she dashed up the narrow staircase.

Suddenly another large beam broke away from the remainders of the roof's rafters and slammed into the floor successfully shutting the trap door leading into the basement. The heavy beam became solidly wedged in the fallen wreckage from the roof and impeded any possibility of escape from the cellar. The trap door knocked Cherry senseless when it slammed shut.

Rose screamed for help until she realized it was not only useless but also screaming used up the cellar's limited oxygen supply. Once again silence permeated the premises until the only sound they heard was the disquieting crackle of burning wood.

As Jim Jam and Big Bob Grumley drove Bob's Jeep the last half mile towards town from the north side, they suddenly saw a red glow growing quickly in the sky reflected from large open flames. They immediately realized one of the small buildings in town was in flames and silently strained to decide which building was on fire.

At first neither man uttered a sound. They simultaneously tried to deny the only rational explanation for what they saw. Nevertheless, there was no mistaking the shimmering light. The big fire was out of control.

The glow grew more ominous and obvious as they drove over the crest of the last, large hill and proceeded rapidly into the small town. "My God, I think it's the shed." shouted Jim. "I should never have left those darn kerosene lamps burning."

They drove the four-wheel drive Jeep as fast as the deep snow-covered streets would allow. Further acceleration would have dispensed of the last grasp of traction.

"Just keep calm," Bob told him. "Maybe it's not your place, but it sure does look like it's in that part of town."

Only when they drove closer and turned the last corner west onto Main Street did Jim see with sudden shock Rose's red pickup truck parked outside the store. "She's come back early, Bob. My God, where is she? I don't see her anywhere. Rose may be trapped in the burning shed. It looks like the whole damn roof has caved in, probably from the weight of the snow. We've got to help her. We've got to get her out."

"Don't panic," Bob yelled. "Stay calm. Maybe she's not even in there. I'll check the store first." By then raging orange-red flames completely engulfed the old wooden shed. Yet there seemed to be no imminent danger of the fire spreading to the larger brick building next door. The solid thick wall on that side of the general store held no windows or doors. With the front door locked, Bob quickly established nobody was inside the general store. A giant of a man, he moved purposefully fast in an emergency. He never wasted motion and within seconds he ran to the back of the store to the burning shed.

Above the loud crackling of the hot wood fire, Jim heard a muffled scream come from below ground in the basement under the shed. "No, she's in the cellar. I can hear her now. Rose is definitely in the cellar," Jim shouted to Bob above the constant crackling noise of the fire.

The men grabbed two of the three heavy canvas tarpaulins they used to cover the generator in the back of the Jeep, and quickly soaked them with wet snow slush. They wrapped the soggy canvas around their shoulders and rushed into the burning wreckage of the old shed. A big man, Bob Grumley was 6'8" tall and weighed 371 pounds, and he was almost as smart as he was strong. The strongest man in the county with biceps of over 20 inches, his deltoids, triceps, and pectoralis muscles necessitated home-made shirts. He had tremendous upper body strength.

By means of superhuman effort from an adrenalin rush the calamity provided, both men heaved together finally to lift the heavy burning wood rafters blocking the basement trap door. On their hands they wore thick canvas and leather work-gloves Bob had previously produced from the Jeep's glove box. Next they grabbed the four corners of the heavy trap door and quickly lifted it to reveal the sealed room below. Smoke poured out from the cellar and temporarily blinded them. Instinctively they stepped back and gasped for air. Their lungs immediately filled with billowing black smoke and for several seconds they could not stop coughing.

In order to catch their breath easier, they ran out of the burning building to clear the hot smoke from their lungs with repeated gulps of cool fresh air. Seconds later, they charged back into the inferno.

"I think the whole damn floor is about to give away," yelled Big Bob loudly above the steady crackling of the flaming wreckage everywhere around them. "We don't have much time."

"It's rotten old wood, and from the smell, I'd say it's soaked up plenty of spilled kerosene. It could collapse any minute, we have to hurry. Go get the long tow rope from your Jeep."

"I've already got it right here. Tie this end around yourself," Bob ordered him. "Make damn sure it's secure. Then I can pull you out when need be."

Firmly grabbing the large shank of inch-thick manila rope, Jim tied it securely around his waist and quickly climbed down into the deep dark cellar. His eyes burned with discomfort from the smoke. He could feel the heat through his heavy winter clothing, though the temperature outside had started to fall closer to freezing again. He could barely see past the tips of his fingers. Smoke swirled everywhere. From above, Big Bob held the other end of the heavy rope which he had now wrapped tightly around his own waist. Jim knew Bob had the strength to pull him up fast out of the deep cellar if necessary - if Bob did not fall through the flaming floor first. The thick smoke reached above his waist, so Jim crouched to his knees to continue his search. He stumbled over broken wreckage frantically looking for Rose. But the faint scream had completely ceased. He shouted to her to keep yelling but received no reply. They only heard the continuous sound of the crackling, sizzling, snow and kerosene-wet wood.

From the light of the fire overhead eating into the floor above him, Jim could finally see two motionless bodies lying on the dirt floor of the cellar. Neither one moved from their side as they lay curled into fetal positions with their backs facing him. They shielded their heads for protection with coat-covered arms and gloved hands. Which one was Rose? Her beautiful soft voice silenced - maybe he was already too late. The smoke-filled air suffocated Jim, and he could barely breath.

He repeatedly asked himself at this moment - this was an important decision, possibly the most significant one of his life - which one was Rose? In the instant of this devastating fire, he repeatedly searched his mind to find in the difficult decision if he ever considered whether one of those unfortunate people on the floor to be his wife, Cherry.

The form on the floor furthest from him finally let out another short cry. Finally relieved to hear the sound of Rose's light familiar voice he loved so well, he quickly reached her by furtively stepping over the other motionless body. He pulled her from the burning wreckage and gathered her closely to smother the flames eating at her coat. Then he handed her up through the flaming trapdoor to Bob.

Bob had just enough free rope to carry her immediately outside the shed and set her out of harm's way in front of the store's front brick wall. Suddenly the north half of the shed's wood floor loosened and fell with a crash into the deep cellar below. The deafening crash echoed throughout the quiet town in the cool night air.

Still in the cellar, the falling, flaming debris rained down upon Jim from above and separated him from the other motionless body still trapped in the burning cellar. Yelling and clawing with controlled fear while focusing his rampant rage, Jim bravely tried to fight his way back to the body through the blockage of thick smoke and flaming debris scattered throughout the cellar. He attempted to use the damp heavy tarpaulin as a shield. The heat had nearly dried out the moisture completely, and now the edges of the heavy canvas began to catch fire.

The heat was too great and permeated the airway deeply into his lungs. His chest burned from the inside as flames caught his clothes on the outside. Jim could not get through the tangled burning wreckage to the unconscious body beyond. She lay five feet too far. The distance may as well have been a mile, and no man could make it through that gap. Jim did not realize he rapidly was being sealed into the burning cellar himself. Suddenly the steep wooden staircase collapsed and crashed into the fiery rubble strewn all about him on the dirt floor trapping him below ground. The fire grew in intensity, fed fast by the dry hay and the other combustible material suddenly falling into the deep dugout basement from above.

A frantic tug on the rough rope tied securely and snugly around Jim's waist alerted him. For a few seconds he had forgotten about the rope. "Not yet, not yet," he repeated as loudly as he could through his smoke strained throat as Big Bob started to hoist him out of the cellar. "There's someone else down here. There's someone else here. For God's sake don't pull me out yet. I can't leave them here to die."

"You've got to," Bob shouted. "We've run out of time or we'll all be goners."

"Just give me few more seconds," yelled Jim. "Throw down the other damp tarp."

The cellar looked like the burning pits of hell - blazing fire and thick smoke were everywhere. Jim coughed deeply, nearly blinded by the smoke billowing upward from the flames around him. He had no broken bones, but his arms and shoulders hurt from the contusions and burns caused by the falling debris crashing down on him. Luckily nothing so far had fallen on his his head rendering him unconscious. He was lucky to have survived his ordeal underground this long.

"It's too late, it's too late, you damned fool," yelled Bob frantically from above with obvious fear clearly showing in his voice. Don't fight me. The whole damn floor is going. It's caving in. I can feel it under my feet right now. It won't hold any longer. It's too late. We're all going to go."

"Just a few seconds."

"It's too late. There's no time left. You're coming up now. You've got to get out now." In a split second Bob hauled Jim up out of the basement with the rope tied securely to him, screaming and protesting. Bob grabbed Jim in a snug bear-hug to smother the flames licking at Jim's jacket and rushed him out of the remains of the fire-engulfed building. The cool night air relieved the heat on their seared, sooty faces. Bob picked Jim up in his arms, held him tightly, and ran him across the street as fast as he could go. Bob finally turned around to look back at the fire when he was well past the sidewalk and 40 feet into the empty lot opposite the store.

Within seconds, the rest of the flaming floor fell into the cellar. The vibration shook the ground on which they were standing. The hole in the ground that once was a functioning fruit cellar looked like a wide-open window to hell.

"There's a new tank full of kerosene stored down there, you damned fool. I helped Cherry move it in less than a week ago while you were working at the plant. Did you know that? Didn't she tell you? We have to stay the hell away from there."

"I don't care. Don't you understand? Cherry may be still down there. She may have driven back with Rose. I have to save her. She's my wife."

"I'm not letting you loose, you idiot. Quit kicking me, damn it. You're not going back down. That would be suicide. You could never survive."

"I have to try," Jim screamed as he struggled to get free of the big man.

Bob's epithet to Jim drowned out as the kerosene storage tank in the basement suddenly exploded. The blast completely demolished everything still standing of the burning shed. Any wood not yet ashes splintered into kindling sized fragments and flew in all directions. For a few moments the force of the explosion completely blew out the red-orange flames. But within a second the fire roared fully back to life with greater intensity than before.

Jim struggled and fought fiercely to get free from Bob until the final explosion. Only then did Bob think it was safe to let loose of Jim. By the time the orange flames restarted, he suddenly relaxed and collapsed in Bob's arms. Jim sobbed loudly as Bob set him down on the wet snow and untied the rope still connecting the two men like an umbilical cord. It had been Jim's lifeline back from the edge of eternity.

"You did everything you could. You did more than most people would even think about doing. Don't blame yourself for not being able to get them both out. Nobody could have done it," Bob said, trying to console his friend. "Nobody could have done it," he repeated.

She regained conscious now. She sat up straight and wiped the heavy black soot from her face as she gasped down great gulps of cool air. She felt she couldn't get enough fresh air deeply into her smoke-congested lungs. She struggled to breathe life back into her body. The damp outside air felt good as she leaned against the cool brick wall. Looking up, she saw Bob coming across the street toward her.

Bob untied the rope from around his waist and reached down to pick her up. He quickly carried her to the west end of the sidewalk in front of the adjoining brick building. He realized she needed lots of clean air and wanted to get her completely out of the smoky wind.

She sat very still in the wet snow and leaned against the cold hard wall. The bricks were damp from dripping melted snow. She couldn't believe she was still alive. Jim had saved her life. He had risked his own life to save hers. He had come from out of nowhere and rescued her from a living hell. She would always remember the moment when he became her hero. How could she ever forget it? Where was he now?

At that point, Jim walked over to her. Shocked and suddenly speechless he finally realized he had not saved Rose. Physically stunned and mentally shaken, Jim realized he had rescued his wife, Cherry, his first love. Rose was dead.

Cherry spoke to him quietly with the sweet high tones of her old voice. She spoke with her voice of long ago, recently restored to her by the doctors. Jim had heard Cherry's voice in the cellar. The restoration of her long forgotten true voice had saved her life. Jim had saved Cherry. She stood up slowly and hugged him closely. Gradually he returned the embrace until it felt so good he could not let go. He held on with the distant memory of his feelings long ago.

The Good Lord works in mysterious ways. Rose was still in the burning basement, and she was dead. Their affair now violently over. Jim would never lie among her daisies again. The triangle had ended. Would a phoenix rise from the ashes?

The Essex Voluntary Fire Department at last started to arrive on the scene. Some of the members came on horseback, some by sleigh, a few in four-wheel drive vehicles and many faithfully on foot. They were a well organized and competent group. Within minutes, the town's 1927 LaSalle fire engine hooked up to the single hydrant and pumped forcefully. The antique truck faithfully worked in all emergencies. The good priest frequently predicted it would function at least for a full 50 years.

Father Schaub drove the engine and directed the operation. With his white fire-chief's hat and yellow fire-proof coat he looked his finest. The gathering townsfolk quickly deduced the rest of the block of red-brick buildings were not endangered by the fire's flames. Parts of the wooden plank sidewalk and several sections of overhanging roof of the general store were badly burned and would need to be replaced. The priest was a recognized expert having worked with fire and brimstone for many years. For the past seven years he had annually been re-elected as chief of the volunteer fire department, even though the majority of members were protestants. He knew his job well and loved the old LaSalle. Within 20 minutes of the big engine's arrival, the last of the flames were extinguished.

The water would need to be pumped out of the basement immediately before Rose's body could be recovered. The pumping would take a considerable amount of time, and therefore removal could not take place until the following morning. They would keep the pumps going all night so Rose's remains would not become encased in a solid eight-foot square block of ice.

Cherry, Bob, and Jim suffered from multiple minor injuries of cuts, abrasions, and first and second degree burns. Miraculously, none of them were more seriously hurt. Ted Lincoln, the Ralston Feed Store owner, offered to ride his best horse to the Olsen farm to bring the doctor back to town. Ted had the fastest horse in that part of the country so the trip would not take very long.

Secrets are poorly kept in a small town and a country doctor's whereabouts should never be unknown. A sign taped to the outside of the clinic door gave the Olsen farm's phone number and location where the young physician could be reached. The town already suspected where he was, however, as he was seen by the entire Lutheran Church congregation leaving the Christmas holiday service after midnight on the arm of young Sharon Olsen.

Ted turned his trusty steed to the long country roads towards the Olsen farm. As soon as Ted arrived at the Olsen farmhouse, he hastily refreshed himself with brandy and coffee while Sharon rubbed down his horse in the warm barn. Then Gerry and Sharon saddled up three of her dad's best horses and the trio quickly rode back into town. The air in town smelled strongly of smoke, but most of the people had left the scene and returned home to finish out the night. The water pumps still ran on power from Big Bob's generator as they slowly emptied the water from the cellar.

When Gerry arrived at the rural clinic on horseback, he hurriedly unlocked the door and went in to set up the necessary instruments and medications used for burn victims. He then sent out word to gather the patients at the medical office.

Father Schaub walked Cherry, Jim, and Bob the short distance to his parish house where he had then started the job of caring for the victims. As a former navy chaplain with the United States Marines in Korea, he had extensive first aid knowledge, and he quickly finished rehydrating the injured victims with fluids and cleansed their multiple burns.

Gerry heard each of their stories separately as he treated their wounds. The doctor let each person talk it out with little interruption. They needed this catharsis, and the sooner they let it out the better.

Obviously Bob Grumley had acted correctly in not letting Jim go back down into the burning basement. Gerry agreed wholeheartedly with Bob that Jim could not have survived any longer in the fire and the smoke in the cellar. Nobody could have survived those conditions as they progressed. Had he stayed there he would have died as well. Bob's decision saved Jim's life. Bob needed reassurance to know he had not let his friend down by pulling him up. The young doctor reassured him in no uncertain terms, as he washed and dressed the burns of the big man's hands, wrists, and face. Big Bob Grimley truly was a giant among men.

Cherry thought Jim had intended to save her life when in his frantic desperation he knew he could only save one of the two women. Gerry let Cherry repeat this over and over again. Each time she repeated it, she more firmly convinced herself until at last she had no doubt in her mind. As with most people, she ended up believing what she wanted to believe. The reason becomes easy if faith is strong, and she sorely needed strong faith in this situation.

The burns to her left hand, both lower legs, and the back of her neck were her worst. The young doctor estimated Cherry's burns encompassed almost 14 percent of her total body area. But with proper care avoiding infection, her burns would heal with little scarring. Besides performing extensive debridement and applying Furacin Soluble Dressings after pHisoHex cleansing and ice water locally, Gerry administered a tetanus toxoid booster to Cherry. Then he started her on oral antibiotics.

Jim obviously suffered from a confused state of mind. He talked continually with his eyes glazed over as the young doctor worked on his wounds. The burns of his hands and lower left leg were cooled, cleaned, debrided, and finally dressed with Furacin cream impregnated gauze. One sizable area of Jim's left leg had third-degree burns and looked as though they would need skin grafts later. He undoubtably would retain permanent scarring from those wounds as deeply as the scars on his soul. A deep two-inch laceration of his neck needed suturing as did a three-inch laceration of his right forearm. The doctor gave Jim a tetanus toxoid booster as well and started him on oral antibiotics.

Jim had saved his wife's life, but he knew he had not chosen to do it consciously at the time. He wondered if it were an unconscious decision, but he would never be sure. In the coming days he still remained confused while he tried to tidy up the facts of the fire in his mind. A mixture of sadness and surprise wove its way into the fabric of his emotions, but this reaction was tempered by both love and regret. He was a changed man, and he hoped to be a better one.

Yes, Jim thought he was saving Rose, but what did this really mean? No man could have rescued both sisters alive, and Jim had never considered his wife to be the person trapped in the inferno. As time moved on, he came to believe the Lord had actually dictated his choice.

———————————————————

The fire was out and the affair was over. Life is for the living. Human beings must go on with the hands they are dealt. It was time to let the old scars heal. Dr. Frank knew it would take time, but eventually it would happen.

Grief is a natural, healthy response to the sudden loss of a loved one. The young doctor knew there were marked and significant differences in the way everyone approaches their expression of grief and universal feelings of denial, anger, anguish, and sorrow. Longing and loneliness accompany confusion, and anxiety mixed with depression can come later. Before grief can pass or be constructively contained, real loss must be accepted and sorrow experienced. Only then can human beings adjust to the loss of a departed loved one's life. Eventually the energy formerly devoted to the deceased will be spent on other relationships. Tincture of time is often the most potent medicine in matters of the heart where passion and love are involved.

Cherry informed Rose's son, Ricky, of the death of his mother when the boy's Uncle Gustav brought him back from

Kansas City where they had spent Christmas together. At first Ricky took it hard. Cherry and Jim formally adopting Ricky helped all of them immensely to heal. By the following spring Ricky called them Mom and Dad. Children often adjust more quickly than do adults. The young boy would always have a good home and an abundance of love and understanding from his new parents, and few orphans ever had it better. Some day the small farm would be his. The Jams became a close-knit family.

Jim refused to have Rose buried in any of the local church cemeteries. He claimed she had never been a religious person and all agreed. He insisted on digging her grave himself. The ground was partially frozen, so he built a small fire and it took all day for it to thaw enough so he could dig the grave. Instead of the usual six-foot deep grave, he dug it eight-feet deep, the depth of the old fruit cellar. Jim buried Rose in the meadow on the side of the big hill bordering their farm - the hill running down to the creek where Jim had first seen her daisies. Every spring thereafter thousands of wild white and yellow daisies would suddenly burst forth sensuous blooms. They blanketed the hillside and were brightest during the spring week of Rose's birthday. Rose's name came from a formally cultivated flower, but Jim ironically always associated her with the common wildflower he had come to love.

Gerry finally understood Rose's difficult life had led to the inevitable tragedy of her sudden death. Rose lived and died like a heroine in an ancient Greek drama. When Jim closely examined the circumstances of her death, he realized little had been purely random or accidental. Rose's life foredoomed the quality and the circumstances of her death - she had probably understood her fate herself. Given the habitually sad circumstances in her short tenure on earth, her destiny demanded a tragic death. She went easily, swiftly, and probably painlessly as anoxia killed her well before the heat of the flames or the concussion of the explosion. The realization of her death's lonely inevitability made her end a tragedy in the classical sense. Poor girl, she was destined to die young.

Scars on the land heal fast in Missouri. By late spring no evidence of the horrible fire remained. The charred portions of the shed were completely torn down and the wreckage carefully excavated from the cellar. Jim busily built a sturdy replacement, larger than the original shed from the same type red brick as the main store building. This would be the first new completely brick-constructed building in the small town in over 40 years. Jim connected it directly to the store with a door cut through, thereby joining the inside of both buildings. They never had to access the storage area by going outside again.

They called the structure, 'Rose's Annex'. Helen insisted on the name and Cherry agreed. Jim never mentioned how he felt about it, but he constructed the building painstakingly with all the skill and care he possessed. Rose would have liked this fitting memorial. Rose would never be forgotten by those who loved her.

Chapter 6
Downstairs Delivery
March 3, 1962

The Bakers were honest, God fearing, poor Missouri dirt farmers wresting a living from 44 acres of hilly, rock-strewn land located about nine miles northwest of the outskirts of Essex. Their minimal contact with the small village was made more difficult because nearly seven miles of the connecting roads were gravel. The rest were dirt roads which turned to mud puddles with the least provocation of moisture. Trips away from the Baker's farm consisted of bimonthly shopping visits early Friday evenings for the staple supplies the farm could not produce and Sunday visits to their Southern Baptist Church for the morning and the evening services.

All week Essex remained a quiet little village until the simultaneously sounding church bells in its three churches' steeples rang with a vengeance on Sunday mornings. By the time the last ringing of the Southern Baptist Church bell faded to silence, almost all of the members of its congregation were safely settled into their worn oak hardwood seats with hymn books open waiting for the first vocal offering to begin.

The Baker family could always be found sitting stiffly in the fourth pew from the front on the right hand side. They could not afford the eye glasses the young wife needed to see the posted numbers of hymns for the day had they sat in seats farther back. Their three girls, ranged in age from seven to three, with their middle daughter having just turned five. The girls sat between their parents in order of age with the oldest next to the father and the youngest next to the mother, with the middle child in the middle. The siblings were always dressed in their best and cleanest clothes for Sunday service. The clothes of the oldest were fresh from the local thrift shop on Station Street. The younger girls wore the dresses handed down from the older girl in order of age. The household head was the husband, Rudy, age 34. A slim 5'9" tall and 154 pounds of prematurely aging protoplasm, Rudy had been weather beaten by seasons of sun, rain, wind, and snow. His black hair already showed strands of white and his calloused hands were stained from the long years of never-ending farm work. He looked at least 12 years older than his actual age. His way of life had become more of a sad sum of his limitations than a real reflection of his true talents. A knowledgeable farmer, he did not have the right equipment or the necessary fertilizer to improve the production of his marginal land. Much of the land was too hilly for profitable cultivation and too rocky to support any serious growth except scrawny scrub pine trees.

His 24-year-old wife, Bridgett, had gradually acquired the look of chronic fatigue relentlessly etched into the 133 pounds of her 5'4" currently pregnant frame. Her light brown hair had been bleached by the sun during the heavy field work of hot sunny summers and long ago had lost its youthful highlights and luster. She smiled limitedly and no longer took part in local social activity. Her face showed acceptance in her fate with melancholic resignation.

Bridgett's obstetrical history reflected that typical of other women of the era and the area. She had para six, gravida seven, miscarriages three, and living children - three. Eight months had been the longest she had gone non-gravid (not pregnant) since her seventeenth birthday. Between her pregnancies and nursing her children, she had not menstruated in the past seven years, and it showed in her overextended body. Many days she felt as though all her blood had been completely drained from her body by other means.

After the unforgettable evening of her seventeenth birthday, she woke up contemplating having lost her virginity the night before. She had not predicted nor planned this event. Bridgett had been head cheerleader in her senior year at Essex High School. With a good academic record of mostly A's and a few B's, her family had considered her their best chance to be the first member to attend college. Financial help from her strict Southern Baptist parents would be needed, but they were willing and enthusiastic about her prospects. Her father managed the Ralston Feed Store on Main Street, and her mother operated the small beauty shop connected to their home on Station Street. They had been saving for their daughter's college education ever since Bridgett showed academic promise by winning the county-wide spelling bee in the sixth grade. They all planned on Bridgett attending the Missouri State Teachers College in Kirksville. She hoped to become a grammar school teacher and then would help send her two younger brothers to the University of Missouri in Columbia.

Rudy had a far different plan, however. The year before he found Jesus, he formed his plan the first time he saw Bridgett do a high-kick cheer at her high school football team's season opener. Essex played against Novinger High School, which won the game in spite of the home crowd yelling itself hoarse. Bridgett wore the uniform short green skirt and tight golden sweater of the cheerleading team. The enthusiasm of her cheering and that of her teammates infected the home team crowd with loud persistent yelling and chanting the home team's name. Her team lost 20 to 19, when Novinger recovered an Essex fumble and scored from the 25-yard line in the last minute of play.

By basketball season, Rudy's plan had become an obsession and he attended not only the home games but also those played out of town. He travelled to some of the away games as far as 70 miles distance from Essex. Rather than risk his old Studebaker pickup truck, Rudy took a job driving the school's team bus. The cheerleaders sat in the front. Though basically shy, Rudy liked to sing and could easily be encouraged to lend his baritone voice to the youthful renditions of the team's favorite songs.

Rudy knew his destiny lay in getting inside Bridgett's pants, preferably the snug, golden ones she wore under her short green uniform skirt. But how could he? Ten years her senior, he had little to show for his life except his high school diploma and a varsity letter from Essex, a bronze star and purple heart from Korea, his well-worn, loan-free pickup truck and tractor, and the back-breaking, 20-year mortgage still owed the Moberly Bank on his father's old farm.

The rocky hillside acres of Stone Hill Farm had harassed his father for years until finally the sloping soil killed him. Rudy's dad had died suddenly in a tragic tractor accident soon after Rudy returned home from his military service in 1953.

Rudy had never known his mother as she had lived a short, sad life of desperate deprivation and rural impoverishment. Her existence had been a endlessly repeated series of never-ending chores. She died following the prolonged labor of Rudy's breach-birth delivery immediately after his birth. He had come into this world of hard luck and hardship butt-end first. In obstetrics this is known as a frank breech presentation and is by no means the preferred method of delivery.

Being his parents' only child meant Rudy would eventually inherit the family farm. But it also meant a childhood of being the only boy to help his father with the hard work of running the place. Actually, they never really ran the place - it more or less ran them. They were always trying to catch up a few months or sometimes only weeks ahead of starvation. Farm children have to grow up fast. Survival is for the fittest, be it animal or man.

Rudy welcomed being drafted into the US Army so he could leave the farm's backbreaking work, though he would not admit this to his father. For the first time in his life, the lad had been guaranteed three meals a day. Occasionally being shot at seemed to be not a bad tradeoff. At least and at last he had his first fair chance in life of dying with a full stomach.

Those chances of his dying increased when he became his platoon's machine gunner. This job frequently goes to the strongest, smallest man in the platoon. He had to be able to carry the heavy gun but be small enough to survive. Big men make big targets. In an infantry firefight, the enemy always tries to kill the machine gunner first since he is the most lethal to their survival. After many days of heroic fighting at Inchon, Rudy was wounded, suffering multiple shrapnel injuries in his left arm and left leg from a Chinese mortar. The superficial pieces were easily removed, but some of the small, deeply lodged pieces would be carried to his grave. Both Rudy and his rifleman were patched up in a Mobile Army Surgical Hospital unit, but his ammunition carrier died in the battalion aid station, having not survived long enough to make it to the MASH.

Rudy first spoke to Bridgett in January at a church supper of the Essex Southern Baptist Church. Staunch church members, her family attended regular services every Sunday and prayer meetings on Wednesday evenings. Rudy started attending the parish to increase his chances of getting to know Bridgett. One of the few single younger men of the church, he had never before considered marriage. He didn't think his small family farm could adequately support a real family.

For reasons Bridgett never fully understood, she found his being older and his quiet attentiveness quite attractive. Rudy also was the first male she had ever dated who was too old to have teenage acne. His eyes held her attention. They were light blue-gray and as changeable as a Missouri daylight sky. Under bright sunlight they paled like well-worn denim. Under storm clouds they darkened like the depths of deep water. They gave a calm yet compelling authority to his glance. Whether looking from behind a 30-caliber machine gun, the steering wheel of a bus, or the controls of a tractor, they signaled the determination of a man with with whom no one should trifle.

Within two months of Rudy and Bridgett's first date, they were going steady, and on the night of her seventeenth birthday the relationship was fully consummated. Bridgett's seduction took place in the back of Rudy's old 1949 Studebaker pickup truck. Not her choice of a location, but on that warm spring evening, it certainly seemed to him be adequate for the occasion.

Rudy had washed out the truck and carefully scrubbed it down in anticipation of the event he hoped would occur. After it had dried, he thoughtfully threw in a new army blanket and fresh hay from a twine-tied bale recently broken open. He cared for Bridgett's feelings, but more than the love in his heart the lust in his loins had led him to this moment of truth. He no longer was shy around Bridgett.

For a full week afterward he could not bring himself to wash the blanket. He kept it more as an altar piece commemorating the moment rather than as a trophy. For reasons known only to himself he later dyed it red - blood red. It had been the second day of her period and her blood seeped all over the new khaki blanket. He had never been with a virgin before and though he had heard there might be blood expected from a girl's first sexual experience, he had never expected anything quite like this. He did not realize Bridgett had been menstruating.

About two weeks afterwards, with intercourse almost every evening in between them, he had her pregnant. Bridgett did not know the exact night it happened. At three weeks overdue she knew it meant her life was irrevocably changed forever. They married on a sunny Saturday in the Essex Southern Baptist Church the month before she would have graduated from Essex High School. The other three cheerleaders were her bridesmaids. When her father gave her away, he had tears of despair and of disappointment in his eyes. He knew the life of hardship his young daughter would be subjecting herself to on Stone Hill Farm.

Bridgett had not menstruated since her first pregnancy, and she never graduated from high school either. If she had done the latter she might still been doing the former. She might even have been teaching school in a town larger than Essex and making money the family had hoped for to help her brothers attend the university. But now that would never would be the case.

There had not been any rural clinic in the village of Essex during Bridgett's first pregnancy seven years earlier. The couple had to drive the bumpy rough road, 62 miles northeast to the medical school's hospital clinic for her prenatal care. Most of the trip took place over pock-marked dirt and gravel roads, until they reached the town of Atlanta and the paved U.S. Highway 63 heading north.

When Bridgett went into early labor late in her seventh month, both she and her husband knew it was a very bad sign. They would not have time to drive to the medical school's main hospital. Rudy drove his old pickup the 41 miles to the nearest medical clinic in Macon taking less than an hour over the narrow country roads. Rudy prayed all the way, fighting fear fostered by his imagination and his guilty consequence. At some point during this wild ride, as they came down the hill five miles from Callao, the greatest truth of his life struck Rudy. He suddenly realized that his feelings towards Bridgett had changed from mere lust. He had, since the marriage, actually fallen in love with his wife. He would never be the same man again.

He tried to make a deal with the Lord. If Bridgett and the baby survived, he would join the church. They both survived and he had joined the church - and he had never missed a Sunday service since then.

Not all the rest of Bridgett's rapidly commencing pregnancies turned out well. The last three had all ended in miscarriages at various stages of fetal development. With each miscarriage since the birth of her youngest daughter, Bridgett's foreboding attitude of depressive resignation had grown. She was hardly a happy woman. Only seven months into her seventh pregnancy, Bridget felt grave trepidation toward the coming birth of her fourth child.

Wilson Miller and James Woodward were the two young doctors on the Essex rural clinic rotation sequence of Tuesday, Thursday, and Saturday afternoons. Doctors Miller and Woodward were partners as were Doctors Frank and Thompson the other three days the clinic opened for patients. The four of them worked the same rotation in the same rural clinic. The partnerships worked opposite each other and were thus never together on the same day.

Dr. Woodward had inherited the Baker family as patients from the prior rotation of young doctors on the Essex clinic's Tuesday sequence. Bridgett had been known to be an aborter and she had Dr. Woodward's full attention from the very first day he saw her at the clinic. His concern about the young woman's chronic fatigue grew when he learned of all the hard work she did on the farm. At first the doctor had thought Bridgett might be anemic, but after laboratory tests showing her hemoglobin to be a healthy 14, her hematocrit a normal 42, and her red blood cell count just over 5,000,000, he ruled out anemia. She was just exhausted, and who could blame her?

In good weather, Bridgett and her husband frequently worked in the fields all day using the back bed of the old pickup truck as a fitting playpen for the youngest of the children. Two of the three children had been conceived there. Rudy had a love-hate relationship with the farm. When he looked at his crops and his children, all growing in his fields, he knew he had been born to that land for a purpose. He just didn't know if it were for the kids or for the corn. Rudy hated his youth as an only child and hoped one day to have ten kids of his own. Had Bridgett realized this goal, she would probably have left him long before.

As a member the U.S. Air Force, Dr. Woodward had flown two years as an enlisted medic and wanted eventually to specialize in obstetrics. Dr. Miller had served as an infantry officer in the U.S. Army for four years, two of them in Korea. He was authoritative and rough around adults, but a soft pushover around children. He wanted to specialize in pediatrics. When the two doctors were not arguing about which branch was the better military service, they made a pretty good working partnership. Good friendships can always survive severe arguments if each side makes sense enough to judge for themselves the winner before the insults start. Besides that, Wilson and James were friends and fraternity brothers, and they both dated girls from the teachers college who were roommates and sorority sisters.

Even for Northeast Missouri, that March had an unusual rainy season. The late afternoon and early evening's prolonged thunderstorm had started with light grayish-purple clouds compacting like bruises in a dark, blue-gray sky. Violence effected the air as lightening flashed and thunder crashed all around the region. Within minutes, hard-driving rain lashed the land like a whip of many tails. Two hours later some of the back roads were practically impassible. That evening Bridgett went into premature labor with her latest pregnancy. From her past experience, she had judged the baby at least a month and a half early - maybe more.

Rudy had called the clinic about 6:00 P.M. after it had closed. The next call he made to the Blue Bell Cafe' found both doctors just finishing up the catfish special with pan-fried potatoes. Rudy Baker quickly and gravely relayed the sudden, severe symptoms of Bridgett's backache and labor pains to Dr. Woodward. There would be no time for his much-anticipated rhubarb pie for dessert. Madge Grumley threw a half dozen donuts in a small paper bag and handed it to Dr. Woodward as he rushed out the door. Close behind him, Dr.Miller ate the last of his pan fries from a thick paper towel.

The Baker's old Studebaker pickup had failed to start up with its dead battery and broken generator. With the local streams rising fast and many of the mud roads already flooded, the plan formulated for Mr. Baker driving his tractor to meet Dr. Woodward's car. Rudy waited at the end of the gravel road at the spot where it turned into the dirt road two miles from the Baker farm, approaching it from the southeast.

Meanwhile, Dr. Miller drove his car from the southwest towards LaPlata where he rendezvoused with the Missouri Highway Patrol. They drove south and brought a portable incubator and two small oxygen tanks from the medical school hospital in the north. Then Dr. Miller drove the remaining miles west with the Highway Patrol directing them to the Baker farm hoping the roads were not impassible from the northerly direction.

When all went according to plan, Dr. Woodward would arrive first at the farm with plenty of time to spare. It is always best an obstetrician arrive first, then the pediatrician when both cannot be there from the beginning. Woodard hoped Wilson, the pediatrician, would not be too far behind.

Unfortunately, the plan did not account for the bridge at the end of the gravel road washing out at the Carol Creek Junction. With rushing water rising and wind swirling, it took another 20 minutes before Dr.Woodward could make it north to the next intact bridge over the fast-rising stream. An additional 15 minutes passed before Mr. Baker could get the old green and yellow John Deere tractor close enough to the car to tow it the last two miles to the farm. Dr. Woodward had his delivery packs and instruments packed dry and safely away in the trunk of his car.

The Highway Patrol members, Sergeant Siegfried and Patrolman Barstow, had better luck. They rendezvoused with Dr. Miller on the outskirts of LaPlata. The big Dodge patrol car with its flashing red lights twisting in rotation seemed to turn the big raindrops crimson in their paths falling from the sky. Siegfried and Barstow had been patrol partners for over four years. They each were over 6'2" tall and weighed well over 200 pounds. Barstow's blond hair and youthful face made him look younger than his 26 years. Siegfried's thick black hair, bushy dark eyebrows, and wide scars running down the entire left side of his face gave him a formidable appearance of sternness. Upon being introduced to this bear of a man, one was more likely to step back in fear than forward in friendliness. Thirty-two-years-old, he generally let Barstow drive while he did paperwork and other required record keeping of their patrol shifts together. Siegfried had lost his love of driving ever since a high speed chase resulted in a serious wreck and the permanent scarring to his face three years earlier.

Like many police officers whose lives may suddenly depend on each other's reactions and abilities, they were very good friends. They laughed at each other's jokes even when they were not funny, and they sympathized with each other's problems even when they were not very bad. With Dr. Miller and the portable incubator now snuggly placed in the back seat of the big brown Dodge, they made it south and west over the increasingly difficult country roads and then arrived at the farm only three minutes behind Dr. Woodward and Mr. Baker. Minimal traffic had impeded their progress. No one without serious need would drive on the rural roads of Missouri on a night like this.

Upon their arrival at the old farmhouse, the immediate problem became not the delivery of a newborn infant but in finding the well-worn mother. Bridgett had disappeared from the small two-story house. They quickly searched throughout it.

The other children were safely asleep in small upstairs bedrooms in spite of the raging storm outdoors. The young girls were oblivious to everything. But Bridgett was nowhere in the house and neither was she in the barn. She had disappeared as totally and as suddenly as if by evaporation.

Mr. Baker himself had finally solved the mystery. "It's the privy, Doc. She's got to be in that damn privy out back yonder in the yard. She must have gone outside to use it."

"What privy? Outside where? What are you talking about, Rudy?" asked Dr. Woodward with concern and excitement in his voice. "I know you have an inside bathroom off the kitchen. I saw it when I came in."

"Right Doc, but our inside flush toilet has not been working properly the last few days, and I've been too damn busy to fix it. We've been using the old privy outside in the back of the house."

Rudy was right. No one had thought to look in the gray, weather-beaten, outside toilet. Rushing out into the pouring rain, Rudy led the way with Dr. Woodward and Sergeant Siegfried following close behind. Patrolman Barstow still searched the barn for a second time, while Dr. Miller set up the incubator in the kitchen.

With the privy door open and banging loudly in the wind and rain it seemed very strange that someone might be inside. A large bolt of lightning ominously struck nearby, temporarily illuminating the darkened scene. The following crash of close thunder instantaneously and temporarily deafened them all as the falling rain persisted.

Dr. Woodward arrived first with his flashlight. Larger than Rudy, smaller than the sergeant, he could move more quickly than either of them. He shined a big bright flashlight beam inside the small wooden building. A clearly visible woman's body slumped over on the pine privy floor. They had found Bridgett.

She lay limp and motionless on her right side with a light yellow nightgown up around her waist. Bright red blood smeared over both of her inner thighs. She did not look good.

"Is she alive Doc?" asked Siegfried with real concern in his voice. "Is she alive?" he repeated somewhat louder to be heard above the noise of the constant wind and torrential rain.

"Yes, but we've got to get her out of here. Help me carry her now. She's lost some blood, and it's getting cold out here."

"Is she in shock?" the sergeant asked.

"No, but she sure will be if we don't get her inside."

Still conscious, Bridgett's pulse maintained strongly as the doctor held her wrist and counted her heartbeats. Her voice barely audible over the noise of the increasing wind and rain, they could not clearly hear her until Dr. Woodward and the sergeant carried her back inside the warm, snug farmhouse to the Baker's downstairs bedroom just off the kitchen. The clean and neat small bedroom was uncomfortably cramped full with a large double bed, an eight-drawer double dresser, two rocking chairs and a old flat-topped steamer chest.

"It's the baby. Where's the baby? I've lost my new baby," Bridgett breathlessly whispered as they put her down on the big bed.

"What do you mean lost it? You're confused. You haven't had it yet," her husband replied as he placed a large heavy blue and yellow patchwork quilt over her to keep her warm.

"I think I passed it out there in the outhouse. I'm sure I did." Everybody there heard her but nobody believed her. "I'm not kidding Rudy. I really did, just a few minutes ago. Please find my baby. Please doctors, find my baby," she kept repeating.

"What the hell?" said Mr. Baker, the first time he had sworn since joining the church. He looked very anxious. His wife never joked about anything, much less a subject this serious. "Bridgett, I don't understand, how could you have had the baby already? The doctors just got here. You haven't had the baby yet." He hovered nervously over his wife and pulled up the large warm quilt over her body each time Dr. Woodward took it down so he could examine his patient.

"Boil water, go boil water," yelled Dr. Woodward in exasperation. "We need lots of hot water, Rudy." Boiling water had been the first thing Woodward learned long ago about medicine from an old MGM movie he saw during a Saturday matinee. Doctors apparently needed lots of boiling water whenever women had babies. However, after four years of medical school, he still wasn't sure what all the boiled water was really for. Maybe it was just to get rid of nervous husbands during home deliveries, keeping up the illusion of real progress produced by a prevailing profusion of meaningless motion. In that respect, it certainly always seemed to serve its purpose and most likely would now. After all, doctors did not use it to boil the babies, and he didn't know of any contemporary cultures that cooked and ate the placenta.

Dr. Miller soon finished setting up the incubator in the kitchen and warming it up as he had done many times before. Luckily the farmhouse had electricity unlike many other rural homes in the area. He came back into the downstairs bedroom just as his partner, Dr. Woodward, completed his examination of

Bridgett. "How is she doing Dr. Woodward?" Miller asked. How soon for this new baby now?"

"My God, she really has passed it. She's already had the baby."

"She's what?" Miller shouted excitedly. "That's impossible. When? How?" he yelled.

"She really has. All that's left here is the placenta inside her, and she should also pass that any minute now. She's lost some blood but she's not really in shock. Go find that baby, Wilson. You're the pediatrician on this team."

"What do you mean go find it? Where is it? How can anyone lose a new born baby?"

"It must still be down there somewhere in the privy pit. She must have spontaneously passed it when she went to the bathroom."

Dr. Miller bound out of the house grabbing the sergeant's long five-battery flashlight. Sergeant Siegfried and Patrolman Barstow were right behind him splashing through the slippery wet mud in the yard to the outhouse. Seventy-five feet behind the farmhouse, the privy sat toward the bottom of a small sloping hill covered with a grove of white birch trees.

The sweetest sound Dr. Miller had ever heard in his medical practice was the cry of an infant coming up from way below the ground through the one-seat hole. Wilson smiled in sudden relief. But the cry was inconsistent, coming and going in waves. Dr. Miller shined the light deeply down into the dark hole, but he and the troopers could not see anything below but shit, water, and used toilet paper. The mixture covered the bottom of the pit at least five feet below the base of the toilet.

"Damn, but Baker dug a deep privy pit," yelled Barstow above the noise of the wind, the groaning tree branches under stress, and the constant driving downpour. "Why did he dig it so deep? He must have meant for this to last for years."

Inside the small privy house the three men were relieved to be out of the wind and the rain. The height of the wooden toilet bench put an additional one-and-a-half feet distance between them and the pit. "We can knock down the privy and tear off the base of the toilet bench. At least then we'll be even to the ground and closer to the bottom of the trench," yelled Sergeant Siegfried. He and Barstow ran outside in the pouring rain again.

"You'll need tools," shouted Dr. Miller. "They're probably stored somewhere in the barn," he screamed even louder at the departing troopers. "Be quick about it."

Dr. Miller thought Siegfried and Barstow had gone to the Baker's barn for tools. The small privy building was soundly attached to the earth by two-by-fours at each corner driven deeply into the ground. Too solid to shake it loose, they would need a heavy axe or a crowbar and large sledge hammer.

The sheriffs thought Dr. Miller was somewhere behind them outside the privy. The rain came down in torrents and the frequent flash of lightening struck close by. By the quickness of the thunder following the flash, Siegfried estimated the last strike to be within one mile of Baker's hill. They were in the center of a severe spring thunderstorm.

The highway patrolmen both ran around in back of the privy and about 40 feet up the incline behind it. "Where is Dr. Miller?" asked Sergeant Siegfried.

"I don't know," yelled back Barstow. "He must have gone to the barn for tools. When was the last time you knocked over an outhouse Sergeant?"

"Not since Halloween in my junior year in high school in Hannibal, so I know the secret. Hit it low and hard."

"I'm right behind you sir," Barstow said, smiling, as they started down the slope between the trees, charging the small building with all of their combined mass and power.

They tackled the poor privy as two line backers would take down a running back. Sergeant Siegfried's experience as a line backer at the University of Missouri 12 years before had finally come in handy. With his 6'4" and 242 pounds combined with Barstow's 6'3" and 222 pounds, they powered into the outhouse. The sudden crash of breaking boards exploded like the detonation of a bomb. The tall, narrow wooden building disintegrated like a small match box under the combined impact of their charging 464 pounds.

Unfortunately, they didn't know Dr. Miller still remained inside the outhouse and had just stood up straight after peering down into the deep hole looking for the baby. He no longer had the big flashlight, having given it back to the sergeant so he could find proper tools. Had the patrolman hit the building three seconds earlier, Wilson would have had his neck broken and could have died right then and there. Still, the impact meant he would be unable to straighten up completely for a couple of weeks to come. When the highway patrolmen saw the doctor among the shards of the destroyed privy, they thought they had killed Dr. Miller. The doctor started moving slowly when Siegfried lifted most of the broken boards off of him. A few moments passed before the doctor appeared to understand where he was and what he was doing. The cool rain falling on his face helped to revive him.

"Are you okay, Dr. Miller? Speak to me. Speak to me." the Sergeant shouted.

Miller thought lightning had suddenly struck and demolished the little building. "The lightning tore down the privy for us. Don't you two understand? It's a sign from the Lord. It means we will prevail," he yelled above the screeching wind as he ignored his pain and started clearing away the rest of the wreckage from himself.

Why not, thought Sergeant Siegfried. There was no reason Miller should ever know that over 464 pounds of Missouri's finest had just run over him. They weren't to blame for his remaining inside the privy.

Barstow, still stunned and groggy from crashing into the building had also not been thinking clearly and felt barely conscious. He tried to stand up again in the slippery mud, but he kept falling down. On the fourth try he finally made it firmly to his feet.

"Are you okay Barstow? It's going to take all three of us to get that baby up out of that pit, and we've got to work fast," yelled Miller above the noise of the storm.

"I'm okay, I'm okay," Barstow replied, still shaking his head to clear his mind. "What's the plan? We still have to get down there into the pit - it looked pretty narrow."

"First we've got to get rid of this bench," Siegfried commanded.

Miller agreed, and he and Siegfried grabbed opposite ends of the toilet bench, tore it from its base, and flung it farther down the hill. Then they ripped off the loose, wet floor boards on either side, revealing a privy pit about five-feet wide, five-feet deep, and two-and-a-half feet from front to back. The steep back bank of the pit slanted at about a 30-degree angle, and water ran off the incline behind the privy and down into the deeper portions of the pit. Miller and Siegfried both flopped down onto the wet, muddy ground and peered over the edge of the dark hole. The Sergeant shined his flashlight back and forth but saw no baby visible in the deep hole in the ground.

By now Barstow had recovered sufficiently to be of real help. He also shined his big five-battery flashlight into the deep pit.

They could still only see mud, water, shit, and old toilet paper below them.

Miller realized if he jumped down into the pit he might jump on top of the new baby somewhere there below. The narrowness of the pit would impede him from bending over if he were standing in it. A tightening cord of fear and apprehension clamped down in his stomach as he realized the risk of waiting. Seconds ran by quickly and each one ticking past decreased the newborn's chance of survival.

They no longer heard any cries coming up towards them from out of the pit. The water level from the rain runoff kept increasing, particularly in the deeper parts of the pit.

"Hold my legs. I'm going in head first. It's the only way," yelled Miller.

"You're gonna' do what?" asked the sergeant with awe and respect in his voice.

"Well, can either of you come up with a better plan?"

"Probably not, but it's dangerous going in like that," Siegfried replied.

"It's the only way that will work. I'll be closer to the bottom of the pit with my hands to find the baby. There's no time to waste."

"Yes, you're right. Someone has to. You're the smallest of the three of us and we're big enough to hold you firmly in there hanging upside down. Get a good grip on your side of him Barstow so he won't fall on his face and drown down there."

There was nothing else they could do - seconds counted. Dr. Miller held the sergeant's big flashlight in his left hand. While Siegfried held Miller's left leg and Barstow his right leg, the big men held on tightly and lowered the doctor carefully into the privy pit head first. He had to find the newborn baby fast, he hoped time had not run out. A baby being born into this world on this poor, dirt-farm was tough enough, but being born like this made it all that much harder.

With his head deeply into the slimy wet pit, Dr. Miller could suddenly hear much better. The walls of the deep hole helped to block the outside howling wind and the constant noise of the drenching rain. Dr. Miller groped along the bottom of the pit with his free right hand, but so far he felt only soft shit and wet mud. Telling the difference in the dark proved impossible as it all felt the same and it all stank. The decomposing wet toilet paper spread over everything giving him the most trouble. The infant seemed to be somewhere under it and the doctor feared the baby might smother or drown in it.

Nothing in his medical studies of pediatrics had prepared him for this night. With no known precedent, he literally wrote the chapter on shit-house deliveries and newborn care in country privies as he dove deeper into the pit. As usual in such circumstances, if a person's character is strong and their resolve is sufficient, they do not need to rely on precedent. Intelligence and instinct soon dictate the proper course of action.

"What do you see?" yelled the sergeant from above. Anxiety and concern sounded clearly in his usually gruff voice. As he bent over additional rainwater from the wide brim of his hat poured down on the doctor.

"I'm not sure. No sign of life so far. Keep the flashlight pointed down here, and try not to let more water run in. There's too much in here already."

"Should we rig a poncho over the pit? We've got a couple in the patrol car," said Barstow.

"No time for that. Just hold me steadily. Don't let me fall on my face in here. I could drown in this mess."

Finally the doctor then heard the faint cry of new life. A sound so faint neither of the patrolmen a few feet above heard it coming from an elevated ledge in the right front corner of the pit. Soon the doctor felt under his probing right hand, the small, warm body of the infant luckily lying on its back. He had his hand on the baby and confirmed it with the flashlight, so he dropped the illuminated flashlight he held in his left hand into the pit. He then had both hands free to grasp the slippery infant and pull the baby up next to his chest. Only then did he yell to the officers. "I've got him. He's a boy. Pull me up now. Get me out of here fast" he yelled. As soon as he accomplished his task, claustrophobia closed in on him caused by the deep narrow pit's walls so close to him. Suddenly he felt fear as a gush of water washed down into the pit from the steep bank. Muddy water covered the baby and dripped down over the doctor's face and head as he perched upside down in the pit grasping the baby to his chest.

Steadily the policemen pulled him feet first from the deep pit. In the years to come, the sergeant would always remember this moment being the first time in his life he had ever seen someone coming up out of shit and mud smiling broadly. Even upside down Miller had a big wide smile on his mud-covered face from ear to ear. He would later admit this to be one of the most satisfying moments of his life. For these first few seconds, the miracle of new life coming up from below ground struck him speechless. Finally he found his voice again. "I think the baby's okay. He's alive and I think he's big enough to make it."

"Are you sure?" asked Siegfried as the two highway patrolmen quickly turned Miller right side up. They placed his feet firmly on the wet ground and steadied him for a few seconds before letting go.

"Pretty sure," Miller replied, yelling over his left shoulder as he placed the infant under his shirt for warmth and ran to the shelter of the farmhouse.

Siegfried let out a loud, shrill shout of triumph which could be heard above the persistent noise of the wind and the rain. The others back in the farmhouse heard it and immediately understood its joyful significance.

Also being a Southern Baptist, Barstow knelt down in the mud and rain to give immediate prayer and thanks to the good Lord for this miraculous delivery. He insisted his sergeant kneel with him and, though Siegfried outranked the man, he obeyed his patrolman's request. With ingenuity and persistence they had circumvented the awesome authority of a sudden spring storm, flash flood and all.

Dr. Miller had already rushed back into the warm house and arrived inside the kitchen just as Dr. Woodward delivered the placenta from Bridgett in the bedroom. She could hear the baby boy's lusty cry. Under Dr. Woodward's watchful care, some of the color had gradually returned to her face. With intravenous fluids running into her right arm, she felt as well as possible under the circumstances. She smiled with a wide grin not seen on her tired face for seven years. As the pleasure of new motherhood flooded her mind and body she felt more alive than she had since the birth of her youngest daughter, now three-years-old. Unexpectedly a few tears of happiness seeped from her eyes. Quickly she wiped them away with her left hand. Only Dr. Woodward noticed.

Then Mr. Baker calmed the two older children who now were awakened by the storm and the commotion and had solemnly tromped down the narrow staircase from their bedroom above. They stood beside their dad in the warm kitchen watching Dr. Miller gently wash the newborn baby in a large metal pan of soapy water on the wide counter of the white sink. The seven-year-old girl, although glad she finally had a brother, immediately realized she would always be big enough to boss him around. He would be no threat to her sibling seniority. The two younger sisters had hoped for another girl. Their initial disappointment quickly subsided as they first viewed with fascination the uniqueness differentiating boys from girls. They giggled shyly in childish laughter. With the birth of this nearly miraculous baby, prayer and hope re-emerged and the Baker household had become a happy home again.

Taking 20 minutes to clean the infant, Dr. Miller estimated the baby's weight at about five pounds, eight ounces. The delayed Apgar score, the method for quickly summarizing the health of a newborn, measured at a surprising seven. Apgar stands for Appearance, Pulse, Grimace, Activity, and Respiration.

He finally placed the infant in the incubator, more for his warmth than for any necessary additional oxygen concentration. Then Dr. Wilson proudly carried the baby into the parents' bedroom, placed him on the old steamer chest at the foot of the bed, and plugged the life-giving machine into a nearby wall outlet.

Problems remained to be solved such as early immunization against possible tetanus, exposure from the minor lacerations and abrasions suffered in the privy pit, and prophylactic antibiotic dosages to prevent infection. But with the worst over, everyone started to relax.

Dr. Miller went to the showers first. Afterwards while he changed into dry clothes loaned by Mr. Baker, the farmer poured hot cups of newly steeped tea from a white kettle on the large black wood-burning stove. He served the two young doctors and patrolman Barstow. Sergeant Siegfried took the next turn in the shower. His tea could wait until he cleaned himself off.

Slowly Rudy Baker spoke, "I can never thank you gentlemen enough. We want you to know we will always be grateful. My wonderful wife and I have decided on the name for the new baby. There is no other possibility. He will be known as Wilson Miller Baker."

The possibilities for Dr. Miller's new nickname were nearly endless. *Shit House Doctor* was not one of his favorites, but *Privy Pediatrician* did have a certain ring to it. He had become used to it because among his fellow medical friends and professional colleagues, this incident would be remembered for many years and became part of the clinic's local folklore. With each repeated telling, the storm would become a little wilder, the pit a little deeper, and the stench a little stronger. One truth never exaggerated in this story was the potential for disaster of a privy pit floor and a young doctor who had brought life forth in this noblest of callings known as the practice of medicine.

Wilson Miller was one hell of a physician. The new infant had a name with a lot to live up to, and Dr. Miller had nothing to live down.

Chapter 7
Fifteen Hands
March 12, 1962

The spring seasonal weather started early in mid march, progressively banishing all evidence of the past cold winter's snow from the warming countryside of Northeast Missouri. Thus, with mixed emotions, Gerry Frank and Harry Thompson drove together the 53-mile drive southwest from the city. Upon arrival in the small village, Harry parked his two-door Chevy next to the now familiar red-brick medical building. Most of the cold winter snowbanks had already melted and thick mud lay where the piled snow had once stood. Extreme moisture in the ground meant it would still be a while before local farmers could get tractors and other heavy equipment into the mud-filled fields and soggy pastures surrounding the picturesque village. Spring plowing and planting might be a bit late this year.

"You know Harry, I never thought I would admit it, but I am definitely going to miss this place. Do you realize April first starts our last two months of rural clinic rotation here as country doctors?"

"I know what you mean," replied Harry as he turned off the ignition and pulled on the car's hand brake. Clicking loudly with a certain finality, it gave an emphasized pause to the moment. Slowly he slipped a cigarette from out of the Camels pack in his jacket chest pocket without removing the pack. Still only using his right hand, Harry placed the cigarette in his mouth and lit it with one hand from a full book of matches he replaced in an ashtray attached to the dashboard. He had learned to carefully twist down one match and strike it without tearing it from its row. This method of lighting a cigarette created an unextinguished lit match still firmly attached to the pack and less than an inch from fresh ones. He could not blow it out because of the cigarette between his lips. He shook it out to accomplish this to keep it from lighting the rest of the book.

Both of the young doctors sat in the car collecting their thoughts about the patients scheduled to be seen at the rural clinic that afternoon. With Harry driving, they generally arrived in the small town 15 minutes before the scheduled opening of the medical office. In spite of the car being ten years old and rust showing through the faded blue rocker panels, the finely tuned engine in the old car had never failed them yet. Over the muddy or snowy Missouri country roads during house call emergencies, the car had always delivered them on time. They called it *Old Faithful*.

"You know that's a damn dumb thing you do." said Gerry.

"Which dumb thing are you referring to?" questioned his partner.

"Lighting your cigarette one-handed like the local ranchers do."

"What do you mean dumb? It takes real skill and fine finger dexterity to accomplish this. It's not as easy as it looks, and it's just as tough as tying surgical knots one-handed. I'm getting better at that too."

"No kidding. Have you forgotten in the last two weeks how you've so skillfully, and with great finger dexterity, singed your complete right eyebrow, half of your left one, the front of your hair, two jackets, and one pair of pants?

"No, but I would forget if you'd stop reminding me," Harry replied as he exhaled a breath of smoke.

"Well, the next time you mistakenly set off the whole damn pack of matches, you may end up burning more than just your face and clothes. I'd sure like to think you learned something besides that stupid stunt from these farm folk around here."

"Well it's safer than taking both hands off the wheel while I'm driving. You have to admit that, old buddy. And, the cigarette lighter in this car hasn't worked for years."

"So get it fixed or better yet, stop smoking," Gerry admonished.

"Maybe some day, but what I'm really perfecting this for," continued Harry, "is so I can light Joyce's cigarette one-handed without taking my other arm from around her warm body. Women seem to think during times of sex-fueled emotion in parked cars or on pull-down couches they can break up a man's timing by asking for a cigarette. Did you realize how important timing is in these situations?"

"Not since I stopped dating women who smoked."

"Well, it's often the critical element between successful seduction and frustrating failure. With this new technique, I'll be able to keep the rhythm of the moment from ever being lost."

Gerry shook his head as he rolled down the car's right-side window to let out the smoke invariably coming his way. Harry had a way with women and he perfected his techniques at all times. His last girlfriend, Joyce Kunz, was a student at the teachers college. Gerry thought the obvious solution was to date women who did not smoke. He would suggest that to Harry sometimes, but not while his friend dated Joyce. She had at least a pack-a-day habit, far worse than Harry's.

Essex had come to mean a lot to the young doctors, and they knew they would be far better physicians for the experience of the nearly four months already spent in the small village. They were sad the externship rotation would only continue for two more months. They would then leave for their year of internship and be replaced with two other student physician externs.

"You said something about a possible vaginal bleeder you had coming to the office this afternoon?" asked Harry with concern in his voice. "Do you have any idea if it's serious enough you'll need to transfer her to the hospital today?"

"No, I'm not sure yet," replied Gerry. "It's Mrs. Richly from out at Hilltop Farms. She's 44-years-old and has been having problems with periodic heavy bleeding from a fibroid tumor of the uterus."

"So how long has she been bleeding this time?"

"She called me earlier this morning to report moderately excessive bleeding starting again late last night. Apparently it had slowed by the time she called, but I told her to meet me here as soon as we opened the clinic. She's had the fibroid problems for months, but she has steadfastly refused surgery. She's already anemic with a hemoglobin last month of 9.6 and a hematocrit of 32."

"Well, nobody's waiting on our doorstep yet," replied Harry, as they stepped from the car. "Why don't we walk over to the cafe and I'll buy you a root beer before we start our clinic day?"

Gerry agreed and as they began to cross the wet street, Weatherford Buntley's purple-painted pickup truck came tearing around the corner splashing mud on both of them as it accelerated down the middle of the street. "You know, that idiot is really a public health menace," muttered Gerry. "Someday he's going to kill somebody with his dumb driving."

"Yeah, and hopefully just himself. But the people of the county probably won't be that lucky," answered Harry, trying to knock the excess mud from his cowboy boots.

"You're probably right, unfortunately."

"Look at the mud all over my boots and pants now. That dummy must have been standing in line behind his cohort, Dexter, when they passed out the brains. Wish we could figure a way to keep him from being behind the steering wheel of that pickup ever again."

"I'm not sure," laughed Gerry, "but I think the wet tan mud goes well with your dry reddish mud. At least it color coordinates with your old brown pants."

Just then Mrs. Richly drove up to the clinic building in her new blue Buick sedan. The doctors immediately forgot about the root beer and walked back across the street as she rolled down the driver-side window of the vehicle and waved at them. She looked slightly pale but greatly relieved to see them both there in the street.

"How are you doing, Mrs. Richly?" asked Dr. Frank. "Are things any worse or any better?" By the time he finished the two questions he stood next to her car.

"The bleeding is less now, Dr. Frank," she replied quietly. "But this time it sure did scare me to death. Maybe that's a poor choice of words for the occasion. But you've been telling me all along I'd probably have to have surgery. I know I've been putting it off too long already. But this time the extent of the bleeding really worries me."

"Well, the good Lord works in mysterious ways. Maybe a little scare is the nudge you needed," said the young doctor.

"I wasn't sure if it would ever slow down when it restarted right after I talked to you on the phone the last time. I'm momentarily better, but I realize this hasn't solved the real problem. My husband and I talked about it early this morning."

"Did you come to any definite decision?"

"We sure 'nuff have. I think while I've got my courage up, if you're willing to drive to the hospital with me now, I'd like to be admitted today and have the surgery tomorrow. Is that possible? If

206

it is then I'll probably be recovered in time to help my husband with the spring planting still needing to be done."

"Let me check my schedule in the clinic first," Dr. Frank replied. "I'll be right back."

"Certainly. I'll just sit waiting here in the car until you know for sure. I'm not weak, but I just don't feel like doing much walking around today."

Gerry realized Mrs. Richly needed the surgery quickly and was glad she had finally made up her mind. "You know, I think I've only got about six patients scheduled for this afternoon, Harry. I could drive in with her now, and you could see my patients. I'll do her history and physical at the hospital when she's admitted, and afterwards get a ride back to the village this afternoon with Sharon."

"Sounds okay to me," said Harry unlocking the clinic's front door and walking inside. Gerry followed him in and quickly confirmed from the schedule the number of patients he had estimated. Though Harry had seven patients of his own to see, four were rechecks so the combined number of patients would be easy for him to handle alone.

"Did Sharon take that secretarial job she had been offered at the hospital?" asked Harry. "I knew she was talking about it late last week. She sounded pretty enthusiastic."

"She sure did," said Gerry. "She's been working for the last three days now, part time in the afternoon after her classes, four hours a day. She is the secretary for the out-patient clinic. I kind of like the idea. She'll become familiar with patient scheduling, procedures, and medical terminology."

"Her knowing all that stuff could help you later on."

"Yes, it might eventually help a certain young doctor I know when he starts his own practice in California. The only bad part is that Huntley character, one of the OB/GYN residents, is already chasing her again. Apparently they dated for a while two years ago."

"With you two practically engaged," said Harry, "I don't see that as a problem. Sharon's probably the most faithful girl in Northeast Missouri. I'm sure she'd never let another man touch her. But from what I know of her and her family, you are kidding yourself, old buddy, if you think she will ever leave this part of Missouri. Maybe she'll visit California but she won't move there. Someday soon, you are going to have to face that problem."

"Well, it's not something I need think about today with Mrs. Richly's condition on the top of my list."

"I know, but it's something you'll need to give close attention to real soon. Don't put it off too long."

Gerry quickly walked back outside and transferred his black medical bag from the trunk of Harry's Chevy to the back seat of Mrs. Richly's Buick. While in the car he took her blood pressure, listened to her heart, and felt her abdomen. He cleared her for the drive.

The patient and her husband were hard working and successful farmers with a sizable spread known as Hilltop Farms, three miles south of the village. They had two boys and a girl, all teenagers. With the help of their children and two handymen, they managed one of the largest, most prosperous farms in the county. They entered prime examples of their produce and livestock and won awards annually in the Missouri State Fair and occasionally in regional contests.

The Richly's were always pleasant company, and Mrs. Richly generally brought a fresh-baked pie to the clinic for the doctors. She had not forgotten this time and had insisted on leaving a deep dish apple pie with Dr. Thompson before the 53-mile drive to the hospital with Dr. Frank. He had offered to drive and she seemed relieved to let him do so. Her excessive bleeding had caused her to be more tired than she cared to admit.

Dr. Frank noticed she still appeared nervous about entering the hospital, so he tried to keep the driving conversation light, interspaced with periodic reassurance that she was doing the right thing. Much of the discussion centered on farming and why her husband had switched to a new hybrid corn that season. She finally leaned her head back on the seat and relaxed sufficiently to fall asleep for the last few miles of the trip.

When the car neared the southern outskirts of the small city that housed the medical school and the associated hospital, Dr. Frank's thoughts became increasingly filled with images of his girlfriend, Sharon. A country girl, the likes of which he had never known, she had really started to effect him. Dr. Frank had been burned badly before in love affairs. Though his heart had hope, his mind cautioned a lot of restraint, but his body didn't receive the message. He knew Harry was correct in his assertion Sharon would want to remain on her family's Missouri land for life. She was not a California girl.

As the doctor drove Mrs. Richly's big Buick through the medical school campus, she awoke from her nap. He dropped her off in front of the main hospital and hailed an orderly with a wheel chair to help her take her immediately to the OB/GYN clinic. Gerry then carefully parked her new car in the side parking lot. Dr. Thompson had called about an hour before to arrange an appointment for her and the receptionist expecting her had greeted her warmly. One of the gyn residents promised to examine her in the afternoon schedule between other patients. There might be an opening in about a half hour.

Dr. Frank had brought Mrs. Richly's chart with him from the rural clinic. A young nurse helped the patient get ready in one of the unoccupied examination rooms. The doctor now completed writing out her extensive OB/GYN history on a hospital form with notes of her current bleeding as the basis of her chief complaint. The staff physician, on whose service she would be admitted, would see her afterwards and then would also write his findings on her chart.

Dr. Frank had done a complete history and physical on Mrs. Richly at the clinic one month before. However, he repeated all parts of the exam to make sure there had been no significant changes. A nurse then helped set up the patient for the pelvic exam procedure.

Considerably suffering from vaginal bleeding, Mrs. Richly felt it had definitely decreased over the past few hours. The heavy bleeding of the previous night and latter part of the morning had worried her, causing her finally to seek help for the problem. During the pelvic examination, the doctor palpated a fairly large fibroid type growth in the posterior wall of her uterus. He felt another possible smaller one within the anterior wall. Her uterus was slightly enlarged but non-tender on palpation. Both ovaries could be felt and seemed normal, as did the fallopian tubes which connected them to the patient's uterus.

"The reason we're a little crowded and rushed this afternoon," volunteered the nurse, "is because the gynecological department is holding an extensive gynecology lab for the senior medical students currently on our service. It starts at four in the student outpatient clinic across the street. Generally we're not this busy or rushed, Mrs. Richly."

"Oh, I don't mind," the patient replied. "I appreciate your fitting me in on such short notice."

"That's a tremendous teaching program," said Dr. Frank. "I remember when I went through it during my hospital rotation late last summer. I saw far more gynecological and pelvic pathology cases in those three or four lab sessions, than I'd ever seen before or have seen since. Who had the good idea to start the program?"

"Doctor Chase proposed starting it in the outpatient clinic three years ago when he became chairman of the OB/GYN department. He didn't claim it as his original idea," said the nurse.

"Whose idea was it then?"

"Dr. Chase said he'd first seen professionally conducted clinics held every three months for his internship class while he trained in Boston. The hospital where he did his postgraduate work kept a running registry of different pelvic diseases and other gynecological pathology, both common and uncommon. Every three months, the staff physicians would put on the lab for the hospital's interns and residents. When I worked as a nurse up in delivery, I had to do lot a pelvic exams before I fully understood dilatation and effacement. I can sympathize with the new physicians about the difficulty of doing pelvic examinations and knowing for certain what they're actually palpating. That's why Dr. Chase also set up the lab here to teach the new student doctors."

"But where do you get the volunteers?" questioned Dr. Frank. "Why would a woman volunteer to have a staff physician, at least one resident, one or two interns, and possibly 15 medical students all do separate pelvic exams on her within an hour? There's no way that is an enjoyable experience for anyone. How do you get patients to agree to being teaching cases?"

The nurse became obviously irritated with Dr. Frank's questions. She strongly respected Dr. Chase since the day she went to work in the department - Nurse Sara Hall completely believed in the gyn labs. Dr. Chase's staunch professionalism and unyielding dedication to teaching carried the day and had overruled the considerable controversy when they had first started at the hospital. Nurse Hall detected a hint of cynicism in Dr.

Frank's questioning reminiscent of early puritanical prejudice others had once raised against the program.

"You know Dr. Frank, this is a teaching hospital," she said with sarcasm in her voice. "Every patient admitted through the clinic service or seen in the outpatient departments is a direct recipient of the services of our nationally renowned medical school and teaching hospital staff faculty. Patients also receive direct and indirect benefits of the extra help of junior and senior medical students serving externships and interns and residents in the post-graduate programs. As recipients of these benefits, they agree to the repeated examinations by the medical students on the particular service.'

"I know all that," said Dr. Frank impatiently. "But the women who participate in these gyn labs are agreeing to pelvic examinations by 15 or more different people. You're certainly not implying that's similar to being a clinic patient, are you Nurse Hall?"

"I certainly am, Dr. Frank," she replied, now more openly hostile and defensive. "In fact, the volunteers are chosen in a selective, professional manner by both the residents and the chief of the department, Dr. Chase. All the chosen cases are accepted only with his final approval."

"You mean there is a formal selection process?"

"Yes. You might say it's like the selection process for medical school, Doctor." Nurse Hall could not resist a little bit of a dig here. "They're chosen keeping in mind their intelligence and their maturity. They must understand the professionalism in which the laboratory is conducted. They must realize the importance of teaching cases and the uniqueness of demonstrating a particular anatomical variation, disease, or other pathological problem to a medical student who can only know the problem by direct participation. A new doctor can't be expected to diagnose even a commonplace pelvic pathology by only reading about it. He or she must see it and feel it. The volunteers we use understand this even if you obviously do not."

By then Nurse Hall had helped Mrs. Richly out of the stirrups, and the patient sat on the end of the gyn table. Mrs. Richly seemed embarrassed by the conversation between the doctor and the nurse. With the examination completed, Dr. Frank took off his rubber gloves, washed his hands of the white powder, and quickly left the room.

Dr. Frank poured a cup of coffee in the alcove near the nurse's station when Nurse Hall walked past him and sat down at her chart desk. She was a beautiful young woman, about 5'8" tall, weighed approximately 135 pounds and had long, wavy blond hair, neatly pinned on her head in a French roll. She had become accustomed to stares and admiration of men whom she knew stripped her naked in their fantasies. She was surprised to see no such reaction reflected in the eyes of Dr. Frank.

"I don't think we should have had that conversation in front of my patient," he said, putting down his coffee cup to add some sugar. "I could detect her embarrassment there in the examination room. Doctors and nurses should not be argumentative in front of patients. Your irritation with me showed."

"You should have anticipated that, doctor," replied Nurse Hall. "You're the one who started the conversation, and I just answered you truthfully." A defiant, feisty tone appeared in her voice the young doctor had never detected before today. However, he knew she was right and he knew she deserved to know that. He added two teaspoons of sugar to his hot cup of coffee. Then he poured in generous amounts of cream and slowly stirred the light brown liquid. Nurse Hall obviously waited for a comment as her cold blue eyes stared intently at the doctor. She suddenly found herself liking what she saw and became irritated with this discovery.

Looking up and directly at her, Gerry smiled. "Rationally, I know what you said in there is right. You're correct, I precipitated the entire conversation. I'm not sure why my attitudes are what they are on the subject. I guess emotionally it's just the question of when is enough enough? How many medical students should a sick patient have to be subjected to during a hospitalization or a clinic experience, even if this is a teaching hospital?"

The young nurse finally smiled, "I'll bet you didn't sound a bit like that when you were a medical student, doctor. I'll bet you were pushing right along with the other students to see and to examine every patient you could get your hands on. Am I right?" she asked as she placed Mrs. Richly's record in the chart rack.

Sitting there slowly sipping his hot coffee, Gerry reflected on what Nurse Hall had said. Yes, damn it, she was right, and he knew it. He broke into a laugh and all tensions between them relaxed.

"I'm right, aren't I? Fess up now. Admit it," she said with a broad smile. The delight reflected on her pretty face made her deep blue eyes sparkle. As she crossed her long legs she pulled her white skirt down over her knees.

"Yes. You know darn well you're right, and I guess that's what bothers me now."

"It bothers you that I'm right?" she questioned. "Boy, you do have a problem, Doctor."

"No. It disturbs me less than a year ago, that was exactly my attitude. And now with only three-and-a-half months into an active practice situation out in the rural clinics, I already see the other side of the coin."

"What do you mean by that?" she questioned.

"I mean some of my hospitalized patients come back telling me tales you wouldn't believe about how they could hardly sleep with all the different examinations they had by so many medical students. I had a ten-year-old girl with an acute follicular purulent tonsillitis infection so bad she could hardly swallow. She became dehydrated with fever, and we had her on intravenous fluids and antibiotics. She had beta hemolytic strep infection with a significant heart murmur possibly meaning endocarditis.

"So what happened to bother you?"

"The fact there must have averaged at least a medical student in the patient's room every hour wakening her up to look down her throat and then to listen to her heart. That was ridiculous. What do you have to say to that?"

By now Nurse Hall had stood up and poured herself a hot cup of coffee, drinking it straight black. Perhaps that's how she kept her slim figure. Sitting down, she again crossed her long legs in a provocative manner while turning her chair to face the doctor directly. "Sure, Dr. Frank," she replied. "That is ridiculous. Student examinations by other than one extern assigned to the case, should only be done under the guidance of a staff physician or a chief resident. They should be done during morning or evening rounds and not waking up a patient to do them. The problem comes when one of the medical students has missed rounds because they may have been on another emergency somewhere else in the hospital, but they don't want to miss the opportunity to see a particularly interesting case. I'm sure that must have happened to you a few times last year."

"Yeah, I can see both sides of the argument," replied Dr. Frank. "It's just I'm surprised at how much my own attitudes and sympathies have changed. Now I find myself overly protective of my patients."

Although the young doctor was now heavily involved with his girlfriend, Sharon, and though they seriously considered marriage, that did not stop him from appreciating the beautiful young woman sitting only three feet away from him. He had heard the local rumor that Nurse Hall had worked her way through nurse's training in St. Louis as a successful model. She won the newspaper photographers photo flash contest two years in a row, but had given it all up to pursue her career in nursing. Patients not only liked her, but she had become Dr. Chase's personal scrub nurse in the mornings for gyn surgical procedures performed at the hospital. She was good at her job and she knew it.

"You had no way of knowing, Doctor, but it is doubly troubling and most unfortunate we had that conversation in front of your patient. You see, we had eight cases set up for this afternoon's gyn lab with the students, but one of them couldn't make it due to some problem at home with her child. Hers was the case of uterine fibroids we were going to use as a teaching example. So when your patient suddenly had been added into the clinic schedule this afternoon, and I saw she was a possible fibroid case, I thought of suggesting to Dr. Chase to consider substituting her into the gyn lab exercise for today."

"What?" said Dr. Frank excitedly. "You were actually considering using one of my patients as a teaching example for the gyn lab without asking me?"

"Yes, I was, and I still am," replied Nurse Hall with a new irritation in her voice. "That is exactly why I had the conversation with you in front of Mrs. Richly about our gyn labs."

"But she'd end up with 15 pairs of hands doing pelvic exams on her. Are you kidding? I didn't bring her to this hospital for that." The doctor was upset again.

Slowly putting down her coffee cup after drinking about a third of the hot black liquid, the young nurse took a deep breath before replying. "No, I'm not kidding, Doctor, and I resent your attitude. What makes your patients so special they shouldn't be subjected to a teaching lab program with their permission, but other physicians' patients should be? You reaped the benefits of the gyn labs when you went through this service, and every one of those women were some other doctor's patient. They all volunteered and contributed to your education. Yet you hesitate to let your patients contribute to some other doctor's education? What is your problem?"

Nurse Hall showed her obvious exasperation. She stood up, turned her back to the doctor, and made busy trying to straighten up certain stacks of medical records on her desk. The conversation bothered her more than she would admit. Known as one of the best physicians in the rural clinic program, if Dr. Frank harbored such anxieties about the gyn clinics, then how many other doctors might also feel this way and lobby to have this practice stopped? None of the students and few of the faculty realized over 50 percent of the cost of the program was directly funded by the donations of Dr. Chase. He had continually paid for the expenses out of his own pocket.

Dr. Frank finished the rest of his coffee in silence. He tried to examine his own values and the contradictions of his own thinking. He knew his opinions were not consistent with his history and this bothered him greatly. Reaching up, he clasped the young nurse's arm and, with gentle motion, asked her if she would please sit down and talk again.

"You know, Sarah," he said specifically, calling her by her name for the first time, "you're really right about this, and I am truly bothered I feel the way I do. I certainly don't know why I feel this way. Do you? You're obviously intelligent and extremely dedicated to this department and to this teaching program. Why should this bother me now?"

"Maybe it's the sex aspect," she said, sitting back down again. She sensed the young doctor's sincerity, and she did want to help him. "Maybe it's the fact since the examination involves a patient's sexual organs, the natural thought is to protect the ultimate privacy and not violate it. It probably wouldn't bother you if you had a male patient in the cardiology clinic and ten different students wanted to listen to a heart murmur he had. But if the same patient were examined in urology clinic for a testicle tumor by five or ten female medical students, it would probably bother us to some extent."

"You think so?" he questioned, deeply in thought over what the nurse had just said.

"Yes I do, but as professionals, we should rise above all that by now. Cheer up. Don't look so sad."

Just then, Dr. Chase came out of one of the examining rooms, walked over to the sink at the nurse's station, and started to scrub his hands. "Well, how're things in the rural clinics, Gerry?" he asked. A big man with a New England accent, Dr. Chase always had pleasant smile on his rough-hewn face.

"I see from the new scheduling, you have a vaginal bleeder in Room Three, with a probable diagnosis of fibroids. How long has she been bleeding?"

"Yes, doctor," interrupted the nurse, "and Mrs. Jensen, the fibroid case you had previously set up for the gyn clinic this afternoon, called in earlier to say she can't make it. I wondered if we could substitute Mrs. Richly as our fibroid condition teaching case. You've always emphasized how important it is to have an example of that type of common pathology in each of our lab sessions."

"That's a damn good idea, Sarah," replied Dr. Chase, as he finished drying his hands and executing a perfect rebound shot of the crumpled paper towel off the side wall into the waste basket eight feet away. "You don't have any objections, do you Dr. Frank?" he asked in a matter-of-fact manner. "You know, these gyn labs are really the best teaching devices we have for medical students on this rotation. Not only do we have good histories and succinct workups on most all the cases we examine, but also with the medical students repeating the exams, we can point out exactly where the pathologies are located. There's no teaching device better than a hands-on examination of a living patient. To understand pathology you have to feel diseased tissue."

"I guess your right about that sir, but…but…."

"No buts about it. You're familiar with my famous mentor, the greatest physician I have ever worked under, who taught me that back in Boston during my internship many years ago."

Oh, my gosh, thought Gerry. He had not seen this coming, and now it was too late. "You mean back in Boston?" he repeated tentatively, but already knowingly.

"Damn right, I mean back in Boston," said Dr. Chase in his broad '*A*' accent of someone from Maine. "That's where I got this great idea for teaching labs in gynecology. We already had them in ENT, orthopedics, pediatrics, and all the other specialties, but your dad, Doctor Frank, Sr., was the first physician with the combined knowledge, professionalism, and personality necessary to start educational gyn clinics for interns. I've just extended the program here to include extern medical students."

"You mean it was Dr. Frank's father that gave you the idea, Dr. Chase?" asked Sarah smiling from ear to ear. She knew now that she had just won her argument with an unbelievable certainty in this unexpected trump card. Her smile nicely accentuated her large, well-balanced mouth and enhanced the elegant features of her high prominent cheekbones and small chin.

"You're damn right, that's what I mean, Sarah," said Dr. Chase. "Dr. Frank's dad was the finest physician and medical teacher I ever had the pleasure of studying under and working with. He developed an intern training program at the Boston teaching hospital recognized as one of the best in the country. Young Dr. Frank here doesn't come by his brains and good sense by accident, Sarah. It's in his genes. Now let's all go see Mrs. Richly."

"Yes sir," replied the young doctor now exhibiting a sheepish grin of reluctant acceptance.

"What we look for in these clinic patients, Dr. Frank," continued Dr. Chase, as he walked down the hallway, "is they not only be a good teaching example of a particular problem such as this fibroid, but also they have the necessary emotional stability and maturity to be a lab subject. They need these attributes to be able to relax under the repeated examination of insecure, unsure, and unskilled medical students learning their trade. Do you think this woman is such a type?"

"Yes, I think so," Gerry replied. "She seems pretty sensible, her current crisis has not panicked her, and she is a strong supporter of our rural clinic programs."

"Then I'm sure she'll agree to participate. I always like to include a case of uterine fibroids in our gyn lab exercises as that is a common problem in gynecology, especially with women aging towards menopause. We sure see a lot of it around here, and with the excessive bleeding that can accompany the condition, it is potentially a dangerous situation out in the rural areas."

By then they had all reached the examination room door, and having heard no negative feedback from Dr. Frank, Dr. Chase opened the door to encounter the patient sitting in the small room at the end of a table. After a friendly introduction, he quickly read her history, asked her pertinent questions, and did a final thorough examination including her second pelvic exam of the day.

"What do you think, Dr. Chase?" asked Mrs. Richly. "Are things worse than we thought?"

"I understand Dr. Frank has already talked to you about the surgery," he said. "Obviously you need it quickly. Each subsequent bleeding episode you have can be more severe, and your laboratory tests show you are already anemic. I understand you have three children and no desire for any more. Is that correct?"

"That's right, Doctor. My youngest child is already 14-years-old and a freshman in high school."

"Then it would be my recommendation we do a hysterectomy on you, removing the entire uterus, but keeping your ovaries intact. I see no problem in those. That will end your menstrual periods but your ovaries will remain with actively secreting hormones until you reach menopause."

Within a few moments, not only had Mrs. Richly signed the proper agreements for her hospitalization to be followed by surgery the next day, but Dr. Chase had also recruited Mrs. Richly as a gyn patient for the laboratory session later in that afternoon. Apparently overhearing the prior conversation between Dr. Frank and Nurse Hall had not discouraged her at all. She had readily agreed to being a teaching case.

"Come on back to my office, Dr. Frank, while I dictate my findings on this case. I've got a good reference book there you can read concerning the surgical approach to fibroids."

After sitting down at his desk and once again reviewing Dr. Frank chart notes on Mrs. Richly, Dr. Chase dictated his own report and signed off the patient's chart. "That should be typed up by my secretary by 5:00 P.M. I still have another case to see before we start the gyn lab, so in the meantime you stay here and read that gyn surgery book while Nurse Hall and I see the last patient. Then the three of us can walk to the lab together."

A half hour later, as Dr. Frank accompanied Dr. Chase and his nurse across the street to the student clinic building, Dr. Chase chuckled under his breath. Dr.Chase asked Gerry, "Can you guess how medical students in the old days were taught pelvic pathology and gynecological problems? Do you know how they used to do it?"

"No, sir" replied Dr. Frank, "I've never thought about it. How did they do it?" he asked stepping up on the curb and rapidly crossing the sidewalk to hold the outside clinic door open for Dr. Chase.

"They did it with prostitutes, my boy. They did it with professional prostitutes. They'd pay to have about a dozen to come in. God knows, you'd always find enough pathology among them to demonstrate most of the venereal diseases and other post-infection problems of their trade. The problem with that is, out of a dozen, you'd generally have three or four with active gonorrhea, a couple with syphilis, and maybe one with more advanced venereal diseases. The rest were good for post infection complications."

"So what was the problem?" Gerry asked. "That mix certainly sounds like a lot of pathology for the students to see."

"What we couldn't get was a good overall sampling of women with normal anatomical or post surgical variations. After all, how many cases of the clap do you have to see before you can recognize someone has gonorrhea?"

"So none of these lab subjects the students see now are paid?" asked Dr. Frank. "They all do this for free?"

"No," said Dr. Chase, "that's not exactly true. The lab lasts about an hour and a half, and each woman is paid 15 dollars for her time."

"That's a lot of money in these parts."

"No, not when you consider the service they provide. We couldn't conduct the lab without them. As you know, some of the younger patients are coeds at the university, and the money does help them as a deciding factor in their agreement to be subjected to the lab exams. But many of the married women and most of the older women, working or not, actually donate their 15 dollars back to the outpatient clinic's general fund."

"They do? Well, I admit, I am impressed with the professionalism of it all," Gerry replied.

"Most of the patients get a real sense of personal satisfaction and value knowing they're contributing to the education and training of a fine group of young doctors. This is particularly true of the cancer patients who may philosophically find some purpose for their disease in some way to make it a positive experience."

By then the group of three had reached one of the larger clinic sections of the building with a hallway running down the middle. There were five examination rooms on each side of the hallway. Rooms One through Eight contained patients in stirrups on gynecological examination tables neatly draped with clean green surgical sheets. Each woman also had a small, clean towel draped loosely over her face so her identity would remain unknown to the students. Located in a small city community, women were more inclined to volunteer for the lab sessions at the hospital if they could be assured their identity would remain confidential.

In Room Nine, separate microscopes were set up along two large tables for the observation of slides made from the tissues of different patients. The separate slides included everything from vaginal smears to blood counts to biopsy tissue cuts. The tables contained three jars full of formaldehyde with surgical specimens already removed from three of the women and culture plates which had been incubated from two of the active infection cases currently being treated.

In Room Ten, chairs for the students were set up and a lecture desk stood in the front from which Dr. Chase or his chief resident, Doctor Huntley, could present the history and the protocol of each case. The cases included everything from a young woman with gonorrhea to a lady in her fifties, six-months post-op from a complete hysterectomy and salpingo-oophorectomy, following the discovery of cancer. The suffix 'ectomy' on the end of the word indicated the removal of that particular organ. Hysterectomy was the removal of a woman's hyster or uterus. Salpingo-oophorectomy indicated the removal of her salpinx (tubes), and oophoron or egg-bearing organs (ovaries).

Dr. Chase asked Dr. Frank to present his case of the woman with the fibroid tumors last, which he readily did from the history he had already prepared. He reminded the medical students to check closely that which he and Dr. Chase had agreed was a possible additional fibroid growth on the anterior aspect of the patient's uterus. Students were also directed to note under the microscope the typical hypochromic microcytic type anemia these patients often suffered from chronic blood loss. This type of anemia is where blood cells are smaller than normal and contain less iron.

Then the students divided themselves up among the eight patient rooms and rotated from one room to the next. They were encouraged to completely examine the vulva, vaginal vault, and pelvis of each patient, and to ask the patient pertinent questions, which could be answered by yes or no. To insure the patient's identity would not be given away by her voice, each patient held a small flashlight in her right hand under the sheets, which she would shine in answer to the questions - one flash for yes and two for no. Each room had a female nurse standing by. Dr. Chase, Dr.

Huntley, and two of the hospital interns circulated among the student doctors to answer any questions they might have.

Some of the students obviously were unsure of themselves. In fact, for some of them, these were the first pelvic exams they had ever done on women with those known conditions. Of particular interest today was a 37-year-old woman with an enlarged mass in her right pelvis, which was probably cystic, but might be malignant. She had already been scheduled for surgery later that week.

"You did a nice job on your presentation of the woman with fibroids, Dr. Frank," said Dr. Huntley. "We appreciate your having her participate in our clinic. Sometimes it's hard to get volunteers for the particular problems we want to demonstrate to our students. There is so much for them to learn, but these lab sessions are a big help."

"Yes, I can imagine," said Dr. Frank. "However, I'm not sure I'd be the first in line for a prostrate examination lab if they decide to start labs for those here." So saying, he bent down to focus one of the new black binocular microscopes on a tissue slide of an infected fallopian tube. Parts of the gross specimen of the tube and ovary involved were in a small, clear glass jar of formaldehyde sitting beside the microscope.

"Do you want to examine any of these patients, Dr. Frank?" asked Dr. Huntley. "It's the least I can do for you today, with your having provided us with one of your cases. I see you're looking at the slides on the young woman in Room Three."

"It looks like an obvious hydrosalpinx, with the gross specimen demonstrating an infected, ruptured fallopian tube and cystic ovary," replied Dr. Frank. "Were you able to save the tube and ovary on the patient's other side?" he questioned.

"Yes, and she does have good regular ovulatory cycles. However, I'm not sure we really did her a favor by saving her other tube," relied Dr. Huntley.

"Why do you say that? I always thought a surgeon should to try to save the best tube and viable ovary for women in their reproductive years."

"Yes, we generally do, but her tube and ovary on the other side seemed thickened with scar tissue, and I, frankly, doubt her ability to conceive."

"At least you left her with some chance for reproduction," responded Dr. Frank.

"Yes, but minimal at best, I'm afraid. She was one of my first patients in my internship, and I scrubbed on her original surgery. Dr. Chase was out of town that weekend at a medical convention in Kansas City. Doctor Cully, then a staff general surgeon, substituted in. He let me do the surgery myself. She's one of the regulars in the lab here every three months. Put on a set of gloves and examine her and give us your opinion. Tell me what you think of her prognosis for possible future pregnancy."

Gerry had never liked Dr. Herbert Huntley because of his attitude. He was 29, 5'10", and weighed 188, but wore it well with a heavily muscled torso. Originally from Chicago, he spoke as if he had seen a few too many gangster movies. Strictly 'Second City', he acted as if he were doing Missouri a big favor with his presence. However, he now seemed generally sincere, and Dr. Frank accepted the opportunity to learn. Chief residents on the cutting edge of surgical cases can always teach their lesser learned colleagues a lot.

As Dr. Frank walked into Room Three, the last medical student had just started his bimanual examination of the woman with her feet up in stirrups, with his left hand on the outside of the patient's lower abdomen and his index and middle finger deep

226

inside her vaginal vault. He obviously tried to feel one side where he knew she still had an ovary and then the other side where she did not. He took a lot of time to complete the examination.

The student seemed confused and in his inexperienced manner he obviously hurt the patient. She reacted to the pain immediately by moving about four inches up the table.

"Doctor," said Gerry, you're supposed to be palpating her ovaries, not her tonsils. A clue to which ovary is missing would be first to look to see which side of her abdomen she has the surgical scar." So saying, Dr. Frank stepped forward and held the patient's right leg, as reassurance to the silent woman.

"I'm sorry," muttered the medical student. "I guess I'm pretty clumsy at all this, and I know my hands are large. But it seems to me the patient's scar is on the right side, but the ovary missing is the one that is supposed to be on the left." The student, Paul Fabian, a 6'3", 263-pound former University of Oklahoma tackle, had hands the size of most people's feet. Dr. Frank hoped the man realized right then he was not cut out for a career in obstetrics or gynecology. Slowly, the student withdrew both hands from the patient and stepped back to take off his gloves.

Looking down at the draped patient with only her naked vulva and lower pelvis exposed, Dr. Frank then saw the woman's six-inch-long and quarter-inch-wide scar from her surgery. The scar ran diagonally over the woman's lower right abdominal side ending in her pubic hair.

"Are you okay, Dr. Frank? I hope you could do a pelvic exam on this patient and tell me what you feel?"

Suddenly Gerry felt faint. He held firmly on to the patient's draped leg up in the right stirrup to keep himself from falling on the floor. It hit him like a ton of bricks. The scar he was looking at, the pelvis they were discussing, the patient who had just been subjected to 15 pelvic examinations by young medical students was his girlfriend, Sharon. Lying naked on the table under the surgical drape sheets, Sharon had her abdomen and pelvis exposed.

Never before had he been struck with such a strong variety of mixed emotions. The combined feelings of fear, anger, embarrassment, pride, and most of all, love flooded him with tremendous warmth. This was a very special woman under those green drapes. The young doctor suddenly startled with a new question to himself. Was he special enough for her?

With gentle, but firm hands, Dr. Frank first palpated the patient's outer abdomen, asking her to take in a deep breath, and then let it all out. This expiration of breath helped her relax the abdominal musculature so he could better feel the anatomy beneath it. Next, he asked her a few questions she could quickly answer by yes or no flashes of the penlight. He used his usual 'patient-talk voice,' empathetic and helpful, but also subtlety authoritative with no sign of recognition for this young woman in his tone of voice. He hoped Sharon would not know he recognized her. With all of the previous examining medical students having applied K-Y lubricating jelly, the patient had enough on her vulva and within her vagina so no more was needed for another exam. With his gloved left hand he firmly held on to the young woman's outside lower abdominal wall, Dr. Frank gently inserted his sterile gloved right hand, index and middle fingers, deeply into her tight vagina. Then slowly and carefully he palpated her uterus, both the cervix and the body. Next he palpated both adnexa areas - where her fallopian tubes and ovaries should have been, one of each on either side of her uterus. One set was missing.

This amazing moment would linger with him for a long time when he would remember of this revelation. The abrupt psychological change from his emotional involvement as the woman's lover, to his intellectual curiosity concerning her patient prognosis came abruptly in seconds.

Slowly and gently his fingers probed inside Sharon's soft, warm pelvis. Looking up at the ex-football player, now medical student, Gerry smiled, "You know, Dr. Fabian, you're absolutely correct. Though this patient's scar is on the right side of her abdomen and though she has considerable scar tissue deep within her pelvis on both sides, the missing ovary is definitely from the left side - just like you said." Dr. Frank could easily feel her normal-feeling uterus, but he discovered the still-present fallopian tube and ovary on the right side were bound down with scar tissue. Chances for this pelvis conceiving a pregnancy were far from good and extremely poor at the very best.

Not until slightly later as he stood up and took off his gloves, did it again sink in whose body he had just examined. This pelvis belonged to a girl named Sharon. Scars or no scars, her body had already given him the most intense orgasms of his life. But he knew life held more than orgasms. He would soon face the question of whether or not he should or could marry her. Regardless of his love for her, if they could not have children together, he didn't think they would have the complete happiness he hoped to find with a woman.

"You two are to be congratulated," said the nurse standing in attendance and smiling at the two doctors. "Of the 16 examiners today, only four realized the ovary this young lady is missing is on the opposite side of her scar.

"How about that?" replied Doctor Fabian with a grin of satisfaction on his face. "And some people say my hands are too big for obstetrics."

The nurse forgave the young doctor's youthful display of enthusiasm and continued, "I think Dr. Huntley wants to have a final word with all of you before the lab session is over. He's in Room Ten, which is used for case presentations and medical lectures."

Confused about what to say at this point, Gerry did not know whether or not Sharon realized he knew she was the patient under the draped sheets, but he hoped she did not. He had to communicate with her somehow. Walking back to the examination table, he put both hands over her flexed right knee before speaking. "Thank you miss, for being part of this gynecology lab session today. I'm sure the students and the faculty appreciate the time and hardship this may have caused you."

From under the draped sheets, the young woman flashed the light once for yes.

Gerry did not see Sharon's response. He had turned to leave the room before she shined her small flashlight. The young doctor could not decide what were his feelings at the time. He did not know if he was being honest to himself, much less to Sharon. He was shocked he had found her there. Shocked and surprised she had apparently subjected herself to being a gyn-lab patient, and as Huntley had implied, she had done it three or four times a year for the past three years. Gerry suddenly knew why the scar had seemed so familiar the first night they were together when he closely examined her scar.

By the time the medical students had all assembled back in Room Ten, they knew they had learned a lot that afternoon, but they also realized how much more they needed to know.

Huntley gave his closing comments about each patient. He loved to lecture and as the chief resident he had become very good at it. "Well, what did you think of the patient in Room Three, Dr. Frank?" he asked. "What's her prognosis for pregnancy?" He smiled, but Dr. Frank knew the smile to be neither sincere nor friendly. Dr. Herbert Huntley had purposely subjected Dr. Frank to his strange sense of humor - dark even for a physician.

"Well, her prognosis is certainly not as good as if she still had both tubes and ovaries. But then again, it's not bad," said Dr.

Frank. "She needs to stay away from the idiot surgeon who operated on her three years ago, making the initial incision on the wrong side. Though the specimen jar in the other room says right tube and ovary, the patient is actually missing her left tube and ovary, regardless of which side the abdominal scar is on." A litany of 'oh's' and 'ah's' went up from the assembled students, but the majority had missed this important fact.

"That's your big lesson for today, class," said Dr. Huntley. "Do not necessarily believe everything another physician tells you about a case before you've had a chance to ask the patient some questions and examine her yourself. Don't believe the way specimens may be labeled in a laboratory as there may be mistakes. Dr. Frank is entirely right. Though the young 20-year-old woman's scar is on her right side, once her abdomen was opened, it was found the ovary and the tube on her left side were in even worse condition. In fact, she had the beginning of an ectopic pregnancy on that side. We elected to remove those and let her keep the tube and ovary on her right side when we did the surgery almost three years ago. Sometimes with an acute, severe pelvic inflammatory disease infection, it's difficult from the outside to know exactly what you are going to run into with surgery once inside. However, in any young female of child-bearing age, we must always try to keep at least one tube and ovary intact, if at all possible." So saying, he started gathering up his books and charts and the class stood up ready to leave.

Gerry waited until the entire class had filed out before picking up his jacket off the back of one of the chairs. "You know, Huntley," he said, "I never really liked you, and now I know why. Your sense of humor is not just sick, it's damn near perverted."

Huntley smiled smugly, put down his books quietly and slowly lit a pipe, which he pulled out of his coat pocket along with a leather tobacco pouch. "Dr. Frank," he said, "you have missed the whole point and purpose of today's lab session."

"What do you mean by that?" Gerry asked.

"I've never seen a lab where even the best of us couldn't learn something. These lab sessions are an educational experience for all the medical students and physicians who attend. You can't tell me you didn't learn something here today."

"Yes. You're right about that."

"And as for the young woman in Room Three staying away from the dumb doctor who operated on her three years ago, I'd say that's pretty much up to her and to me. Back then when I operated on her, I made the original incision on the wrong side, and you are right - that was pretty dumb. But don't forget, I've learned a lot about women and about gynecology and surgery in the last three years. Now, if you'll please excuse me, Doctor," he said, blowing a puff of pipe smoke in Gerry's face as he walked past, "I've got rounds to make at the hospital. Give my very best regards to Miss Olsen when you see her again. Even a dumb doctor like me recognizes she's of a class and quality you don't fully appreciate nor deserve. After you've matured a little, come back and we'll talk again."

Chapter 8
Lost Lens
March 12-15, 1962

Doctor Gerry Frank walked out of the student clinic medical building at 5:30 P.M. and crossed the street to the front entrance of the main hospital. The separate outpatient clinic was run by senior medical students under the supervision of school staff physicians. The hospital outpatient clinic in the east wing of the hospital, run by hospital staff attending physicians, could only be entered through the front hospital entrance at that time of day.

With spring definitely in the air, it had, however, turned colder within the last hour with a northwest wind bringing heavy rain. Even though the walk was short to the hospital, the young doctor's jacket was soaked with rain by the time he reached the hospital foyer. Quickly he took it off and hung it on a coat rack next to the receptionist's desk before proceeding to the east wing.

In the hospital outpatient section, he stopped by the head nurse's desk and picked up the typed report Dr. Chase had dictated earlier and signed regarding Dr. Frank's patient, Mrs. Richly. Dr. Frank would keep one copy for the patient's rural clinic record and make sure to have another copy placed in her current hospital chart. For now he had some serious thinking to do not involving his patient.

The sudden weather change reflected how Gerry's emotional state had also quickly changed within the last hour. He had gone from an intellectual high always associated with his medical studies and work to an emotional low over the recent clinical demonstration and revelation in the student gynecological clinic laboratory. He had discovered his girlfriend being used as an example of a case of probable sterility due to past serious pelvic inflammatory disease. He still found it hard to believe what he had seen - but he knew he had seen it. He had actually felt it when he did a bimanual pelvic exam after 15 medical students had done their examinations on the young woman. He also had it confirmed by the assistant surgeon who had operated on her. His girlfriend, Sharon - the woman he loved - undoubtably suffered from sterility and would probably never be able to have children. For the first time firm restraint fought the fierceness of his love for this woman.

Gerry quickly knew he must get a handle on his emotions so he could deal with the problem rationally. He knew he loved Sharon more than any woman he had ever met. But he also knew someday he would want a family as much as he now wanted a medical career. The unfairness of the situation already gnawed at him inside. He had never considered adult life without eventually having a wife and three or four children.

When the young doctor first brought in his patient, Mrs. Richly, from the Essex Clinic with fibroid tumors of the uterus, he had never expected to end up in the gynecology lab to present his case. Finding his girlfriend there as an example of pathology had evoked extreme emotion in him.

Gerry must first figure out if Sharon knew that he knew she was the patient on the examining table. All the women used as teaching examples were lying on the various gyn tables, naked on their backs with their legs spread and in stirrups. Other than their pelvic areas, their bodies and heads were draped with sheets so their identities would remain anonymous. Gerry thought if he waited to call Sharon on the phone until later she might not realize he had recognized her from her lower abdominal scar. She had apparently not wanted him to know of her probable sterility or of her participation as a demonstration case in the labs or she would have told him so long ago. She had never mentioned it.

He couldn't wait to call her and the phone was busy the first time, but when he dialed back 30 seconds later, another secretary answered to say Sharon had quit work for the day about two hours earlier that afternoon and would not be back until tomorrow. Gerry made it a point of leaving a message with his name, the time he called, and the fact he was in town unexpectedly from the rural clinic. He said he had originally hoped to have dinner with her that night, but instead would see her tomorrow. He thought when she received the message it would relieve her anxieties if she thought he had recognized her. Also it would give him time to straighten out his own emotions before he and Sharon would meet again.

As he stepped out of the phone booth, Dr. Frank almost collided with Doctor Anthony Gillespie, the new anesthesiology resident, already quite popular with students and staff. The fact he had been in general practice for five years had not hurt his reputation and had given him a more mature outlook on life and the knowledge of the proper place of specialists in medicine. Sometimes doctors lacked in professional maturity when they went from an internship directly into a long residency in one of the specialties. Their boundaries often were as confining as their scope was narrow.

"Hey, Frank," he said laughingly, "just 'cause I'm a resident now and you're a big student staff referral physician out there in the rural clinics, don't start pushing me around." Doctor Gillespie stood short and had a dark complexion, with a pleasant smile never far from the surface of his rounded face.

"Hey, Tony, I didn't see you. I'm sorry. You know I'd never intentionally knock over a gas passer. You can't always tell what may suddenly come out of them during surgery or otherwise," Gerry joked.

"Talking about surgery, I just got the schedule for tomorrow and I see you have one on the list for a hysterectomy. Want to walk up to the third floor with me while I do a pre-anesthetic exam on her?" Tony asked.

"Well, actually," said Gerry, "I've been with her for most all afternoon and I thought I'd go down now and get supper here at the hospital. Not all of us are lucky enough to have Italian wives like yours who can cook so damn well. No wonder you're 30 pounds overweight."

Dr. Gillespie chuckled. He was 5'7" and at least 208 pounds. "Okay, old friend," he said, "but anything I should know about her in particular? Any allergies or pertinent medical history of respiratory problems?"

"Nothing really, except her having only one lung, TB, being asthmatic, and known allergies to most anesthetics," Gerry laughed.

"Come on," said Gillespie, "with that attitude I'll have to do my own history. You keep that up and I may never invite you and Sharon over for another spaghetti dinner."

"That really was a great meal. Hope your wife will give Sharon the recipe for those meat balls she served."

"You know," Tony continued speaking softer as if in conspiracy, "Sharon may not be Italian, but I really approve of her. That woman would make one damn fine doctor's wife and the statistics are clearly significant. Married doctors do live longer than single ones. Think about that." Dr. Gillespie walked over and pressed the button for the elevator up to the surgery floor. The doors opened instantly.

Dr. Frank waited until the elevator left and realized it might not be headed back down for a couple minutes. So he walked quickly to the nearest staircase. The hospital kitchen and dining room were in the basement of the building's west wing.

The hospital dining room was busy, and after picking up his food in the cafeteria line, Dr. Frank chose a table by himself in the far corner of the room. Half way through the corned beef and cabbage entree, Nurse Sarah Hall walked over with her food-laden tray. She had a huge vegetable salad as her main course, a dark soup of unknown flavor, fruit juice, coffee, and two dessert bowls of rice pudding.

"Mind if I join you?" she said, already pulling out a chair. Gerry nodded but said nothing. "What did you think of the gyn lab?" she continued. "It's come a long way in just the six months since you were in the service. I particularly like the idea of having the pathology residents pull all the old slides and specimens of the different cases. In fact," she chatted on, "next time we're thinking of pulling all the old X-rays of the patients and putting them up on display view boxes, if there are any pertinent abdominal or pelvic films. What do you think?"

Gerry still said nothing. He continued to eat slowly and methodically. He was not very hungry, though the entree was one of his favorites.

"Okay. So I guess you just want me to shut up?" Sarah said, buttering her bread and avoiding the young doctor's accusatory gaze. "You looked a little upset sitting here by yourself, and I thought maybe you needed some company. I know sometimes it helps me to talk when I'm upset about unexpected circumstances."

"Why should I be upset?" replied Dr. Frank, looking directly into the nurse's deep blue eyes. "Is there something I don't know to be upset about? Is there a real reason for my sudden anorexia you might have some inkling about?"

Putting her fork down, she reached for her glass of ice water. Returning his gaze, she answered, "Doctor, I'm not sure you have anything to be upset about. But if you're not, then why do you look like you saw a ghost?"

"You know damn well what I saw, Sarah. In fact, as the gynecology nurse in charge of the clinic demonstrations with access to all of the histories and patient identities, and as - I hope - a young woman with feelings, you, more than anybody, know exactly what I saw. Anyway, it sure doesn't seem to have inhibited your appetite at all."

Suddenly the tears started. flowing, slowly at first, and then in a definite cascade down the young doctor's cheeks. Quickly Sarah reached out and grasped his right hand. She touched him firmly but with a very cold hand. She had been holding her glass of ice water but had not drunk from it yet.

"I'm sorry," she said sympathetically. "I'm really very sorry. I didn't know you were going to be at the lab, and I'm sure Dr. Chase didn't either. It should not have happened - it was a tragic mistake."

So far no one else in the dining room watched them, but suddenly Gerry knew he had to get out of the room. Doctors were not supposed to cry. "Excuse me," he said, pushing back his chair from the table and standing up. "I'm not as hungry as I thought." He threw his napkin down on the table and quickly walked out the door to his left, dropping off his nearly untouched tray of food on the stand as he left.

It took her five seconds to decide. Then, after three un-ladylike gulps of her hot black coffee, she walked from the dining room but then ran down the hallway. She caught up with the doctor at the door to the physician's lounge.

He heard her approach. Quickly he stepped inside with her coming in right behind him. No one was in the empty lounge though the television set was on.

"I believe it says 'Physician's Lounge' on the door, Nurse Hall," he said quite formally. "I've got some thinking to do and I do it better by myself. Now, if you'll please excuse me. No, wait a minute. I am curious about one thing. Why did you let it happen? You obviously knew the identities and case histories of all the women who would be subjects this afternoon. You even encouraged me to have my patient be your eighth case."

Sitting down in a soft lounge chair, Sarah grasped her knees together tightly with both hands and paused for a few seconds while staring at the gray concrete floor. Then she looked up directly into Gerry's face. "You're right, Doctor. I do know all the case histories. And besides that, I know some of the women who have been in repeated clinics very, very well. A couple of them are two of my best friends and I look upon all of them with great pride and respect. I just thought you would be there to present your case only. I never thought Dr. Huntley would ask you to examine any of the other patients. Had I anticipated it, I would not have permitted it. I had little respect for the man before; I have less now, though he has finally become a pretty fair surgeon."

Then, standing up, she put her hand on the door to go. With her back to the doctor, she continued talking. "I know you feel very badly, Doctor. I can empathize with you. But please don't do anything to hurt this program or Dr. Chase's reputation. This program already has its enemies in the administration, and if news of such a goof got out it would really hurt us. But maybe even more importantly, don't harm Sharon. I haven't known her for very long, but I already know she's a wonderful woman. I'm not sure you deserve someone as fine as her."

Putting his hand against the door, Dr. Frank stopped her from opening it. "I understand what you are saying, Sarah. There's no sense in making more people feel bad. You don't owe me any apology. You are a true professional and a mighty fine nurse. The gyn department and the patients are lucky to have you here."

She turned around and surprised him with the tears now in her eyes. "It's not an apology, Dr. Frank. It's a plea from the bottom of my heart. For God's sake, don't hurt the program and don't hurt Sharon."

With that she opened the door and stepped into the hallway as it started to swing shut behind her.

Gerry called to her quickly, this time reaching out to hold the door open. "I must know," he said, "does Sharon realize I recognized her there in the lab? Does she know I know everything now, including her case history?"

"She was pretty sure you did. She said something about you putting pressure on her leg in a reassuring way. But she wanted to know for sure."

"She did?"

"Yes, that's one of the reasons I followed you over here to the hospital. I promised her I'd find out and tell her the truth. I plan on calling her later this evening from home. She's driving down to Moberly this evening where she plans to stay with her aunt overnight."

Gerry went back into the doctor's lounge and hung up his clothes in an empty locker. He took a long, refreshing shower and put on a clean pair of surgical greens. They would be good to sleep in on one of the extra bunks in the surgical lounge. He already felt physically tired and emotionally drained from the activities of the day. First, however, he would make a final check on Mrs. Richly before the nurses handed out sleeping medication to her and to the other patients scheduled for surgery in the morning.

When he arrived up in the surgery wing by the elevator, Dr. Frank ran into Mr. Richly, the patient's husband who had been with his wife during visiting hours. With calm reassurance, Dr. Frank told the man the details of the upcoming surgery for his wife the next day and joined the couple to make sure they both understood the surgical consent forms they had signed together. After reviewing the patient's chart including the notes of the intern, surgical resident, anesthesiology resident, staff surgeon and staff anesthesiologist, the young doctor left the patient with a half hour's visiting time remaining to spend alone with her husband. Gerry assured her he would be there during her surgery in the morning, scrubbing as the second assistant surgeon on her case.

When Dr. Frank left the chart at the nurse's station, he ran into Nurse Hall again as she reviewed some physician's orders with Dr. Chase. From the lightness of Dr. Chase's conversation with her, obviously Dr. Chase had not learned of the afternoon's goof where Dr. Frank ended up examining his own girlfriend in the gynecology lab demonstration. Dr. Chase's nurse did not want her boss to know of or be burdened with any additional problems as the chief of the OB GYN department. Not wanting to make Nurse Hall feel any further embarrassment, Dr. Frank excused himself as quickly as possible and headed for one of the empty bunks in the physicians' lounge.

Gerry slept well that night, being awakened only twice by phone calls for other physicians catching catnaps while their patients were in labor during the evening. Worry never interfered with his sleep. In the early morning, after a big breakfast, a hot shower, and changing into fresh surgical greens, he presented himself in the surgery suite, where he confirmed he would be scrubbing as the second assistant to Dr. Chase, with an intern scrubbing as the first. His good night's sleep had helped clear the young doctor's mind and he concentrated his thoughts on the patient and her upcoming surgery. He necessarily put Sharon far from his mind.

From the initial incision through the lower abdominal rectus muscle, until the time the uterine arteries were ligated and the uterus later delivered through the abdominal incision, all went well. Visualization of the outside of the uterus would seem to confirm the palpable masses were typical fibroid tumors and non-malignant. After that revelation some relaxation of the surgical team's tension occurred.

Then disaster struck in a way before unknown in any operating suite of that hospital. Blood pooled in the space where her uterus had been. Additional bleeders would have to be tied off, but that was not the problem. Dr. Frank saw a sudden splash in the pool of blood. Looking up and across the table at the intern, Gerry noted the stark horror on the upper portion of the intern's face that could not be hidden by his white surgical mask.

"My God," said the intern. "I just dropped one of my contact lenses in the patient's abdomen. My eye watered and I blinked. I can't believe it."

"You did what?" questioned Dr. Chase. He remained calm, but you could tell the deep irritation in his voice. His attention had been diverted momentarily examining the uterus now outside the patient's body so had not seen the incident.

"I've got my finger on the place, doctor," said Dr. Frank, "but I can't feel it yet. It may have slipped behind her intestines."

"Nurse," said the intern, "reach up under my gown and you'll feel some keys tied to the drawstring of my surgical pants." Surgical pants have a drawstring like those in pajamas. "Find the key to locker number seven, my glasses are in there. Could you please bring them here and put them on me."

"Stand back from the table, doctor," said the nurse, "so I don't contaminate the sterile field." Reaching under his gown and around his pants, she pulled the string. However, in her concentration in finding and freeing the keys and then selecting the right key, she forgot his pants were now loose, and a moment later the intern's pants fell to the floor. He wore no underwear - only a jockstrap.

"Get the glasses, nurse. The front of my gown is still sterile, though I may freeze my ass off in here now." The laughter of the rest of the operating group slightly relaxed the atmosphere. Dr. Frank had taken over the intern's duties and put hemostats on additional bleeders. With Dr. Chase's help, he also coagulated them by electric cautery.

"It's probably somewhere behind the bowel and we may have to run the bowel to find it," said Dr. Chase. "I can't believe this - losing a lens in a patient's open pelvis."

"I'm sorry," said the intern. "I'll never wear the damn things again. They were dark green, so that may help in finding the lost one."

"Not much, I'm afraid," replied Dr. Chase. "As soon as the nurse gets your glasses, we'll run the bowel."

"I'm afraid that's not going to help much, gentlemen," said Dr. Frank. "If he puts his glasses on, then he won't have correct vision in his other eye because he'll have both the glasses and the contact lens on that side. Instead, why don't you just drop out of the surgery, Doctor Carter, and I'll finish for you."

The intern knew he'd screwed up beyond redemption and stepped back from the table, took his gloves off, and reached down to pull up and tie his pants. Unhappy with himself, everybody enjoyed scrubbing first assistant with Dr. Chase who was a gentleman physician and a fine teacher. He let the new surgeons in training do as much as they thought they were capable.

Two-thirds of the way through running the bowel, they found the contact lens adhered to it. They quickly removed the lens and both doctors changed to sterile gloves before continuing with the procedure.

"We now have to treat her as a contaminated abdomen," said Dr. Chase. "Nurse, give me some penicillin for irrigation, usual concentration. Dr. Frank, she's your patient, I'll expect you to tell her what it happened - she has a right to know the truth. If she has any further questions, she can ask me and I'll explain it to her again. If there is any treatment for post-operative infection or increased length of stay in her hospitalization, she is not to be charged for it. I'll document the incident in my surgical report. Any questions?"

"No sir," both young doctors answered simultaneously. "Dr. Carter," he continued. "have you ever had a contact lens fall out like that before?"

"Well not in surgery, doctor. But I have been having trouble with them, and the left one has dropped out two or three times in the past week when I blink."

"Then you're a damn fool to wear them in surgery. You should have anticipated this possibility. Have you any infection in that eye?"

"No, doctor, none."

"Well, as soon as the patient is out of the recovery room, I want you to stay with her like a special duty nurse until she's awake, and Dr. Frank will advise her of the situation."

"But why, sir? Even if she gets an infection, it won't show up for a couple of days. What good will my staying there do?"

"It will make me feel better and it will make her feel better to know you stayed with her from the time of this incident until she is fully conscious. Dr. Frank will take over the rest of your surgical assisting duties for the rest of the day."

They finished closing her abdomen without a word. After completion and dressings were applied, all three physicians helped move the unconscious patient to the recovery room gurney.

After this, Dr. Chase dictated the surgical report in the doctor's lounge. Gerry walked out to the nurse's station for a cup of coffee where Nurse Sarah Hall had been coordinating the surgical nurse for the first operation in Suite Two. She had now returned from Suite One after making sure everything was set up for Dr. Chase's second surgery of the day - an anterior and posterior repair.

"I want to thank you, Gerry," she said, "for not upsetting Dr. Chase with yesterday's foul up. Maybe it's best we all try to forget it."

"I haven't discussed it with him yet, but I sure as hell haven't forgotten about it. I doubt I'll ever be able to rid the scene from my mind. I make no promises about not discussing it with him, but I certainly wouldn't do it today when he has a full surgery schedule."

"Thanks," she said, putting her right hand over Gerry's. "I am about to bring a cup of coffee to the doctors' lounge for Dr. Chase. May I get you a cup?"

"You take pretty damn good care of him, don't you? You're his head office nurse, his surgical scrub nurse, and even hustle him hot coffee between operations."

"I'd do anything for the man, Doctor. Anything. He's the finest physician and gentleman I've ever known. This hospital doesn't know how lucky it is to have him here. He's a born teacher and a great surgeon. Now, do you want cream and sugar or not?"

"Yeah, two cream and two sugar, please," said Gerry turning and walking back into the lounge.

The rest of the day passed like a wonderful dream with Dr. Frank scrubbing as first assistant on four additional gyn surgeries and one scheduled caesarian section. Gynecology surgery had always been one of his foremost interests and he spent the day scrubbing on the biggest number of cases he ever had in one day as first assistant. One of the two OB/GYN residents generally grabbed the first assistant position. However, one of the residents had been away writing a state board exam and the other busy in obstetrics all day. One of Dr. Frank's favorite instructors, working with Dr. Chase all day provided a pleasurable and memorable learning experience.

Only after the last case around 8:00 P.M. as he took off his gloves did he realize he had not thought of Sharon since the first surgery began that morning. *My gosh,* he remembered excitedly, he'd never even called her.

"You look worried, Doctor," said Sarah, noting his expression as he looked up at the clock over the scrub sinks. She carried a tray of instruments back towards the nurse's station for sterilization.

"I just realized I never called Sharon all day." The starkness of this reality shocked him.

"It's okay," said Sarah. "I called her during one of our breaks. I told her you'd be in surgery all day and you would have no chance to get to a phone."

"You called her?" said Gerry, questioning her. "But why? What more concern is this of yours?"

"I promised her I would call her and I did. It's my concern if your future actions will in any way bring discredit to Dr. Chase or to the OB/GYN department. Even worse would be if your reaction to yesterday's goof up causes the gyn labs to be canceled."

"So what did Sharon say? Did she seem upset?" Gerry asked as he untied the face mask loosely hanging from his neck.

"Doctor, I'm holding about 30 pounds of instruments in this tray. Can I finish up my work and then we can talk about it later?"

"Oh, sorry about that. I didn't realize how heavy all those instruments are."

"She's staying with her aunt in Moberly for a couple of days and would rather not see you while she's there. Look," said Sarah, finally putting down the heavy instrument tray, "just give me some time to finish up here, and then we can talk. In fact, why don't you meet me in the bar at the Traveler's Hotel in about an hour? I'll be done by then, and it's only three blocks from here."

"Yeah, okay," said Gerry. "It'll give me a chance to check on Mrs. Richly again." During a break between surgeries that afternoon he'd already told her about the temporarily lost lens. She laughed lightly until she realized any laughing hurt her surgical incision.

When Dr. Frank looked in on her this time she appeared to be dozing, so he did not awaken her. Instead he returned to the doctor's lounge, changed into his street clothes, and put on his jacket. He avoided the elevator and walked down two flights of stairs to the ground floor and out into the evening air. He had been in the hospital almost 27 hours.

A light spring shower filled the air again, and by the time Gerry walked the three blocks to the local watering hole, the rain had soaked and refreshed him. Shaking out his jacket as he entered the hotel pub, he immediately saw two of his fraternity brothers, Claude and Worth. They were drinking at the bar, laughing loudly, and watching Ben Casey, the medical drama on the television behind the bar.

"I can understand you both drinking," Gerry said, "but why spend your time watching a doctor TV series? No women to chase tonight?"

"Well," drawled Claude in his southern Illinois accent, "according to this series, medicine is supposed to be a glamorous profession. We're trying to appreciate that."

"Besides," said Worth, "look at all the good looking girls that guy has chasing him every week. We think it's because he wears tailored white uniforms, not those old baggy ones we have to wear in the hospital."

"I can't believe seeing you two guys here," said Gerry. "You have the best moonshine business going in this part of the state. This is like finding the chef of fine restaurant eating in someone else's dive diner."

"Well, actually," said Claude, "we do have the white lightning business down pretty good. I admit to that. But occasionally

Worth and I just like to sauce it up on the local brews like a good old Bud and some Bush Bavarian. We don't make beer."

"I'll drink to that," said Worth.

"Besides, those big Clydesdale horses down in St. Louis need our local support. Tonight is support-your-local-Clydesdale evening and Worth and I are big supporters."

"I'll drink to that too," repeated Worth, adjusting his glasses as he looked up at the large TV set. The two of them had obviously already been drinking for a considerable amount of time. "Another round, Murphy, and one for the good surgeon here," he continued.

"And keep 'em coming for the Clydesdales," added Claude raising his glass in salute. "Mighty fine horses, but too big for light duty plowing." Claude was still a farmer at heart.

Within the next hour Gerry found himself having drunk three large glasses of Budweiser. He forgot he had not eaten all day and was relieved when Sarah walked in before his fraternity brothers could pour him a fourth beer. Gerry gorged on pretzels while Sarah shared one big glass with Worth and another with Claude. The three doctors all agreed after watching the TV show that Los Angeles County Hospital was the place to intern, especially if all the nurses look like the ones in the Ben Casey series. Gerry and Sarah stayed until the show was over at 10:00 P.M. Claude and Worth remained, having one more beer and watching the late news before walking back to the fraternity house.

"You need to eat, not drink," Sarah to Gerry as they left the bar. "I don't think you've eaten all day. I have some cold chili to warm up at my place and plenty of French bread if you're interested. I didn't know you were a drinker."

"Sounds good," said Gerry. "The bar didn't seem conducive to talking. And you're right. I hardly drink at all since I've been in medical school. I used to drink a fair amount during my pre-med days at Colgate. Fortunately I grew out of the habit. Heavy drinking and serious doctoring don't mix very well."

Sarah lived in a compact trailer on the north end of town. They drove to her trailer in his car, which had been parked at the medical library for three days. Gerry felt better after using her bathroom. It had been years since he had drunk that much beer.

Sarah went into her bedroom and changed into a light blue blouse and black wool skirt before coming out and busying herself in the compact kitchen.

"How do you like your chili?" she asked. "Mild, hot, or extra hot? I can't promise you a gourmet meal this time, but I have enough here to save us from certain starvation."

"Oh, just average hot, I guess," he answered while exchanging smiles and picking up a bottle of Napa Valley red wine she placed on the counter. By the time he had read the label, Sarah had two frosted glasses taken from the refrigerator and indicated he should pour the cabernet.

"More drinking is not a good idea," said Gerry. "Neither of us has eaten all day and I already feel half smashed from the beer. What do you think?"

Looking straight at him, she ignored his question, and touched his glass with a toast. "To a better gynecology department," she said, instantly putting her glass to her open lips and finishing it off with a few fast swallows. "Maybe it's best we do get half smashed before finishing the conversation we started at the hospital. We weren't doing that well sober."

"What's to finish?" he asked. "I'm just not sure a gynecology lab for medical students is a good idea using volunteers in a small city. No matter how professional you try to be, there's too much risk of possible embarrassment over subject patients being recognized. You even said some of those women were repeat performers."

"They're not performers, Doctor. Not at all. We tried it with performers in the beginning when we had prostitutes. They were professional performers," she said sarcastically as she poured another glass of cabernet for herself.

"What do you mean?" he responded, sitting down on the nearby couch and sniffing the obvious odor of burning French bread, which Sarah had put in the oven to warm.

"Oh shoot," she yelled while turning around and bending over the stove to open the oven. Pulling out the large pan with the bread slices, she held them over the sink and tried to scrape off the more burned portions.

"What do you mean performers?" he repeated. "You mean Chase wasn't kidding about prostitutes in the beginning?"

In disgust, she realized she couldn't salvage the toast. Throwing it in the garbage, she put six new pieces in the oven, closed the broiler door and started setting the small dinette table. "No, he wasn't kidding. I guess I should know better than anybody because I'm the one who recruited them."

"You did what?"

"That's a long story so let's eat our chili first. I don't have any more toast to burn and I know we're both hungry. I put a salad together yesterday, and it still looks pretty good. Do you want some?"

"Sure. Guess I'm hungrier than I thought."

"Good, because we have canned peaches for dessert."

The meal was tasty, and they were both hungrier than they had originally anticipated. The wine made the occasion feel festive, relaxed the tension between them, and contributed to an informal familiarity they might otherwise not have felt. Their conversation stayed light until Gerry once again brought it back to the problems at the gynecology lab.

"What about the prostitutes you were using as subjects?" he asked. "I would like to hear about that."

"They were out of St. Louis," she answered as she refilled her glass again and seemed to be recalling the details. "Of course, for demonstrations like ours, it's almost impossible to have ongoing cases of pathology needing immediate surgical intervention. But we try to demonstrate chronic conditions of some of the post-surgical cases who have either complete or partial hysterectomies or salpingo-oophorectomies."

"So, couldn't you get a mix with the prostitutes? I would think they should have many of the same problems as other women would, with the exception of a higher incidence of active or chronic sexually transmitted diseases."

"No, it's not that," she said laughingly. "Doctor, have you ever had anything to do with prostitutes?"

"No," he answered truthfully. "In fact, I don't know if I've ever met one, although I may have seen a couple of hookers on Hollywood Boulevard last summer."

"Oh," she said, with a laugh in her voice, "well, the first thing you have to realize is they're always on stage. Put them in a situation where they have their panties off and they can't stop acting. We had a really beautiful, dark-haired woman, who'd been faking orgasms for so many years, every time a student touched her crotch to do a pelvic exam, she couldn't stop faking them."

Drinking more wine, she continued, "Her orgasmic act not only included much moaning and groaning with verbal obscenities, but also pelvic movements like you wouldn't believe. Then one day during a pelvic exam by a particularly clumsy medical student she almost become unglued. Right there in the lab she actually had the first genuine orgasm of her life, although she had been a pretending them as prostitute for six or seven years."

"That's incredible," said Gerry, getting up from the table and going over to sit on the couch a few feet behind the kitchen dining area. "I'll bet that broke up the lab."

"No, but what happened next certainly did." Coming over to the couch and carefully setting the now half-empty wine bottle and her glass on the coffee table, Sarah sat down beside the young doctor and continued with the story. "Our working girl then sat up, pulled off the towel we had covering her face, threw off all of her other drapes, jumped off the table, and started hugging the embarrassed doctor."

"You mean love at first orgasm?"

"Well, something like that. She started demanding to know the doctor's name, and of course it was on his white jacket pocket. To make it worse, he was married, and she started calling him at home and making obscene phone calls in the middle of the night."

"Is that the worse thing that happened?" asked Gerry, laughing loudly for the first time that day.

"No, it's not the worst, and it's not even the funniest. We had one working girl who had tremendous control over her lower pelvic musculature. With some of the doctors, she'd clamp down on the speculum so tightly the doctor could barely draw it out of her. Then she'd claim they were trying to pull her insides out. They were so unpredictable you'd never know what they'd do. And they did almost anything for a laugh. One day, two of them had a $50 bet over whether or not one of them could get a physician to have his head in her crotch."

"Well, that's a bet she must have lost," Gerry said as he put the cork back in the wine bottle. He felt they both had enough to drink for the night.

"No, in fact she won," replied Sarah, "just as the doctor drew the speculum out of her, she pulled her legs free from the stirrups, draped them over his shoulders, wrapped them around his neck, and pulled him down onto her. The poor man almost died of embarrassment. Then she tried to fake an epileptic seizure and claimed her assaulting him was all part of her seizure. But she won the 50 bucks."

"Well, that's one doctor who probably decided right then and there never to go into gynecology," Gerry said.

"Yes," said Sarah. "I think he became a psychiatrist."

"So that's how the gyn lab started here?"

"Yes," said Sarah, "and then we slowly phased out the prostitutes as we found local women willing to be subjects who had the type of clinical entities or post-surgical anatomy we needed most for teaching classes. I guess the real break came when one of the hospital staff physician's wives volunteered for the lab. She ended up with cancer requiring a complete pelvic clean out, post-surgical radiation, and the whole ten yards."

"And she volunteered for the lab?" asked Gerry. "A doctor's wife actually volunteered?"

"Yes, she was one hell of a fine lady. When she heard about the lab, she realized its significance as a learning source. She thought the least she might do would be a good demonstration case for the medical students. That made the teaching staff more aware of the program, and I think most of the staff doctors tried harder after then to recruit legitimate subject cases."

"Well, you still haven't convinced me, and I'm making no promises on whether to report yesterday's incident to Dr. Chase."

Looking down at the almost empty glass in her hand she said, "I know how you must feel, Gerry. It must have been a great shock to you yesterday, finding your girlfriend as a subject in the lab."

"Bullshit," he said, "there's no way you could know how I felt or could imagine how she must have felt. Don't give me that clinical stuff about being a valuable teaching exercise. I'm talking about two people in love."

Finishing the wine in her glass, she placed it empty next to the corked bottle. Then she turned towards Gerry and placed both hands on his arms, "You're wrong doctor, I do know how you must have felt. And even better, I know how she must have felt. I know because it happened to me in the same lab three years ago. I was engaged to a senior medical student who recognized me during a pelvic examination. He freaked out and complained to Dr. Chase. Chase said if it ever happened another time, he'd discontinue the whole program. That's why I'm worried. That's why I'd do anything to influence you favorably about keeping the program. The thought of it of being in jeopardy makes me feel sick."

Gerry didn't quite know what she meant by '*anything*'. However, it surprised him to learn she had once been a lab subject. He also knew damn well the effects of the wine and the desirability of the woman next to him weakened his defenses. The fact she hadn't let go of him and now reached up and rubbed his head didn't help.

With some embarrassment and in attempt to be humorous, he said, "Maybe we should define what you mean by 'anything'. Or maybe we should just put the discussion off until tomorrow when we're sober."

"No," she said, "I just want to say…damn, I really do feel sick." She kicked off her shoes. She tried to stand up but did not see the phone cord and tripped over it. She fell back across the table smashing both wine glasses. Then she vomited all over herself with a gut-wrenching type of emesis, emptying everything from her stomach she had drunk or had eaten since arriving at the trailer.

Quickly Gerry gathered her up, carried her to the small trailer bathroom, and held her head over the toilet while she finished throwing up. He tried to stand her up, but she kept falling down.

Oh Lord, he thought. *This is all I need now, a drunken nurse to nurse.*

"Can you stand up in the shower by yourself?" he asked. "Sarah, you're a mess. You threw up all over yourself. You can't go to bed like this."

However, Sarah just laughed as she tried to say something completely incomprehensible and slowly slid down the bathroom wall against which he held her. Finally in desperation, Gerry put her in the shower, clothes and all, and turned the faucet on to cold.

The cool water started to bring Sarah out of her stupor and, giggling and laughing, she started to take her clothes off. The shower also completely soaked Gerry. He had revived her sufficiently so she could hold on to the side of the shower stall without falling down. Gerry quickly stripped to his shorts to prevent his outer clothes from becoming more soaked.

In a way it was funny. In a way it was romantic. However, Gerry was too involved with Sharon to enjoy intimacy with someone else. He always considered himself a one-woman man. He figured if he could start Sarah talking again it would help.

"Get the damn vomitus off me," she said. "It's even in my hair. Help me get clean. Agh...I can't stand it."

"Can you hang on to the side of the shower okay without falling down now?" he questioned. "Use the soap dish to steady yourself. But it's not strong enough to lean your full weight against it."

"Yeah, I'm doing better." By now she had her blouse and skirt off and she surprised Gerry to see she was not wearing a bra.

Soon she stepped free of her panties and remained with her back to him. He lathered up her arms and shoulders.

"So, what happened to your medical student friend?" he said. "Did you two break up?"

"No, no," she said, "but our relationship sure as hell has changed drastically. We were dating for about a year, and he gave me his fraternity pin for an engagement promise. In our relationship up to then I had always been the dominant one. Then he said we would have to change. I realized I loved him and didn't want to lose him. I said I'd do anything to keep him. Nobody should ever have to say that."

"So what drastic means did you have to submit to in order to keep this fine fellow?" Gerry laughed, as he bent over, soaping her lower back, buttocks and upper legs. Difficult to remain clinical with a beautiful naked woman in her shower, the young doctor tried to be objective about it by bringing up her boyfriend.

"Damn, that water's cold," she said, turning up the hot faucet. "Well I don't know. I guess some people would say I took a drastic tactic. Anyway, he said I'd have to immediately stop being a subject in the gynecology lab, and he'd give me an engagement ring I'd have to promise to wear forever. He left two months later for an internship in Texas, which he has since followed up with an OB/GYN residency there.

"So you don't see him very often with the distance separating you?"

"Oh, often enough to keep the romance going. He sends for me about every three months. The plan is if I'm still as submissive as he wants or needs in a woman when he finishes his residency in fifteen months, we'll get married."

"And that's what you want?" asked Gerry.

"It's strange, Gerry," she said. "I'm not sure anymore. I've always considered myself a pretty straight person, and I'm certainly no man's mistress, much less a slave. Here I am an OB/GYN nurse with every reason for a healthy outlook on sex and male-female relationships."

"And you don't think you have a healthy outlook anymore?"

"I don't know. I can't believe the changes in me in the last three years since it happened. I used to orgasm easily, but now I can't unless a certain threshold of pain is present. Yet the orgasms I do have are of much greater intensity than anything I'd had before. They are almost overwhelming, and I really need them."

"Is that progress?"

"I don't know. I don't know," she said, answering his question, which she had asked herself often enough.

She certainly sounded like she was sobering up, thought Gerry, but he wondered about the validity of what she said. He finished kneeling down and soaping the backs of her lower legs as she reached back with her left hand to rub her thigh in a sensuous motion.

Then it hit him. What promise never to take off an engagement ring? She didn't have one on. She certainly could not wear one in surgery. He could never remember seeing her wear one in the gyn clinic where she was head nurse. He was sorry he had drunk so much wine. Had he heard her correctly? Was he confused? Maybe he should turn up the cold water again.

"Okay," he said, straightening up. "That finishes your back, now turn around."

"I can't," she said, her voice so low he had to ask her to repeat it. "I can't," she said, "I'm embarrassed."

"Hey," he said, "this whole conversation is unreal. What do you mean embarrassed? You're a nurse. I'm a doctor. We're both engaged to other people, and we're here in a shower together only trying to scrub the vomitus off each other."

"I know, but I'm still self-conscious about it and feel stupid I drank so much."

"Well," he continued, "you're really a nice person, but the story doesn't have a ring of truth to it. In the first place, you could have worn his engagement ring and still participated in the gyn labs. Who the hell would know one way or the other? Certainly he wouldn't, being in Texas."

Just then Gerry slipped on the wet floor falling backwards first into the small trailer's sink and then onto the floor. Worse than the noise of the fall, he twisted his right knee and ankle. The light blue bar of soap went flying across the small room and ended up behind the toilet.

Quickly, Sarah turned around, stepped from the shower stall and tried to help him. "Can you stand?" she asked with the sincere concern of a nurse in her voice. "Did you hurt your knee or your ankle?"

"I think I twisted my ankle, and now I'm sitting on it," he said. "Can you help me up?" Though his ankle hurt more than he would admit, the humor of the situation struck him. He smiled up into the expressive features of her down-turned face. Whether sober or drunk, clothed or naked, dry or wet, Gerry knew he was in the presence of a beautiful, special lady. Though proud of her body, a red flush spread quickly across her face. Gerry kept his eyes glued to hers, though his lower peripheral vision inadvertently wandered to her beautiful naked breasts dripping water on his chest.

Spreading her long bare legs apart, she braced herself and reached down with both hands while she grasped his wrists. Then she pulled him partially up, while he extracted his hyper-flexed right leg and slowly extended it out in front of him. Examination elicited a mild tenderness along the lateral portion of his ankle. "I don't know if it was worth it," he moaned. "A shower with a beautiful woman like you may have cost me a sprained ankle."

"But I never lied," she said, sitting down on the floor in front of him, extending her long, wet legs on either side of his. "I haven't lied to you Gerry, and I never would."

"The engagement ring. The engagement ring," he repeated. "You promised your boyfriend you'd wear it forever. Hell, I don't see it on you now, and I have never seen you wear such a ring."

"I know," she answered. "Nobody has. That's how he knew I could never be a subject in the gyn labs again."

Gerry still didn't understand. He looked at her quizzically. "I guess I'm confused," he said. "Maybe I did drink too much."

"No, no," she said. "You're not dumb. In fact you're smart and very nice. And I'm not as confused as I used to be." She smiled again with the happiness of anticipated pleasure. Already she could feel a warm tingling sensation starting to concentrate in her pelvis.

Taking his right hand in both of hers, she gently placed it on the hair and lips between her legs. It look him a few seconds to realize he felt more than the warmth and wetness of an adult female vulva. He felt the cold hardness of a gold, labial ring, securely stapled through her right labial lip, waiting to be pulled. She waited to be fucked.

Chapter 9
April Fools
March 15, 1962

Sarah softly asked as she affectionately snuggled closer to Gerry in her warm double bed, "I wonder if it's appropriate we did this today?" The large bed almost filled the small bedroom at the back end of her 32-foot trailer. She gently rubbed the young doctor's bare chest as he lay on his back under the bed clothes looking up at the low dark ceiling. Sarah could faintly see the features of his face illuminated by the distant lamplight shining in from the living room at the other end of the mobile home.

Gerry's facial expression fixed between mass confusion and utter amazement over everything that unbelievably had happened to him over the last two days. He felt stunned at finding himself already in bed with Sarah. "I don't know what you mean by that," he replied. He tried to stifle a yawn but then gave in to it. Opening his mouth widely, he slowly moved his lower jaw from side to side.

"Am I already boring you, Doctor?"

"Certainly not. The yawn is only a symptom of exhaustion over the events of the last two days. What did you mean by your remark about our sleeping together? Are you referring to the fact that it's only one day after I found you using my girlfriend as a clinical case specimen in your gynecology lab?" A deep disappointment clouded the young physician's face as he spoke these words. The shocking vision of Sharon lying on her back on the hard gynecological examination table with her bare legs spread wide in cold metal stirrups and her naked vulva and pelvis fully exposed for examination by 15 medical students still proved to be more than he could bear. Gerry kept forcing the picture from his mind but it ruthlessly returned to haunt him. He wondered if he would ever be able to forget the memory of that afternoon.

"No, dummy," Sarah replied with sudden light laughter in her voice as she raised her head and propped it up with her left arm. "I mean, is it appropriate we ended up fucking in my bed here at 1:00 A.M. on this particular day?"

"What particular day is it?"

"Well, today is actually the anniversary date of my engagement - March fifteenth," she continued with delighted mirth. "Maybe we should have waited until April Fools Day, though I don't think I could have waited another two weeks."

"Okay, now I get it. You think I'm some sort of a surrogate boyfriend or maybe just a dumb romantic fool? Is that what you mean?" Gerry reluctantly questioned as he turned to take a long look at Sarah. Then reaching out, he held her blond head next to his face and deeply inhaled the faint scent of lemon from her freshly shampooed hair, still slightly damp from their recent shower together. The lemon-like smell reminded him of the citrus groves back home in Southern California.

"No. It's not like that. It's not anything like that at all," she said wrinkling her forehead in an accentuated frown.

"So what did you mean?"

"I just wondered if we were both romantic fools for becoming sexually involved like this. After all, we're each engaged to other people and they are both good people, well respected by their peers and co-workers. Sharon is definitely one of the finest women in this part of Missouri and I'm lucky to be engaged to my OB/GYN resident in Texas, even if his sexual fantasies are a bit kinky. What do you think about this or are you reserving your professional opinion until later?"

"Do you really want my honest opinion now?" Gerry asked.

"Yes, I do. It can't hurt me to know."

"I think your boyfriend is far past mere kinky. He sounds crazy to me. Putting that damn labial ring in you showed his true colors long ago."

"What do you mean by that?" Sarah questioned with concern in her voice. "What 'true colors'?"

"I mean for an enthusiastic gynecology resident he sounds more sadistic than empathetic. You're kidding yourself to think otherwise. I don't want to hurt your feelings, Sarah, but your boyfriend sounds like a sicko."

"But for every sadist to survive there needs to be a masochist to foster their ambitions," she whispered. "Always remember that, Doctor. So the fact that I let him put a gold ring through the tender flesh of my labia may actually say more about me than it says about him." Her faint smile hid what she really felt as she waited for Gerry's response.

For a few seconds the young doctor did not know what to say. He knew Sarah was an intelligent, super-competent, and compassionate nurse. He found it difficult to understand how she could have become involved with her doctor boyfriend whose sexual practices obviously included severe sadomasochism. Could professional people be crazy in their personal lives and not have the effects spillover into their professional lives? As the silence between them continued, it emphasized her last sentence as a statement in request of an answer.

"Should I interpret your silence as an agreement or as a statement of 'no comment'?" she asked.

In moments of doubt, Gerry's method of operation had always been to switch to humor. Humor helped to dissipate the immediate embarrassment of a situation or helped to change the subject. "Well I hope he used a lot of Xylocain as a local anesthetic. Otherwise putting that gold ring in your labia must have hurt like hell," Gerry continued with a forced laugh. Actually appalled by the whole horrible idea, he had never seen such a ring before.

"No, he did not use a local anesthetic. You still don't understand do you? The use of local anesthetic would not have been proper. That would make sure I would appreciate the pain and would know complete submission. This is the ultimate gift he forced me to give him to reinforce his newfound dominance over me and made his power over me complete. The ring visualizes the sexual acquiescence between him and me."

"Does it?"

"Yes. With the imposition of this ring in my labia, I became a sex slave to his desires and fantasies," she said as she gently continued to rub Gerry's chest. "He is a sadist of sorts, but he is not randomly cruel in an arbitrary way. With his patients he is a completely compassionate and very empathetic physician. And he is becoming a damn fine surgeon with all of the additional training he's receiving in Houston."

"But what's in it for you Sarah? Why, for heaven's sake, do you continue to feed his fantasies this way?" the young doctor asked as he kissed her damp forehead and pulled her warm body closer. "Why do you need that kind of abuse?"

Sarah had asked herself this question on many previous occasions, but she had yet to find a satisfying answer. "I don't know why," she began as she slowly brushed tears from her eyes. "Thinking about it now makes me sad. But I do know since the pain of that dreadful night he forced the gold ring through my right labial lip, I can no longer have an orgasm unless a certain threshold of pain is achieved."

"You're kidding?" Gerry exclaimed in a barely audible voice.

"No I'm not. But it's not all bad."

"What could be good about it?"

"Because when I do come, the release is so fantastically greater in intensity than anything I've ever felt before the ring. I know I could never be easily satisfied as I was before. I need the pain now. I have to suffer first as it heightens my sensory input. I need it to set off my neurological response of pleasure. It's hard to explain and harder for you to understand."

"Well you must be a pretty damn good actress because I sure thought you climaxed nicely with me here a few minutes ago. It certainly seemed like all pleasure without any pain and even sounded like it. I thought for a minute you would wake up the neighbors in the next trailer. It's less than 25 feet away."

"Yes, you're right. The pleasure of my cumming with you was fantastic, but it was proceeded by pain. You just didn't realize the pain I had to suffer first."

"You lost me again. Run that by me once more," Gerry replied.

"When you were above me and I had my left hand on your balls, I simultaneously pulled my labial ring with my right hand. The pain it caused really opened me up. I could feel the flood of my own juices. Then I know I had to really fuck. Nothing could have stopped me." She said it without embarrassment, almost as if she was proud of the fact. The room's low level of light hid the schoolgirl blush spreading across her fair face.

"You do like to talk dirty, don't you?" Gerry asked. "You're normally proper and professional with your clothes on, especially with your pure white, stiffly starched nurse's uniform and hat. I don't think I've even heard you ever say '*damn*' outside this bedroom. But with your clothes off you're an untamed animal."

"We're still all animals underneath the thinly layered veneer called civilization," she replied. "But that's not why I revert to four letter words in bed."

"So why do you?"

"Because they're the original words of my ancient heritage. They're the strong, short, expressive words of Saxons, uninfluenced by Norman French."

"What ancient heritage? I thought you mentioned earlier today both of your parents were English and migrated to the US after World War II."

"That's correct, and I was born in England before they left their native land. I'm a naturalized citizen of the United States by choice, not by chance."

"So what's this stuff about Saxons?"

"My heritage and blood is still purely Saxon on both sides of my family. In fact, on my father's side, we go back to the famous Saxon warrior, King Cernig. Don't you Americans still study English history here in the colonies?" she asked with a laugh and a faintly affected English accent. "At one time the sun never set on the British Empire. All good children of the many colonies throughout the world were expected to know about Mother England."

"Well I thought I knew a little. My mother's parents both immigrated from Cornwall - Land's End to be exact. But I guess most of my knowledge of English history came from reading a few of Shakespeare's plays in high school and college."

"You can be sure there is damn little Saxon or Celt in Shakespeare's work. Once Saxons were the dominant tribe and the noble warriors of England. Their language is laced with many short, one-vowel words. But when the hated Norman French finally defeated the island's natives at the famous Battle of Hastings in 1062, many of the short simple words were socially ostracized from the Saxon's own language. Cunt became vagina, cock became penis, fuck became fornicate, shit became feces, and piss became urine. However, even as the two latter examples changed to Norman French, they did not smell any better.

"What smell better? The human waste products or the Norman French?"

"According to Saxon legend there was little difference between the two," she replied with a wide grin.

"The old short Saxon words were relegated to the bedroom and the bathroom, no longer to be used by anyone other than peasants. Is that what you are saying?" he asked.

"Exactly. When I'm naked in the privacy of my own bedroom and my own bathroom, I will continue to use the expressive language of my proud ancient heritage. I think it helps get blood and other body juices surging through my system. Someday Saxons will have enough courage to bring this part of our language back into respected circulation." Sarah did not laugh as she said this, making Gerry wonder how serious she was about the subject.

Now did not seem to be the right time to tell her the father's side of his family was one-fourth French. But as he knew very well, Normans were not really French. They were the descendants of Northmen or Vikings who had headed south in the Tenth Century to colonize the Atlantic Coast of France, and in doing so lost most of their own ancient language.

Maybe a little humor would help, Gerry thought. "Well, you're the first woman who ever needed to be motivated by pain to sleep with me. Generally pleasure turns women on, and I hope the experience equals the anticipation."

"No, no. Don't think of it like that. No pain factored in my decision-making process. I certainly do find you physically attractive and have wanted to fuck you for months. But yesterday, I found more than just a physical attraction to you. I saw a sense of compassion with vulnerability, and it made me want to reach out and comfort you. Women have to feel needed, you know."

"I guess I sure did need someone."

"You needed me. You're too damn macho for your own good or for anyone else around you for very long."

"So you're here in your bed after some really fine sex just because you feel sorry for me? If you're this good out of sympathy, then I don't think I could handle what you must do when love is involved. You still just don't seem like a masochist to me."

"Don't confuse your perception with my reality," Sarah replied. "It's very difficult to know anything certain about another person."

"What do you mean by that?" Gerry asked.

"Generally other people have an image in our heads based on limited information, or at best based on a few isolated incidences. Then we use it to justify our conclusions. No wonder so many of our conclusions about each other, whether we are lovers, relatives, or friends, are wrong." Sarah paused before continuing, "And if I didn't feel so relaxed right now, I would sit up and hit you for thinking I would ever fuck out of sympathy."

"So you do feel better?"

"Even my stomach feels much better after the oral Maalox you made me take. Is that stuff an aphrodisiac besides being an anti-acid?"

"Not that I know of, but I'll keep it in mind for future reference. Whatever works well without unnecessary risks is the drug of choice."

"Seriously, I would never fuck anybody out of sympathy. That is a real sin. I wanted you, Gerry, I hope you understand that.

You're really a very passionate and compassionate man, in spite of your occasional arrogance."

"What arrogance? Who said anything about being arrogant?" he injected with an extra-loud voice but with a big smile on his face.

"Be nice now, and I might even want you again in the morning," she replied as she rolled over toward him, put her right arm around him, and hugged him closely. "We've had enough physical excitement and emotional reflection for one night. I'm falling asleep. I've already talked far too much for one evening."

"Did you set the alarm clock?" Gerry asked as he looked over Sarah's right shoulder at the faintly illuminated radio-clock on her night table. "I have rounds to make at the hospital at 7:00 followed by lectures and clinical conferences until 11:00. Then I have to leave for my rural clinic in Essex. It's going to be a busy day for me."

"Don't worry. I have to be at the hospital myself by 6:45. Dr. Chase has a C-section scheduled for 7:00 with two complete hysterectomies to follow. I set the clock for the alarm to ring in time for sex before six."

"How much before six?" he asked in a sleepy voice with his eyes already closed.

"How much sex or how much time before six?" she replied. "Or how much of both?"

"I set it for 5:30 A.M. Will a half-hour of me be enough to make your day start out right? Anything more might make us both too tired to start the day after tonight's activity."

"You know," he said reflectively, "I don't want to impose or keep you awake any longer, but you were supposed to help me figure out what to say to Sharon when I see her tomorrow. This evening hasn't given me any new insight on the problem."

"You're on your own on that for now. A hard man is as good to find as a good man is hard to find. If you can fuck me a few more times like you did tonight, then maybe I won't encourage you to go back to Sharon right away. I really like your girlfriend as a person, but I think your brand of love could be therapeutic to this girl. Maybe it's what I need for a week or so. Sometimes a person must look out for herself first." Before Sarah finished her last statement, she realized Gerry's quiet rhythmic breathing signaled he suddenly fell fast asleep.

Sarah's last thought of the night centered on trying to remember the first time she had used the word '*love*' in her bedroom. Before she could contemplate the answer to her question she also fell fast asleep.

The next day dawned damply and unseasonably warm for mid-March in Missouri. After raining briefly during the dark early morning hours, clouds were cleared by the warm southern wind. A moist, delicate haze hung in the air as the sun arose.

After Gerry drove Sarah to the hospital to make sure she would be there well before 6:45, he had 20 minutes of free time before surgical rounds started at 7:00. It took him three minutes to find a close parking space. Then he headed down to the doctor's dining room in the basement of the building's west wing. Food served to the student doctors at cost was always surprisingly tasty. Needing time to do some serious thinking, Gerry passed up offers to eat with two different groups of staff physicians and medical students sitting at long crowded tables. Instead he took a small square table in the back of the room. The table had one leg shorter than the others so most other personnel avoided it unless all the other tables were full. Before sitting down, Gerry quickly drank his glass of orange juice so it would not spill if the table wobbled under the weight of his elbows and food. Better to drink the juice first rather than end up wearing it before finishing his meal. He had the same experience at this table in the past.

The sex before six with Sarah had been good for Gerry with them both spontaneously aroused to mutual orgasm at the same time. But he could tell it had not been as good for her as the night before. Their short foreplay upon awakening had been sufficient to arouse them both quickly. However, Gerry would not let Sarah put her hands on the labial ring. He wanted to show her that she could orgasm without the pain threshold she claimed she needed. Though he held out for over 20 minutes before his own unstoppable release, Sarah had not reached climax. She tried to make light of it, but he could sense her disappointment. Gerry didn't know why he should he care so much, after all, she was the kinky one, not him. But he did care - and it came as a surprise how much he cared.

"Hey there stranger," Harry called out a few minutes later carrying a full metal tray of food as he approached Gerry sitting alone at the table. "Why are you sitting so forlorn looking eating alone at the one wobbly table in the whole room? Won't the big boys let you eat with them at the long tables?"

"Look partner, if you drink your full glass of orange juice before it spills and slurp down your coffee below half way I'll let you sit here too. Don't you remember what happened last summer? You, Woodward, and Miller helped me file one leg of this table shorter than the rest during our internal medicine rotation."

"I do remember. We figured we could always depend on finding an empty table since rarely would anybody else want to at that table even when the room is crowded. Everybody already knew the table tilted a little. We just helped it tilt even more."

"All it takes to stabilize this old rocker is a couple of quarters temporarily stacked under the short leg. Do you have any change?" Gerry asked. "I don't have any with me this morning."

"Yeah, that was one of your better ideas," Harry replied after he carefully put down his tray and quickly drank his tall glass of orange juice before it could spill. "Nothing better than a little OJ to start the day." Reaching into his pants pocket, he took out two quarters. Then, pulling up a chair opposite of Gerry, Harry bent over and placed the stacked coins under the short leg. "Yeah, that was a good idea. But not calling Sharon for the last two days is a bad idea, and it's getting mighty worse every hour. She called home twice last night."

"What did she say?" Gerry asked though he was not sure he wanted to know. "Did she seem upset?"

"Well, I could tell she had been crying, but she didn't have much to say at all. She did mention she still planned to stay with her Aunt Helen in Moberly, but she would be back at college today. I'm not one to pry, old buddy, but if you need someone to talk to, you know I'm always available."

"I do know, old friend, and I appreciate it. I just don't feel much like talking yet. Maybe I will later on."

"No problem," Harry replied. "Now about breakfast. Your fried eggs look better than my scrambled ones. Don't suppose you'd want to trade would you? I know this is asking a lot, but then we have been friends for over three-and-a-half years."

"Partner, they don't make friends as good as you anymore. But trading anything for those scrambled eggs goes way beyond friendship. You will realize this the moment you taste them. I've had them before and they're not Cooky's specialty. I think she serves them as punishment to all the doctors who arrive late for breakfast."

"Well, just thought I'd ask," replied Harry with resignation in his voice as he reluctantly dug into the warm, wet yellow mass on his plate. "Of course, maybe on the other hand, you've already found another friend to tell your troubles to? Yeah, that's probably the case by now."

"What makes you say that?"

"I just saw Worth in the hospital parking lot on my way in through the emergency department entrance. You know he lives out in the new trailer park in the north end of town. Said he drank too much beer last night, so he had Claude give him an injection of B-complex and B-12 back at the fraternity house about 11:00 P.M. Then he slept on the couch there 'til about 3:00 A.M., until he awoke sufficiently sober to drive home. He claims your car was parked all night next to some 32-foot home on wheels registered to and domiciled by one Sarah Hall, R.N. Of course, I replied you must have been there on some house call emergency. Don't think he bought any of it though."

"Probably not, since Sarah and I had a few beers with him earlier that evening at the hotel bar," Gerry replied.

"You know the story is she's engaged to the OB/GYN resident in Texas who did his senior year here three years ago. He must be a cheapskate as nobody has ever seen her wearing an engagement ring, but I've heard she doesn't date anybody else. That's all I'm saying on the subject."

"Well, I appreciate that," Gerry said as he finished his first fried egg and started on the second. "Want some of my toast? Cooky gave me two extra slices, and they're already buttered."

"Thanks, I will take one. Maybe I should mention one more thing passed on to me by Worth this morning." Harry spread strawberry jam all over the toast as he formulated what he needed to tell his best friend.

"So what's this one thing more you feel compelled to tell me?" Gerry asked. "What could possibly upset me any more?"

"The guy carries a gun," Harry responded gravely.

"Who carries what gun?" Gerry replied in astonishment as he put down a forkful of fried potatoes and almost knocked over his coffee cup. "You mean Worth does?"

"You know damn well what I mean. Don't play games with your old buddy. I'd hate to see you end up stupid and dead with less than two full months to graduation. No night in bed with any woman is worth that, not even with the beautiful and brilliant Nurse Sarah Hall."

"Okay, so her boyfriend carries a gun," Gerry anxiously replied. "But he is in Texas, which is still one very long ride from Missouri if I remember my geography correctly. The entire state of Oklahoma is between us, and Texas is a sizable state."

"Well, Worth got so worried when he saw your car out there past 3:00 A.M., he actually called the switchboard operator at Houston Community Hospital. It seems '*Tex*' has a habit of periodically appearing on the scene here in Missouri, unannounced at Sarah's trailer. Worth wanted to make sure the guy was still in Texas."

"Is he?" Gerry questioned.

"Yes, for now, but Worth went further than just finding out if Tex were on duty. He's a good friend and you owe him a few beers for this one."

"I realize Worth is a damn good friend but why do I owe him a few beers?" Gerry asked as he finished a doughnut at the end of his meal.

"Because Worth had enough sense to ask the switchboard lady at H.C.H. exactly what on-duty nights Tex has at the hospital this month. Worth said he needed to know so he could reach him later on about something important. Worth found out Tex was pulling double night-shifts the next two weeks, covering for another resident, but then three weeks from now, he will be completely off schedule for a full week."

"So he may be heading north this way then? Is that what you think?"

"I sure don't think he took the time off to study for his Boards. They're not given until August this year. What I'm saying is we don't need another shoot 'em up in town. I still get shaky thinking about the one last year during our junior year."

"Hey, I can take a hint. I appreciate your concern, but don't worry. I have enough problems right now with Sharon. I sure don't need any new ones with anybody else around here or in Texas."

"I think you better call Sharon today. She said she had classes this morning at the teachers college but would be doing typing at her hospital job this afternoon. Why not call her from our clinic in Essex around three o'clock?"

"Good idea. I'll do it. Or maybe I should wait until she drives back home to the farm this evening. She should be back home in Essex by 6:30 P.M. and we'll still be at the rural clinic then."

"No. Call her first. I think you two may have problems a mere tincture of time with caring conversation will not solve. Take it from your partner, call her soon."

"Okay, okay, I'll do it," Gerry grudgingly replied with a frown on his face and resignation in his voice. He realized the longer he put off calling Sharon, the harder would be the outcome.

After Dr. Frank finished his surgery seminar at 11:00 A.M., he walked over to the administration office of the Rural Clinic

Program, composed of three adjoining rooms in the basement of the east wing of the hospital. From the receptionist/secretary's room just off the main hallway, the door to the right opened into a small classroom for lectures and case presentations. A door opening into the medical director's office of the Rural Clinic Program sat to the left of the secretary's office.

"Morning, Boss Barbara," Gerry announced cheerfully. "Is The Ghost in and working or do you truly run this department?"

"Don't let him hear you call him that," she said shaking her finger at Gerry, "or you'll be less than a mere spirit around these hallowed halls. His name is Doctor Tripton Casper to you, and do not forget it, at least not until you've finished your six months on the Rural Clinic rotation."

"I suppose you're right. Maybe I should be a little more humble to our benevolent Director of Rural Medicine."

"You'd better believe it. I've seen a few Faustian bargains made around here where souls were sold for a medical degree." The stern coldness of her voice contradicted the warm welcome of her smile. Barbara merely stated for the record the official protocol of the office, though she had long since realized all of the externs referred to her boss as "Dr. Ghost." Not just because his name was like the cartoon character's, but also because his bald head and cherub face looked like *The Friendly Ghost* in the comic strip. He also had a bad habit of sneaking up on people, appearing suddenly, silently, and ghost-like at rural clinic offices for unannounced inspections. Sometimes these inspections ended up far from friendly. The Ghost never drank in the mornings or the afternoons around the hospital, but in some afternoon rural clinic inspection runs, he had been known to show up in such a high state of alcoholic intoxication the student doctors would have to drive him home.

"Yeah, you're probably right," Gerry said. "A little discretion being the better part of valor and all that stuff. After all, another few months and I'm gone. I'll be comfortably back in warm, sunny, southern California. Why should I care if The Ghost drinks too much white lightning? It's just embarrassing when he shows up to inspect the clinics and is so drunk it would be murder to let him back behind the wheel of his car. At least he doesn't try to give medical advice or to take care of patients when he's intoxicated. Why does the administration tolerate his drinking like that? Can't they make him stop?"

"Well, maybe you'd drink too if you had the medical/legal responsibility of 12 rural clinics spread over hundreds of square miles of Northeast Missouri staffed only by student doctors. Some people think anybody would have to drink pretty hard to take on that job."

"You know that's not true, but I promise to say no more on the subject," Gerry replied. "I realize he's your boss and your friend."

"Now you're thinking with a clear head," Barbara Mueller said as she raised both hands, palms-first in supplication of surrender. She had the habit of accompanying much of her conversation with visual analogues. As a part-time, professional puppeteer it had become natural for her to move her hands as she spoke. She hailed from Maine and still spoke with a decidedly down-east accent. With her pageboy haircut she looked much younger. Already 33-years old, she was the mother of five-year-old twin girls and the cherished wife of a junior-year medical student from Germany.

As the oldest student in his class at age 42, Gunnar Mueller had been a fighter pilot in World War II. He was shot down over Africa in the desert battle of l'Allemagne. Gunnar's personality made him the most pleasant and personally popular student among the third-year students, and he had been elected class president twice. The inequality of veteran's benefits was the only thing ever to cause him to complain. For some reason, the United States Government refused to offer Gunnar any veteran's benefits or G.I. college tuition fees since he had been piloting a Messerschmitt 109 fighter plane at the time he was shot down. He wore the gray uniform of a young Luftwaffe airman when his parachute landed him unceremoniously behind the American lines, which didn't qualify him for United State's G.I. Bill to attend college.

Immediately captured, Gunnar eventually had been shipped off to a large prisoner of war camp in Maine, from which prisoner trustees were furloughed out to individual farms. Farm work being critical during the war, the shortage of field-hand workers occurred in many rural agricultural areas where most able-bodied male Americans had been drafted into the military to fight. Gunnar had been raised on a German farm, and he considered the work and the delicious American food a blessing from heaven. Compared to what he had heard about combat on the Russian front, he preferred the easy farm duty from which only an idiot or an S.S. fanatic would try to escape. A pacifist at heart, Gunnar didn't miss the front lines and he felt he had found a home for the duration of the war.

Slightly plump at 5'4' and 145 pounds, Barbara had put on considerable weight during her pregnancy and had kept most of it on since the birth of her twins. She had shoulder-length, dark-blonde hair with most of it combed over to the left side of her head. Long bangs covered her forehead helping to hide permanent scarring on the left side of her face and neck from third-degree burns on her left shoulder and upper arm. But these were generally hidden by the long-sleeved blouses she made for herself.

Barbara had been raised on her father's fairly large family farm, well run before the war by him and his two younger brothers.

Her father's left leg had been amputated due to a farming accident below the knee keeping him out of the war. Both of his brothers volunteered to fight and had been accepted into the U.S. Navy. Barbara's father continued through the war to make his way around the farm fairly well on his peg leg, but the farm was more than he, his young daughter, and his wife could manage alone. As a prisoner of war. trustee, Gunnar had been furloughed to the custody of Barbara's parents for wartime farm work.

Gunnar had never been much of a fighter pilot, but there were two things he knew well - agriculture and hard work. Within one month, his help had become indispensable to the farm's operation. At first he ate in the kitchen after the family members had finished their meals. But midway in his second month they invited him to eat with the family. They knew he was supposed to be the enemy, but with his shy mannerisms, broken English, friendly smile, and enthusiasm for hard farm work, they could not help but to like him. Besides, with Barbara's two uncles serving on battleships in the Pacific Theater, the family's attention primarily focused on fighting the Japanese. After all, Japan had openly attacked the United States, not Germany.

Barbara had been 13-years-old the summer she fell out of her playhouse in an old, oak tree on the property. She needed a short leg cast due to the fracture of her left fibula at the ankle joint. She could not bear her weight on the left leg for six weeks. Within a week of her injury, she had become quite proficient on crutches. One evening, during the third week of her convalescence, a bull escaped from his stall in the barn, knocked over a lantern into dry hay, and started a fast-raging fire. Barbara became trapped in the burning building's hayloft into which she had climbed in spite of specific instructions by her father never to go up there. At great risk to his own life, Gunnar saved Barbara's life, thereby earning her undying devotion and her parents' everlasting gratitude.

Following the fire, Barbara spent the next two weeks in the local community hospital for her burn injuries. Her leg had to be cast with a protective shell of plaster and bandages, molded to protect the broken limb as it healed, and daily dressings were applied to her scalp and neck for first and second degree burns. There were small areas of third-degree burns, which eventually needed grafting. She still exhibited these permanent scars.

The next summer, at 14-years-old, Barbara injured her leg again when she once more fell out of her shady, oak-tree playhouse. This time she needed a full-leg cast due to the severe spiral fractures of her right leg's fibula and tibia bones. She could not bear any weight on it for eight weeks. When not working in the fields, Gunnar carried Barbara everywhere she wanted to go. By the third week of her convalescence, she realized how much she liked being carried by Gunnar. That summer she had changed from a girl into a woman and had also started wearing a bra. She suddenly became too old for the oak-tree playhouse.

During the following summer in her fifteenth year, in the daytime, Gunnar taught Barbara to drive the farm tractor. It would have been best to teach her to drive the car during the day, but warm summer evenings were the only time Gunnar had time to teach her. Gasoline was rationed during the war, so they had very little gas for driving the personal vehicle. Subsequently much of her lessons took place with little actual movement of the car itself, but considerable movement within the car.

By the summer of her sixteenth year, Barbara and Gunnar were deeply in love. With the war finally over, Gunnar was scheduled for repatriation back to Germany in September. Instead, with her parents blessing and a Lutheran Church minister officiating, the couple quickly married in Lewiston, Maine, a week before Gunnar's ordered departure back to his homeland. He still had to be sent to his old home in the British Occupied Zone of

West Germany, and it took almost three years before Gunnar could obtain official permission to return to the United States as an immigrant considering his marriage as a qualifying factor. Once he returned to Maine, and working part time, it took Gunnar eight years to finish his pre-medical studies at Bates College in Lewiston and three more years of full time work on Barbara's family's farm to save enough money to start medical school.

By the end of the first semester of Gunnar's second year at the medical college in Kirksville, the couple's savings were gone. The family lived on Barbara's wages as a secretary at the school and on earnings she and Gunnar brought in from their puppet shows. Gunnar had constructed a miniature, temporary portable stage they could attach to the back of their Volkswagen van. Most weekends and all school vacations were spent touring small towns of Missouri, Iowa, and Illinois, putting on puppet shows for the public. Besides the usual Punch and Judy characters there were numerous other puppets Gunnar had made. Many of them were of religious significance, and frequently the local parishes of the Lutheran Church Missouri Synod would sponsor the couple.

"Do you know about our puppet show in Essex this weekend?" Barbara asked Gerry. "We'll be putting on two shows at the Lutheran Church on Saturday evening. I hope you and Sharon will be able to make it."

"Yes, I remember seeing a poster about it in the front window of the Blue Bell. What will the two shows be about? Knowing you and Gunnar, I'll bet there will be something about the clinic in at least one skit."

"Correct. Gunnar already has a red-headed wig for one of the doctor figures we use as a puppet. It should be a good show. I hope the whole town comes to see it," Barbara said. "We sure could use the money good attendance would provide."

"At least you'll have all the Lutherans there. Maybe if you could put on a skit involving Father Schaub you would draw the Catholics too. For a priest he is a damn good fire chief."

"We have one already with him and a toy red fire engine," she replied while smoothing a stray lock of her shoulder-length hair over the scar tissue of the left side of her neck. "Before we ever put on a puppet show in any small town, we scout the place for local folklore and harmless gossip. Reverend Bishop of the Lutheran Church and a lady who runs the Blue Bell Cafe' gave us enough information to make the evening enjoyable without insulting anybody."

"Sounds really fun," Gerry said smiling broadly in anticipation. "You can count on Sharon and me being there. We'll also make sure Harry comes along too." Gerry thought he would call Sharon to invite her to the puppet show and not say anything about the gynecology lab episode. He would wait for her to bring up the subject if she wanted to talk about it.

Stopping by the split Dutch door of the hospital pharmacy, Dr. Frank picked up four prescriptions he had refilled for specific patients he would be seeing the coming afternoon in Essex. Next he went by central supply, turned in 12 used, glass syringes and needles. He picked up a dozen more newly wrapped and sterilized, checked out three freshly sterilized minor surgery packs, and then headed for his car in the back parking lot of the hospital.

Sharon waited for him at the side of his car. Dressed in a gray skirt with heavy black sweater and short red jacket, she looked great except for the slight edema around her eyes, hardly noticeable as long as she kept her sun glasses on. As soon as she saw Gerry, she ran forward, threw her arms around him, bent slightly and buried the side of her head against his warm wool jacket. They held onto each other tightly for a full minute.

"I guess you're angry with me," Sharon said more as a statement than as a question. She could feel her heart rate increasing with a heavy thud deep in her chest. "My continuing on as a lab subject is something I probably should have discussed with you after we became lovers." Sharon relaxed her hug and straightened up as she spoke. A dryness in her throat made it difficult to continue. Shaking her head, she let her dark auburn curls fall freely around her face and took off her sun glasses. "Please say something."

"Yes, I think telling me might have been appropriate. I know I've never given you a diamond ring, but you do wear my fraternity pin and we are supposed to be engaged. A certain amount of truthful sharing generally goes with serious commitment."

"Could we at least get in the car to continue this conversation? It may be a little too personal to finish in a parking lot. Would you like to go for lunch somewhere close?"

"I would, but I can't. I'm supposed to pick up Harry at Ely's Cafe' in ten minutes. He's having Ely make up some sandwiches for us to eat on the drive out to the rural clinic. "We figured on getting there early today for some elective minor surgery patients. We each have several scheduled for particular procedures." By the time he finished explaining his excuse, Gerry had the Thunderbird unlocked and they were both sitting inside the small sports car.

"Do you want your pin back?" Sharon asked quietly, with resignation and sadness in her voice. She reached inside her jacket as she spoke and felt the gold pin attached to her heavy wool sweater just above her left breast.

"No. Not now anyway," he replied with obvious sadness in his voice while looking directly at her face. He thought by seeing Sharon while she spoke he might better understand what had happened. He needed to find a good reason for her actions, something he might see deeply in her eyes or the set of her jaw or the movement of her mouth. "I just want an explanation. I want to know why you do it. How could you subject yourself to being a naked pelvic specimen for all the medical students to stick their fingers in your vagina? Do you need the money that badly? Does it give you some sort of pleasure? Just tell me why you do it?" Gerry couldn't think rationally about it all. He knew he should but he could not, and his voice became harsher with each cruel question.

"I don't think you really want to know," she replied raising her hands to her face and wiping away the tears starting to form in her eyes. "I think you're just mad about the whole situation right now and just want to yell at me. You're upset and need to vent your anger," she continued, her voice becoming husky as she stumbled in a hurry to verbalize her thoughts. Sharon wanted to make Gerry understand, but she didn't know what to do or what to say. An explainer's lot is never easy, especially when love is at stake.

"Well, I'd be lying if I said I was happy about all of my colleagues and half the junior class having done pelvic exams on you in the last year and a half. I know I should be more objective, but it is hard for a man, even a physician, to be objective about the vagina and pelvis of the woman he loves." Realizing how ridiculous his statement sounded, a small smile relaxing the tension came to the young doctor's face in spite of his anger.

Suddenly reaching across the front seat of the small car, Sharon put her arms around Gerry's shoulder and hugged him closely. "You're not really as mad at me as you're acting, are you?"

"Maybe not as mad. I'm actually quite proud of you for offering yourself as a subject for the necessary education of physicians. But if I'm not mad at you, then you'd have to say I'm mad at fate. I'm mad for the circumstances probably making you sterile, disappointed for the near certainty we could never have children together. It's not your fault and I know it. But it's not mine either," he said in resignation of realizing their problem.

"What do you think after doing a pelvic on me yourself, after feeling all the scar tissue around the only fallopian tube I have left? Do you agree with Dr. Huntley I'll never have kids? Are my dreams of having children fantasies?"

"Did Huntley tell you that? Are you sure?"

"Yes, he has told me that many times. He was there for the surgery and has been my gynecologist ever since. He said the only way to be sure would be to do a hysterosalpingogram where they put dye in one remaining tube and see if X-ray shows the dye as threading all the way through, or if it shows blocking somewhere by massive scar tissue. The nurses say it hurts when they push in the dye, but I'm not scared. I can tolerate pain. I have in the past and am sure I will do so in the future."

"So why haven't you had the test done? What scares you? We could schedule the procedure for next week in radiology, and then we'd both know for certain."

"Because I'm afraid to know. I'm afraid if you knew I could not have children for sure you would leave me. Be honest. You would, wouldn't you?" She asked the question as if already knew the answer.

"It's a tough question. You know I love you as much as I've ever loved any woman, but you also know I want my own children. I've never considered not having them." He rubbed the soft hairline of the back of her neck as he spoke, thankful she had stopped crying.

"It's not a tough question," she whispered. "Not really. It's a simple and direct one. It just demands a tough, honest answer. I deserve to know the answer from you. You have known me as intimately as a man can, objectively and subjectively, you know me as a woman. Don't answer now, but I do want to know within this week."

"That's not a very long time. In fact, it's not much time at all. Don't you think we should both think about this for at least a couple of weeks? Maybe we can make the final decision on April Fool's Day." As he spoke, large raindrops started falling on the Thunderbird's broad front windshield. Within seconds they had coalesced into small streams running down the outside of the glass.

"I have to go now," Sharon replied avoiding his question. "I'm not dressed for rain. Maybe you can stop by the farm on your way back tonight, or I could drive into Essex and have supper with you at the Blue Bell."

"Sounds good," Gerry said as he grinned with approval. "Things will work out. I'll meet you at the cafe' at 6:30. Don't get out of the car here. I'll drop you off under the overhead at the ambulance dock. No sense getting wet."

"Thank you. You do give good service, Doctor, in all respects."

"Now promise me, Sharon, you'll eat something in the hospital dining room before you start work this afternoon. You look like you're losing weight."

"I will eat. I promise. If not lunch, then I'll get a sandwich and a milkshake later this afternoon. I have time for at least a half hour of studying on my accounting homework. We have a big test next week, and I have a lot to review."

As Gerry turned his car hard to the left after letting Sharon out as close to the emergency department entrance as possible, he noticed the blue Ford of Dr. Herbert Huntley pull quickly into the hospital driveway coming to a sudden stop in the physicians-on-call parking stall. Already out of sight, she was halfway up the interior staircase on her way to the clinic office where she worked. Huntley's attitude about Sharon really bothered Gerry. He knew

285

they had dated for a while, and it was now ancient history. Obviously Huntley still had feelings for Sharon, but from her attitude towards him, it seemed she only considered him her gynecologist and perhaps a friend. Though he didn't want to admit it, just the idea of his girlfriend having a gynecologist for a friend troubled Gerry.

Harry leaned against the old oak tree standing on the corner of the block outside the front door of Ely's Cafe'. Rain stopped as suddenly as it had started. Harry held his black medical bag in his right hand, a couple of medical books under his right arm, and a brown bag of sandwiches in his left hand. He stepped down from the curb as the black Thunderbird pulled up next to him.

"Did you call Sharon yet?" Harry asked as soon as he sat in the car before he shut the door. "If you haven't, you had better do it here from the cafe' before we drive out to Essex."

"Shut the door. I've already seen her back at the hospital, and we'll be having supper together tonight at the Blue Bell after she gets off of work." Turning right, Gerry headed the car south, accelerated through second gear, and then shifted into third.

"Maybe I should also take my car. Then you can stay in Essex longer after the clinic closes," Harry offered as he handed his partner a roast beef sandwich from the brown bag.

"Not necessary, old buddy. Anyway I do want to talk to you on the way out to the clinic. Sharon and I have a serious problem, and I don't know what I want to do about it."

"I'll bet it can't be any bigger problem than I've had with women in the past. If you'd like a country boy's comments, let me know. Do you have enough gas in this thing for the trip to Essex and back? I heard the new gas station just ahead at the highway junction dropped their price two cents a gallon last night, and it's my turn to buy."

"Don't worry. It's still three-fourths full," Gerry replied as he turned off the windshield wipers. There was still considerable cloud cover overhead, but it looked like the rain would not start again for awhile.

"About you and Sharon. That good girl loves you like no man has been loved in these parts of the country for many a year. Marry her, start a family, and forget California. Live the quiet life as a country doctor here in Missouri. You will never be financially rich but you will always be romantically happy. In the long run, it's probably a far better choice."

"That's the problem. Apparently Sharon can't have children, and I don't know if I could marry her. I've always wanted to have at least three or four. I can't imagine being married without having a family."

"Wow, are you sure? Why can't she have children?" Harry seemed shocked by the news.

"She had a tube and ovary surgically removed on one side and has enough scar tissue around the other tube to inhibit any chance of pregnancy in the future." Gerry could feel the rage rising within him when he vocalized his fear, while thinking it unfair this tragedy would happen to someone like Sharon. Such a sincerely good person, he knew they didn't come any better.

"So, when did you find out? You must have seen her surgical scars. Have you ever done a real pelvic examination on her?"

"I knew about the surgery since the first time we were in bed together, but I never did a pelvic exam on her until this week. The ovary and tube on her right side are heavily bound down with scar tissue. I doubt the tube could possibly be opened up, and she refuses to have a hysterosalpingogram to find out once and for all. She said she's afraid to know."

Harry suddenly stopped eating his second sandwich of egg salad and lettuce. He carefully rewrapped the remains in the used wax paper and placed it back in the brown paper bag.

"You're right. You do have a real problem."

Neither of the two friends spoke for several minutes. Gerry turned on the car radio already set on a Moberly station, which soon came in loudly and clearly. At the end of a Marty Robbins song he turned down the volume to barely audible, but he still did not speak.

"Could you be happy adopting kids?" Harry asked.

"No, definitely not. I want my own children," Gerry replied. "I don't think I could ever compromise on my desire for having my own kids."

"Then you have answered your own question of what you have to do. It wouldn't be fair to you or to Sharon for the two of you to marry. No matter how much you love her now, the feeling of resentment and disappointment over the children issue would eventually destroy the relationship. Love would soon be lost."

"I'm afraid you're right."

"You know damn well I am." Reaching back into the bag, Harry continued eating his egg salad sandwich. "You only ate your roast beef. Ely knows how much we both like his egg salad so he made a couple of extra big ones today. I've got one in here for you, too. Now eat. In times of crises one has to eat properly to keep up one's strength. Clear thinking takes calories."

"No thanks. I'm not very hungry. Maybe later."

"Other than some massive heartache on both sides, your main problem now is how to bring the affair to a proper end without hurting Sharon any more than necessary. You should concentrate your efforts there. You have Sarah to fall back on for company and comfort."

"Sarah has nothing to do with this, nothing at all."

"Right. Nothing at all," Harry repeated with droll sarcasm.

"No. Really, she doesn't, Harry, at least not in any direct way. I'm sure of that."

"Then you're dumber than you look. Her OB/Gyn resident, Tex, is considerably bigger than you, and he's upset easily. I've seen the plastered-over holes in the Theta House library wall where he put his fist through three years ago when he was only a little bit angry at some noisy freshman pledge. Your heading for real emotional injury no matter what you do. Don't increase your probability of physical injury along with it. Nobody needs that."

"You think I should tell Sharon it's over as soon as possible?" Gerry asked, purposely ignoring Harry's talk of Tex who was too far away to worry about. Gerry had bigger problems much closer needing his full attention.

"Well maybe not this weekend, but soon. And talking about this weekend, Barbara and Gunnar have a big puppet show they're putting on in Essex Saturday evening. I suppose you've already heard about it?"

"Yes. In fact I talked to Barbara this morning at The Ghost's office. Sure hope it's a success. Those folks really need the money. The two of them and their twins are a fine family."

"Talking about good people, did you know they'll donate half of the proceeds of the first Saturday night show to our clinic?"

"You're kidding?"

"No, they always donate whatever they can when they put on a show in a town or village with a rural clinic in it. It brings out a bigger crowd and helps the community."

The partners said little more during the drive to Essex. Gerry turned up the car radio when a Hank Snow number came on. Harry methodically finished the rest of both their sandwiches. As they drove the last two miles into the small village, they saw tractors in local farmers' hillside fields working to break up clods of damp soil. The bottom land was still too wet for such activity.

"Oh, by the way," offered Harry as his partner parked the small car in front of the clinic, "guess who I'm bringing to the puppet show as my date?"

"Joyce Kunz of course. You have been dating her for almost two months now."

"Nope. She asked for one cigarette too many last night and I burned my good tan shirt with the one-handed match-lighting trick. Hate to admit defeat, but I think it's time to stop that stunt, too."

"The Bloodstone girl from St. Louis? Is she home on spring break?" questioned Gerry. "You haven't seen her since February."

"No, not her either. That's on hold for a while."

"Why? You were pretty excited over her a while ago if I remember correctly."

"I was, but it became a question of compatibility," Harry replied. "Compatibility and priorities are where it's at."

"As in sexual compatibility?"

"No, that wasn't the problem, though with her living in St. Louis most of the time, our occasional coupling was more erratic than erotic. What bothers me about her is she apparently thinks my being a good and patient listener requires her to be an unstoppable talker."

"Yes, I can see where that could be tiring - especially a woman who never stops talking but says very little."

"So, I give up. Who are you bringing to the show? Is she a flame from days long ago?" Gerry asked with a abroad smile on his face.

"I'm bringing Purity Jones. In fact I have a coffee date with her tonight when we get back home. I think she has finally forgiven me for the episode in the parking lot, and I've come to gain a lot of respect for her over the months since. She's the best nurse on the surgical wards. All my patients say so, and I sure agree. You know what's funny?"

"Other than life in general?" Gerry replied in a questioning voice.

"Women in general," Harry answered. "They are simply unpredictable, which is the only thing you can predict about them. They always have been and they always will be. But no matter how beautiful, ingenious, sexy, or affectionate they are, damn few realize what they need for the long haul is loyalty and brains. Smart women turn me on, and Purity is one smart lady."

Chapter 10
Last Supper
March 15-16, 1962

Sharon finally arrived in Essex at the Blue Bell Cafe' on Main Street at 6:25 P.M. The noisy supper crowd filled nearly every table in the small cafe'. Above the mixed voices of the crowd the western ballad, Marty Robbins singing *Big Iron* could be heard coming from the elaborate juke box in the corner. Only one stool stood empty at the left end of the counter. Just as she approached it, Sharon saw two men from the Purina Feed Store dressed in overalls and red and white checkered shirts finishing their desserts in the back booth nearby.

"Evening Sharon," shouted Madge from her place in front of the cafe's large black steaming stove. "Doc Frank just called over from the clinic about ten minutes ago. He said he would be no more than 20 minutes late for supper and for you to grab a booth when one is empty. Daryl's booth ought to open up right soon if he'd stop gabbin' and finish eatin'."

"We'll be done here in a few minutes, Miss Olsen," offered the older of the two men from Purina. Daryl is going to have one more piece of the rhubarb pie and I'm gonna' finish my coffee and cigarette while I hear out the other Marty Robbins selection I punched up on the juke box. I suppose you're waiting for Doc Frank?" Noticing Sharon's look of disapproval at his half-smoked cigarette, the man jabbed it out in the ashtray beside him by pushing it around in quick circles amid the gray ashes.

"Yes. It seems when you date a physician you spend a lot of time waiting," she replied with a girlish smile and nervous toss of her head. "Think I'm finally getting used to it now."

"Well he's a mighty fine doctor, Sharon," said Daryl in soft low voice as he looked down at his empty pie dish and waited for

Madge to bring him the next piece. Then after stirring his coffee he continued, "I know. My folks and my good wife and I all go to him when we need any medical fixin'." These were the most words Sharon had ever heard Daryl Dawson say at one time. He graduated in the high school class just ahead of hers and always had been considered the shyest person in the school.

"Shove over Daryl, and let the nice lady sit down with us until we're through," said the older man gesturing for Daryl to move over. The older man was Daryl's father-in-law, and since he weighed 295 pounds no room was left over on his side of the table.

Daryl blushed as he moved to his left and almost upset a large glass of ice water. Sharon grabbed it just in time. They all laughed, though in embarrassment over his clumsiness, the young man's face brightened to crimson.

By the time Gerry arrived ten minutes later, Daryl and his father-in-law had finished supper, paid their bill, and left the cafe'. Sharon helped Madge bus the dirty dishes from the booth's table to the open kitchen and Madge completed wiping down the table and setting up the two new places. "Got your favorite tonight, Doc," she said. "Lamb stew and lots of it."

"You know me well Madge," Gerry replied, "and a big bowl of it for the lady, too. I'm trying to get these cow farmers to appreciate eating some lamb now and then for a little variety. They think beef is the only type qualifying as real meat."

"I've also ordered a good green salad for you to start with," said Sharon. "You don't eat enough vegetables. Maybe you should read more medical books on nutrition instead of surgery."

Neither of them spoke for a few moments while they ate their meals. Gerry grinned warmly and reached out across the table to hold Sharon's hand. A smile came to her face and her fingers quickly squeezed tightly against his before relaxing. The unmistakable awareness of each other's touch created the aura of quiet intimacy. Sharon was a beautiful person in all respects. She was everything a man should want in a wife, if the man did not want children. But Gerry wanted children, and suddenly he knew without a doubt Harry was right. No matter how much love he now held for Sharon, his feelings of resentment and disappointment over her inability to become pregnant would eventually destroy any attempt at a lasting relationship with her. He would soon have to tell her, but not tonight.

"Can you stop by the farm for a while on your way back to the city this evening?" she asked hopefully in a voice demonstrating unabashed vulnerability. "It doesn't look like you're too busy at the medical clinic this evening. In fact, I only saw three cars parked outside when I came into the Blue Bell."

"No, that's not the problem. We should easily be finished by 8:00 P.M., but I gave Harry a ride today in my car, and he promised to be back for late evening date with a new girlfriend. I don't want him being too late because I know he has a tonsillectomy patient scheduled for early surgery tomorrow with one of the ENT residents."

"That's right," Sharon replied. "I forgot you only brought one car down here today. Will you be staying over in Essex Friday night after the clinic closes?"

"Is that an invitation, I hope?"

"It sure is," she answered quickly without any flirtatious verbal sparring. "My dad may be staying down in Moberly for the weekend helping Aunt Helen and her husband build the new garage they have planned for their house. Will Harry be seeing Trish Bloodstone on Saturday?"

"Why do you ask?"

"Well, I heard today he and Joyce have just broken up and I understand Trish will be home for the weekend from St. Louis. I haven't seen her here in town for at least a month, now that I think about it."

"No. Harry has a new love interest, and I doubt he'll be dating Trish any more, either here or in St. Louis."

"Who then?" Sharon asked with enthusiasm. She liked Harry as a friend but thought he needed a woman with less expensive tastes than Trish Bloodstone who was too spoiled by her parents' obvious wealth.

"Well, not an entirely new interest. Actually he's liked this particular lady for a long time. He will be with Purity Jones, R.N. on Saturday.

"I think she's neat. Good for Harry. Tell him I heartily approve, even if she's not from Essex. Did you know she used to be a really good basketball player for Greentop High? She could have played girls varsity for the teachers college. The coach wanted her, but she had no time with all her part-time jobs."

"No kidding? I've talked to her a lot but I don't remember her ever mentioning anything about basketball."

"There is a lot more to that young woman than meets the eye," Sharon said with a meaningful grin on her face. "Though what meets the eye is all some of you guys ever see when someone is as pretty as she is and fills out a sweater as fully."

By the time the young couple finished supper and had talked about things of local and academic interest to both of their schools and work they had discussed nothing about the problem now critical to their relationship. Obvious to each of them was the other pretending as if the revelations in the gynecology laboratory had never happened. Soon enough they would have to face the reality it had brought home and crucial decisions must follow. Without being verbalized, this thought lay heavily on their minds.

The young couple held hands as they walked across the village's quiet street and then headed west to the clinic on the corner. Waiting until a slow-moving pickup truck passed them, they embraced in a warm hug and kissed passionately. Neither spoke as they held each other closely until interrupted by the headlights of an approaching car. Letting go of her, Gerry watched silently until Sharon entered her car and drove out of sight before letting himself into the medical office.

Three more patients waited to be seen before the young doctors could head north and back home for the night. Two of Harry's patients were scheduled for student athlete physicals before being permitted to try out for the high school varsity baseball team. The remaining patient scheduled for Gerry was Rudy Baker. He had been having considerable local discomfort in the upper lateral fleshy part of his left leg. It bothered him to drive his tractor, and the pain had become worse during the past week.

"So what do you think it is Rudy? Did it come on suddenly?" Dr. Frank asked, he had a bad habit of asking two questions before the patient could answer the first one.

"Well Doc, to tell the truth, I've always had some discomfort in that part of my thigh whenever I overuse the leg or sit too long on a jouncing tractor. It has been going on at least since I was wounded in Korea back in the early fifties. I wonder if it could be old shrapnel finally working itself out? I know the surgeons in the field couldn't remove all of it when I was wounded."

"Let's take a look. Sometimes it takes years for a deep foreign body to work itself free, and sometimes the body isolates it harmlessly behind scar tissue, and you can carry it forever. Take off your boots and pants and lie down on the examination table."

"Should I lie on my back?" Rudy asked after partially undressing as requested.

"No. It will be easier to examine the area if you lie down on your right side with your left leg on top."

There were numerous scars from the old wounds on Rudy's left arm and left leg. Closer examination with deep palpation of the farmer's left lateral quadriceps muscle revealed a firm, well-demarcated mass about two inches in diameter.

"That's it Doc. You're right on it now. How about cutting it out this evening?"

"Are you sure you want me to do it now? It may smart a bit afterwards, even though I'll use a local anesthetic for the procedure and give you some pills to take afterward for the pain."

"Yeah, Doc. I've carried that damn war souvenir around in my leg long enough. Take it out."

"Okay, but someone else should drive you back to your farm when I'm finished," Dr. Frank replied, pleased for the opportunity to do a little surgery. "Anybody still in town who might be heading home out your way? You live off County Route J, right?"

"Right Doc, and Daryl can give me a ride. He and his wife now live on the small farm just north of us. Fact is, I anticipated that and dropped by the Purina Feed store on my way over here to ask him. He'll be coming by here to pick me up before he heads home. I've already told my wife Bridgett not to wait on supper for me. She sure has her hands full lately with our new boy."

Minor surgery can sometimes not be quite as easy as a young doctor anticipates. The doctor surgically scrubbed the patient's leg with Phisohex soap, draped the area with sterile towels, and injected a local anesthetic with epinephrine, which helps minimize local bleeding. Dr. Frank did a ten-minute hand and forearm soap scrub and then gowned and gloved up. He started the surgery by making a two-inch-long vertical incision over the spot where he felt the hard metallic mass imbedded. Local bleeding was minimal except for a small artery which the doctor easily clamped with a sterile hemostat and then quickly cauterized. The scar tissue of the old wound, however, was much more than the doctor had anticipated. Now was no time to let his ego interfere with his work. Any patient should always receive the best medical service possible under the circumstances. "I'm going to need a little help on this one from my partner. Mind if I call in Dr. Thompson?"

"Not at all Doc, and if you need more help, Daryl will be coming by around eight o'clock."

"Well, we'll try to keep this particular surgery restricted to the local medical community, if possible, but I do appreciate your suggestion, Rudy," replied Dr. Frank as he yelled for Dr. Thompson to come in from the examination room next door.

Within seconds, Harry came into the room with a questioning look on his face. "I didn't realize you had a leg amputation scheduled for late this evening. Do you need any help?" Without waiting for an answer, Harry started a surgical scrub of his own hands and forearms after taking a quick look over Gerry's shoulder at the exposed incision in the patient's leg.

"You medical guys are really funny sometimes," laughed Rudy. "But please remember I walked in here this evening and I plan on walking out when you're through cuttin' on me."

"Are we looking for anything in particular?" questioned Dr. Thompson. "How about giving me a hint. What are we looking for, Rudy?"

"Pieces of an old Red Chinese mortar from Korea, I'm afraid," Rudy replied. "I've been carrying it for far too long already. Go for it guys."

"If you would glove up and use the retractors, Dr. Thompson, I would appreciate it," suggested Gerry. "I will have much better visualization. There is a lot more old scar tissue than I had first anticipated."

"No problem," Harry replied, spreading the incision apart with small rake-like retractors he picked up from the sterile green cloth on the Mayo stand. "See if you can separate the deeper layers with blunt dissection first, but you may have to do some sharp resection to get down around the lower borders of the foreign body."

The wound needed sharp resection, but with Dr. Frank's careful persistence and Dr. Thompson's helpful assistance, they fully removed the large piece of metal and had the patient's fascia and skin closed before 8:00 P.M. As Gerry started putting the exterior sterile dressing on the patient, Harry went back to his office to finish the physical exam of the last baseball player. They nearly finished another rural clinic day's work. Gerry put ten Empirin with Codeine tablets into a small brown medicine bottle for Rudy to take - one pill every four to five hours, as needed for pain when the local anesthetic wore off.

By the time Daryl arrived to drive Rudy home at 8:10 P.M., Harry had finished his examination of the new third baseman for the Essex High School varsity team. Within five minutes of the patients' departure, the two young doctors had collected their medical instruments, shut off the interior lights, walked outside into the damp evening air, and locked the heavy front door behind them. Carefully they stowed their small black medical bags in the Thunderbird's trunk before getting into the stylish sports car.

Gerry drove over the Clariton River bridge heading east before they spoke as they were both deeply into their own thoughts.

"Mind if I make a suggestion old buddy?" Harry tactfully asked.

"No, but I know what you're going to say. You're going to tell me at first that looked like a minor surgery, but it was a two-man job from the beginning if I had adequately thought about it."

"You are partly right. What I want to suggest for your consideration is there is no such thing as a '*minor surgery*'. If you're doing it or it's being done on you then everything is a major surgery. There are minor surgeons, however, and you are too fine a physician to let yourself get caught in a trap."

"And I almost was trapped. Is that what you are saying?" replied his partner with slight irritation in his voice.

"You just didn't think far enough ahead. In an emergency it's different. You have to go with what you have. Seconds may count and mean the difference of a patient living or dying. But elective surgery is different by definition. No matter how small it may seem at first, you should take your time and anticipate potential problems before they happen. The only way you could have properly done that procedure as a one-man job would be to use small self-locking retractors or to extend your incision to twice the size it needed to be if you didn't have them."

"And our clinic does not have them along with a lot of other stuff we could use."

"Right on, old friend. So it automatically made it a two-man job. One of us had to hold the small, old rake retractors to give the other the proper visualization. Always remember, sometimes in surgery, having an extra pair of hands can go a long way to make up for not having the best and the latest equipment."

"Well said, old friend. Tonight's experience taught me a good lesson. I won't forget it. But what are our chances of getting a few extra dollars to buy some more surgical instruments for the clinic? What we have is basic and adequate, but we could sure use a lot more."

"Now think about it for a minute. Every surgery we do out here in the rural clinic, especially an elective procedure, is one fewer done in the medical school's hospital, either as an inpatient or an outpatient. So we can't expect much help from the hospital for expanding our surgical capability on the local level."

"The puppet show could really raise some money for the clinic," replied Gerry with new enthusiasm in his voice.

"Now you are thinking. You and I both like surgery, and I know a doctor's widow in Quincy wants to sell a good used set of very expensive surgical instruments owned by her deceased husband. If we can sell enough tickets for Gunnar and Barbara's show, we could buy those instruments for the clinic."

"But what about The Ghost? Would he approve?" asked Gerry apprehensively.

"Who knows? He used to have a pretty fair sense of humor and was quite understanding when sober, but lately his drinking is out of hand. I'm afraid he's going to kill himself soon in an auto wreck on a rural clinic run some afternoon."

"Yeah, I'm thinking he's an accident about to happen."

"It is really sad, because in the beginning, he certainly did an awful lot of good for this rural clinic program. But now he is living on reputation and his latter bad behavior is quickly cancelling out his formerly good behavior. By the way, are you going to take this curvy road all the way to Atlanta before cutting north on Route 63? The sharp curves may be fun to drive in this sports car but they sure interfere with serious sleeping."

"No, I thought I'd cut north on Rural Route 3 and then take old 156 into LaPlata. We can pick up 63 there, and that's a much straighter drive."

"Sounds good," said Harry leaning back in his seat. "Wake me up in LaPlata. I'm supposed to have a coffee date with Purity when we get back to the city." Harry fell asleep within a minute and Gerry turned the Moberly radio station on faintly for some music to keep him company. The night had cleared with a bright moon and very few clouds filled the sky. The well-tuned engine of the low-slung Thunderbird made it a dream to drive. With the special overdrive cutout switch Gerry had installed on the car's floor-mounted gear shift, he could easily switch in and out of free wheeling when he drove.

Harry slept soundly and Gerry did not wake him until he was well into the city and almost at Ely's Cafe'. "Wake up, old buddy," Gerry alerted Harry.

"Are we home already?" Harry responded through a stretch limited by the small confines of the car.

"Just about, and Purity is probably anxiously awaiting your expected arrival. Is your car at our apartment or in the parking lot of the cafe'?"

"It's at Ely's place. Drop me off there on the corner. Boy, will she be surprised when I'm the perfect gentleman tonight. This should be interesting. I'm not even gonna' kiss her. She's gonna' have to beg for it."

"Goodbye, goodbye," said Gerry still laughing as he let his friend out at the corner across the street from Ely's and then turned east on Jefferson Street. Three blocks later, he arrived home at his apartment. After retrieving both medical bags from the trunk he made sure to lock the car and then started up the front walk.

Gerry did not see her until he climbed the four steps to the large outside porch running around two sides of the old, gray-shingled building. She sat on the weather-beaten porch swing hanging by chains attached to a large overhead crossbeam. "I hope you're going to invite this tired working girl into your house. She's been patiently waiting here in the dark for you for the past 20 minutes, and this old swing has almost put her to sleep with its restful rhythm."

"Sarah. What are you doing here sitting out here by yourself?" he asked with surprise in his voice.

With a sly mischievous smile, she looked Gerry up and down from head to toe. She replied, "Waiting for you, dummy. Isn't it obvious?" Slowly she undressed him in her mind as she fantasized what pleasure the next hour might bring.

"Here," he said, handing her one of the two medical bags. "Hold on to this until I get the keys out of my pocket and open up the place." As soon as they were inside, Gerry turned on the lights in the front living room and took Harry's medical bag from Sarah. He then stowed both leather bags under the combination bar-bookcase, which sectioned off the room - leaving the back half for his bed and dresser. Taking off his jacket he threw it on the brown plaid spread of his double bed.

"Interesting place you and Harry share. I take it your bed is in the corner, but where does your roommate sleep?" Sarah asked as she followed Gerry through the front room and into the kitchen. "Oh, I see," she said, answering her own question as she passed Harry's bed inside the entrance to the back room. "So Harry, the food-hound, really does sleep in the kitchen next to the refrigerator?"

"Be kind now and watch your manners. This place only has two rooms with a bathroom off the kitchen. Originally the house had been a big private residence, and about 20 years ago they converted it into five apartments with a couple of private rooms as it is now. We use the front room as a living room/bedroom combination and the back room as a kitchen/bedroom combination. That way we have at least some limited privacy."

"The kitchen is actually bigger than the front room," she said walking around to the sink and stove area.

"Right, so we also have both of our desks in the kitchen. In the winter it's too cold to do anything in the front room besides sleep, but it stays nice and warm back here with the large radiator and the gas stove. If I'm up late studying and Harry wants to sleep, he just shoves his bed forward eight feet into the front room and sleeps behind the bar."

"Well, I have to admit," Sarah smiled, "it's neat and clean, but obviously from the furnishings, it looks like a bachelor pad. At least you have two rooms. Bet it's easier if one of you wants to socialize with a girlfriend some night, as I am sure you both frequently do." She sounded simultaneously amused and intrigued as she finished the sentence.

"Have to confess it may have happened on occasion," replied Gerry opening the cabinet above the counter, pulling down two thick glass water tumblers and setting them on his desk. "My desk also doubles for a kitchen table. In fact, it's a converted picnic table bought at auction after they made improvements at the Thousand Hills State Park. Hope you don't mind sitting on a bench. Do you want a cold beer or some wine?"

"I'll take a Busch Bavarian if you have one," she replied sitting down on the far end of the bench and straddling it to face him.

"No problem," Gerry said reaching into the refrigerator and handing her a bottle. He also rummaged around on the lower shelves until he found Ritz crackers, celery, and two kinds of cheese. Then, opening and pouring both the Busch for her and a Miller for himself, he took off his tie and joined Sarah sitting on the other end of the bench. He straddled it and faced her as he drank from his glass. He filled the cavities of two pieces of celery with cream cheese, handed her one and quickly ate the other. She ate only half of hers before laying the rest on the table next to the plate of crackers. Sarah wore a light blue skirt and an oversize lavender pullover sweater. When she sat on the bench with one leg on either side, her skirt provocatively rose to well above her mid-thigh level. She seemed to realize this but made no attempt to pull it down over her bare legs.

304

"If your skirt were up any higher, I could tell the color of your panties," Gerry said with a grin, reaching for his beer again. Setting it down after finishing half the glass, he spread cream cheese generously on three Ritz crackers and handed Sarah one. He ate the other two before she answered.

"If your eyes were better or your glasses stronger you might realize by now that I'm not wearing any panties. And, though I appreciate the beer and the goodies, they weren't exactly the goodies I came here for. How long do we have alone here before Harry comes home? I can have my fill of cheese and crackers back at my trailer."

"Maybe you and I should have a small talk first," said Gerry, though the effect of her appearance and comments already stirred excitement deeply within his groin.

"What's to talk about? I want you again, and from the obvious bulge now developing in your tight pants, I'd say the feeling is mutual. Let's get to it. Why waste valuable time?"

"I thought you only talked dirty in bathrooms and bedrooms. I thought you acted like a nice girl in kitchens and living rooms."

"Well, the setup of your apartment has confused me. I'm not sure if this room is more of a bedroom or a kitchen. But we can always move into the front room if you prefer. When does Harry come home this evening?" she asked again. "I'm serious."

"I believe you are, Nurse Hall."

"I've been thinking about this all day long and I hope it's crossed your mind at least once." Reaching out, she grasped Gerry's right hand and placed it under her skirt high between her legs. She surprised him with how moist she was already. Gently he slipped his middle finger deep within her and then gradually forced in a second one as she willingly pulled her skirt up to her waist and spread her legs wide on either side of the smooth bench. Slowly, with intermittent pressure he grasped her clitoris between his thumb and index finger and steadily stimulated her until her pelvis responded in rhythmic motion. He could feel the metallic gold ring against the side of his thumb but was convinced she would soon cum without need for it to be pulled in any fashion.

"Take off your pants," she whispered in a husky low voice.

"I need to be fucked here and now. Take them off," she pleaded as she pulled her loose sweater off over her head and leaned back against the wall. Perspiration formed on her braless bare breasts.

"Later," he replied bending forward and licking her skin just above her pubic hair line. "This one is just for you. Now lean back and enjoy it."

"But your cock, your cock, I need it. Please Gerry," she begged, "let me have it. Let me have it. Don't you see I need it now? Don't make me beg any more," she pleaded making no attempt to minimize her tumultuous passion.

"Later Sarah. Now relax and stay there." Slowly he straightened up, stood up and started undressing himself.

She stayed extended almost flat lengthwise on the bench, but her shoulders and head leaned against the wall behind her. Her legs were now spread widely apart. Reaching down to her feet, she kicked off her loafers and slipped off her white bobby socks, quickly throwing them under the table. Her only remaining clothing was the short light blue skirt perched high around her waist.

As Gerry undressed he dropped his clothes all over the apartment, and he quickly walked around both rooms to turn off all the lights except a lamp on Harry's desk. He purposely left his pants on the floor just inside the front door as a signal to Harry, should he come home early and open the door, signaling a few minutes wait would be required before entering the apartment.

Grabbing a folded blanket off the bottom of a shelf, Gerry threw it on the floor at the opposite end of the bench for Sarah's head. Putting her legs together, he lifted up her buttocks and slipped off her soft cotton skirt. Then he pulled her down lengthwise and flat on the bench as he once again spread her legs widely apart as he sat between them. *Sex in uncomfortable positions is unnecessary when all it takes is a quick, satisfactory rearrangement of the surroundings,* he thought as he once again reached between her warm thighs.

Sarah's cheeks now flushed bright pink and her anticipation made her even more moist during the wait watching Gerry walk naked through the apartment. She had also been pulling on her own nipples, which were now considerably larger and much more tender than when she first sat down. Within three minutes of his tongue finding her clitoris Sarah came. With his mouth on her, her orgasm of previously unknown intensity threw her into a unfathomed depth. Her hands did not once look for her ring as they were too busy rubbing Gerry's hair and pushing his head back and forth between her legs.

"So you can cum without pain," he said proudly, "You can cum without ever pulling your damn ring, and we just proved it once and for all."

"Yes, it was great," she said while trying to catch her breath. "In fact it was great, but it was not real fucking. You've got a huge hard on and I need to feel your big cock inside me. I need it now and you need to be inside me."

"Why don't we take a break, get dressed and drive out to your trailer for the night? Harry might be coming in here at any moment. I'm starting to feel nervous."

Sitting up, she smiled and reached out for his testicles and penis. With both hands, she gently drew him close. A strand of soft blond hair fell down over her forehead. "I'm not going anywhere, Doctor, until I've sucked on this for a while." Looking down at her upturned face as he stood naked in front of her, Gerry could see the pupils deep within her blue eyes visibly dilate with pleasure as she licked the end of his penis and drew as much of it in as she could into her warm, wet mouth. Gently he stroked her hair as she sucked him off, but just before he came he reached down and firmly seized her breasts in his hands. As his spasms of ecstasy ceased, Sarah swallowed all of his sperm not letting any escape over the lips of her soft mouth.

By the time Harry arrived home just past midnight, Sarah and Gerry had showered, dressed, and shared another beer. Then they had cooked and ate a hearty omelet. As they finished washing the dishes Harry came into the kitchen through the front room. He tried not to look too surprised, though his concern for his friend briefly clouded his face as he took off his jacket and hung it up on a hook beside his bed.

"So, how did your big date with Purity go?" Gerry asked with enthusiasm in his voice after pleasantries were exchanged between them all. "Did you have a good time?"

"Fantastic," Harry replied as he sat in the apartment's only soft chair and leaned back comfortably in pleasant contemplation of Purity's charms. "I think I'm in love. Now I know what you're both thinking, but this time I really mean it. Not only did we not eat at Ely's but I actually took my favorite nurse out to Elaine's Inn for a late steak feast. That may be my first meal with her but I'm betting it won't be our last together. So, what did you folks eat this evening?"

Chapter 11
The Ghost
March 24-25, 1962

Doctor Tripton T. Casper drove his black 1956 Plymouth sedan south on U.S. Route 63 toward the small village of LaPlata, Missouri. The generalized headache he had woken up with in the morning gradually subsided. He swallowed two pink Darvon 65 capsules just before leaving home and their analgesic effect had finally kicked in. *Thank God*, he thought, *for the pharmacology industry in general and Eli Lilly in particular*. Temporary relief for his problems came from ingesting only a couple of pills. He wondered how many it would take to cure all of his troubles forever.

Dr. Casper momentarily slowed his Plymouth and he came up behind a big red semi-trailer truck loaded with squealing hogs, the good doctor reflected on this latest headache. He knew very well what had caused it, and his body asked his brain how he could continue to treat it so poorly. He had been drinking excessively again. These morning headaches came on more frequently and severely over the last two months. His binging also caused his blood pressure to elevate. One did not have to be a genius or a physician to figure out the correlation between his problems and his pain. His body and his brain demanded relief for his craving for alcohol right now. Two or three fast shots of vodka before starting out that morning might have helped his head, but he knew the liquor would raise hell with the burning he felt deeply in his stomach. Even the white liquid Maalox he had taken an hour ago had failed to extinguish his acute gastritis discomfort. *That's all I need*, he thought, *another activated peptic ulcer bleed. Life sure is getting complicated.*

Quickly Casper accelerated around the market-bound hogs and concentrated on the straight stretch of black-top road ahead. He ran behind schedule to monitor the rural clinics. Many physicians are deeply in denial about their own health problems - and Casper was no exception in spite of being a smart man. He had always been able to rationalize the big difference between a controlled alcoholic and an uncontrolled one. He realized his own alcoholism but he considered himself one of the former type, since he could frequently go many weeks without drinking any liquor at all. Even when he fell off the wagon, he never drank before noon. Less than an hour away from noon, Casper counted down the minutes. Like many a drinker, he suffered from the delusion he could control his addiction.

Many years earlier Tripton had admitted to himself he was an alcoholic. He had 'dried out' on three extended occasions in the prior 15 years by committing himself to the psychiatric sanatarium in Macon. He still shuddered when he remembered the huge copper metal doors of the facility slamming shut behind him and the isolation he felt on being locked into his room every night. Having been registered under a false name in a special isolated wing of the sanatorium, his convalescence had been a fairly well kept secret, though certain members of the faculty and of the medical school administration knew of his problems. With the medical school being a very close-knit community fiercely protecting its own, little ever was mentioned of these episodes outside of personal consultation with his psychiatrists. The staff personnel of the mental health departments were excellent, both at the medical school and at the psychiatric sanatarium in Macon. With their assistance, Dr. Casper at age 56, still functioned as a useful and knowledgeable physician.

On the road to LaPlata in quick succession, he overtook and passed two small pickup trucks also filled with live hogs heading south. *Must be an auction in Macon this afternoon,* he thought. If he had the day off he would have liked to go to the auction. Tripton was still a good old country boy at heart. Unfortunately he had married a city girl, Rosalyn, a fine woman five years his junior. She taught English at Novinger High School for the past 26 years. They were not been blessed with any children but otherwise life had been quite good for them. They lived comfortably in a neat, one-story brick home just outside of the town limits of Novinger, and they played a passive role as aunt and uncle to the seven children of Rosalyn's two younger sisters.

Now overweight with 230 pounds packed on his sturdy 5'9" frame, it was hard to imagine Tripton had once played left tackle for the varsity football team at the teachers college. Only his wide, brawny shoulders and thick neck gave evidence of his bygone glory days as an athlete. Occasionally he would get his old college yearbook down from the attic and look at the photos to remind himself of the old days when he was 194 pounds of muscle mass and motivated destruction. His 1927 football team had won the Missouri State College championship in the fall of his senior year. Afterwards Tripton had gone on to graduate in June 1928 and to become a science teacher and the head football coach at Novinger High School.

His interest in athletic injuries first motivated the coach to consider going back to college to become a physician. He finally accomplished this at an age older than most of his classmates, and he graduated from medical school in 1941 soon after his 35th birthday. Still single without family obligations, Tripton had been engaged to the one greatest love of his life during the first half of his senior year at the teachers college.

His fiancee' studied to become a French teacher and finally broke the engagement when she became worried about his heavy drinking, though at the time it had been confined only to weekends. She later married a teammate who played left halfback on his football team. After college graduation, the newlyweds moved to the halfback's home and farm in the village of Essex.

Though happily married to Rosalyn in Novinger, Tripton often thought of the beautiful girl of his youth and of the young dreams still occupying a lot of room in his mind. When she broke their engagement, she shattered his heart in so many pieces he wondered if he would ever piece it back together completely. He especially thought of her when he drove to check in on the rural clinic in Essex. He still associated his alcoholic problem with her, though he realized this was neither honest nor fair to the fine woman's memory.

Rural medicine had been the life and substance for Dr. Casper for almost 20 years. He once had been one of the best all-around country doctors in Missouri. By the time he finished one year of a rotating internship and an additional year of general surgery residency at Normandy Hospital in St. Louis in 1943, the United States was completely involved in the World War II. The nation's commitment to military medicine produced a serious shortage of civilian physicians in rural areas. Entire counties were without doctors to provide the health care of local people. Casper had a deferment from military service due to a pan-systolic heart murmur originating from an episode of rheumatic fever at age 12. Though rheumatic fever killed a lot of children during his youth, Dr. Casper always wondered how many young boys' lives it ultimately saved when they were ineligible for the military draft. The residual heart murmurs caused by the disease often excused them not only from the draft but also from possible death on distant foreign battlefield - a fate difficult to escape for many who served in the military during the early days of the war.

After filling in at the large general practice for a physician in St. Charles for six months, Dr. Casper had returned to Novinger

Town. He then found himself immediately busy as the only physician in the small Missouri village. He did all of the birth deliveries, all of the minor and some of the major surgery cases, plus the care of the pediatric and internal medicine patients. Only the most serious cases were referred to the medical center in Kirksville for specialist consultation and treatment.

After the end of the war, the era of medical specialization soon increased at an accelerating and unprecedented rate. Many of the young physicians returned from their experiences in the military and went on to specialize in various medical fields. Even the new doctors graduating from medical school were less interested in general practice than the graduates of previous classes. With the gradual movement of populations from small country villages to the large growing cities, fewer and fewer physicians returned to practice in rural communities of those shrinking population bases.

Because of Dr. Casper's love for the small town and the rural village lifestyle in America, and due to his fervent conviction general practitioners were the real physicians, much more so than the supra-trained technologists of the specialties, Dr. Casper was invited to join the faculty of his old medical school, Kirksville College of Osteopathy and Surgery. The college had long emphasized its dedication to producing some of the best educated and well-trained general practitioners in the country. Dr. Casper had been appointed to start the very first Department of Rural Medicine in a major medical school anywhere in the United States. From this small beginning in 1948, the program had grown to one of national recognition. The good doctor had a right to be proud of the innovations in medical education he had started.

So why did he drink? What was Tripton's problem? Did the alcohol merely provide a temporary escape from the stress of work and overwhelming responsibility of the job? After all, he was chief of 12 small rural clinics, spaced throughout Northeast Missouri and staffed solely by senior medical students still in the early learning phase of their careers. No, the students in general did not worry him. Any physician worth his salt always continued the learning phase of his or her career.   Casper rationalized his current problem had started his most recent bout of heavy drinking.

No, it was the Essex Rural Clinic worrying Dr. Casper. He knew Frank and Thompson were on duty on Mondays, Wednesdays, and Fridays, and Woodward and Miller were on Tuesdays, Thursdays, and Saturdays. They were four of the best of his senior medical students, though only two were actually in the top half of their class academically. But all were highly motivated. With the largest rural clinic practice in the history of the clinic, he knew they were very well liked in the small village and were taking excellent care of their patients. But rumors he heard lately had given him cause to think they might be putting the entire Rural Clinic Program in jeopardy. He heard twice of the possibility that besides the clinical care of human patients, these student doctors had established a veterinary medicine practice and actually treated sick and injured animals at outlying farms.

The first time Dr. Casper heard this rumor came two months earlier from a fellow classmate of the senior student assigned to the medical practice in Eden, the rural clinic closet to Essex. Eden, Missouri, a slightly larger village than Essex, was located about nine miles to the northeast. A student known as a perpetual grumbler, Windsor Fox, had complained of a diminishing number of practice calls in Eden for him and his three partners since student doctors in Essex were stealing his patients. Fox claimed they offered the extra service of veterinary medicine for their patients' farm animals. Dr. Casper had not given the story much thought because Windsor always had a big mouth and continually bitched about something. His obvious jealousy of the success of his nearby classmates was apparent. Fox had a reputation as the class snitch, even among the faculty.

But when another teaching physician, Doctor Wiley Parsons, suggested the medical college should buy each of the rural clinics a maroon-colored *Merck Veterinary Manual* to keep next to the blue human medicine version, *The Merck Manual,* in the clinics' small libraries, Dr. Casper started to take the rumors seriously. The clinics didn't need local veterinarians claiming the medical students were cutting in on their animal practices. He considered any medical student who would also practice veterinary medicine would be lowering himself in the public eye and putting all of the clinic programs in jeopardy of unlawful activity. As senior medical students, they all practiced under Dr. Casper and his two staff assistants' licenses as physicians and surgeons. One of the three seasoned doctors visited each rural clinic every day to review all of the current patients' charts and to countersign the latest chart notes and prescriptions. Nobody in the system had a veterinary license.

Dr. Casper did not know, nor had he taken the time and trouble to find out, that the young student doctors in Essex only saw an occasional sick or injured animal on an emergency basis and then only if a licensed veterinarian were not available or not affordable. In fact, both of the vets in Macon and the one in LaPlata had approved of this arrangement, and Dr. Parsons at the hospital had actually donated his personal copy of the Merck Veterinary Manual to the Essex Clinic when he became aware of this valuable service the students occasionally offered to local farmers. For some of the poorer rural folk the loss of a good cow could be an economically devastating event, and the loss of a breeding hog might cause serious financial repercussions for months.

After driving the Plymouth into the paved parking lot of the small grocery and liquor store on the north outskirts of LaPlata, Dr. Casper hurried inside for his purchase. Behind the counter his old friend Charlie Rales worked on solving the crossword puzzle in yesterday's paper.

"Morning Doc, what brings you out on such a fine Saturday morning before noon? Kinda' early for a clinic run isn't it?"

"Morning Charlie. Has my good colleague Dr. Parsons been in yet? I'm supposed to meet him here at 10:30. Guess I'm running a little late."

"He's been here and gone. Had a cup of coffee with me and then said he'd be going over to Ted's Barber Shop for a haircut. Told me to tell you to meet him over there when you came by. Can I get you a hot cup of strong coffee?"

"No. Give me a bottle of cold milk and a fifth of vodka. Milk's about the only thing helping my ulcer from eating a hole through my stomach."

"Well Doc, I'm not a physician like you are, but I'm willing to bet the vodka won't be doing you or your ulcer any good. Did you want anything else? Maybe you should try some baking soda."

"Yeah, here's a five. Also take out for a St. Louis newspaper and some peppermints. And you can keep the unsolicited comments on drinking to yourself."

"Well, I think they're comments worth studying on for a while. We've been friends long enough to be blunt with each other."

"Hell, if you had half my worries you'd be smashed all of the time, too," Tripton said as he picked up the paper, the candy, and his two bottles. Both the vodka and the milk were in individual brown paper bags concealing their contents. "Think I'll leave my car here and walk around the corner to Ted's. Hope Dr. Parsons is still there."

"Take care Doc," said Charlie as he bent over the counter and concentrated again on his crossword puzzle. "You can let your car sit out there in my parking lot as long as you want."

After he rounded the corner, Tripton sat down on a bus stop bench and opened the cap from each bottle. Just out of the Charlie's icebox, the cold milk soon relieved the burning in the doctor's stomach. *It's funny*, he thought, *the best a person will feel on a bad day is when they feel just a little better after feeling really bad for a very long time.* Looking at his watch, he noticed it was not quite 11:45. He still had 15 minutes before he would let himself have his first drink of the day - and some people thought he had a drinking problem. Standing up slowly, he continued to walk along the tree-lined street of the sleepy village to the small barber shop just up the block.

Doctor Wiley Parsons sat in the first chair with his haircut nearly finished. "Morning, Casper. Figured you'd be able to find me okay after you checked in with Charlie. How are you doing?" Noticing the two brown bags in his colleague's right hand, he knew it meant Tripton was not doing well. He had apparently started drinking again - even before noon.

Sitting down in the back of the shop, Tripton took another big swig from the milk bottle he kept within one brown bag before replying, "So why the haircut? It's going to take more than that to make you beautiful. I wanted to get over to Essex with you to talk to some of my old friends there before any of the students arrive at the clinic today."

"You should have showed up at Charlie's on time. Don't blame me. It's my day off, and I'd rather be home on the farm."

"Yeah, I know. Forgive me. My peptic ulcer's acting up again. I'm not feeling too great. Took some Maalox this morning and the cold milk helps," said the doctor as he took another three or four large swallows from the bottle in the bag. Some of the white milk imprinted on his lips and he let it stay there long enough to make sure Wiley saw it before Tripton wiped it off with the back of his hand.

"Looks like you need a haircut too, Dr. Casper," offered Ted as he finished up with Dr. Parsons.

"I'll be done here in another five minutes and then we can start on you."

"No thanks, Ted. It will have to wait until later. Dr. Parsons and I need to be in Essex as soon as possible," replied Dr. Casper as he picked up a Time Magazine and started reading the Letters to the Editor column.

They soon left the small barber shop together, and Dr. Parsons offered to take his new, big white Chrysler on the run to the clinics.

"You must admit, Tripton, it will certainly be more comfortable on those rough back country roads than your old Plymouth. You should trade up at least to a Dodge."

"Good Idea. I'll leave the Plymouth at Charlie's. That way the students won't spot it in Eden or Essex until I want them to know I'm there. It's tough trying to keep a step ahead of them most of the time."

As Dr. Parsons started the powerful Chrysler and headed west on Route 156 out of LaPlata, he worried deeply about his medical colleague sitting next to him. "I'm not buying that ulcer crap, Tripton. You've started hitting the juice again. Bet you have a bottle of vodka in the other brown bag there on your lap, don't you?"

"Just a little, and I don't need any lecture from you about it," Tripton answered as he looked to the north out the passenger window of the car. "It's those damn students and the specter of a clandestine veterinary practice going on in Essex that's got me drinking again. That's the last thing I need to worry about. It could set my rural clinic program back at least ten years."

"Bullshit! That's pure bullshit, and you know it."

"What bullshit? I'm serious. Frank and Thompson are two of the best doctors in their class, but they're jeopardizing the entire rural clinic program for everybody by treating sick animals there."

"Says who?" asked his friend as he put the heavy car into a controlled 40 mile an hour slide as he took a curve in a gravel road marked at 30 miles an hour.

"So says one Windsor Fox - that's who."

"And you believe him? Hell, Tripton, he's always been the class snitch. I sure wouldn't trust him as far as I could throw him, and since he probably weighs 210 pounds it wouldn't be very far. Besides, he's just jealous Essex has a bigger patient-load than Eden, even though Eden is the larger community."

"Do you deny they are treating farm livestock in Essex? You deny it, Wiley?"

"No I do not deny it. In fact I confirm it and agree with it. I think it's a great idea, as long as it is not taken to extremes, and I know those boys are not taking it to any unreasonable extremes. Frank first asked me about the legality of treating a cow three months ago. It belonged to a poor family with no way to afford a vet. They would have faced financial disaster if they lost the animal, and they didn't know what to do. Frank treated it and saved its life."

"So what happened?" asked his friend now completely confused to learn Dr. Parsons not only disagreed with his concern but apparently agreed with the students' actions. "Did you actually help them?"

"I called a couple of veterinarians I knew in the county, but they were too busy with spring lambing problems to do any free charity work with somebody's sick cow. They saw no problem with the medical students trying their hand. After all, most of the local farmers try to treat their own sick animals before they'll ever call in a vet. Farmers can buy all kinds of veterinary medications, from antibiotics to steroids, in large local pharmacies. They don't need a license as long as they're treating their own animals."

"I know all that. But I understand Frank actually charges the farmers to treat their animals. He charges two dollars a visit. Don't you need a license to charge legally - and they're doing it under our medical licenses."

"Relax, Tripton, before you do have an ulcer bleed all over my fine leather upholstery. Frank is smarter than you think. He knows the law better than some attorneys and he's worked out a method not only completely lawful but also advantageous to all parties concerned."

"So what's his method?" asked Dr. Casper, now taking a good swig of vodka from the bottle in the other brown bag in his lap. The dashboard clock of the Chrysler had just switched to one minute past 12:00 noon.

"Like I said before and like Frank quickly figured out, you don't need a veterinary license to medicate or otherwise treat any of your own farm animals. So, Frank makes a deal with the farmer where Frank buys the guy's sick animal, for one dollar. Then, depending on the number of times he sees and treats the animal, at two dollars a visit, he sells the beast back to the farmer after the animal's recovery at the price of two dollars times the number of farm calls plus the dollar he originally paid for the animal. Once Frank pays the farmer the dollar on the first visit, Frank owns the animal. For all legal purposes, he is then treating his own

320

livestock. The farmer willingly provides the necessary veterinary medications and supplies, which he would have done anyway.'"

"And the farmers needing help all agree to this, I suppose?"

"They sure do. Those four student physicians are the most respected and trusted new citizens in Macon County. When Frank saved the Baker's good Holstein after three visits, Rudy Baker was so grateful he insisted Frank take ten dollars when he sold the cow back to the man. Frank flatly refused. Said the price was seven dollars and that's all he would take. But later I learned he and his partner accepted a homemade apple pie Rudy's wife personally delivered piping hot to the Essex Clinic five days later."

"Damn, I thought I had him. I thought I really had him for sure this time. That is clever. It even sounds legal. That boy should have been an attorney. The barrister profession lost a good man when he took up medicine."

"Maybe someday he will also become an attorney. With all the government interference I see on the horizon descending on the medical profession, we will soon need physicians who are also attorneys. Mark my words on this."

"Damn," repeated Tripton taking a big swig from the concealed vodka bottle in the brown paper bag. "Thought I had him for sure."

"It is clever and funny the way Frank and his buddy Thompson do it. Thompson is an old farm boy himself from West Virginia, but Frank tells the farmers he's city bred and considers all livestock, horses, sheep, hogs, etc., as only worth a dollar a piece anyway. Even jokes with them saying he can only just barely tell the different animals apart, the horses from the hogs. He has a great sense of humor," chuckled Dr. Parsons. "I sure do like that boy."

"Of course, the farmers obviously know he's kidding them, but they go along with it," replied Dr. Casper now better appreciating the humor. "Maybe I have misjudged that boy's innovative thinking."

"Right, but he uses his claimed ignorance as an excuse for paying them only a dollar, regardless of the animal or it's condition. Furthermore, it keeps the bookkeeping easy."

"But what if an animal dies on him? Then what?" questioned Tripton. "How does that smart aleck handle that little problem? Face it Wiley, sick animals, just like humans, sometimes die no matter what you do for them."

"Well so far he's been lucky and it's only happened once. A goat got into some barbwire and ate it, and it did die on him," replied Wiley.

"Bet that gave the goat a sore throat and a stomach ache."

"Anyway, the farmer bought the carcass back for the three dollars for the visit and the original sale. Then, after the farmer autopsied the poor animal to make sure it was safe meat, he and his wife invited Frank and Thompson over to their home where they barbecued the goat and ate it. Frank told me later he was sad to lose the goat but an obvious advantage to veterinary medicine is the occasional ability to eat your failures. I sure admire that boy's attitude."

Deeply in thought, Dr. Casper did not reply. Already he felt better and his headache started to clear as his blood absorbed the alcohol directly into his bloodstream from his stomach. "Do you like the group we have at Essex? You think they really are a good bunch?"

"You know damn well they are, Casper. Why are you so down on them? What's your problem?"

"It's Frank. I worry about him. He lacks humility. He's too much California for a Missouri boy like me. I was poor too long to appreciate any student who shows up his freshman year in a

Cadillac convertible and then trades it in his junior year for a Thunderbird. Hell, I'm still driving a Plymouth."

"So you're jealous? Is that what you are saying? Don't you realize he bought both of those cars used and probably for no more than a new Chevy would have cost? Is it out of jealousy you're trying to get something on him?"

"Yeah, partly. But it's more than that, and it's for his own good."

"I don't understand. You will have to explain that one a little more, Tripton."

"I want to get him put on some sort of probation where he won't be allowed to graduate unless he takes an internship here in Missouri and agrees to practice in these parts. Instead he wants to go back to California and become a surgeon - Thompson and Woodward, too. Even Miller wants to specialize in pediatrics. We can't afford to lose our finest students to specialties. We need them as family physicians. We need doctors of this caliber in general practice. That's the whole point of this rural clinic program, and sometimes it seems like I'm the only one around here who remembers this."

"For that reason you would actually try to hold students back against their will?"

"I would with Frank. We need to keep him here. I must find a way to keep him here in Northeast Missouri. You wouldn't understand."

"Okay, tell me the entire story, Tripton. What's going on? Stop swilling the vodka and tell me while you're still sober enough to remember."

"Maybe that's my problem, Wiley. I still can't talk about it when I'm sober and it's been over 15 years since it all happened."

"What happened? I don't follow you."

"Have you ever met the girl Frank is engaged to? Her name is Sharon. She's not just beautiful. She's intelligent, kind, and gracious."

"Sure, Sharon Olson. She's a student at the teachers college and works as a part-time secretary in the clinic. Fact is, I even know her dad, Gustav. Showed some of my prize Herefords against some of his in the Adair County Fair last year.

"Bet he won."

"Yeah, as usual, but I did get the red ribbon."

"Well, years ago I was engaged to Sharon's mother."

"You're kidding."

"Hell, I wasn't fat and mushy like this back then," Casper replied as he took another long draw from the vodka bottle.

"Yeah, that must have been during your football days. I have seen the old pictures of you then."

"I got intoxicated after the big game in Columbia one night. It was the first time we had beaten U Mizzou in five years. They threw me in the drunk tank down there in their jail. She broke the engagement later that month."

"Just because they threw you in jail for getting drunk? Doesn't sound like a very compassionate woman to me."

"No, for staying drunk for almost two weeks afterwards. It was my first severe and prolonged bout of insatiable drinking. She realized then I really was an alcoholic, and even I hadn't realized it yet. I killed a man while I was sobering up in the county jail drunk tank. I've never been able to forget it nor to forgive myself."

"Like murder? You actually killed a person?" Wiley asked in stark disbelief as he slowed the car and turned quickly to look at his passenger.

"No, more like manslaughter, and I wish I were kidding. Oh, I was never arrested. In fact nobody but me realized I was connected to the poor man's death. But I knew. Hell, I could never forget. I still can't. That man's death has weighed heavily on my mind and my soul ever since."

"So how did it happen? Who did you kill?" Wiley asked as he brought the big Chrysler to a temporary stop for a dozen cattle crossing in the road.

"I killed an old drunk I met in the drunk tank. Hell, he wasn't really old. The newspaper later claimed he was only 47 and I was only 21. He had been drunk for most of 30 years, and I swear he looked at least 67."

"I still can't believe you actually killed a man. What happened?" asked Wiley as the cattle cleared the road, and he started the car forward again, steering the vehicle carefully around the last couple of slow moving cattle.

"He sobered up and had a bloody dressing around the right side of his neck. Claimed he had tried to cut his jugular vein to commit suicide. Didn't come anywhere near close to making it. But he had bled a lot and the police took him over to Boone County Hospital to have him sewn up and bandaged before bringing him into the drunk tank."

"Go on. What did you do, tear the dressing off him?"

"Well, I was only a senior at the teachers college, but I had taken a course in advanced first aid, and as a potential coach, I had had a small course in anatomy and kinesiology. The guy made so much damn noise feeling sorry for himself, he kept all of the rest of us in the tank awake all night. I finally told him if he didn't shut up he wouldn't have to try suicide again, I would simply kill him myself. Remember, I was pure muscle and terror back then."

"So, you hit the poor guy? I can't believe you would actually hit a drunk. Did you?"

"No, I wanted to strangle him to make him shut up, but I didn't. However, I was sober just enough to get interested in his damn story of how he tried to kill himself. He went for his right internal jugular with an old half-dull razor in his shaky right hand while turning his head away from his right side and looking to his left. So, of course, he missed the intended blood vessel completely because by turning his head left he pulled the sternocleidomastoid muscle group over the large vessel."

"Which protected it from the half-dull razor."

"Exactly. So when he cut himself he just got a branch of his external jugular vein and not even very well."

"So how did you kill him? I don't understand."

"I stupidly told him how to really cut his own internal jugular. You turn your head toward the side you're cutting instead of away from it. Then it's not protected by that muscle. That shut him up for the night. I can still see him practicing with his bare dirty right hand, head turned to the right as he sat leaning against the cell wall. That was the last thing I saw before I fell asleep that night long ago, and it's been the last thing I see in my dreams before awakening on many a fitful night since then."

"Then you didn't personally kill him that night in jail?"

"No, but three days later I picked up a Columbia paper. On the front page - the story told how the poor drunk successfully cut his internal jugular and bled to death in some back alley off the Strollway. In my head I killed that man just as sure as if I'd strangled him there in the drunk tank."

"Look Tripton, You didn't really mean to kill him. He killed himself. If you hadn't given him a little anatomy lesson that night he would have found some other way to do it. You're being silly. Don't blame yourself for that one."

326

"Do you wanna' hear 'bout the next one...the next one I killed?" Tripton asked with speech beginning to slur and with tears starting to swell up in his puffy blue eyes. "It's...it's an even worse story...even more tragic."

"Not if you keep swilling vodka. You'll be too drunk to tell me anything." Already Dr. Parsons developed a plan. He figured at the rate Dr. Casper drained the vodka bottle, his colleague would be too drunk to get out of the car in either Eden or in Essex. Then he could not do any useful spying on the students and Dr. Parsons would let Tripton sleep off his intoxication in the car while he checked in on the clinics. To facilitate this plan, Wiley had already slowed down the speed of the Chrysler.

"Hey, won't this damn car go any faster?" Tripton asked as he looked up from the two bottles in the brown paper bags on his lap. "I wanna'...I have to get there soon. Have to...have to be at the clinics before those students get there."

"Look here, friend. I'll be damned if I'm going to take a chance of wrecking my new car on one of these stray Herefords just so you can go spy on some of your best students. The students don't need spying on any more than these loose Herefords need hittin'. Somebody's fence must be down close by. We'd better call the highway patrol and let them know right away. It's like an open range up here."

"You're right. Pull inta' the nex' farmhouse. Pick one with phone wires...lines. If this loose beef is not rounded up by evenin', they could total a car that might be runnin' fas' and hit them in the dark."

"Fact is, Tripton, we could hit them ourselves on the way home," Wiley replied. "Time to practice a little preventive medicine."

"Yeah, so...so I... just turn...turn in, right here. It's the Halbertson place. I know them, know 'em well. Delivered their two oldest kids. Musta' been 15, 16 years ago.... Seems so long, so long ago."

As Dr. Parsons drove up the narrow private road toward the gray shingled house in the distance, he debated whether or not he should make the call or let Dr. Casper do it. By the time Wiley reached the farmhouse, his friend had placed the two bottles from his lap onto the car floor, and even before the car came to a complete stop, Dr. Casper stepped out onto the dirt driveway.

That was a mistake. Dr. Casper fell flat on his face. The stupidity of not realizing the car was still moving was hard on the doctor's dignity, but the sharp sudden pain of his left ankle was harder on his anatomy. He had twisted the ankle in the fall.

"Are you okay, Tripton?" asked his friend as he ran around from his side of the car after it finally stopped. Why didn't you wait until I had it fully braked?"

"Because I'm already half smashed and showing damn poor judgment," replied Tripton as he slowly got to his feet and hobbled over to the car. With the door still open on his side, he carefully eased himself back in the passenger seat. "Make the damn phone call. Then let's...let's just get the hell out of here."

Within five minutes, Dr. Parsons had made the phone call to the Highway Patrol. Mrs. Halbertson accompanied him back to the car with some ice wrapped snugly in a blue towel. "Dr. Parsons told me of your fall, Dr. Casper. He said you hurt your ankle and maybe some ice would help. Put this on it right away."

"Thank you very much, Mrs. Halbertson. This is very kind of you...very thoughtful. Don't worry 'bout me. It was my own fault. I'll be okay. Very nice of you."

"Well, I have another wet towel here. Let me wash the soil off your face where you hit the ground," she said as she gently scrubbed the dirt off his left cheek and forehead. "OK, that's better," she said standing back to survey her work. "But get some merthiolate on that abrasion on your forehead when you get to the clinic in Eden."

"I will, Mrs. Halbertson. Don't worry. I'll be okay," Dr. Casper replied as he quietly shut the heavy car door. Within seconds Dr. Parsons had the large car turned around and headed down the narrow rutted dirt road back to state Route 156. "Keep the ice on your ankle. Do you think you broke it?"

"No, but I sure did sprain it. Anyway don't worry. It gives me a whole new excuse to keep on drinkin' today. Besides, I'll be too lame to do much spying on your friends in Essex. So...now for some...some serious drinkin'," Tripton said as he leaned over and picked up both bottles from the car floor. Knowing his stomach needed more protection from the alcohol, he quickly drank half the milk left in the bottle. "What did the highway patrol people say? Do they...do they realize the potential problem?"

"Damn right. I got Sergeant Siegfried on the phone. He said he and his partner, Patrolman Barstow, would be going back on patrol within the hour and would check it out. In the meantime, he would call all the farms and ranches bordering this road for four miles back to find out whose cattle they were. The owner will be responsible for rounding them up and repairing the fence break."

"They're both good men," said Casper as he finally figured how to let the leather seat on his side slant backwards farther, helping him stretch out more. "I've known 'em both, known 'em both for years. Siegfried used to be quite a football player. Played with the University of Missouri. He's big enough to bulldog any damn Hereford himself."

"Patrolman Barstow?" Isn't he the one who helped Woodward and Miller in the outhouse delivery a couple months back?" asked Dr. Parsons, still maintaining a much reduced rate of speed in case some of the free-roaming livestock had wandered this far.

"That's him. That's him. Both he and Siegfried helped." Casper started to repeat himself, slurring his words even more than before. "Now don't you see...don't you see what I mean 'bout the Essex Clinic bunch? Woodward and Miller are naturals for general practice. It hurts...it hurts my very soul to think of 'em wastin' their talent and initiative in some highly technical specialty. What a waste. What a waste," he repeated with tears welling up in his eyes. Slowly he picked up the brown bag with the vodka bottle in it, removed the cap and took a few large swallows. "Now where was I? Where had I stopped in my long tale of woe 'fore we were were so rudely int'rupted by those damn fool Herefords?"

"You were telling me about all of the people you thought you had killed, but I'm still willing to bet that it's not as many as most other doctors. Hell, our ignorance will always kill a few - no matter how much we learn and remember. It only becomes a moral crime when we let our ego and our arrogance kill patients. You're too nice a person to ever do that."

"No, you're wrong. You're wrong, Wiley. I did do it. I let my ego...my damn ego and my arrogance get in the way one time and the young mother died. She died 'cause of it, 'cause of me."

"Do you want to talk about it? Maybe it's something you should discuss with a psychiatrist first," said Dr. Parsons as he slowed the car to turn south on State Route 3.

"No, I think I'm doing better right now discussing it with an old friend and faithful colleague. And the vodka helps too. Never did have much truck with the head shrinkers. Have more faith in vodka."

"So what fine lady did you lose?" Dr. Parsons gently asked.

"I lost Nina Truitt, and thereby left her three-year-old daughter motherless. I lost her to an ectopic pregnancy. She bled to death internally right there in my arms in the back seat of her husband's car as he rushed us to the hospital. We didn't make it...didn't make it to the hospital in time." Gradually the sobs came forth from deep within Tripton's chest as the tears flowed freely down his fat puffy face. As he concentrated on his tale of woe, his speech became clearer as he talked slower.

"Look Tripton, ectopic pregnancies are tough in a rural practice. You have to get in fast and do the surgery. Many of them will bleed to death. That's not your fault. That's just fate."

"No, it was arrogance and ignorance. I knew the young couple well. They had called me out to their place the night before when Nina vomited and had mild generalized abdominal discomfort. There was a lot...a lot of gastroenteritis goin' 'round. I examined her and figured that's probably what she had. At worst I felt...maybe an early appendicitis. She did have some...some mild, right, lower-quadrant tenderness, but no rebound. I swear to this day, Wiley, the woman had no rebound pain." Reaching into his coat pocket, Tripton found a folded white handkerchief and slowly wiped his moist face.

"What did you do?"

"I gave her a shot of Thorazine to stop the vomiting. I thought she would become dehydrated from fluid loss. Thorazine was a new drug back then. It dropped her blood pressure a little but she seemed to do better. Nevertheless, I was worried, I sure 'nuff was. They were good friends, so when they offered me the living room couch to sleep on for the night, I accepted."

"Had you been drinking at all that day?"

"Yes, but not heavily. I certainly wasn't intoxicated, and believe me, I know intoxication as few men do. Doc Weaver had originally been on call for the weekend. I was supposed to have Saturday and Sunday off. Only late Saturday afternoon, poor Weaver was in a car wreck on a bad turn just east of Goldsberry. Broke his right wrist. Suffered a concussion. Ended up in the hospital himself. So we were short on physicians, I had to finish out his call schedule for the weekend. That's where my ego and arrogance interfered. I knew I had a few drinks, and maybe my reflexes and coordination were not 100 percent, but I actually thought my cognitive powers were fine enough to cover his calls."

"Did this Nina lady know you had been drinking?'

"Hell, yes, I'm sure she did, but she was...she was much too polite to say anything. Later her husband told me she had fainted in the early morning while getting up to go to the bathroom. He wanted to awaken me but she refused to let him....Said I needed my sleep and she would be OK. Said not to wake me 'till mornin'."

"But she wasn't. Is that what happened?" Wiley questioned his friend.

"By 7:00 A.M. she was in such acute pain her husband woke me anyway. Her abdomen was guarding and splinting. It was definitely a surgical situation and even...even if my damn hands had been steady enough to open her up right there, I did not have the instruments nor the blood she needed. I started IVs in both her forearms and we rushed her to the hospital in the back seat of her husband's big Packard. I worked on her all the way while he drove as fast as he could. I couldn't believe I was losing her. I didn't declare her dead until we reached the emergency room, but I think...I do think she died just north...just north of LaPlata. I started drinking heavily again that evening. Resigned from the hospital the next day. Two weeks later, ended up almost comatose at the Macon Sanitarium. That was the first time I committed myself. As you know, it wasn't the last. No, it sure wasn't."

"That was a tough one. And you say you knew her? You knew her as a good friend?"

"Even in the biblical sense of the word. Her maiden name was Truitt, but her married name was Olson. She was my fiancee'. Her husband - Gustav - my old football teammate. I'm the reason Gustav raised Sharon alone from the time she was three-years-old

332

without a mother. Now she's engaged to that smart aleck, Gerry Frank, and he's gettin' ready to go back...to go back to California.

"Yeah, I hear that's true."

"But Sharon is a Missouri farm girl. Don't you understan', Wiley? She needs to stay here. She needs to stay where her roots are. I've gotta' keep him here for her. I gotta' get that boy on probation. I owe it to Nina. God, but I failed that poor woman - in every, every way possible." With the last few sentences spoken more slowly than his previous speech and more slurred from the increasing effects of the alcohol, Tripton's head slumped to the side. Finally he fell quiet in a relaxed state of semi-sleep.

By the time Dr. Parsons stopped the new Chrysler in front of the Eden Clinic, Dr. Casper had fallen fast asleep and snored loudly with his mouth half open. Wiley planned to let Tripton sleep it off. Sleeping would do him more good than anything Wiley could do, and it would keep him from interfering with the medical students. Quietly Wiley opened the heavy car door. He left it ajar and walked toward the short front staircase of the Eden clinic.

"Hello there, Dr. Parsons," yelled Windsor Fox perspiring profusely as he opened the clinic door and bounded down the four stairs to the sidewalk. "Boy, is it good to see you here. Is that my good friend Dr. Casper asleep in your car? I need to wake him up and say hello."

"Down, Windsor, down boy. Dr. Casper needs a nice nap now. Just let him be," replied Dr. Parsons in open disgust. He had never liked nor trusted Windsor. It would be just like Fox to foster discontent amongst fellow medical students within the clinics. He was a pompous bore with opinions as damp as his handshakes.

"Let me wake him up. I need to talk to him about those guys over in Essex. That veterinary practice they have going is terrible. Someone with some authority has to shut it down."

"You'll wake him up over my dead body, boy. Now be quiet and come inside quietly before I shut you up and down."

"But...but I...."

"But nothing. Just do what I tell you if you ever want to see Oklahoma again. Now come along." Turning his back on the flabbergasted student, Dr. Parsons walked into the clinic and loudly shut the door as soon as Windsor had stepped inside. "Are there any patients in the office?"

"No Sir. I'm here early by myself. We don't open up for patients today until one o'clock. My partner won't be here for another half hour."

"So why did you come out here to Eden before 1:00 P.M. today?" Dr. Parsons asked suspiciously.

"Dr. Casper's secretary told me he might be out here early, and I wanted to see him privately. Somebody has to do something about those doctors in Essex. The veterinary practice they have going on the side is a disgrace to medicine. Maybe you can help me make them quit. Windsor Fox waited until Dr. Parsons had seated himself before pulling his own chair out from behind his desk and sitting down in the small office.

Dr. Parsons pulled his chair close to the front of the desk and stared across at the student doctor. For a few seconds there was silence. "Why do you really want to shut them down, Windsor? Are they bad doctors?"

"Well...well, no sir, but that's not the issue. They're treating farm animals on the outlying farms of their patients. That's degrading and brings shame on all of us. It's a reflection on you and the other rural clinic staff physicians."

"And a damn good reflection I might say," Dr. Parsons replied in a quiet manner. A damn good one."

"What sir? What did you say?" asked Windsor with his nose suddenly twitching in nervous fear and worried anticipation he might not have an ally in Dr. Parsons.

"I said it's a damn good reflection. Their concern for a few dumb animals is a hell of a lot more sincere and caring than your phony concern for the rural clinic system."

"But sir, I thought you'd be pleased by my bringing this matter to the attention of you and Dr. Casper. I...I just don't understand."

"Well listen up, my young friend, so you won't ever forget what I'm about to tell you," said Dr. Parsons in a loud voice as he suddenly slammed his right fist down on the desk top. The vibration scattered pencils and tipped over a narrow jar of paper clips.

"Yes, sir," replied Windsor with his facial twitch now completely out of control. "Whatever you say, sir."

"I don't ever want to hear even a hint of you bad-mouthing a medical colleague again. Do you understand?"

"Yes, sir."

"I don't ever want you to bother Dr. Casper with this poppycock bullshit again. Do you understand?"

"Yes, sir."

"And I want you to buy your own *Merck Veterinary Manual* and start reading about diseases of hogs. There is some trichinosis in this county, and if some hog farmer ever asks you about how it affects his pigs, I want you to be able to give him a halfway informative answer. Do you understand?"

"Yes, sir. I do understand, sir."

"And just to make sure you learn something about hogs, I'm going to give you a test on that chapter next Saturday. Understand?"

"Yes, sir. Hogs it is, sir. By next Saturday, I'll be an expert on them. You can count on me, sir."

"Now let me see the clinic charts for yesterday, and while I read them, you just sit there quietly and think about this little talk we just had." Reaching across the desk top, Dr. Parsons took the stack of medical folders the student doctor nervously handed to him. Wiley could not help but notice Windsor's facial twitch and felt genuinely sorry for the hapless individual. But he did not feel sorry for having yelled at him. Windsor needed this lesson and Parsons hoped he would learn from it.

It took Dr. Parsons about 15 minutes to finish going over all the records of the previous day. The clinic had seen six patients. The differential diagnoses were well reasoned, and the treatment plans were in-keeping with the well-documented histories and physical findings. "Your group here in Eden does good work, Windsor, including you. You'll be a good physician someday. So quit being a damn snitch. Grow a pair and show some maturity. Talk well of your medical colleagues or talk not at all of them."

"Yes, sir. I appreciate your advice, sir."

"That's better. Now with an improved attitude like this, you just might become president of your state medical association some day. There's a need for a man like you in Oklahoma, and I hear you plan on practicing there after your internship at Tulsa."

"Yes, sir," replied Windsor, now smiling from ear to ear. His nervous facial twitch suddenly disappeared. "My girlfriend is from there, and we plan on making the Muskogee area our home."

About ten minutes later, Dr. Parsons drove his car carefully across the county bridge over the Chariton River. He slowed down the big Chrysler as he guided the heavy car across the rough wooden planks and waved at the two young teenage boys fishing from the edge of the shore bank. The noise of the loose planks banging against each other awakened Dr. Casper from his sleep in the front seat of the comfortable car.

"Where are we, Wiley? Where...where are we?" he said as he sat up straight and looked out the window. "Hey, we've gone way past Eden. Why didn't you stop there? I wanted to see Windsor Fox."

"We did stop there. You slept through it. Now drink up the rest of your bottle of milk before it becomes too warm and spoils sitting there on the floor of the car. You're lucky if it's not turned to buttermilk by now." Reaching down with his right hand, Dr. Parsons grabbed the paper bag nearest to him, fished out the bottle of milk, and handed it to Tripton.

Dr. Casper suddenly felt thirsty while deeply inside his stomach it started to burn again. Carefully he took off the cap and drank about ten large swallows. Next he replaced the melting ice pack closer around his swollen ankle. "Think I did sprain it a bit. Damn, but it's starting to smart."

"Keep the ice on it. I picked up an ace bandage at the Eden clinic. I'll wrap it for you when we get to Essex, but I want your word on something first."

"What kinda' word do you want?" Tripton asked with slow and slightly slurred speech.

"Throw out the rest of the vodka, and stop picking on those students about the veterinary practice matter."

"Well...I didn't know you...you approved of the veterinary stuff. I really had no...no idea. So if you...if you think it's okay, then I'll stop my bitchin' 'bout it. But since I started drinkin' early, my day is already shot, so let me...just let me enjoy a good drunk." By the time Tripton had finished the sentence he had passed out again and fallen back against the reclined leather seat of the big Chrysler.

When Dr. Parsons finally arrived at the Essex clinic, he surprisingly found all four doctors in town. Woodward and Miller were on duty, but Frank and Thompson were there with their girlfriends helping paint one of the examination rooms. They had already finished the ceiling in an off-white color and worked on painting the four walls a light green.

"What do you think of it, Dr. Parsons?" asked Purity, dressed in an old, light-blue jacket. She had green paint spattered all over her jacket and the left side of her face. She had tripped over Harry's outstretched legs and fell against one of the freshly painted walls. "Of course we will have to do the smudge marks over on the wall there."

"Looks mighty good, Purity. It sure is nice to see young people's enthusiasm on your day off."

"Well, Mr. and Mrs. Richly donated the paint," offered Sharon. "They said they had bought too much for their new kitchen and knew we could make good use of it here in the clinic."

"How much longer before you finish the job?" asked Dr. Parsons. "Looks like you're nearly done 'cept for one wall."

"About 15 minutes sir, if the girls will stop gabbin'," Harry replied, now furiously painting over the large smudge spots. "Why do you ask? Do you need something?"

"Yeah, Harry. I need the room for a patient. He's sound asleep now stretched out in my car, but I don't want him seen there when Drs. Woodward and Miller open up for patients in about 20 minutes."

"Right, sir, especially if it's someone people around here might recognize. Let's bring him in right now," offered Gerry Frank who already suspected the patient's identity.

Carefully putting down their paint brushes, Gerry and Harry followed Dr. Parsons outside to his Chrysler parked about 15 feet from the clinic's entrance. With some difficulty, the three men finally were able to lift Dr. Casper from the car and carry him into the clinic. They placed him on the large treatment table in the middle of the newly-painted examination room. The good doctor seemed to awaken for a few seconds, but he quickly went back to sleep with his mouth partially open. He seemed at peace with the world.

"We could finish painting the room some other day, I suppose," offered Sharon in a soft voice as she carefully spread a light brown blanket over the sleeping man.

"That's not necessary. There's no real problem now that we have him safely inside. He won't wake up for hours. Just go ahead and finish the job," said Dr. Parsons.

"His left ankle looks swollen, sir," Harry said as he removed both of Dr. Casper's shoes. "Did he fall recently?"

"There is also a definite abrasion and a contusion developing on his left cheek and the left side of his forehead," said Gerry. "Why don't you strap up his ankle with an ace splint, Harry, and I'll get his vital signs right now. What happened to him, Dr. Parsons?"

Harry already shined a light into Dr. Casper's eyes as he gently spread the man's lids apart. Both pupils responded immediately and equally to the light. Then with an ear speculum attached to the small diagnostic instrument, Harry looked into both ears of the sleeping doctor and found each drum clear with no evidence of blood behind either tympanic membrane.

"Look guys, I do appreciate your examining old Casper here but I've been with him all morning. I saw him fall. He did not lose consciousness then, and I think we all know why he's asleep now," replied Dr. Parsons as he sat down on the side of the examination table and looked at his reclining friend.

"But I don't smell any alcohol Dr. Parsons," said Purity as she bent over the sleeping doctor and wrapped a blood pressure cuff around his left arm. "His blood pressure is now 168/98 and his pulse is 96."

"That's because the good doctor's beverage of choice is vodka. Am I right, sir?" asked Harry as he faced Dr. Parsons. "That's why the alcohol is harder to smell."

"Right son, he drank almost half a fifth between LaPlata and here. And I'm not sure who's the bigger fool. Him for drinking the booze or me for letting him. We were having a talk of some importance, and I thought the alcohol helped him say what needed to say."

"I understand, sir. Could you elevate his left leg while I get the ace splint on him now?"

"Right, Dr. Thompson. Let me hold it up for you." Dr. Parsons held Tripton's injured leg at a 45-degree angle until Dr. Thompson had the ace splint applied and then let the leg rest at a 30-degree elevation on some pillows. "Now lets put the ice around the ankle again to keep the swelling down."

Sharon had stepped aside and gone back to finishing painting the remaining unfinished wall. She felt badly for poor Dr. Casper. She knew he had been the doctor who delivered her as a baby, and she knew far more about the connection between him and her parents than she had ever let on, even to her father.

"Why don't you, Dr. Thompson, and you, Dr. Frank, walk over to the Blue Bell Cafe' for a cup of coffee with me right now? Purity can monitor Dr. Casper's vital signs for a while, and Sharon can finish painting the wall. Seems like she does the most careful painting job of any of you four."

At almost 1:00 P.M. the three doctors walked into the cafe'. A Marty Robbins ballad played on the jukebox. Only a few people were still eating lunch and Drs. Woodward and Miller were just finishing their coffee. Shifting around the half-round bench seat of their booth table, they quickly made room for the newcomers.

"I thought Dr. Casper would be making the southern clinic run today," said Dr. Miller as he signaled Madge to bring over three fresh cups and a pot of coffee. "To what do we owe the privilege of your visit? Don't tell me The Ghost is sick?" All the medical students loved Dr. Parsons. As a way of letting him know of their open admiration and affection for him, they frequently referred in his presence to the other staff doctors by their pet names for them. Dr. Parsons had only recently learned their pet name for him was 'Whistling Wiley,' a habit he had when walking alone, and he liked it.

"We heard he was doing a big investigation of the veterinary practice he suspects we have going on down here. Is that true, Dr. Parsons?" asked Dr. Frank.

"Enough. You guys - enough. Just how big is the veterinary side of what you do down here? Be honest about it now. You can all level with old Doc Wiley."

"Well, speaking for my partner Harry and me, I'd say maybe we see two or three livestock cases a week. The vets don't object and the poor people sure appreciate it. At least we don't mind taking a look and giving an opinion."

"Miller and I might see one or two," offered Woodward.

"It's generally when farmers or ranchers already have us at their place to see a sick person. Then on the way out of the house they ask us down to the barn to see Old Bossie or some lame horse. They really do appreciate our help. So we've all started to carry a copy of the veterinary manual in the back of our cars."

"It's sort of an all-win, no-lose proposition," offered Harry. "If we're right in our diagnosis and treatment and the animal lives, they thank and pay us. If we're wrong we still get paid and sometimes we're invited to supper to eat the unfortunate critter. Come to think of it, we actually do better when the animal dies when it's still edible."

"I'm not sure I want to think of it in those terms," said Gerry, "but I do admit none of us had any problem eating the cooked goat we lost to the barbed wire. Barbecued to perfection, that was surely some gourmet meal."

"I think we had better get back over to the clinic, Woody," said Miller to his partner as he finished up the rest of his coffee and put his cup down on the table. "Time to start work."

"What I wanted to say to you all is don't flaunt your little sideline in veterinary medicine in front of Dr. Casper. I talked with him about it today and he does at least understand, so it's okay to do it. But he still doesn't feel comfortable about it, I can tell. So don't flaunt it, guys. Let it run a quiet course."

"By any chance, did you talk with Fox when you passed through Eden?" asked Woodward. "He is the one trying to create bad feelings around these parts and between the rural clinics."

"Yeah, I sure enough did. Don't worry, he will suddenly have a big change of heart I predict. By this time next week, he should be an expert on hogs if you need any consulting on that subject. Now get on over to the clinic, you two, and do your usual good work. Just don't use treatment Room One today."

"You mean the ladies haven't finished painting it yet?" Miller questioned. "I thought with all four of you working on it, you'd have it done by 1:00 P.M. Can't you two guys keep your hands off your women long enough to get some real work out of them?"

"Just let it rest, Miller. Let it rest right there," said Dr. Parsons with a sudden serious inflection to his voice.

"Yes, sir, you can count on that, sir. Come on Woody. Time to go to work, and stamp out disease."

"Do you want to take a pot of coffee over to the clinic with you, Dr. Miller?" called Madge from the kitchen. "I know how

342

you and Dr. Woodward like to have your coffee handy, and I have some extra left over from lunch."

"Thanks Madge. Don't mind if I do," Wilson replied as he and Dr. Woodward stood up from the table. "Will the rest of you be sticking around for the puppet show Gunnar and Barbara are putting on tonight at the Lutheran Church?"

"Sure 'nuff," replied Harry. "In fact, as soon as we're finished painting the treatment room, we are all going over to the church basement to help Gunnar set up the stage and his props. After all, he's donating half the proceeds to our clinic. See you two guys there this evening."

For the next half hour, Dr. Thompson and Dr. Frank stayed at the cafe' drinking coffee with Dr. Parsons and listening to his medical stories of the old days in that part of the country.

"After I've checked the medical charts and prescriptions at the clinic today, I'd like to drive out to the Olsen farm and take a look at some of Gustav's Herefords. Do you think Sharon could call her dad and see if it would be okay?" Dr. Parsons asked Gerry.

"No problem. In fact I know he's due in town here at 2:00 P.M. to pick up some feed at the Purina store. Why don't you meet him there and drive out with him?"

"Good idea. Casper will probably be sleeping it off for at least the next six or seven hours. Might as well let him do it here. I can visit with Gustav and catch Gunnar's early puppet show at the church before driving back home to Kirksville this evening."

They all agreed, and by the time the three of them walked back to the clinic, Sharon had finished painting the room. She already had cleaned the brushes and most of the spattered paint from her forearms with turpentine. She met them at the door and quietly escorted them all in to see Dr. Casper who peacefully slept and snored with a slight smile on his flushed face.

"His vital signs are good," said Purity. "I think it's safe now to leave him here by himself. Dr. Woodward promised to look in on him every half hour or so between patients."

"I'll just sit here quietly and read yesterday's charts," said Dr. Parsons. "Then I'll see Gustav at the Purina store around two o'clock"

"You mean my dad, Dr. Parsons?" asked Sharon.

"Yes. Dr. Frank said he would be in town then, and I hoped he might take me out to your place and let me see the new prize bull Hereford I heard tell of. I understand the animal has grand championship potential."

"Oh, I'm sure Dad would love to show him to you. He was originally going to Moberly to stay with my Aunt Helen for the weekend. But since the new bull arrived, Dad hardly leaves our place. He claims it's the best breeding stock in the county."

As Dr. Parsons settled down to read the stack of charts, the four young people gathered up their things and left for the Lutheran Church.

The entertaining puppet show played to an enthusiastic full house in the Lutheran Church basement hall at 6:00 and 7:30 P.M. performances. Gerry with Sharon and Harry with Purity attended both shows. Each were slightly different, with the first performance concentrating on the student doctors and the rural patients in general, and the second concentrated on some of the more prominent businesspeople of the village and the two ministers and the priest of the three village churches. The humor was in good taste and everybody enjoyed it, especially the principals whom the puppets represented in their roles and their looks. Dr. Miller saw the first show while Dr. Woodward covered calls at the clinic and then they switched places for the second performance. Woody reported Dr. Casper had only woken up once to use the outhouse and then had immediately gone back to sleep.

But when Dr. Miller checked in on Dr. Casper at approximately 8:25 P.M., he was gone and the examination room was empty. Dr. Parsons' big white Chrysler was also missing. He had left it in front of the clinic all afternoon through the early evening while he visited Gustav at the Olsen farm. Gustav had insisted on taking his pickup when the two of them drove to the farm to inspect the prize bull and some cattle around 2:00 P.M.

"Well, maybe Dr. Parsons came back and picked up The Ghost and they drove home together," offered Harry as an explanation to the two couples who returned to the clinic with Woody at 8:45. "Does seem, though, Whistling Wiley would have let you know they were leaving, Miller."

"No, it didn't happen like that. After I made sure The Ghost hadn't fallen or passed out in the back yard on the way to the privy, I called Sharon's dad to confirm he and Gustav were still out at your place, Sharon. They were and still are," said Miller.

"You mean they're not disturbed by The Ghost just flat out disappearing?" questioned Woody. "That seems kinda' strange."

"Hell, I didn't have the guts to mention Dr. Casper's name to Gustav. Never could figure out what their problem is, but I know they don't speak to each other. The rumor is Gustav threatened to make a real ghost of Casper if he ever found him on his property."

"Yeah, I always thought it was kinda funny," responded Harry, "because they did play college football together years ago. Am I right, Sharon? Did The Ghost miss a block one time and your dad was thrown for a loss?"

"It's a long story, and I don't know it all," answered Sharon as she sat down in a waiting room chair. "I think dad thinks Dr. Casper threw their whole friendship for a big loss years ago. So my dad doesn't permit him on our property, nor does he permit Dr.

Casper's name to be spoken in our home." Sharon had worry on her pretty face as she spoke softly causing Harry to drop his ready smile and to reflect quietly for a moment on what she said.

"Well, did you talk to Dr. Parsons, Miller? Did you tell him his new Chrysler is missing?" asked Woody as he pulled down the window shades to indicate the clinic would be closing even though the inside lights were still on.

"Hell no. I hoped The Ghost would come back any minute. Thought I'd wait for a powwow with all you Indians before making any big chief decisions." Though Miller spoke in a semi-joking way, he worried as much as any of them and perhaps more than the rest of them. As a former military officer, he felt complete responsibility for Dr. Casper's disappearance. After all, he reasoned, it had happened on his watch, and he had not heard The Ghost leave the clinic. Miller had been busy in the other examination rooms seeing sick patients.

Gerry instinctively realized how Miller must feel. "It certainly isn't your fault, Wilson, and I'm not sure we should panic about it yet. Let's spread out. Each of us pick a street and walk the village in the central area for the next half hour and see if we can spot the car. If it's here it will be easy to find. If we don't, we can notify the highway patrol."

"Good Idea," replied Miller. "Gerry, Sharon, and Woody will each take an east-west street and Harry, Purity, and I will each take a north-south one. It should take no more than 20 minutes. Then we'll all meet back here and exchange reports." Gerry briefly stopped in the Blue Bell Cafe', but no one there had seen the white Chrysler leave the clinic.

Purity stopped in the yarn shop at the eastern edge of town on Main Street to talk to the Widow Munster. The widow always kept the shop open until 9:30 on Saturday nights and remembered seeing the car. "She said it was being driven erratically and almost hit the telephone pole in front of her place as it took the right turn out of town heading south," reported Purity.

"So, maybe he is heading out to your home, Sharon, to pick up Dr. Parsons and head back to Kirksville," offered Woody.

"No Woody, Dr. Casper would not dare confront my dad on our property. But it does give me an idea."

"Anything you can share with us?" asked Miller. "Maybe now we do have to call the highway patrol office in Macon. Sure hope Sergeant Siegfried is on duty tonight."

"I agree we have to now," said Gerry, "but first I'll call Dr. Parsons at Gustav's and tell him his car is missing. He's not going to like it one little bit, but we have to let him know. He loves that big highway locomotive." Standing up, Gerry walked into the first examination room where the phone was located and quickly dialed the Olsen farm.

"Anybody have any other ideas?" asked Harry. They all looked at Sharon and waited for her to offer more information on what she had alluded to earlier. However, they all respected her privacy concerning the problems between Dr. Casper and Sharon's dad.

"He may be on his way to Macon for more vodka," offered Purity. "There's no liquor store open this late in either New Cambria or Callao. Why don't Harry and I drive Harry's car the shortest way to Macon, which would be the route Dr. Casper would take if he wanted more booze tonight."

"Good idea," replied Harry, "but let's wait until Gerry and Miller finish their phone calls." As Harry finished the sentence, Gerry walked back into the room looking worried.

"Dr. Parsons took the news about his car surprisingly well," Gerry said, "but he is very concerned about The Ghost. He offered to have Gustav drive him over here immediately in Gustav's pickup, but I thought it would be best to have him stay there with your dad, Sharon, until we know more. I told him we would call back in an hour or so with an updated report. If something really strange has happened to The Ghost, I think it best your dad have an iron-tight alibi for his whereabouts tonight. This way, Dr. Parsons can provide one. Did you say you were ready to call the highway patrol now, Wilson?"

"Right. We've got to do that, but I sure hope we're not getting the poor Ghost in trouble," replied Miller with a worried frown. "He's probably just passed out and is harmlessly sleeping off his drunk in the Chrysler parked somewhere along the highway."

"I think Whistling Wiley is blaming himself for letting The Ghost drink all morning," suggested Gerry, "and for leaving his keys in the Chrysler, and for leaving the rest of the bottle of vodka in the car. I should have poured out the remains this afternoon when Harry and I saw it laying on the floor of the front seat. It would have been so easy to do," continued Gerry as he sat down in a chair next to Sharon and reached to hold her hand.

Nobody spoke while they strained to hear Miller's voice emanating from the adjoining room as he spoke on the phone to the highway patrol office in Macon. From the sound of the conversation, obviously he talked to Patrolman Barstow, whom he addressed by name. Miller and Barstow would never forget the infant they rescued from the privy that dark, stormy night. From one of Miller's responses accompanied with loud laughter, his friends listening understood Barstow had just asked Miller if he had looked into the clinic privy hole for Dr. Casper.

"Maybe we should," offered Woody to break the tension in the waiting room.

"I will as soon as I'm finished using it," replied Harry as he headed out the door and around to the back yard.

"He's not in the privy," Harry said as he returned to the clinic just as Miller finished his phone conversation with Patrolman Barstow.

Miller returned to the waiting room with a local map and a clipboard. "Okay now, we're about to get this hunt organized. Barstow will take his patrol car and head toward Macon continuing farther south to search the roads east of the Chariton River. He'll have his two patrol cars in the north search Route 63 all the way up to Millard. Woody and I will search County Roads F to the J junction and then east to State Route 3, and then on south to Callao. Harry and Purity do 149 south to Route 36, and Gerry and Sharon free lance wherever Sharon thinks might be appropriate. How does that sound?"

"Sounds well organized. Should we check in with the Highway Patrol office at any particular time?" asked Woody as he stood up and reached for his jacket from the coat rack in the corner.

"Yes," replied Miller. "Each car will stop and phone in every hour for the next four hours. If we haven't spotted him by then we will notify his wife and call off the search until morning. I hate to scare Rosalyn, but The Ghost might be home by then, safe and sound, with us still running all over the countryside."

Sharon stayed seated until all others except Gerry had left the room and drove off in their respective teams. Neither she nor Gerry spoke until the last car had left.

"So, do you think you know where he is?" asked Gerry as he looked at Sharon with a grin on his face. "I'm betting you do, though I have no idea where or why." Giving her hand a quick squeeze, he stood up and put on his reversible jacket, green on the inside and tan on the outside - the rain-protective side. It become colder outdoors so he turned up the collar.

"Well, at least it's an idea. Glad I brought my comfortable old shoes and old slacks to paint in today. Let me change back into them and out of this nice dress I wore for the puppet show."

"Mind if I watch?" laughed Gerry.

"If you watch then you will want to help, and if you start helping I'll end up with more clothes off than on," she answered with a smile on her pretty face. She came closer, unbuttoned the front of her blue dress, and let it slip to the floor. She quickly stepped from it and gave Gerry a big hug while still in her slip. Soon that also hit the floor as Gerry held her closely. "See what I mean? Now you had better turn me loose and let me finish changing or we'll never find The Ghost tonight." Kicking off her high heels, she sat down on a soft chair in the waiting room, undid her garter belt and stretched out her long legs. Slowly and carefully she took off her thigh-high nylon stockings.

Gerry could not keep his eyes off of her. *She sure is one beautiful, sexy woman*, he thought as she stood up and pulled her old pair of green, paint-spattered slacks up over her pink panties. Then she pulled her gray, college sweatshirt on over her head, over her pink bra, and down to her waist. Next came the thick white bobby socks and the comfortable white tennis shoes. She neatly folded her dress and placed it in a small cloth bag along with her high heels, hose, and garter belt.

"I'm ready. Get your keys to the Thunderbird and let's go. We'll head out toward our farm. Do you still have the big flashlight in the trunk of your car?" she asked as she turned to look at him. "We may need it."

"Yes, but why? How dark is it where we are going? The moon is almost full. Will that help or will we be indoors?" he asked as he opened the clinic door and held it for her as they walked outside into the mild spring night.

"We will be outside and in a fairly rugged area. We might have to walk for a while. There is an old abandoned wagon road going in part way to where we're going. But I don't think the Thunderbird has a high enough ground clearance to make it safely."

"Know what you mean," Gerry replied as he locked the clinic door, walked to his car, and unlocked and opened the passenger door for Sharon. "Hand me your clothes bag. I'll put it in the trunk while I dig out the flashlight. Should I also dig out the small axe I have back there with my car jack?"

"No, just the flashlight for now," Sharon replied as she rolled down the side window before closing the door. With considerable certainty, she felt she could find Dr. Casper. She hoped she was right and The Ghost had not hurt himself, accidentally or intentionally.

Gerry climbed into the small car, handed Sharon the big five-battery silver flashlight and turned on the car's ignition. "Put your seat belt on and we're off," he said. "I'll head toward your farm."

Sharon made sure the flashlight worked before she turned on the radio to the Moberly country western station, it took a moment for the radio tubes to warm up. Then she turned the volume control way down until the Everly Brothers record being played could only be faintly heard. "We'll actually pass the entrance road to the farm. Then you have to drive very slowly. The old wagon road entrance is hard to spot and we'll have to take down a couple of fence posts to get in."

"What you're implying is Dr. Casper is actually somewhere on your farm property tonight. Hell, I hope your dad doesn't find out. The Ghost may become a real ghost if he does." Gerry would have liked to ask Sharon more, but he knew she would tell him in due time, more or less, on a need-to-know basis.

As Gerry finally passed the Olsen farm entrance on his left, he slowed down the small sports car immediately. Two hills, three curves, and 500 yards later, Sharon put her left hand on his right thigh. "It's about 50 yards ahead on the left, just past those two big oak trees standing closely together."

A split-wood rail fence bordered this part of the property. At one time it had been an all-hardwood forest, but the trees were timbered back for a good distance at least ten years before, and the land converted to rough pasture for grazing. The moon slowly traversed through a cloud-cluttered spring night sky, and the available light varied from fairly good to nearly none. Fortunately, the moon shined brightly with no cloud interference.

As Gerry slowly and carefully pulled the Thunderbird off the road, he down shifted into second gear and stopped the sports car just short of the fence. With his headlights on high beam intensity, pointing almost perpendicularly at the split rails, he could see between them. On the other side started a rutted parallel road running up a slight incline and off into the distance. "I never knew you had this old road here. What's it used for?" Only then did he notice the bottom wood rail of a section of the fence had its right end laying against the ground.

"Turn off your headlights now," Sharon commanded but in a quiet voice. "I think he's taken the Chrysler up the road."

"Sure," Gerry replied as he reached forward on the dashboard and pushed in the light switch. He shut his eyes tightly for a few seconds to acclimate to the darkness.

"The old road is used only for funerals. It heads up into the woods across this rough pasture land, then winds around a couple of small hills, and finally ends up at our family cemetery. The graveyard is on the other side of the big hill behind our farm house."

"You're kidding," Gerry exclaimed in surprise. Suddenly it struck him why The Ghost might be here, half drunk, in the middle of the night. He had to ask Sharon to make sure, but before he had the chance, she jumped out of the car and quickly took down the two wooden crossbars of the fence. Then she stepped quickly aside and motioned for the car to be driven forward.

Gerry shifted into first gear and drove the car past the fence and inside the pasture. Though the grass between the parallel tire tracks grew high, the ruts were not deep and the oil pan and both axles of the small car cleared the rough ground.

Sharon quickly replaced the two loose fence cross bars and climbed back into the car. "Can you navigate in the moonlight without your headlights? If not, I can walk slowly ahead and guide you."

"No, I'm okay. We can make it for a while as long as the mid-road portion doesn't get higher. How far do we go from here?"

"About 200 yards up into the trees. We can pull off to the right there and hide the car. Then we'll walk in the rest of the way. If Dr. Casper is up here, and I think he is, we should see the big Chrysler pretty soon. There's a cul-de-sac turn-around to the right in among the walnut trees just past those huge boulders."

Gerry steered the small sports car in behind the rocks, when the parked white Chrysler loomed up suddenly in front of them. Neither Sharon nor Gerry spoke at first, but they just sat quietly straining their eyes to see ahead in the darkness. Gradually the moon came out from behind a large fluffy cloud and illuminated the area sufficiently to see no one was in the Chrysler. Sharon quietly got out of the passenger side of the Thunderbird and Gerry stepped out of the driver's side. They advanced slowly toward the Chrysler. Silence permeated the night except for the sound of a slight wind moving the branches of the tall trees. They could not possibly see into the Chrysler below the level of the windows.

Gerry tried the passenger door - unlocked, it opened easily. Opening the door caused the car's interior overhead light to come on with an intense suddenness scaring him. Instinctively he jumped back, eliciting a quiet laugh from Sharon standing on the other side of the car.

"That's not funny," he whispered loudly.

"It sure looked funny from here," she answered.

She quickly opened the passenger door and smiled at the young doctor as they stood looking across the empty seat at each other. No one sat in the car, neither in the front seat nor the back, nor on the floor. Thoroughly searching with the flashlight under the seats, between the seats, and in the glove compartment showed the vodka bottle was missing.

"I don't think we will find the bottle there, but let's look in the trunk just to make sure, then we'll walk the rest of the way over to the cemetery," Sharon said quietly. "The road used to go all the way but it's been 15 years since the last funeral and most of it's grown over with brush now."

"The keys are still in the ignition," said Gerry as he took them out, walked to the back of the car and opened the trunk. The trunk had nothing inside it except a spare tire, a jack, and a coil of large rope. He quickly shut the trunk, and the sudden slam echoed in the evening quiet.

After closing the front doors of the Chrysler as gently as possible, the young couple stood there together, holding hands, and letting their eyes re-acclimate to the darkness. "I know the way, so I'll take the flashlight," said Sharon as she took it from Gerry, "but we'll try not to use it so we won't scare the poor Ghost away." There was sadness and empathy in her voice as she spoke.

"I have to ask you. You know one time you told me about your family cemetery and its friendly Ghost. Is this who you meant? Did you actually mean, 'The Ghost' - Dr. Casper?"

"Yes, I've known for seven years. In another hour it will be midnight. Tomorrow is my mother's birthday. I was nine-years-old before I asked my Aunt Helen what date my mother was born on. For some reason, Dad would never tell me. He said I was too young to know, and if I did I would always be sad on that day every year. It sounded like a reasonable explanation at the time so I never pressed him on it. But I was curious, and when I found out, I decided to make sure to visit her grave on that day every year. It seemed like I should."

"And that's when you first saw The Ghost?" asked Gerry.

"No, I didn't see him that year. It had been raining for a couple of days just before her birthday. I had turned ten-years-old that year the first time I climbed up here after school on her birthday. The ground was still soaking wet. I immediately noticed fresh boot prints imprinted in the wet, soft soil. I knew they were not my dad's. His boot prints are all over the farm and are easy to recognize."

"So you knew someone visited the graves. But how did you know it was your mother's grave in particular? He could have been visiting your Grandparents."

"No, it was my Mom's. I knew right away. Knee indentations showed beside the headstone and toe marks from the tips of his boots dug into the wet soil where he knelt and prayed. I measured the distance, further proving they didn't belong to my dad."

"How, from the distance apart?"

"Yes, from the knee prints to the toe marks. Two months later I found my dad in a kneeling position like that. He was nailing the lower boards alongside the barn's bull pen. His knees were flush up against the stall, and he didn't realize I marked a line where his boots' toes rested. When I went back and measured it later that day, the length of his lower leg was almost two inches longer than the grave's prints."

"You were pretty damn clever," said Gerry as he reached out and hugged her closely. The closeness of her body and the smell of vanilla excited him in this strange dark setting. "So you actually missed seeing The Ghost that year?"

"Right. But in the dark early morning hours of her next birthday, I slipped out of the house and climbed up here with a flashlight and carried my dad's 12-gauge shotgun. I didn't need the light. The moon shined much like it does tonight. As I snuck up here, I hid in the trees, staying in the deep shadows. I didn't need the gun, but at age eleven, I was scared."

"Did he see you?"

"No, he never saw me. I actually heard him crying before I saw him, a pitiful grown man weeping, almost sobbing. Like his heart was broken. He stayed for almost two hours after I got there. Of course I didn't know how long he had been there before I arrived."

"Just praying all that time?" Gerry asked in wonderment.

"No, but kneeling and praying about half the time," Sharon answered.

"And then what? What else would he do?"

"He would sit on the iron railing around the plot, look at her grave, and drink vodka almost ritually. Apparently he would have already had about a third of the fifth drunk before he got here. He drank about another third while he was here, and just before he left he would pour the last third on my Mother's grave. He did the same thing every year."

"Do you think he came here at other times?"

"Well, back then, I visited the graves in the day time about once a month. Half the time my dad or Aunt Cherry or Aunt Helen would come with me. I never told them about The Ghost, but I never saw any strange footprints around the grave again."

"So he probably came only once a year," said Gerry.

"No, he comes twice a year, but I was 14 before I figured it out. Aunt Helen told me the date in September my mother died - on the thirtieth. I suddenly had the feeling The Ghost might come on that night also, so I snuck out of the house and came up here. He was here in the darkness of the early morning again. He acted out the same ritual every year, it never varied."

"Did you know who he was?'

"No, not until I was 15. We needed physicals at the medical clinic to play high school basketball. He was monitoring the two student doctors and gave me my physical that year. I recognized him immediately, but he didn't frighten me at all. I guess I knew I would someday meet the man, and he obviously loved my mother very much. He was very nice and considerate in doing his exam of me. Then at the end, he looked at my name on the chart, and he dropped it on the floor. I leaned down to help him pick it up, but before I could, he bent down and kneeled on the floor to retrieve all the pages. When he looked up at me he had tears in his eyes. He looked so much like he does at the cemetery I almost started to cry."

"Did he say anything? Did you?" Gerry asked squeezing her hand.

"He said, 'You're Sharon Olsen?'"

"I couldn't speak. I only nodded, Yes. I really choked up inside and afraid my own tears would start."

"He said, 'I knew your mother. In fact, I delivered you as a baby girl many years ago. Now you're a beautiful young woman

and already an outstanding athlete. She would be proud of you.'
Then he suddenly put the chart down excused himself, and walked
away. By then tears ran down his face."

"Wow. When did you see him next?" Gerry asked in a
whisper.

"After my rape I saw him as a patient in the hospital. He
stopped by to see me every day. He was very, very nice.
Somehow he always knew when my dad would be there and he
came in after Dad had left. Of course, now I see him quite often
since I work there part time as a secretary. He always stops to say
hello, but I realized it made him sad to see me."

By the time Sharon had quietly finished her story, the couple
had walked the rest of the rugged distance to the hill at the base of
the cemetery. The moon hid behind gathering clouds again as they
started to climb the last 100 yards up a fairly steep incline. They
stopped talking and tried to be as quiet as possible.

"My mother's grave is in the back corner on the right,"
Sharon whispered. "The cemetery is in a large clearing over the
crest of this last hill. I know he will be there. Should we say
anything or should we just watch to make sure he's okay?" she
asked as she picked up the pace and walked faster.

"Maybe we should just watch to make sure he is okay, and
then meet him back at the Chrysler. But there is no way I am
going to let him drive the car home tonight," Gerry said. "I have
the keys. We'll leave the Thunderbird here and drive him in the
Chrysler." As he spoke, the wind increased in its intensity, and
they heard the first few drops of rain striking the spring foliage
above and around them. A bright reflection of a nearby flash of
lightning suddenly lit up the sky as nearly simultaneously a crash
of thunder drowned out the sound of the rain for a few moments.

"Geez." Sharon said above the dissipating thunder. "That
sure came on in a hurry." The intensity of the rain had already

increased as it hit the treetops above them. "Looks like we may get wet tonight after all. With lightning striking so closely maybe it's best to wait here a few minutes before climbing any higher."

"Is the cemetery near the top of this hill we're climbing now? Don't forget, I've never seen it before," said Gerry.

"No. It's in a large clearing over the crest of this hill and about a-third of the way down the other side. From the edge of the trees at the top of the hill, we'll be able to see down into the cemetery below us. I've always watched The Ghost from there before," Sharon replied.

"I think you're right about not climbing any higher yet if thunder and lightning is about to start," Gerry said. "Most of the scattered clouds seem to have coalesced. But the wind from the west is picking up so it may all blow over pretty rapidly." As if to emphasize this possibility, moonlight suddenly shined brightly though a break in the clouds as the sound of rain lessened on the leaves. "Let's just make sure we're not standing near the highest tree around. In fact, let's get back down to lower ground right now at the base of this hill."

Sharon agreed and while holding hands the young couple quickly retreated downhill to a small grove of cottonwood trees, which were not as high as some of the surrounding tall hardwood and pine trees. Holding each other closely, not only out of affection but also for the warmth they provided each other, they waited around ten minutes. By then, the sudden rain shower ceased and no more lightning strikes occurred. Faint thunder could still be heard occasionally far in the distance to the east.

"Shall we try to get up there again?" Sharon asked as she let go of Gerry.

"Sounds good, but I'd rather have you holding me in a big hug like that." The night moisture had dampened and accented the curls of Sharon's hair and felt good against Gerry's face.

"You can always try again later," she laughed. "But for now, be very careful because after that quick rain, the hillside might be pretty slippery. Be careful so you don't fall."

"Okay, you lead the way and I'll follow," replied Gerry as they started back towards the top of the hill.

By the time they reached the crest of the hill, the clouds had blown past, and the moonlight shined considerably brighter in its intensity for a few moments. Sharon carried the large flashlight but had not used it. The trees started to thin out with increasing space between them.

"The cemetery clearing is only about 35 yards ahead," Sharon whispered back over her shoulder. "We can see it better from behind the group of tall pines to the right. There's a ridge overhead and then an embankment dropping off suddenly just in front of the cemetery."

"Can we get down the embankment there?" Gerry asked as more clouds moved quickly across the sky partially blocking the moonlight again.

"No, but let's look from the ridge first. Then we can take the path down about 20 yards to the left. Remember, it will be very slippery in that wet grass on the hillside."

"I hear you," Gerry replied as he followed closely behind her for the last few yards.

When Sharon reached the pine trees, she stopped suddenly and Gerry stumbled into her, knocking them both to the ground. "Sorry," he said as he stood up and helped her to her feet. "You stopped so quickly. Did you see The Ghost?"

"I'm not sure, but he's not at my mother's grave. Hold on tightly to the trunk of that tree and peer around it. The ground is steeper and slipperier than you think, and I don't want you falling over the edge here."

Grabbing the two-foot tree trunk with both hands before leaning carefully against it with his chest, Gerry looked around the thick tree and down into the open clearing just below them. At first he could not see much for a few seconds until the moon came out again from behind another cloud. Then he saw it all - the small cemetery, the white gravestones, the spiked iron fence around it, and The Ghost. The gravestones stood upright and still in the night. The Ghost lay still, sprawled on his back just outside the iron fence gate. He was not moving.

"My God," said Gerry. "He looks dead. Let's get down there right away. Turn the flashlight on."

"What do you think happened to him?" Sharon yelled above the swirling noise of the constant wind. They no longer had a reason to keep their voices quiet.

"It doesn't look good, I can tell you that much from here. When a person falls on their back with their arms outstretched it means they went down so fast they didn't have a chance to protect themselves...to protect their head."

"So what does that mean?" she asked.

"It generally means they were unconscious before they fell, rather than becoming unconscious because of the fall, like from hitting their head when they fell. That is not a good sign."

Within a few seconds, Sharon had found the path to their left. Their feet slipped in the grass and they each fell twice before reaching the cemetery fence and The Ghost lying before it. Gerry took the flashlight from Sharon as he knelt down beside Dr. Tripton Casper. With his left hand, he felt for a right side carotid artery pulse, while with his right hand he shined the flashlight into the unconscious doctor's upturned face.

"Is he alive?" Sharon gasped. "Oh God, don't let him die like this. He's a good man, Lord. He meant well. Please don't let him be dead." Quickly kneeling in the wet grass and mud on the other side of the doctor's outstretched form, she picked up his left hand and rubbed it between her own two hands to warm it with friction.

"Do you think we're doing the right thing, Gunnar?" asked Barbara sleepily as she rolled down the Volkswagen van window on the passenger side of the small bus-like vehicle. A cool breeze flowed in from outside waking her fully.

"We don't have any choice," her husband replied as he drove the small van east on County Route J. "The Ghost is gone and we have to bring him back. I can't explain it but since I packed away the puppet of him we used in the show tonight, I had the feeling he is in grave danger. He is our friend and he is also your boss at the hospital. Were it not for the salary your job pays you and for the tuition money he has personally loaned to me, I would have had to drop out of school last year. You know that's true."

"I know, and I do agree with you that the poor tortured soul of that good man is in grave danger. I knew the minute Reverend Bishop came out to our van when we were resting after the show telling us Dr. Casper drove off drunk in Dr. Parsons's Chrysler."

"Yes, and it's strange that you should use the word 'grave' to describe the danger, because now I'm beginning to see in my mind he's standing next to a grave in a small country cemetery."

"Do you see an open grave or a closed one?" Barbara asked, turning to stare at her husband as he concentrated on driving.

"I can't tell yet, but as we drive north the vision becomes much more clear. Keep looking for that old cemetery we saw on the way down to Essex. We need a cemetery for the ceremony."

"Do you still have the headache?" she asked with wifely concern. "There's some aspirin in my overnight case if you need it."

"Not any longer. I know it must seem strange to you, and I can't give myself any scientific explanation for it, but the headache at the start of these visions always clears as as they begin to reveal themselves in my mind. The headache is almost completely gone now."

"Why didn't we just use the cemetery near the Lutheran Church in Essex? When Reverend Bishop woke us up to tell us about Dr. Casper, all we had to do was drive a block to the cemetery there and set up the small stage on the back of the bus."

"It wouldn't have worked there. We need a small cemetery without a church. The Ghost is a man without a church. He's a man who has lost all his religious faith. That's how I see him now. Make sure you have five puppets ready. Yes. I'm seeing much more clearly now. With a threat this strong, we definitely need a cemetery for the exorcism. Besides, if we had done it in Essex, the townspeople would think we were crazy and get in the way. They would not have understood. Sometimes I wonder if I'm crazy myself, but I do know what works."

"Well, I still have a *Father Death* puppet all dressed in black, but which puppet will I use to represent *Life*?" Barbara asked. As she spoke, she quickly ran over in her mind the inventory of puppets packed neatly away in the back of the van.

"I see the *Life* puppet as one of the Essex doctors. Yes, it's definitely Dr. Frank, and he has a helper. It looks like...like Sharon Olsen. We used a Dr. Frank puppet in the first show tonight, but do we have a puppet that looks like Sharon?" Gunnar asked as he carefully steered the van around a sharp turn in the road. Though the bright moon had risen high in the sky, large clouds periodically blocked it.

"Give me five minutes with a needle, thread, scissors, and a crayon, and I will be able to convert one to look like her. Does *Death* have a friend? I hope he doesn't."

"Oh but he does," Gunnar sadly replied as he concentrated on the bend in the road ahead. "His friend is *Hate* and somehow it looks like that man we saw with Dr. Parsons this afternoon in front of the Purina store."

"That's Sharon's dad. Their farm is nearby. But this puts *Death* and Mr. Olsen on one side and Gerry and Sharon on the other. I don't understand. Sharon and her dad will be on opposite sides?"

"I don't understand it either, yet that's the way I see it. Their faces in the vision are very clear to me now." Though cool evening air came in the side windows of the small VW bus, Gunnar perspired profusely. "There are some tissues in the glove compartment, could you wipe the sweat off my face before it starts running down my forehead and into my eyes?"

Barbara quickly found the open tissue packet and reached over to Gunnar's side of the seat and gently wiped his wet face. She worried as her husband had not had a serious headache and vision this strong in over a year.

Barbara had hoped they were done with his visions. They had no rational explanation for them and they scared her. But she realized Gunnar's visions were portrayals of impending trauma and the tragedies were symbiotic with the puppets. She knew this, but when she tried to tell Gunnar, he would vehemently deny any such possibility. This had been the only thing they seriously had argued about since the beginning of their marriage.

Gunnar loved his puppets, to him they were nearly living things. He had become a very fine puppeteer over the years since he had started with his first three puppets as a teenager in Germany. He used some continuing characters over and over in his short skits, their faces were so carefully carved out of wood no one would mistake whom they represented. Others had quite generalized common features and interchangeable wigs and clothes. Barbara would dress them to alter their appearance from one person to another depending on the subject matter to produce the different characters Gunnar needed for the each new skit he saw in his visions.

"I'm going to need more illumination than this map light to finish remaking this puppet. Can I turn on the overhead for a couple of minutes?"

"Sure," Gunnar replied, "but put it out quickly if a car comes towards us or it will reflect off the window."

"You don't think this is a vision we could ignore, do you Gunnar?" his wife asked anxiously as she finished converting the puppet in her hands to look like Sharon. Earlier that evening the same puppet had been Cherry Jam, Sharon's aunt, during the late show in Essex.

"No Barbara. I still remember last year when we performed the skit at school about Ely and his cafe'." That vision came on just like this one with a profound feeling of dread and apprehension. When I picked up the Ely puppet after the show, I knew he would be in great danger soon, and I failed to warn him. He almost died two nights later in the shootout and other people did die. How can you possibly forget that?"

"Well, it's one thing to sense through your puppets people you know are in danger and want to warn them, but it's quite another thing, Gunnar, to think you can prevent it by exorcising the danger through a puppet skit. Don't you realize that?"

"I know. I know. I'm a medical student, and next year I'll be a physician. Here I am involved in something rather supernatural for which I have no explanation. That's why I don't tell people about it. But it works. What more can I say? You know it works. There is no way we can possibly find The Ghost in time tonight to warn him in person, so we have to do a fast skit to exorcise the danger. Remember your two uncles?"

Barbara would not argue about that. During the Second World War, when she was a teenager, Gunnar had visions her uncles were in great danger on a ravished tropical island in the Pacific. He could not warn them, so he put on a small puppet show for her and exorcised the threat to them. After the war when her two uncles returned home she found out they were in danger that very week, both were wounded while serving as volunteers from their ship to drive amphibious landing craft during the bloody invasion battle on Iwo Jima. Barbara had never seriously considered trying to dissuade Gunnar from the exorcising skits again. Having finished the new Sharon puppet, she picked up another, dressed it in blue overalls, and started to make it look like farmer Olsen.

"I think the cemetery is about three miles ahead," Gunnar said. "We should be there in another five minutes. I'll set up the small stage and lanterns as soon as we park. You finish converting the puppets to the new characters we need. We have to hurry or The Ghost will surely die tonight."

At 2:25 A.M., Miller and Woody drove carefully north on Route 63 toward LaPlata. Neither of them had spoken much on the ride. Woody drove and finally broke the silence. "We did see what I think we saw tonight, didn't we?" He asked. "I mean, you were there, too. You saw it all - you saw more than I did. Right?"

"Yes, but I'll be damned if I'll ever admit it to anyone else. It gives me the willies just thinking about it. Gunnar and Barbara out there by themselves in that old cemetery at this ungodly hour, putting on some strange puppet show. At least it looked like them. From a distance those damn puppets looked so real. I still can't believe I actually talked to those puppets. Promise me you will never tell my girlfriend what I did." Miller still shook his head in wonderment.

"Nobody in his right mind would believe us anyway, so I'm certainly not going to tell anyone," Woody replied. "But when we drove past that cemetery, and I saw their Volkswagen bus with its back window all set up with the small stage and the lantern lights, I had to investigate. I'm sure no one else is crazy enough to go driving around in a country cemetery on a stormy night by themselves."

"You know, Woody," replied his partner and friend, "I saw a little combat in Korea, so I know real fear and what that's all about. But that damn *Death* puppet worried the hell out of me tonight, I was scared. It was so eerie, a bunch of puppets fighting and yelling on a small stage, attached to a Volkswagen bus in the middle of a deserted cemetery."

"The puppet handlers must have known we were there, right?" asked Woody. "I know it was dark and all, but they must have been able to see through that puppet stage curtain and recognize us. Why didn't they answer you when you walked up to the van and tried to talk to them?"

"Well they did answer us. They answered us through the puppets. Hell, I must have spent ten minutes talking to the damn puppet dressed in all-black, holding the sickle. He called himself *Death*, and he claimed he was looking for Dr. Casper."

"But Gunnar's actual voice answered you. It had to be him. Right?"

"Did that voice of *Death* sound like Gunnar to you Woody? Be truthful. Did it sound anything like Gunnar with his faint German accent?"

"No, I admit it. It sure didn't," Woody replied as he pushed in the dashboard cigarette lighter and took a Chesterfield from his inside jacket pocket. "But it had to be Gunnar. Who else could it have been? It was man's voice, I think, and it certainly wasn't Barbara."

"Well the puppet that looked like Sharon did have a voice a little like Barbara's. I'm sure Barbara had to be behind the black curtain manipulating that puppet and talking for it," Miller said, deeply in thought as he stared straight ahead into the darkness. "Turn up the heater a notch. I'm getting a cold chill just thinking about that scene again. Let's just forget the whole crazy episode."

"No. Let's talk about is as rationally as possible just one more time," Woody replied as he exhaled a gray cloud of cigarette smoke. "As far as we know, Gunnar and Barbara always do the shows by themselves. So, between the two of them, they had to be doing all the puppet voices, right?"

"Right. But there were five different puppets on the stage at once," Miller offered as he finally reached over and turned up the heater himself. "I'm sure of that. I counted them all moving at certain times."

"So what?" asked Woody as he dimmed his bright beams for a semi and two cars passing them in the opposite direction heading south.

"So everything," Wilson replied. "Don't you know anything about puppets?" Each puppeteer can handle two at once. But they had five going - all yelling and fighting at once."

"I'm not sure you're right, Wilson. I think a good puppeteer might be able to control two puppets with his dominant hand. Anyway, that puppet obviously representing Dr. Casper didn't do much moving around. He seemed pretty dead to me most of the time, lying next to that white slab that looked like a tombstone."

"Hell, he moved pretty damn fast when the shooting started," Miller said. "I know he did."

"How could you tell? You were moving pretty fast yourself then," laughed Woody as he exhaled another cloud of cigarette smoke. "You should have seen how it looked from my perspective."

"Well, I've never before been shot at by a puppet holding a tiny Derringer. Those things can kill you at that close range. I thought the puppet was kidding when he told us to leave. I admit, though, once that character dressed in black grabbed the Derringer from the puppet that looked like a farmer, I lost any idea of tearing down the stage curtain to see if Gunnar and Barbara really were hidden behind it. But the gun still looked like a bluff. I mean, the puppet couldn't have been acting on its own. Right? We know that. It had to be Gunnar at the strings. Damn, Gunnar shot at me." Miller could not believe what had occurred.

"Okay. Let's take it from the top one last time again," said Woody. "When we first drove into the cemetery with our headlights on, I stayed in the car after we stopped about 30 feet from the back of the van and its stage, and you got out and walked up to them. What did you see first?" Woody asked.

"Well," Wilson replied, "at first I saw only four puppets yelling and fighting on that small stage with the fifth puppet lying between them and moving occasionally. They must have seen me walking up towards them. Hell, I was silhouetted by your car's headlights. How could they miss me?"

"Right, but as a silhouette, they could not see your features, so they had no way of knowing who you were," Woody offered, "unless they finally recognized your voice when you started talking."

"Okay, but they still must have seen me. And strangely they just kept on yelling and fighting. In fact, they didn't seem to take any notice of me until I stood about eight or ten feet away. Then I yelled at them asking what the hell they were doing. Then the fighting stopped and the one who called himself *Death* walked over to the edge of the stage and stared at me."

"So what did you say next? Your back was to me, and I couldn't hear you, but I sure could hear the one called *Death*."

"I said, 'Hey, it's me guys...Wilson Miller', and, 'I know it's you Gunnar and Barbara behind the stage curtain, so come out now and tell me what you're doing putting on a puppet show in a deserted cemetery in the middle of the night.'"

"And then what?" asked Woody, patiently prodding his friend for more information.

"Well, at first all the puppets started yelling and *Death* and the one I'll call *Farmer* started shaking their fists, first at each other and then at me. Got to admit it unnerved me."

"And next...."

"Next, the one that looked like Sharon came over to the edge of the stage and told me I would have to leave. She said Gunnar and Barbara were not with them tonight, they were back in Essex sleeping at the church. She said the puppets had done such great shows in Essex earlier that evening that Barbara and Gunnar had given them the night off."

"Yeah, so then what happened?" questioned Woody as he quickly glanced at his partner.

"So the puppets all chimed in and told me they had driven the van there by themselves."

"But why a cemetery?" Woody asked. "Did they ever tell you why they had gone to a cemetery?"

"See," said Miller, "See what I mean? Now you're starting to talk like it really was the puppets talking to me."

"Okay. Okay. We won't even try to get into that yet. Just tell me the rest of what happened. I'm certainly not in any better position than you to judge the reality of it all."

"Well, the Sharon puppet kept trying to talk me into leaving. Next to her, the puppet that looked like Frank tried to get me to leave also, but he did give me an explanation of why they were all there." Wilson's lower lip twitched in nervousness as he spoke.

"Why were they there?" Woody asked anxiously as he took a last drag on the cigarette and stubbed it out in the ashtray. He knew cigarettes were bad for him but the nicotine rush did calm down his anxiety.

"He said they were there for a fight between *Death* and Dr. Casper. He said it might get pretty bloody, so they had purposely picked a cemetery for that reason, and one of them would be buried out there tonight. He said one would die within the hour."

"One who?" asked Woody. "One of the puppets or one of the real characters they represented?"

"He didn't say. I was about to ask him, but then they all started fighting again. Already I started to feel kinda' foolish standing there talking to a bunch of puppets. But they really did seem so damn alive." Miller spoke with an apologetic air as if he needed to explain his actions both to Woody and to himself. "Well, didn't they look almost real?"

"So then what?" Woody asked, as he dimmed the Pontiac's high beams for another couple of oncoming cars.

"Well, by then I could see it was not just a free-for-all. The puppet dressed in black who called himself *Death* and the puppet who I learned called himself *Hate*, seemed to be on one side of the fight and the puppets of Sharon, Frank, and The Ghost were on the other side. They all yelled loudly and talked quickly like a bunch of excited children."

"How did you know he called himself *Hate*?" Woody asked. "Sharon told me...I mean...the Sharon puppet told me. There I go again. But they did seem so real to me."

"Yeah, I know what you mean. They looked even more real at a distance from inside the car where I sat," said Woody. "From my perspective, they looked just like real people from far away."

"Then the puppet dressed like a farmer who was called *Hate*, got a club and started beating the puppet that looked like Dr. Casper. Frank, I mean, the puppet that looked like Frank, got clobbered a couple of times trying to take the club away from *Hate*. Finally he succeeded. Then *Death* went over to a small box on the stage that looked like a trunk. He said if I didn't leave, he would shoot me. Obviously I thought he was kidding. But the next thing I knew, *Hate* opened the trunk and pulled out a tiny but very real, deadly Derringer pistol. Then *Death* grabbed it away from him and started after me. *Death* wasn't kidding."

"That was the shot I heard?" asked Woody.

"You know it, old buddy, and right then I lit out of there. Figured the bullet passed about two feet over my head, but that was all the motivation I needed to move out at double-time plus. Luckily you kept your motor running. I have never traveled in reverse as fast as you did in that Pontiac backing out of that cemetery, it was surely the fastest ever." For the first time in the past hour, Miller allowed himself a smile.

"What do you think the second shot was?" asked Woody.

"You mean the one we heard after you insisted on pulling the car off the road around the next curve and talked me into sneaking back there again? I still can't believe I let you talk me into that. I must be losing it."

"I have a high index of curiosity," said Woody. "Let's stop by Millard's for a beer - they're open 'till 3:00 A.M. on Saturday nights. Then we'll call the Highway Patrol like we promised. Do you think we should mention any of this?"

"Well, I agree with the idea of a beer or two, but no way am I going to tell Siegfried about that cemetery scene. We'll just report in to the rest of the search crew and hope someone had better luck finding The Ghost."

"You never answered me about what the second shot was, the one we heard when we sneaked up on the east side of the graveyard. It sure seemed to end the fighting among the puppets."

"Obviously one of them shot another one. Wish we knew which one got it. Damn it. There I go again, talking about them like they were real people." Wilson had a hard time thinking of them as not real. His lower lip curled in as he spoke, indicating his own confusion over what he had seen.

"At least by sneaking back we proved one thing. Though the lights on the stage were turned off and the Volkswagen van was dark, I'm sure only an adult could have made all that noise digging in the ground with a shovel. It had to be Gunnar or Barbara," said Woody. "No puppet could break the ground like that."

"We may never know since the digging was on the opposite side of the van from us. The van blocked our view. But if we go back in the daylight and dig in that spot, I'll bet we come up with some buried puppet shot through the heart."

"Which puppet do you think it will be?" asked Woody as he slowed down and pulled off the road in front of the Millard Tavern. Do you think it will be Dr. Casper?"

"I'm afraid to guess. Hopefully it's not him or Frank or Sharon. You know, I just figured out who the face of that *Farmer* puppet looked like."

"Who?" Woody asked.

"The one they called *Hate*. It looked like Gustav Olsen."

A loud voice came from the kitchen of the Olsen farm house. Though he could not understand the words, the noise had awakened Gustav. It might have been Dr. Parsons, but it sounded higher pitched than his voice. He wondered who Wiley could be talking to. Gustav had given him the guest room to use in the hope that his Chrysler and Dr. Casper would be found safely and soundly in the morning. He wondered if the voices were Dr. Parsons and a highway patrolman with news about Dr. Casper. Or maybe Sharon had come home from her date with Gerry.

While Gustav quickly pulled on his gray wool pants and blue denim shirt, he thought of his long evening with Wiley Parsons. For a physician, Dr. Parsons sure knew a lot about cattle. By the time Gustav had shown him around the farm that afternoon, the two men were on a first-name basis. They already had broiled and eaten a couple of large Hereford steaks for supper and enjoyed their third shot of Jack Daniels bourbon at the kitchen table when the call came in about the missing Chrysler and Casper. Gustav had never seen a grown man cry before and it had surprised him. At first he thought Wiley was crying over the probable loss of his new car. Inconceivable to him why Gustav hated Casper so much, Parsons was concerned over his fellow physician's welfare. But Wiley blamed himself for letting Casper drink so much that afternoon.

Maybe the liquor was talking, or maybe Gustav felt he could really talk to Dr. Parsons about the loss of his wife and the hate he felt for Casper. Whatever it was, Gustav found himself first consoling Wiley about his missing friend and then admitting his own feelings about Casper. At one time back during their college days, Casper had been Gustav's very best friend.

"He's paid that debt in spades," Dr. Parsons had said. "Oh, not to you personally, Gustav. No one could ever make it up for the loss of your wife, but Casper has paid back to society in pluses for the drinking indiscretions of his life. The rural clinic program he started has saved hundreds of lives in these parts, and it needed Casper to come to fruition and to survive. Now he needs your forgiveness for himself to survive. There probably isn't a day in his life that he doesn't think about the death of your wife. I know because told me about it this morning. If he is still alive, please find it in your heart to forgive him for what happened and welcome him back as your friend. He needs that and maybe you do as well."

Gustav would not promise Wiley he could forgive Casper, but he did promise him he would sleep on it and give him a firm decision in the morning. Gustav had not been sleeping much that night and kept having a crazy dream awakening him. His dream was populated by characters called *Death* and *Hate* and they all mixed in with Casper and Sharon and young Dr. Frank. As he walked from the bedroom, he finished buttoning his denim shirt and then headed down the front staircase. The muffled voices from the kitchen grew louder and sounded more animated as he crossed the empty dining room to push open the swinging door into the kitchen. It had been a long time since he had heard that many excited voices in his own kitchen, and he found it a pleasant sound no matter the circumstance.

Sharon first saw her dad come into the room to see him face the four people sitting around the circular table drinking coffee. She quickly stood up and faced him. Dr. Frank sat to her right and Dr. Parsons to her left also stood. "Sorry we woke you, Dad. In the excitement of it all we must have been talking pretty loudly. Gerry and I have been out looking for Dr. Casper."

Patrolman Barstow stopped writing, stood up, and turned around. "Sorry for the intrusion at this late hour, sir, but while I was here, I thought I might as well finish up my report on this Dr. Casper matter."

"What are you doing here?" Gustav asked as he stared at the big highway patrolmen. "Did you find him? Did you find Casper?"

"No sir, at least I didn't. Your daughter and Dr. Frank found him about an hour and a half ago outside of Dr. Parsons's Chrysler."

"That's right," said Sharon shaking her head up and down. "We found him laying stone still on the wet ground stretched out on his back. A big bolt of lightening had just struck close by."

"So you came out here to tell Dr. Parsons?" Gustav asked the highway patrolman as he pulled up the kitchen stool to sit on.

"No, I just found out about him myself from your daughter," Barstow replied looking embarrassed. "She's the one who found him. She and Dr. Frank are tonight's heroes."

"So why did you come all the way out here at this hour? Is there some other trouble going on?" Gustav sounded more attentive and concerned than irritated.

"I'm not sure, sir. We took a call at headquarters about an hour ago from Dr. Miller, who was with his partner, Dr. Woodward. They called from Millard's Tavern and admitted to a beer each. Frankly, sir, I think they must have lost track of time and quantity. You know how it is sometimes when you start drinking. They were off duty after a long afternoon's work and I'm sure they deserved a few beers."

"What did they say?" Gustav asked as he added sugar to the hot cup of coffee Sharon had poured for him.

"Something about I had better get out here to your farm fast...they expected trouble. They were all confused. I'm sure the beer was talking. They are both nice guys and certainly didn't mean any harm. They've always kidded around with me ever since that outhouse baby delivery we all did together. Guess I never will understand medical humor. I should have known they were putting me on. They yelled something about a fight out here between the forces of hate and death and life and Dr. Casper. Kept saying how they finally figured it out. They figured you were the farmer in the play, whatever they meant by that. They really sounded out of it."

"What are you talking about?" Gustav asked with a puzzled expression on his face. Squinting his blue eyes, he looked closer at Barstow as he sipped hot coffee from his cup.

"See what I mean, Miss Olsen. If your father doesn't understand, how will my Sergeant ever understand? Hell." he said standing up and tearing his report into shreds. "There won't be a report on this. I really shouldn't have come out here to bother you. Except they mentioned Dr. Casper in their phone call, and there was an All Points Bulletin on him. Anyway, thanks to Miss Olsen, we can cancel that."

"Would you like more coffee, Officer Barstow?" Sharon asked as she reached for the large pot on the back of the stove.

"No thank you, miss. I'll be leaving now," he replied. Picking up his trooper hat from the coat rack beside the back door, he put it on, gave them a quick salute, and let himself out. No one spoke until they heard the big hemi engine of the patrol car start and then head out of the driveway.

"So you found the old drunk passed out somewhere near Dr. Parsons' Chrysler?" Gustav asked. "That figures. Tripton sure has a bad drinking problem."

"Not any more," Gerry offered as he sat back down at the table. "Not any more."

"And I suppose you still want me to forgive the old S.O.B.?" Gustav asked as he looked at Dr. Parsons. "That's asking a lot, you know. That's really asking a lot."

"I think you'll have to now, Dad," Sharon said as she opened a fresh box of sugar doughnuts and set them on the table. "There's no choice left in the matter. Not any more. Not after tonight."

"Why not? Where is that old S.O.B?"

"He's upstairs asleep in my room. It's a miracle he's alive, but he is."

"He's in MY HOUSE? He's here right now? Who gave YOU the right to bring him here under MY roof?" Gustav shouted at his daughter for the first time in her life he had ever raised his voice at her.

"Mother did," she answered calmly.

"Who?"

"My Mother did, that's who. She gave me permission tonight, out at the old family cemetery. She called down one strike of lightning. It struck the iron arch over the cemetery gate, and enough of it bounced back and zapped The Ghost, knocking him flat and senseless. Gerry and I found him that way an hour ago."

"I have to admit, sir, I thought he was dead," Gerry said as he picked up a doughnut and shook off the excess sugar before it could land on his shirt. "I still don't know how he could live through something like that, but he did. Maybe the power of that wild electricity dissipated as it jumped from bar to bar of the old iron fence, with part of it going into the ground each time, before it finally hit him. Anyway, he is alive and asleep right now upstairs in Sharon's room. I just checked on him again before you came down. He's okay."

"And he's promised to stop drinking," Sharon said. "He told us all about it on the way back to the house here. He really is a new man."

"I only talked with him for ten or 15 minutes when they got here and woke me up," Wiley said, "but he is different. He has changed and I believe him. I don't think he will ever partake of alcohol again. He's looks like someone who has experienced a religious miracle. Something like that can change a man's life."

"What do you mean about '*seeing your mother*'?" Gustav asked.

"He saw Mother tonight in the cemetery. He saw her after the lightning struck him," Sharon replied.

"He did what?" her father asked in disbelief.

"He saw Mother and he talked with her. He had an out-of-body experience only people very close to death have reported. He told us he was ready to die and didn't care if he did when the lightning struck him. But mother told him he had to come back to life. She said they were not ready for him in Heaven yet, and he still had a lot of work to do with the rural clinics here on earth."

"She did? What else did she say?" Gustav asked, not knowing what to expect any more, but wanting to hear what his Nina had reportedly said.

"She told him there were a few more people whose lives he would save here on earth. Those people needed him, and there were many more medical students whose lives he would influence for the better, and how they were needed in General Practice."

"Did she say anything about me?" Gustav asked, now convinced of the truth of Casper's vision.

"Yes, she did," Sharon replied softly.

"What was it?" her dad asked.

"She said you had to forgive him, to forgive him completely for everything that has happened, and he had to stop drinking immediately or you would die before your time. She said if you forgave him and he gave his solemn word to stop drinking, a miracle would occur in our family within the year."

Reaching out for his daughter's hand, Gustav Olsen took it between the calloused palms of his own two hands. Then looking straight into the beautiful face of his daughter, the face of this young woman who reminded him so much of his wife, he said, "As

God is my witness, and now before friends in the humble kitchen of my home, I do forgive that S.O.B. Tripton Casper." Everyone smiled and Wiley and Gerry let out a cheer.

"Do you think you could repeat that without the S.O.B. part?" Sharon asked.

"Not this year. No, not yet. But maybe next year after we see what the miracle brings," he laughed. "But I will keep my oath. Casper is forgiven and from this day forth he will always be welcome in our home. AMEN!"

Amens were echoed by all present and a toast with coffee followed.

"Now can I go upstairs and talk to the S.O.B?" Gustav asked. "Maybe my wife told him more."

"He said she did but he would not tell us what it was about," Gerry replied. "You will have to wait until morning to find out. Dr. Parsons said and I agree, he needs at least six to eight hours of sleep right now." Everyone smiled and agreed as they stood up and stacked their dishes in the sink. The Ghost had finally come in from the night and would be warmly received indoors forever more.

Chapter 12
Lost Love
March 30-April 3, 1962

The first week full of early spring had started out well for everyone concerned after firming up the truce between Gustav and Tripton. The renewal of their old friendship commenced instantaneously, punctuated by laughter and tears throughout that first Sunday at the Olsen Farm. Intermittent thunder showers cleared by 10:00 A.M., and the sun shined brightly. Their celebration lasted all day while they first barbecued a hind-quarter of one of Gustav's prime beef for the occasion. However, the week wasn't ending well for Gerry and Sharon with the foreboding probability of great sadness to come.

Mr. Olsen, Dr. Parsons and Dr. Casper had all left early that afternoon for a big cattle auction in Kansas City going on all weekend. The three friends drove down together in Dr. Parsons's Chrysler and would be gone until late Sunday night. The young couple had the big house to themselves as the doctor stayed overnight at the farmhouse with Sharon starting Friday. They would not have to worry about the animals as Gustav had hired a full time farmhand to help with chores and fieldwork. The new hire and his wife lived in a house trailer moved onto the property parked just north of the barn where it was plugged into the farm's electricity and water supply.

The last weeks of the young doctor's rural clinic externship were winding down to a precious few. Gerry felt he had already been in Essex for a many years, rather than just a few months. The village became an significant part of his existence. Its people were far more important to him than just as a medical practice's population. The village introduced Dr. Frank to general practice, and he enjoyed it very much. But deeply in his heart he still desired to specialize as a surgeon. He knew he must soon return west to California for the many years of his training stretching ahead. Nagging questions constantly haunted him - should he take Sharon with him? Could their happiness together last?

"What are you thinking?" Sharon asked as Gerry completed drying the last of the dishes she had washed after supper. They finished a fine meal of broiled farm-bred sirloin steaks smothered in mushrooms with mashed potatoes and broccoli. Gerry knew there were a couple of frozen blueberry pies and some vanilla ice cream in the freezer he wanted to save if either of them were hungry again later that evening.

"I thought about the horseback ride we took all over your farm this afternoon and then up into the hills this evening to watch the sunset. It sure is beautiful up there. Can you imagine what it would be like to have a house in that location, one that looked to the west?" Gerry asked.

"I have thought about that on many occasions. But to make it complete, I'll need you in the house with me - then it would be a real home. Even without children, I could make it a good and happy home for us. Have you thought any more about our problem, or should I say my problem, of not being able to have children?" Taking both of Gerry's hands in hers, Sharon looked up at his face as she spoke. He saw the kindness on her face, but it now held an aura of unspoken sadness.

Looking down at her, Gerry remained silent. Tears formed in his eyes as he paused and fought for control. His throat felt as if it were closing, cutting off the air to his lungs. Pulling Sharon forward for a tight hug, he held her closely as they wrapped their arms around each other. The smell of vanilla strongly saturated her soft hair. The fragrance would forever stimulate the inner recesses of his mind.

They stood silently in the kitchen for a few minutes. Sharon could feel Gerry's wet tears on her cheek. Turning her head slightly, she whispered in his ear, "It's okay. It's okay. I do understand. Really I do. You have obviously thought long and hard about marrying someone who can't have your children. And you can't do it, not even if it's me. Am I right?"

He could not answer out loud. Slowly he shook his head up and down. Letting her go, he turned his back and walked slowly to the coat rack by the back door.

"Where are you going?" Sharon asked with surprise in her voice as she watched Gerry take down his jacket and put it on. "What's with the jacket?"

"I guess I'd better head back north to the city. That's what you want now, isn't it?"

"And waste what may be our last weekend together? Nonsense. I may not have you for a lifetime, but I'm sure going to make every minute count we are still together. Now take off your jacket and let's go to bed." Sharon had no tears in her eyes. She had used them all up in the past few weeks since her surprise exposure in the gynecology lab. She knew now that her life after June must go on without her young doctor. Slowly they climbed the back staircase side by side holding hands.

"Do you remember our first night here in this bed together last winter?" Sharon asked as she turned down the green plaid spread.

"How could I ever forget? That night will live in my memory forever."

Taking off her penny loafers, she sat down and leaned back against the pillows. "You were so nice, even more so than I dared hope for. At least you got me over my fear of sex, the fear I'd had almost constantly since that man raped me."

Kicking off his shoes, Gerry sat down on the other side of the large bed and lay back with his head on her abdomen. Then rolling over to his left and straightening himself out beside her, he reached over and pulled her close to him. "I will always remember that night. I will always remember you. But at least this way, by my leaving for California alone, I won't be taking you away from your beloved Missouri and from your close-knit, extended family. Cherry once warned me you would not be happy if any man tried to influence you to leave these parts."

"Well, I would have been willing to go to California with you for your internship and residency. Afterward I would have tried to get you to come back here to live and work. Maybe that's not what you're destined to do."

"What do you mean? What do you think is my destiny?"

"I'm not sure. I know you're a dreamer. But you're more than just lucky. You have the brains and the abilities to make those dreams come true. Do you ever think of how your life may turn out and what it might include? I'll bet it will be a fascinating story, one of adventure and accomplishment."

"Right now I'm not thinking much past this weekend. It's been far too long since we were alone in this house." He spoke quietly while he rubbed the back of her neck.

"Then let's get started and make it as fine a weekend as the very first one we spent together here in my bed," Sharon whispered as she started unbuttoning the young doctor's shirt. Once again looking deeply into his brown eyes, she saw the gentleness combined with the look of longing she loved so much.

Lifelong dreams are made from these kind of weekends, far too good to be let go voluntarily. But by late Sunday evening, Gustav telephoned the farm from Columbia. He called Sharon to let the young lovers know he would arrive back by 10:15. Gerry left just before 10:00.

As Sharon's father, Gustav probably loved her more than any man alive with the purest and selfless love fathers reserve for daughters only. Not even sons are offered such caring. Fathers far too frequently love sons as an extension of their own egos and genes. Sons are loved dearly, but with the obligation of biological destiny meant to carry on the family name. Sons are to complete the ambitions and the dreams of their fathers. But daughters are for happiness, and mostly their own selfish happiness. Less was demanded of daughters in those bygone years of the early sixties, because less was expected. Whatever daughters would achieve was welcomed as an additional blessing neither owed nor anticipated.

Sharon had been a special blessing to Gustav's life. He wanted only for her to be happy, and he knew she was happy with young Dr. Frank. But lately Gustav feared the young couple's relationship would not last. He had purposely left them by themselves in the big farm house for the weekend, hoping it would give them sufficient time to be alone together any way they wanted. Maybe then they could work out their difficulties and compromise on them.

"How did your weekend go?" Gustav asked as soon as he entered the back porch door. Taking off his jacket, he sat down at his kitchen table, and Sharon poured him a hot cup of coffee. Then reaching into the nearby cookie jar, Gustav pulled out two ginger snaps and dunked them in the steaming liquid.

"It was one of the nicest weekends of my life, Dad, but in a bittersweet way. Gerry and I said goodbye as lovers this evening. From now on we will only be friends." Sharon's eyes glistened with moisture, but no tears fell. Sitting down at the round table, she reached out to hold her father's worn and calloused hand for a few seconds before letting go and picking up her own cup of coffee.

"You know, honey," Gustav began and then cleared his throat before continuing, "I could not love that boy nor think any more of him than if he were my own son. He saved my life. For the last four months, he has made my little girl the happiest I've ever seen her. I know you will miss him but life goes on. Maybe the good Lord meant you to have someone else."

"Any idea who?" his daughter replied with a light, forced laugh, but a sincere smile.

"Well I don't know at this point," Gustav replied.

"Anyway, who needs another man in her life when a girl has a dad as fine as you? As a father and a man, you are the greatest. Dad, you do realize how very much I love you, don't you? You have always treated me with a dignity of mutual respect emphasizing the proud kinship we share."

"Yes, I've done okay by you. You haven't turned out half bad. You're a real keeper. Casper even said your mother told him she was proud of me and of the fine job I'd done raising you. Can you imagine that?"

"Did she tell him anything else?" Looking into the kind, work-hardened and weather-worn face of her father, Sharon did not want to cast doubt on his faith. His feelings were so obvious and open for the world to see.

"I know what you're thinking, daughter. You're a doubter. What can I say? Just after spending time with Tripton since his experience so close to death last weekend, I do believe he had one of those out-of-body experiences people talk about. I really believe he did see your mother. Does that sound foolish?"

"Dad, I have no problem with that. After all, Gerry and I found Dr. Casper and he sure seemed dead at the time. If Gerry had not pounded on his chest and forced air into his lungs he probably still would be dead, dead and buried. But what does that have to do with us?"

"I'm not sure at all, Daughter. Casper would not tell me everything my Nina told him, but he did imply you'd be married before Gerry steps one foot back in California."

"Mother said that? Are you sure?"

"That's what Tripton reported, but it will only come true if you stop being with Gerry and don't see him for the rest of this March and April. It's not in Nina's plan for you to see him again until May."

"I can't believe it," Gerry said as he hung up the telephone at the apartment he shared with Harry in Kirksville. "Here it is Tuesday, after one of the best weekends of my life with Sharon, and she just called up to say goodbye. Damn, but I hate trying to talk sense to a woman on the phone."

Putting down his Thoracic Surgical Diagnosis, Harry looked up at his friend with sadness on his face. Reaching for an open pack of cigarettes from his desk, he slowly removed one and used his two hands to strike a match to light it. Harry took a couple of deep drags and exhaled faint clouds of smoke toward the ceiling each time. He tried to pick his words carefully. "Guess I'm confused, but I thought last Sunday night when you drove home from Essex you two were through as lovers and had already said goodbye from that standpoint. Are you saying now that she doesn't even want to see you as a friend?"

"You think you're confused? How about me? Sharon said she does want to be friends but she just doesn't want to see me for a couple of months. She's moving back to the dorm at the teachers college and will confine herself to campus hitting the books for A's and working on her honors project in accounting.

"That sure sounds like mighty heavy academic motivation," Harry answered.

"I don't understand her at all. When we parted on Sunday, we agreed to keep seeing each other...just to stop sleeping together. Fact is, I was supposed to have a coffee date with her at Ely's this evening." Walking across the kitchen, Gerry opened the porch side door to let in the spring breeze. He could hear the pleasant rustling of the wind in the trees of the yard. "Any more coffee in your pot? Guess I'll be having my evening cup here with you."

"Sure, pour yourself all you need. There is plenty of cream in the refrigerator. You know something, old buddy? Maybe it's best this way. She's a pretty smart woman, so you ought to listen to her."

"You think so...even about this?"

"Yes. Also, it was your decision to break the engagement, so you should defer to her to choose the way the breakup is the least painful for her. You're both hurtin', that's for sure. But for, her it's worse. You still have medicine as your mistress and the real love of your life. She's lost the biggest love she may ever know. Let her be. Let her adjust any way she wants."

"You really think this is the best way to do it? Just stop seeing each other in any capacity for a two months?

"Yes. I really do," Harry replied.

"Well, maybe you're right. Maybe it does make sense." Adding two spoonfuls of sugar to the cup, Gerry stirred it in and sat down in his easy chair waiting for the coffee to cool. "But it sure will be lonely without her. I miss her already."

"And have I got the loneliness cure for for you. Purity gets off at 11:00 tonight. Thought I'd catch a piece of pie at Ely's with her then. Why don't I have her bring Sarah along?"

"She won't be working late. She's probably home writing to Tex."

"No. She is working late. They were short handed in OB tonight so Sarah pulled a double shift. I'll call Purity now and tell her if you think you're up to it."

Chapter 13
Tex's Trip
April 6-8, 1962

The following Friday evening found externs Frank and Thompson sitting in their favorite back booth at Ely's Cafe' on West Jefferson Street. They waited for their late evening dates with Sarah Hall and Purity Jones. The two young doctors had driven back to Kirksville from the Essex Rural Clinic arriving home about 9:30 P.M. After first stopping by their apartment where they showered and changed, they walked the four blocks to the cafe' for a fill of Friday night catfish and fries.

They had just finished the main course when Ely came out of the kitchen. He headed directly to their booth bringing a large, warm cherry pie and a full steaming pot of freshly brewed coffee. He sat down to join the two doctors, cut the new pie in thirds, and poured the hot coffee. "Nothing is too good for my old friends," he said, "especially now that they're scheduled to be leaving our fair city in less than two months. You guys are really graduating aren't you? They wouldn't dare keep either of you two around here any longer, would they?"

"Do I sense sadness in your voice or only sarcasm from your soul, Ely?" questioned Harry. "I'm betting you'll miss your two favorite customers before we're gone a week," he continued with a combination of humor and patronizing patience. He slowly stirred a spoonful of sugar into the white coffee mug sitting in front of him.

"I admit it. I'll miss you guys," replied Ely as he placed the three huge pieces of pie on separate plates and handed two of the plates to his friends. The cafe' had been a special part of the young doctors' lives with many a meal and a cup of coffee taken there during their four, long years at the medical school. Ely knew this as well as they did. The three of them had become good friends over the past four years, and, though both Harry and Gerry often enjoyed complaining about the food, they also generally enjoyed eating it. Ely and his beautiful wife, Delta-Sue, had always tried to make the doctors feel like the little cafe' was more than just a place to eat. At the cafe' they could relax with friends, be refurbished with food, and be entertained by the latest new tunes or old favorite songs in the big 220 Selection Seeburg stereo jukebox. Still his pride and joy, Ely loved his three-year-old, '59 model jukebox. He only loved his family more than his jukebox, they were all his pride and joy.

Such relaxation, however, had not always been possible in the small restaurant. Many a meal taken here in earlier days had been most stressful. The cafe', located directly across the street from the basic science building of the college, often was the place of last-minute study with medical students sharing critical information just before a big examination. And the stress had not always been academic.

Though these three friends had never fully discussed the events of the 'Coffee Shop Shoot-Out' (as it was locally called), since the night of the duo of deaths, the scene of that homicide-filled evening forever imprinted on all of their minds. They could not believe the killings were almost a year old.

"What time are your dates coming by?" Ely asked as he attacked his pie with compulsive zeal. He loved his own cooking. "I hear now you're both dating nurses from the hospital."

"Well, their shift is not over until 11:00 P.M. So by the time they finish up reports and drive on over from the hospital, it will probably be at least 11:20," replied Harry. "We all have the day off tomorrow so we can afford a late night now. Why don't you get your wife and head to Millard's with us for some dancing and some beer? No sense keeping this place open if we're finishing off your last cherry pie of the day. Nothin' much else left that's fresh enough to sell tonight."

"No, Delta-Sue left a couple of hours ago. She's probably asleep at home by now, and anyway she wouldn't leave the kids all alone. You know, Delta-Sue and I always figured a couple of good looking, corn-fed Missouri women would have married off with you two long ago. Instead there's now less than two months to go and you both will be out of here free of local matrimony. How did you manage do that?"

"It hasn't been easy," Harry replied, taking several slow swallows of coffee. "I do keep asking your good-looking wife to run off with me, Ely, but so far no luck. When you get home tonight you tell her she has only a few weeks more to make up her mind. I'm not ever coming back to this town after I leave here for good on June 1st, and that's the truth. If she wants to get out of here, now is her chance."

Ely laughed long and hard, with a wide-mouth grin showing off his big, white teeth. His good nature was his trademark. "Yeah, you'd probably try to take her away and leave me with the two youngsters crying themselves to sleep every night and wondering what happened to their momma."

"No, that's not true Ely. I'd be glad to take both the kids too if Delta-Sue would agree to run off with me."

"Well, I am starting to ponder on whether she is getting appreciably older and past her prime now," said Ely suddenly furrowing his forehead as if in deep thought about his wife.

"Why do you say that, Ely?" questioned Gerry, now willing to enter the conversation since he had finished his pie. He knew he had just eaten the last piece.

"Well, for the past five years, Delta-Sue has always averaged five or six serious proposals a year from medical students, and I do mean serious ones."

"I believe it," Gerry replied as he pushed his empty plate aside. "She's a beautiful, gracious woman."

But this year she only got three. I'm afraid she may be losing her looks," Ely continued but now with a large smile on his face. "What do you guys think?"

"Maybe she actually gets a lot more than that but just doesn't want to tell you for fear of causing you needless worry. Some people in these parts say you have a powerful temper when riled up." All three of the friends smiled at this reference, but Harry went no farther with the conversation nor its implications.

"You're probably right, Harry," Ely replied. "Of the four most lied-to people in the world, I'm filling the job description of two of them."

"How do you figure that? What are the four? asked Gerry.

"A spouse, a bartender, a priest, and a barber. I'm a husband and a bartender. I've probably heard it all by now."

"And done it all, or at least most of it," Gerry added. Then getting up from the table and stretching, Ely grabbed the tab left by the waitress. "This one is on me guys. Just leave a good tip for Helen, the new girl. She's a student at the teachers college and really needs the money for her books and tuition next semester."

"Hey, why this compulsion to grab the check all the time lately? We actually do have a few dollars now. We can afford a real meal occasionally. You're never going to get rich here in the restaurant business if you don't let the customers pay for the food," Harry said.

"Because if it hadn't been for you two guys, I'd be a dead man by now. Sox would have murdered me and probably my wife too. Just because we never talk about the night of the killings doesn't mean I've forgotten about it."

"We know. None of us have forgotten," replied Harry.

"By the way, Delta-Sue and I would like to have you two out to our place for a barbecue some weekend before you leave in June. Bring your girlfriends along with you."

"It will be a pleasure," Gerry answered as Harry nodded in agreement. "Tell Delta-Sue we'll try to get together with her by next Thursday to decide which weekend would be best for us all."

After Ely left, the partners spent the next 20 minutes over a second cup of coffee talking over various medical cases seen that day at their rural clinic. Foremost in the discussion, were the two proposed patients for probable elective surgery they would be referring into the hospital early next week. One was a post-laperotomy patient needing an abdominal wall hernia repair and the other a heavy-set female in her forties who had suffered repeated gall bladder attacks and needed a cholecystectomy.

As Gerry stood up to put a quarter in the jukebox and punch some selections of his favorite Jim Reeves records, Purity and Sarah entered the cafe' laughing loudly. As soon as she saw Gerry, Sarah came over and put her arm around him. She noticed he still had one selection left on his quarter. Quickly she punched the buttons for the song *Sincerely,* by the Moonglows. She rubbed her nose against his cheek and then kissed him long and hard. They walked back to the booth holding each others' hands. By the time they reached the table, Purity had already sat down next to Harry and dived deeply into a conversation about a former patient of his recently readmitted to the hospital.

"You're pretty open in public with affection towards my medical partner," said Harry in a good mood but with a ring of concern in his voice. "I don't think that's a good idea with you being engaged to an easily enraged boyfriend who's heading back here from Texas next week."

"Can I help it if your roommate turns me on?" Sarah asked with a demure smile as she reached up with her free right hand and brushed her blond hair back from her forehead. "I'll know in advance exactly when Tex is heading north. Until then I want this good doctor for my roommate." Already Sarah had her other hand on Gerry's leg under the table and rhythmically rubbed his inner thigh.

"I just don't want him shot to death," Harry replied. "Let's be blunt. This affair between you two bothers me. Sarah, rumor has it your boyfriend carries a pistol. I talked with a couple of guys in the Guard last week who claimed Tex used to target practice with them at the old armory once a month when he lived here. They called him Deadeye Doc."

"Actually he carries a revolver, a .38 Colt Special to be specific," Sarah responded.

"Well that's not exactly a big difference Sarah," Harry continued. "People have been known to have been shot to death with those things, too. Don't get too technical with me when I'm being serious."

"Harry is right," Gerry added. "When it comes to handguns, I don't want to be looking down the receiving end of one of those things again."

"Oh my gosh. I forgot. This is where the big shoot-out occurred last year. You were the two students involved, weren't you?" Sarah asked excitedly. "Isn't this the booth it all started in?"

"Let's change the subject. That's another story for another time," Purity suggested. "I may have just finished an eight-hour shift on the surgery ward, but I'm ready for some beer and some dancing at Millard's."

"And that's all?" Harry asked with a sly smile on his face, which quickly switched to one of studied concentration as he carefully lit his first cigarette of the evening.

"Well, maybe a little hanky-panky, but nothing big in the parking lot. Especially in that parking lot, not even if it's pitch dark and totally deserted."

"Still keeping your guard up against this guy?" Gerry asked Purity.

"Yeah. Along with my underpants. At least for a while, but maybe I'm weakening, just a little bit," Purity replied as she affectionately put her hand on Harry's wrist.

Later in her trailer, Sarah sat on the couch and once again brushed her wavy blond hair back from her forehead. Then flipping her head back and to the side she let her hair spin around her face for an instant in a seductive motion. "It's been a long time since I spent a late Friday night dancing and drinking beer until the 2:00 A.M. closing time at Millard's. That was fun. Thank you for taking me."

"It was my pleasure," Gerry replied as he sat down on the couch next to her, "though it always amazes me how a woman can be tired from walking all day on her job and then still enjoy a couple of hours of dancing at night. Here, put your feet up on my lap, and I'll give you a good foot treatment."

Quickly taking off her black loafers and wooly bobby-sox, Sarah stretched out on the couch and put her feet up for a much-welcomed massage. "You really are a nice guy. Are you trying to make me addicted to all of this physical attention?" she asked while stifling a yawn.

"Is that yawn of yours out of pleasure rather than boredom?" Gerry asked.

"It's a yawn of pure contentment," Sarah replied. "So what do you think of Harry dating Purity? They certainly seemed to be having a good time tonight at Millard's. I think they're both really great people, and I'm glad to see them finally getting together. Do you think it could become a serious relationship?"

"No, I'm afraid not," Gerry replied as he continued massaging Sarah's right foot. "It's too late in the college year for that. We'll be out of here June first and headed for our internships. That's less than two months away. Harry is trying for an internship at Corpus Christi and then on to a three-year surgical residency somewhere else in Texas."

"It's too bad they didn't start getting serious about each other sooner," Sarah replied with a dreamy expression of pure contentment on her face. "This foot massage is great. What's it going to cost me? I'll do anything you want," she stated eagerly.

"A good back rub when I'm done by a beautiful, naked nurse. It's one of my continuing fantasies. Now put up your left foot and tell me the latest news about your old boyfriend. When can we expect Tex to be arriving on the scene here in Missouri?"

"In two weeks, I'm afraid. Wish I could put it off until after you're gone, but I am engaged to the guy. I can hardly stop him from coming here to see me now and then."

"Yeah, I can remember the feeling of engagement bliss. It's not very long since I had it myself," Gerry replied. Though he had tried to keep busy, both with his medical work and his fast and furious affair with Sarah, the young doctor found himself thinking of Sharon much of his free time.

"Look Gerry, I know I should be disappointed you and Sharon broke up, but how can I ever fake being sad when your breakup means you will be free to spend your nights here making mad, passionate love with me? Does it make me a bad person that I want you so much? I'm certainly not going to feel guilty about your breakup because I don't think I'm to blame."

"You're not. Don't ever assume that guilt. It's not yours to bear."

"Why did you break up? Do you want to talk about it? Did it have anything to do with the gynecology lab?"

"Only indirectly. The gyn lab just gave confirmation to the facts I had already realized subconsciously but refused to admit to myself."

"What, that Sharon's chances of pregnancy are pretty slim?" asked Sarah. "She will probably never have children?"

"Yes, the lab proved to me it was time to focus on facts, not just feelings. I want my own kids in my life. I had to be honest with her and with myself. We still love each other, but it wouldn't have been fair to either of us to continue the relationship under those circumstances."

"Where is Sharon now? I heard she doesn't work at the hospital anymore."

"She moved into a dorm on campus and is concentrating on her college honors project. She may go to summer school to earn enough credits to graduate early by midterm next year. I'm done talking about that, and this is the end of your foot treatment."

"Let's take a shower together now. Then I'll give you my special nurse back rub. You will forget every other woman you've ever known. You can count on that, Doctor."

"Is that a threat or a guarantee?" Gerry said now rubbing the inside of Sarah's smooth, firm calves. She prompted his question by the passion of her promise.

"A little of both," she replied impatiently, sitting up and quickly undoing the front buttons of her light-blue blouse. Within seconds she had it off, reached behind her back, unsnapped her bra, and let the straps slip baring her shoulders. Then leaning forward she unbuttoned Gerry's shirt. When she had it off she placed it neatly over the back of a nearby chair. Then she stood in front of him as she slipped out of her gray cotton skirt and pink panties.

She stood provocatively, tilting her pelvis upward and spreading her long legs wide apart.

"You are a sexy woman, Sarah. Now start showering or we'll be doing it here on the couch," Gerry said stroking the sides of her firm thighs.

Only when he stopped touching her, did she turn and walk to the bathroom. She liked the young doctor. In the inner core of her subconscious, she knew her attraction to him was much more than just sex. She hoped to hide the deeper feelings and already dreaded Tex's return.

The two lovers awoke late the following morning at nearly 10:15 A.M. The sun striking the metal trailer heated up the small bedroom. Gerry stood up to open a window on each side of the trailer for cross ventilation, helping to to cool it down a little.

"Do you want breakfast here?" Sarah asked as she reached for a short, bright-red robe falling to her mid-thigh. As she tied it with a wide black belt, she stood up and yawned. Her fine, tall posture accentuated her beauty and her height.

"Sure do. I'll grab a shower first while you start cooking," Gerry responded enthusiastically.

"What did you think of last night?" She asked, yelling into the bathroom, but not sure Gerry could hear with the shower running. Turning up the gas burner, she pulled out her favorite Revere Ware frying pan, dropped in a scoop of fresh butter, and placed the pan on the stove. She realized Gerry had not heard her question as she could now hear him whistling in the shower. Retrieving a carton of eggs out of the refrigerator, she cracked four into the pan of heated butter and watched as their outer edges turned white. She quickly added a dollop of tomato sauce, two shakes of A-I sauce, and then started scrambling the contents of the pan.

"What did I think of what?" Gerry asked as he stood beside her with a large Turkish towel wrapped around his waist and a big smile on his face. He rubbed the back of her upper thighs under her short robe with both hands and licked the back of her neck lightly with his tongue as she bent over the stove.

"Don't play with me when I'm cooking or I'll burn the food. What did you think of our fucking last night?"

"It was fantastic, but then it always is for me with you. Just when you get your hands around my balls, I know you're probably pulling on that damn ring of yours. I don't like that."

"But that's what I wanted to tell you. I had a real breakthrough. I had a great orgasm last night and never even once touched my ring." Her face flushed deeply pink as she spoke. Neither of them knew whether she flushed from the heat of the stove or the memory of the night. Backing up, Sarah divided the ranch-style eggs on two plates as Gerry buttered a short stack of whole wheat toast. Sitting down at the small table, they quietly held hands for a few seconds before starting to eat.

"What will you do when Tex comes back? Why not get rid of the labial ring once and for all? Do you want me to cut it? I could get a ring cutter from the clinic and have it off today."

"No, Gerry, no. I'm not ready for that yet, but I am starting to think I can really enjoy sex without pain. You have been really great for me. I want you to know how much I appreciate the kind concern and gentle affection you have shown towards me."

"So when exactly does Tex come back?" This time Gerry emphasized the word 'exactly.' He realized he wanted to enjoy being with this woman right up to the last possible moment.

"You're not scared of him are you?" Sarah asked.

"I'm scared of anybody who carries a gun. When it comes to handguns I've had my fill of looking at the business end of one."

"Yes, I guess the shoot-out at Ely's Cafe' would have been enough to scare anybody. But they say you were pretty damn brave during all the excitement the night of the shootings."

"Brave, HELL. The only reason I didn't shake uncontrollably during the entire affair is because I was scared stiff. I was too damn scared even to shake. Harry was the brave one of the two of us. When Sox, the escaped con, started waving his gun around, Harry at least could move. I was too afraid."

"But the girl Sox killed was Harry's girlfriend, wasn't she?"

"Yes, she saved Harry's life. Marlene jumped in front of him just as the gun went off. That gave Ely time to reach for the .357 magnum the con carried and he immediately unloaded it on Sox. Have you ever seen a formerly healthy body after it abruptly interrupted the flight path of six slugs from a .357 magnum at point-blank range?"

"As a matter of fact I have," Sarah said. "I went down to the anatomy pit when the two pathologists did the autopsy on Sox. He probably never knew what hit him."

"No. You're wrong about that. He lived long enough to know what hit him and that Ely shot him. Ely wanted him to know, and Sox deserved to die. His demise was no loss to anyone. Marlene's death was the tragedy. But that's another story."

"Since it's Saturday and we both have the day off again tomorrow, let's drive over to Hannibal," Sarah suggested. "Let's take my Crown Vic Ford rather than your T-Bird so we have more room. I can pack a lunch and we can have a picnic along the Big Mississippi."

"Hey, sounds great. Sharon and I had talked about a trip to Hannibal, but we never made it."

"She called on Wednesday to say she had moved into the girls' dorm at the teachers college while taking classes," Sharon said, "and she was studying full time on her honor's project. She said she wouldn't be volunteering for any more gyn labs. She thanked me for my kindness and told me you two had broken up. She told me you may need a kind shoulder to cry on, or at least a good friend to talk to," Sarah explained. "She also told me she heard we are seeing each other, and she thinks it's nice for both of us. She wants me to be good to you and, and if I get a chance, to take you to Hannibal some weekend. I then realized that Sharon is a far finer person than I am and probably a better friend than I deserve."

Gerry was not ready to share his reaction the ladies' conversation, so he avoided responding to Sharon about it. "You look like you are dreaming about something," Gerry said as he finished his breakfast, stood up, and cleaned off the table. "Want to talk, or just be mysterious and provocatively sexy?"

"No, I'm just thinking of Sarah. Let's get the dishes washed right away. We can go buy some fried chicken out at the highway truck stop and head east for the Big River."

"Okay, but I'm going to run the T-Bird back to the apartment and let Harry know I'll be gone in case he gets any calls from Essex. In fact, since we both have the weekend off, let's take a small suitcase and stay overnight in Hannibal."

"Are you expecting anything of medical significance to happen in Essex this weekend?"

"No, though the Sullivan girl should have her baby next week sometime. She's the only obstetrical case I have left who is due to deliver before I leave for California."

"Do you think Harry and Purity would like to come along? They're a nice couple. All we need is more food."

"No, they're going out to her folks' farm for supper tonight. Purity actually invited Harry to meet her family."

"Maybe their romance is getting serious," Sarah replied.

On their weekend trip they did all the tourist things Hannibal provides. They saw the home of Mark Twain, the whitewashed back fence of Tom Sawyer, and the cave where Indian Joe died. Early Sunday evening they traveled back to Sarah's trailer park.

As they approached the front gate of the park around 8:00 P.M., Gerry spotted Worth's car parked alongside the left side of the entrance road facing them. "Slow down, it's Worth's car and he just blinked his lights at us," Gerry said.

Pulling over to the side of the road, Sarah stopped the Ford and shut off the ignition. Before she could set the hand brake, Worth bounded out of his car and dashed alongside the driver's window of Sarah's car.

"It's Tex," he said anxiously. "He's back in town early, he's a mite more than merely mad, and he's looking for you, Sarah. Better let Gerry out here right now. I'll drive him home."

"When did Tex get to town?" she asked with worry in her voice.

"Last night about 9:00 P.M, he flew from Houston into Kansas City sometime late Saturday afternoon and rented a car. Drove it up here from there. My contact at his hospital said he didn't realize Tex had left until Saturday evening. Tex apparently switched schedules with another OB/Gyn resident and left a week early. Fact is, I didn't learn he was on his way 'till 11:00 P.M. yesterday when my friend at Houston Community Hospital called. By then Tex had been here in town for two hours."

"How long have you been waiting here by the roadside?" Gerry asked.

"Since five this afternoon. Harry and I decided to pull four-hour shifts waiting to make sure we reached you before Tex did.

403

Thank God you didn't come back late last night. This guy is really mad."

"How do you know?" inquired Gerry as the full realization of the possible danger finally sunk in.

"Because he banged on my trailer at midnight asking me if I knew where Sarah was. I'm three trailers down from Sarah," Worth said. "He'd apparently hit both homes in between before he got to mine."

"What cover story did you give him, Worth?" Sarah asked. "Knowing your reputation, I'm sure it's a good one, and I better start memorizing it right away."

"I told him you went to a funeral of a woman patient being buried in Hannibal. Told him I didn't know her name, but she was someone you'd cared for in the hospital here last year. I said she died suddenly on the family farm Friday and would be buried in their farm cemetery today."

"And since there'd be no phone at a small family cemetery he couldn't call. Right?" Sarah laughingly questioned. "That's a good cover for me. It should work."

"Right. So get your stuff out of Sarah's car, Gerry, and I'll drive you home. Don't even think about kissing her again. Just grab your suitcase, and let's get the hell out of here. And you, Sarah, go home, change your clothes and pick up Tex in ten minutes at the hospital emergency room."

Gerry stepped out of Sarah's car, grabbed his overnight bag from the trunk, and climbed into Worth's Ford. Sarah then drove her car into the trailer park, "Is that idiot really mad?" He asked turning to look at Worth. "Why is she picking him up at the emergency room?"

"He's mad all right, but not just because she wasn't here to greet him. Seems Tex needed company so badly this afternoon I decided to give him some."

"Oh no. I don't think I'm going to like this. You didn't did you? Not really?" Gerry asked as he slouched down on his seat and rested his head carefully against the back of the seat.

"Don't worry. He hurts too badly right now to be looking for you. I introduced him to Rover. Rover liked Tex, but then that pit bull terrier generally likes anybody she gets a real sizable bite out of. Guess Tex must have tasted pretty good to her."

"You sick'd that damn pit-bull bitch on the guy?" Gerry questioned.

"Hey, he asked for trouble. Who the hell does he think he is anyway? He tried to make trouble for my neighbors and then woke me up at midnight. You know how Rover hates to be woken up at night once she gets comfortable with those massive jaws around her favorite black angus femur."

"So what did River do? Give me the bloody details."

"Well, by late this afternoon, Tex was really pissed. He had already been down to my trailer twice more, early in the morning waking up me and my girlfriend, on our only Sunday morning together for the whole week. Christy was so mad she threatened to get up, go to church, and then move back in with her ex-husband."

"So you were desperate?" Gerry asked.

"Right. So I went down to where Tex parked his rental car and got one of his shoes he left on the back seat. I took it home to Rover and let her smell it and chew on it for a good quarter hour. Wanted her to fixate on his scent real good."

"Don't tell me," Gerry interrupted. "Then you took the shoe and struck Rover across her hind legs with it. That bonds her with the place to bite and the shoe smell of whom to bite. Afterwards you turned her loose to do mischief. Right?"

"Almost right. By then I was so mad I missed and hit her across her ass. Then I set her out in front of my trailer with the old quarter-inch chain - the one with the two loose links."

"Rather than with her regular chilled steel, three-eighths-inch chain?"

"Right, and then Tex came down a third time around 4:30 and started yelling again. Well, she ran out after him pretty fast. Rover chased him for at least three blocks. She apparently likes to get a little adrenalin profusion in the muscles of her meals. Then she bit him on the ass. She got so excited she wet herself, and Tex did too."

"How do you know?"

"I took him to the emergency room. Rover got a three-inch chunk out of the left side of his butt. They were still sewing him up an hour ago. Figure they should be done in another 15 minutes."

"That ought to slow him down for a while."

"Yeah, the only piece of ass he got today was his own, chewed up by Rover. If I hadn't called her off of him, old Tex would have ended up a half-ass for life," Worth said through a full smile of gleaming white teeth.

"So why all the excitement about getting Sarah home right away and me away from her? We could have spent another 15 minutes together."

"It's Rover. You know how upset she gets after she's bitten someone. I think she feels guilty even though this time it's obviously my fault. I have to quarantine her for the next ten days to make sure she no problem with rabies. Hell, I know she's clean.

She's had all her shots, and if she had rabies half the dogs around here would be dead by now."

They pulled up in front of Gerry's apartment and Worth climbed out of the car, grabbed Gerry's suitcase and started to carry it up the front walk for him.

"Hey, I can carry that," Gerry said. "You don't need to accompany me to my front door, though I do appreciate the courtesy. Next thing you'll be expecting a tip for all your super service."

"I thought as long as I'm here, I may as well drop in for a couple of beers and say hello to Rover."

"To Rover," yelled Gerry. "Not to Rover."

"Yeah, why not? She probably misses me already."

"OK. Break it to me easy. Where is Rover?" asked Gerry as he unlocked his apartment's front door." Rover quickly answered his question as she jumped off Gerry's bed and ran to meet the two doctors. Her stubby tail wagged happily as she jumped up on each of them and licked their faces.

"I think she'll enjoy spending her quarantine here," Worth offered in explanation.

"What do you mean, '*spending*'?"

"Well, what else could I do? The animal authorities wouldn't let me quarantine her at the trailer park. You know you owe me on this one."

"Yeah, I suppose I do," Gerry agreed.

"And besides that, Rover sure seems to like lying on your big bed. Bet she'll sleep like a baby," Worth said.

"So where do I sleep for the next ten days?"

"Well, Harry and I figured there's just enough room for you to sleep in your sleeping bag on the top of your living room bar.

Just don't roll over in the middle of the night, you might fall on the floor and break an arm, or worse than that."

"Worse than what? What could be worse than breaking my arm?" Gerry asked.

"Well, you must remember, Rover doesn't like to be awakened in the middle of the night by sudden banging or thumping noises."

"Okay, I'm glad to know that."

"Her old jaw bones don't comfortably wrap around the dead bull's femur bone. You'll be okay. Don't worry. She can't fully chomp on you," Worth explained.

"Anything else, old friend?" Gerry asked, "Just to make sure I don't worry."

"Okay, I almost forgot. There's raw hamburger for her in the refrigerator. She likes it medium rare with just a touch of garlic, but generous on the A-1 sauce. Give it to her at least once a day. And maybe, until she gets used to staying here, keep her on the Thorazine - 25 milligrams every eight hours. Now give me a couple of beers. I noticed some cold ones in the refrigerator."

"Two at once? Have you become a two-fisted drinker?"

"No, one's for me and one's for Rover. Why not? This has been a big day for her. She deserves a cold beer."

Chapter 14
Train Wait
April 13-May 4, 1962

Senior medical students who served their six-month externships and worked in one of twelve rural clinics of Northeast Missouri had great pride in their personal black medical bags. They crammed their leather bags full of every known small diagnostic instrument a student could afford. This equipment represented concentrated thought, careful planning, and considerable investment. Whenever medical students on extern duty staffed a clinic you could be sure their black doctor's bag sat close by.

In the village of Essex, each of the rural clinic's two exam rooms had a leather covered examination table, a dark wood desk, two matching metal chairs, a round metal stool, a large gray filing cabinet, a counter area for routine lab work, a sink with cold running water, a standing scale, and white cabinets with glass shelves and glass doors for medical instruments, medications, and clean linens. Conspicuously absent, unfortunately, were X-ray and EKG machines. In this respect, the small clinic of Essex was not comparably equipped with larger city clinics during the period during of the early 1960's. Costs prohibited convenience.

That which the student doctors lacked in expensive machinery, they made up for in endless enthusiasm. The local people of the small country towns in Northeast Missouri received some of the finest health care that that of anywhere else in the state. If EKG's and X-rays were needed, sick and injured patients were promptly sent to the city campus of the nearby medical/ educational complex. This nationally recognized medical school, then known as the Kirksville College of Osteopathy and Surgery with its adjoining three hospitals and busy outpatient clinics, was located 53 miles away from Essex. Though many of the medical students had frequently discussed getting additional equipment for their respective rural clinics, they could not afford to buy it themselves and village residents were quite conservative with the money their proud but independent citizens could offer for such health care expenses.

On a particularly warm and clear sunny afternoon, the workday had proceeded like any other during the spring of 1962. Dr. Gerry Frank had seen seven office patients at the rural clinic and made two house calls within the small village. His partner, Dr. Harry Thompson, had seen four office patients and made three house calls to farms nestled around the rolling wooded hills and fertile green valleys of the outlying countryside.

House calls were an important service in rural medicine, since many of the older and chronically ill patients could not easily travel any great distance from their homes to the clinics. During time of inclement weather, gravel and dirt side roads became nearly impassable. Four-wheel drive vehicles, tractors, and occasionally horses were needed to reach distant locations deeply nestled into the country districts within the gentle hills and the hidden valleys.

At the end of the clinic day, Gerry locked the heavy wooden exterior door of the faded red-brick clinic, turned right, and walked east down Main Street before crossing over to the Blue Bell Cafe' for supper. Three pickup trucks, an old brown Jeep, and a new red tractor were all parked out in front of the small, neat restaurant. The Blue Bell survived on solid food and prompt service. No fancy advertising or bold pretense brought in its faithful customers. Only the large black and gold painted block letters on the front plate glass window announced its presence and purpose. Regardless of the name, there no blue bell was in sight. Rumor inferred 'Blue Bell' had been the name of a cat persistently hanging around the restaurant when it first opened in 1886. Food in one form or another had been served there continuously for well over three-quarters of a century.

Since all three side booths and the front four tables were already filled with early customers eating their evening meals, Gerry sat down at a round red swivel stool at the end of the empty counter. He loosened the buttons on his blue denim jacket. The enticing aroma of lamb stew cooking on the stove drifted out from the open kitchen. Suddenly he knew exactly what he would have for supper.

Madge Grumley, age 48, wife of Hank Grumley, who owned the local Texaco gas station, did a '*double*'. She not only waited on customers at the counter, but she also cooked at the stove. The old timers remembered she had been a local beauty of about 5'6" and 125 pounds in her day. But ten kids, 20 pounds, and 30 years of hard work had pushed that day to an early twilight. However, her years of troubled toil and blighted hopes had dulled neither her enthusiasm nor her cheerfulness. Her pleasant smile had been permanently etched on her face, and she always seemed as if she had just been told a good joke.

"Got your favorite lamb stew again tonight, Doc," she called out loudly as she quickly served up a generous bowl of stew without being asked. She immediately followed this by a putting down a big cup of steaming hot coffee, which she placed on the red laminate counter next to the stew. A large pot of baked beans simmered on the old black stove's back burner, but Madge already knew they would not interest Gerry.

"Now that's what I call lamb stew, Madge. I sure do love your cookin'. All stews should be thick like this so you can eat them with a fork."

"Where's your partner, Dr. Thompson, this evening?" she asked. "I know he doesn't much like lamb, but I have some fine beef hamburger and fresh home fries. I can fix 'em up real fast for him." Besides the perpetual smile on her face, she had a softness in her large brown eyes as she spoke. She felt each set of new doctors brought a fresh breath of life to the small town as they stayed for their six-month rotations in the art and science of rural medicine. At the end of the six months most of them would disappear forever for their internships and their other graduate training or general practice. But even as their careers might take them anywhere in the United States, they would always remember how their practice of medicine truly had started there in Essex or the other rural villages near the university.

"He's just finishing up the last of today's house calls," answered Gerry as he finished buttering a slice of dark brown bread and picked up his fork to attack the thick stew. "I'm expecting him to be along in just a few minutes if his old Chevy holds out that long. Do you think maybe your husband could take another look at that clutch? I'd hate to think of Harry stuck out on some deserted county road at night with a no-go car."

"Well, Hank's specialty and preference has always been Fords and Jeeps, Doc. He never did take kindly to workin' on Chevys, but I sure will ask him if you want. I know Harry would have a kind'a hard time forgiving Hank if he had to walk all the way back from a remote call some night."

The doctor seemed deeply absorbed in thought as he added double cream and sugar to his hot coffee and stirred slowly. "You know, Madge, I crossed the railroad tracks about 2:20 this afternoon, and that damn Silver Streak passenger train, the one you folks call the Mainliner, must have come roaring around the east curve and on straight away through town doing about 60 miles an hour. Then it headed west again without even a hint of slowing down. Does it ever stop here any more?"

"No chance, Doc. That's the Santa Fe's finest train in these parts of the Lower Midwest. I understand it even does 70 to 75 on the straightaways west of here. The train doesn't stop until it hits Kansas City, 163 miles southwest of here." She said this with the authority of a local who had traveled to the big city and back quite a few times.

The railroad tracks ran along the lower half of town parallel to the Main Street, swung two blocks south and then down a straight, sloping hill. The old railroad station was a two-story Victorian style building, now painted dull tan with black trim, topped with a steeply slanted blue-gray slate roof and large overhanging eaves. Twice a day a freight train stopped there to pick up and discharge produce and cargo. The morning freight train went through Essex from the east at 10:32 A.M., and an evening freight train went through from the west at 11:36 P.M.

Rusty Rails, the 63-year-old emphysematic station master would drive over from Moberly, 33 miles away, to feed Old Max, the graying, semi-retired German shepherd railroad dog, and to supervise the cargo loading and unloading during the local train stops. At all other times, the station would be deserted except for Old Max who thought he still worked there. Few people were willing to argue with him, especially if he were hungry. Max never refused a meal and had flatly ignored banishment to junkyard patrol. He knew his duty and purpose in life ever since his birth under a baggage cart on the station platform 14 years before.

The two local freight trains were the only trains that ever stopped in town. Madge informed the young doctor that no passenger train had stopped in Essex for well over 20 years. She considered the subject closed and walked back to her stove about five feet behind the counter. She slowly stirred the baked beans. The fragrance of their faintly burnt brown sugar sauce soon drifted throughout the small cafe', which was her way of letting all the customers know the hardy beans were also a special on the evening's menu.

Gerry took in a few more mouthfuls of the lamb stew and continued, "It sure would be nice if I could get the Mainliner to stop here some day soon, because I want to take about a week off of work to go back out to California."

"You planning on a vacation of sorts?"

"No, not a vacation, but I have to interview and then finalize my decision on the internship offer I received from the hospital in Los Angeles. Their big county hospital out there offered me a spot for my residency. If I half'ta drive all the way down to Kansas City to catch the train heading west, it's gon'na take me at least an extra half a day driving down there and another half a day driving back."

"You're right about that Doc. It's a sizable drive down to the city."

"So, I'm just gonna half'ta somehow stop the train right here in town. Then I won't be wasting the extra day. Yup, that's just what I'm gon'na half'ta do." It had recently dawned on Gerry earlier that week it was time to go home because he already started to talk like the locals. Another year here and his California surfing friends would not be able to understand him. Even his California physician friends might have trouble communicating with him. On a recent long distance phone call to a doctor in Los Angeles, Gerry had described his patient load for that day as including two *'down in the heart'* farmers, and four with *'bone miseries'*, the local lingo for congestive heart failure and rheumatoid arthritis.

"Look," said Madge with a patient pause in her voice as she focused on how to answer without offending Gerry. "I know there's nothin' as all knowin' and as all powerful as a new doctor, but the fast train hasn't stopped here or in any other way acknowledged the existence of this town in over 20 years."

"Is that a fact? Well, then it's time it does stop," Gerry said.

"Hey, it wouldn't have stopped even back then if the old steam locomotive hadn't hit deaf Charlie Brown's hay wagon. Now that was somethin' to see," Madge exclaimed.

"What happened?" Gerry questioned as he shoveled in another forkful of the thick lamb stew.

"Well, witnesses said his two stubborn Missouri mules decided to stop pullin' his wagon full of hay half-way across the tracks. In fact, the train didn't come to a complete stop even then. I think it just kinda' slowed down while it scattered hay bales all about and splintered up the remains of the old wooden wagon on either side of the right-of-way. Sure was a mess. I saw the results about ten minutes after it occurred."

"But what happened to the mules and to Charlie?"

"Well it sure made those two mules most of more worthless than they were in the beginnin'. Charlie wasn't hurt at all 'cept his feelins'. But from then on, he could never really slow them stubborn mules down once they saw the railroad tracks. They'd just take off runnin' fast no matter what they were pullin'. Finally caused the old man to turn them in for his first Ford pickup truck. Funny the way progress comes to a small town."

Gerry tried to visualize the iron train versus wooden wagon accident, and Madge said a silent prayer for old Charlie Brown who had just recently been run over by his own truck. He recuperated at his daughter's home in Moberly with multiple contusions and abrasions.

"Heck, Doc," she continued with a pause after pouring herself a full cup of hot, black coffee, "if the Mainliner would stop here occasionally, this place wouldn't be the ghost town it is today. It sure would help the local economy, and it would give some people around here more faith in their old home town." Madge's manner of speaking showed her faith had been terribly tested on

416

many previous occasions. The lines on her face of 48 years were already deeply etched from her past reflections on frequent hard times. Yet the broad smile lines around her mouth were even deeper.

"Well, Madge, maybe that's the problem, and if so, the solution is obvious. Don't you understand? That's a problem we can sure 'nuff fix up right soon," Gerry declared.

"Understand what? Not sure I see what you're drivin' at Doc," Madge responded.

"Maybe it really is just a question of faith. If the good people here would have enough faith that the fast train hasn't forgotten this tired old town, then maybe the train would begin to stop here again on occasion." The young doctor's voice rang with the enthusiasm only young people can bring to an impossible situation. He put his fork down for a few seconds and stopped eating as he silently reflected on the words he had just said. Suddenly he realized how in most situations he wanted to ignore the probability of bad if there were any way to reflect on the possibility of good. Here was a situation with considerable potential for a good outcome.

"I gotta' admit, Doc, those are powerful thoughts. People don't have the faith in their own home town like they used to in the good old days. Why, even young folks leave here 'bout as soon as they're out of high school. I know. My oldest five kids sure 'nuff left. Some even before they graduated. You're right. It would be a mighty big boost to all of us if the fast passenger train would stop here just once - even if it were to take on only one passenger."

Just then the silver bell jingled at the front door of the cafe' as Harry came back from finishing his house calls. He smiled in quiet anticipation of one of Madge's excellent meals, though he had no idea what she had cooked. He took of his brown sports coat, loosened his tan tie, hung his coat on a wooden wall peg near the front door, and sat down on the empty round counter stool next to Gerry. Madge put a couple of fresh hamburgers on the stove without even asking Harry what he wanted. His wide smile showed a mouthful of large white, nearly square teeth. Harry loved hamburgers, especially the way Madge made them smothered in chopped onions.

One of the most important aspects of small towns is that everybody knows everybody so well, they also know what they like for supper. But at Madge's place, it did not really matter because they were going to eat whatever she cooked and wanted to serve. She generally was well in tune with her customers distinctive digestive desires, and her food always filled their tummies with delicious, plentiful portions.

"Now that he's here, let's ask Harry what he thinks, Madge. As my partner I feel obliged to consult with him on any issue of this magnitude."

"What I think about what?" asked Harry, suddenly realizing he may have interrupted a serious conversation.

"Do you think if we could get the Santa Fe's Mainliner to stop here in town to pick up a passenger at the old railroad station, it would help this town regain some faith in itself? Might it even put this place back on the Missouri map? I remember last February looking at a recent big map of this state I couldn't even find Essex mentioned or listed. I'm not rightly sure the rest of Missouri knows this town is still here." Gerry realized it would take a while for Harry to answer, so he returned his full attention to finishing up the last of his large bowl of lamb stew and the two slices of dark bread Madge had served on a separate side plate. The generous, meaty stew had been a specialty of the cafe' and one of the young doctor's favorite meals. Since he had spent most of his meal thinking and talking, he found himself only half way through the soon-to-be-cold stew and a third slice of bread without the benefit of butter.

Probably one of the finest new physicians the village had ever seen on a six-month clinic rotation, Harry had planned on dedicating himself to rural medicine and on going back to a country practice in his native West Virginia's hills and hollows after first taking a rotating internship and surgical residency in Texas. However, once he had set his mind on eating, he did not like to entertain any serious conversation until well into the first course of the meal.

Gerry respected him for this. After all, every man has his priorities, and the sooner in life he sorted them out, the more smoothly his life went. Therefore, he let Harry wolf down both of his large hamburgers and finish most of his first cup of coffee before diverting his attention again. Harry always completely finished one item on his plate before starting on a different one.

Madge, by now familiar with Harry's preference for eating over talking, had taken advantage of this break in the conversation to serve three new customers at other tables and to take payment from another two. Then she returned to the counter with a side order of baked beans that she put down next to Harry's coffee cup, stating as she did, "Let those cool a couple of minutes or you'll burn your tongue."

Late into the panfried potatoes, Harry brushed back the reddish-blonde hair from his forehead with his free left hand and finally replied. "Yes, I do definitely think it is a question of faith, Gerry. That's just what it is. We both know that. But it's a complicated, circular argument. The old town lacks faith in itself because, among other things, the fast train won't stop and the Mainliner won't stop because the train knows the town doesn't have any real faith in its future. Essex was an important place during the cattle drive days here at the end of the Old Chisholm

Trail, and the town had all kinds of faith in a real future. Even when the town fathers purchased the old LaSalle fire engine back in 1927, the town still had faith in itself. But how can any town have faith in itself if the train blasting through doesn't ever bother to stop and its fire engine won't always start? That damn fire truck is almost 40-years-old."

Harry found the issue of the derelict fire engine a sore subject, and he managed to mention it at as often as possible. Harry loved fire engines, and though he would not admit to it anymore, he really did love the old LaSalle. The town's people trusted him and Gerry with their children's health, with epidemics, and with traumas of their very lives from birth to death. But the town counsel in its calm, collective, and infinite wisdom had seen fit to rule against Dr. Thompson being allowed to drive the local fire engine. They appreciated the good doctor making house calls on gravel roads at 75 miles per hour in his own car, but they did not appreciate his potentially being behind the steering wheel of their beloved 1927 LaSalle fire engine. "Yes, it is a question of faith," said Harry, "but I just don't think there's enough faith left in this old town to stop that train."

"You really don't think so?" his partner asked.

"I'd sure like to think so, believe me I would, but I'm really not sure." Shaking his head repeatedly, Dr. Thompson once again looked down at his dinner plate and attacked the last of his fried potatoes.

"I don't agree, Harry. I think there is fairly enough faith around here, but we'd sure have to start a serious search for it and really scour down to the base for it. I think there's enough faith in this here good old town to stop the fast train, even some time within this very month. Yup, I'd almost be willing to bet on it." With that statement, Gerry banged his empty milk glass on the counter for emphasis, so hard it chipped a small piece from its thick bottom.

By now Madge was so fascinated with this conversation she overlooked the damage to one of her few remaining matching blue glasses. She had not said much more as she took it all in and turned from facing the doctors to suddenly busying herself cleaning the big stove.

Even his old pie auction foe, Dexter Wilkinson who had come in for his evening cup of coffee and deep dish apple pie grew intrigued as he sat at the counter two seats down from the doctors and listened to every word. He had forgotten to make his usual complaint about the apple pie not being deep-dished enough. He finally gave a loud shout of laughter and slapped the clean counter top with his large dirty hands. These doctors sure did sound dumb to Dexter. "Oh hell," he said with a sarcastic laugh, "the fast train hasn't stopped since my mammy and pap came back from celebrating after their wedding in Kansas City and that must have been 30 years ago." Dexter's comment verified what Gerry had always thought of him as he knew Dexter was 32-years-old. *So Dexter really was a bastard literally and not just figuratively,* Gerry thought to himself.

"I can drive you all down there to Kansas City to catch the train straight away in my truck about as fast as the train can make it there anyway, Doc," continued Dexter. "In fact, we could borrow Buntley's new Chevy pickup, which is even faster than my Ford. Just let me know when you need that there ride, and I'll haul you down for the price of the gas and, of course, a little extra." Dexter was not necessarily all bad - just mostly bad. Some folks could almost forgive him for foreclosing on the mortgage to his own parent's farm as they were just as mean as Dexter. Seems like the 'meanness' gene had been destined to be passed on from generation to generation.

The matter of Don Powell's dog's death, however, was hard

to forgive or to forget, and many attributed it to Dexter. The big bull dog reportedly had a vicious streak and on occasion had attacked a couple of deer hunters from Iowa. Still, nobody considered that a good reason enough to tie it with a leash to its collar onto the back bumper of deaf Charlie Brown's pickup, resulting in a horrible sight. The fact Charlie had not found the remains of his dog until two days after he sobered up from another drinking binge was something Charlie could never forget. That experience had one good side effect being Charlie's last drinking binge. Deaf Charlie never drank again. From that moment on, Charlie fanatically did an airplane pilot-style walk-around inspection of his pickup truck before he would ever start his motor. He had also rejoined the local Southern Baptists saying they were not much different than the Lutherans since he could not hear either minister anyway.

"That's it then. I know what I'll do," announced Gerry to his partner, "Though I'm not yet the world's greatest doctor, they're going to remember me around here as the man who re-instilled big faith in this small town." With this said, Gerry pushed back his dirty dishes, stood up and with unsmiling eyes steadily surveyed the room. Solemnly he announced in a voice loud enough to be heard throughout the small café, "I am going to stop the fast passenger train. The train is going to stop, pick me up, and not only take me to Kansas City, but also take me all the way to Los Angeles, California." With this statement made, the doctor carefully sat down, sipped on his second cup of hot coffee and started his first piece of apple pie.

For a few moments, silence permeated throughout the restaurant as nobody spoke. Even some of the diners at the front tables stopped eating with full forks midway to their mouths. They were all locals except for the John Deere dealer from Macon who had been trying to sell the new tractor parked out front to a

Ferguson tractor farmer.

"That's impossible," yelled Dexter. "That's the damn dumbest thing I've ever heard any of you college boys say yet. That's the trouble with you guys with too much education. You got no common sense, Doc. Boy, I sure wish I could talk you into playing with us in my Wednesday night poker games," he laughed while he banged his dirty left fist on the hard laminate countertop.

Poker was Dexter's forte - a really good player, he had already cleaned Harry out on two separate occasions. He ran the Wednesday night card sessions in the local pool hall down the block. He also reportedly played serious cards on different nights in three or four other surrounding small towns within a 20-mile radius to the extent most of the people who knew him thought gambling to be his true means of livelihood - a good guess, since his family farm had pretty much gone fallow to raw pasture.

"Well, Dexter, if you're so damn pessimistic, then you're the first one we should try here to convert. You've just got to get some faith the fast train will stop for me," said Gerry. It seemed like an appropriate time to memorialize this as a solemn occasion - one long to be remembered. Gerry stood up again, walked over to the old juke box in the corner, dropped in a quarter, and hit the button three times for *Amazing Grace*, his favorite hymn. The music inspired him as it filled the small café, and brought a large smile to Madge's face.

"Yeah, Dexter, show a little faith in something good for a change," challenged Harry. "Listen to that old time hymn, give up your life of sin."

"No way, no way," persisted Dexter, yelling louder to be heard above the music. "It ain't gonna happen. It just ain't gonna happen. That Mainliner will never stop in Essex again. You'll be wastin' your time if you start waitin' for that distant day."

"Might you be willing to bet on that, Dexter?" questioned

Harry boldly. "Say in the form of a small cash wager?"

"Sure am. In fact, I'm willin' to bet right now against all the money y'all can put up tonight, or any other night, that there's just no way you guys can ever stop that fast train in this here slow old town, short of throwin' a living body or large object onto the tracks. Yup, I'm even willin' to give ya good odds on that." Smiling smugly, he attacked the second dish of apple pie Madge had put down in front of him. "I'd even bet that one over my own dead body," he repeated for emphasis.

"Quit talking to me about the scenic route, Dexter. All I want is the fastest route to get me to Kansas City and on to California," Gerry responded.

By then Dexter's crony, Weatherford Buntley, had entered the restaurant and sat down at the far left end of the counter, with Dexter to his immediate right. Their mothers were sisters so these two winners were cousins. They even looked alike, though Dexter had a darker complexion, was three years older, two inches shorter at 5'9", and about 20 pounds lighter at 180. They both dressed wore old plaid shirts, faded blue overalls with black suspenders, well-worn black boots, and bright red caps advertising their respective choices in Midwest fertilizers. Just as tough and as thoroughly mean as Dexter, Weatherford had been considered by most in the small town as a less dangerous threat since he was too stupid to do anything original. On the few occasions he smiled, it looked more like a grimace of pain out of the left side of his mouth. This hid his shortened, right upper lateral incisor and canine teeth, which were noticeably worn down from his bad habit of twisting off beer bottle caps with his teeth. Some of the town folk thought he had long since completely cooked his brain smelling fumes at the local rendering plant in the northeast corner of town where he worked and lived in the first house downwind of the plant.

His method of driving his new Chevy pickup, however, worried the young doctors as a definite menace to the health and safety of the entire county. The ten-month old truck was Weatherford's pride and joy. He had been able to buy it cheaply in a recent Kansas City bank repossession auction because it had been painted purple by previous owners. It was the only purple pickup in all of the state of Missouri and no one else wanted it.

"Well, then," said Harry banging a spoon loudly on an empty water glass for everybody's attention, "maybe we really ought to put a small wager on this venture. Now everybody admits that faith here in Essex is damn scarce, and since that train hasn't stopped for at least 20 or maybe even 30 years, I think the Frank and Thomson syndicate, as the good guys, should get at least five-to-one odds. We're willing to hereby bet that our own Doc Frank can put on his Sunday go-to-meeting suit, pack a small suitcase, pick it up, walk down on that old deserted railroad platform, stick his right thumb out on some agreed-upon day, and stop the fast Mainliner of the Southern Pacific right here in the center of town."

Dexter nearly fell over himself trying to get his well-worn wallet out of his right hip pocket, but at the same time yelling over and over again the odds were, "Too high, much too high." By now he stood up from the table even though he had not finished his second piece of apple pie. He looked through his wallet to see how much money he had available. As he opened it, three copper pennies, four wooden matches, and a tattered prophylactic pack fell out on the green laminate counter.

Weatherford kept spooning down his baked beans, which by now were about a 50-50 mix with ketchup and tabasco sauce he had added in abundance. He grunted and yelled too, but no one could understand him through the food in his open mouth, and the excitement of the bet made him even hungrier. Adding to the confusion, a large fan on the floor whirred just behind the counter which Madge always turned on whenever Weatherford or others from the rendering plant sat down to eat. The big fan turned back and forth like a spectator at a sporting match, first watching one side and then the other. Gerry thought Weatherford deserved a little extra watching as he seemed paranoid at times, he always suspected everyone and expected the worst in them.

When the noise quieted down, Gerry asked for her opinion. Madge smelled a rat, but she did not know where it came from. She thought the docs were getting in far too deeply, and she knew these two town boys were never to be trusted about anything. But having been asked for her opinion, and being a strictly honest and conscientious person, she said she estimated about three-to-one odds were more fair. Dexter Wilkinson and his sidekick, Weatherford Buntley, would have to put up three dollars for every one dollar the doctors put up on the bet.

Dexter returned his wallet to his hip pocket and sat down again finally to finish his pie, obviously deep in thought while everyone else also quietly finished their meals. The only sounds in the cafe' were the metal utensils hitting the plates and the fan's whirring mingled with music from the big juke box in the corner. The Ferguson farmer had added more change and the machine now rendered *Your Cheatin' Heart* sung by Hank Williams.

"In that case, I'm going back to the card game at the pool hall after supper 'cause all I got here is about $63 and that won't cover more than $21 of yours," said Dexter. His sidekick had even less - about $42.

"Hell," said Harry, turning toward them on his counter stool, "that's only going to cover about $35 of ours. The odds are three to one. I thought you guys were big-time. The doc and me here were thinking about putting up a $1000. We're talking about some real faith right up front. This isn't child's play or back-room foolishness."

"Jeezus." said Dexter getting so excited he jumped up again, this time knocking over Weatherford's coffee. This score was like nothing he had seen before. This was big time, right now and right here in this remote village. Suckers like these dumb doctors did not come every day, and suddenly Dexter clearly knew deep into the very meanness of his bone marrow, somehow he and cousin Weatherford would have to raise plenty of money. But how would they obtain it?

"We'll take it, Doc, on a 1000 bucks at three-to-one, but y'all gotta give us a few days to raise the money. That's a lot more than just walkin' around change."

"Okay," said Gerry, "that's fair, and one place I suggest you start is by taking out the maximum loan you can get on that crazy purple pickup." Making Weatherford wheelless would certainly enhance the community citizens' long-term chances for survival on the local roads. In fact, his losing his truck would be a bounty and benefit to all mankind within driving distance. "Now pick up that condom pack you dropped on the counter, Dexter. We surely don't need you diluting the gene pool any further in these parts."

The word of the bet spread like wildfire throughout the town and beyond. Since Gerry had already picked a definite date on which he wanted to go west to California, he had tied himself to a time frame of leaving exactly three weeks from Friday. He also agreed the large bet between the two doctors and the two town boys would be covered by two weeks from Wednesday. Others of the town could bet as they saw fit right up until the final day at noon.

Gerry and Harry had not realized the full ramifications of their venture on the small town to renew local faith in itself until the next Wednesday night - an unseasonably warm spring evening with a hint of thunder in the air and distant flashes of sheet lightning reflecting across the hills into the distance in the west.

They made a medical call visiting 84-year-old Miss Agatha Martin and her younger, 82-year-old sister, Miss Martha Martin, at the sisters' home. The two ladies did not like having to walk the distance to the medical clinic and then the possible wait in the reception room. They lived together in a large weather-beaten, brown-frame house set a fair distance back from the main road and halfway up a large hill slightly north of town. Originally built in 1885 by their father, the outside looked like it had seen better days, but the inside showed as meticulously neat and clean as could be. The ladies never allowed neither disorder nor dust. Both women were dedicated to the proverb of *Cleanliness being next to godliness* as a primary concern. Most of the fine Victorian antique furnishings were original to the rooms with high ceilings and tall narrow windows. Entering from the open front porch with its ornate spindle railing felt like walking back in time to a distant era. Martha always wore black skirts with white blouses and reportedly had since the sudden, accidental demise of the sisters' father. He had been killed after breaking his neck when he was thrown from a wild quarter horse over 50 years earlier. The ladies' eccentricity seemed more easily tolerated in the small town where it weaved itself firmly into the fabric of the local folklore.

Agatha generally wore bright combinations of vividly contrasting colors. This evening she had chosen a red and yellow striped skirt and a bright blue blouse with her favorite light green shawl draped loosely over her slightly stooped shoulders. Agatha would always be young at heart.

The doctors arrived for a routine check of Agatha's chronic arthritis and Martha's congestive heart failure with periodic pedal edema. Being persistently hungry and generally broke, the young doctors timed each two-week checkup of the sisters for around six in the evening. The ladies were always pleasant and tried hard to look sincerely surprised at each visit, though by now they would have been quite disappointed had the doctors failed to show up every other Wednesday as an informal ritual. As usual, the sisters insisted the young doctors stay for supper, which just happened to be almost ready to be put on the table. Both women were fantastic cooks. The easy, open hospitality of this area of Missouri contributed itself to a more southern-style hospitality than a northern persuasion. Likewise, the cooking seemed far more Dixie than Des Moines.

During the main course of southern fried chicken with fresh homemade biscuits and brown gravy, Martha brought up the subject of the train bet. "We want to tell both of you fine young doctors how much we do appreciate your goal of reviving full faith in this here old town. Now sister and I sincerely believe Essex has a fine future once again, but for many years we had been well nigh to worryin'. Many's the time we've chewed on this railroad problem both here at home and at our weekly Tuesday afternoon sewing bees. Isn't that true, Agatha?"

"Yes, Martha. I waxed nostalgic just to remember the good old days and the excitement in town when the big passenger trains with their loud, gray steam locomotives stopped at our little station on their way to or from Kansas City. Oh, to see them stop again. Those were the good times. It even brings back memories of my young Timmy Rivers and how very handsome he was on the fine spring day in May when we ran off together to Kansas."

"Agatha. I'm truly shocked. I thought we had agreed 60 years ago this coming July never to mention that again. Yes, it was in this home of our very own father, God rest his soul. You promised never to discuss again the disgraceful two months of your life when you lived in total sin. And Timmy already married to a woman in St. Louis, even if you didn't know about it. Yes, you've shocked me again, sister." From the way she said it showed Agatha had shocked Martha on numerous previous occasions, and she probably would again.

"Well, these two, fine young gentlemen are our physicians, Martha, and I'm told you should never have any secrets from your doctor," she replied with a shy grin brightening up her pleasantly lined face.

"But about the train bet, Agatha? Didn't we all decide yesterday about it?" Martha said in her hurried attempt to steer the conversation away from the past indiscretions of her older sister.

Harry looked at Gerry. Gerry looked at Harry. Then they both looked deeply inside themselves. Where was this all leading? Harry hated to discuss important things until well into his second helping of food, and three legs and a large thigh still sat on the serving plate. He knew Gerry would grab at least one more of the legs, but with a little luck, Harry felt he could get the other two for himself, and then they could split the last thigh.

Agatha answered with a gentle nod and continued the discussion. "Though as good Christian ladies, my sister and I don't approve of gambling, we do know the good Lord takes various means to demonstrate his learned lessons in faith and good works. And anyway, three-to-one odds ain't bad at all. Those odds demand some bread be cast on the waters to see what comes back."

Harry sheepishly shrugged his shoulders and apologized in feigned contrition as he slowly reached for another chicken leg. Those were the best odds they could get, he explained, though they had hoped for four-to-one in the beginning.

Gerry laughed loudly, seeing through Harry's plan for the remaining fried chicken. Bending over the table, quickly took both the last two legs for his own plate, leaving Harry the thigh.

"Well," continued Martha, "sister and I did indeed discuss it at our afternoon sewing bee yesterday with the rest of the girls [not one under 70], and the 12 of us are all putting up $20 apiece. We hope we'll be getting back 720. That sure ought to finance a lot of quiltin'." Chuckling to herself, her kind old face radiated pure pleasure.

"Or a fine weekend in St. Louis for all of us ladies," said Agatha with a sudden new gleam in her pale-blue eyes. Though the fire in her furnace had been tamped down considerably by the passing years, her spark for romance refused to be smothered. Unbeknownst to Martha, Agatha had recently read in a St. Louis paper the obituary of Mrs. Timothy Rivers who had died last month. Her widower husband, age 88, had moved into the local old soldiers' home, and he reportedly was in excellent health. Well, with the good Lord willing and the trains running, he better be in good health because she finally had plans to be on her way again.

"But who is the stake holder?" asked Harry. "That's your girl's $240 against $720 of somebody else's money. That's a lot to hold, darn close to a $1000."

"Don't worry," said Agatha as she stood up from the round dining room table to bring a fresh-baked, hot apple pie in from the nearby kitchen. "It's as safe as can be. You can all rest assured of that." Sitting back down, she slowly cut the pie into four large pieces and then subdivided one piece in half to share with her sister.

"Well, tell them the rest, sister," said Martha. Once again she refilled the doctors' now empty glasses with cool milk from the large green glass pitcher on the table. She enjoyed watching those two boys eat. Martha knew the two doctors would finish the rest of the pie before leaving. If not, she would send the rest of it home with them.

"Madge Grumley's husband, Hank, at the Texaco station, has agreed to hold all the stakes wagered and everybody in this part of the country knows his reputation. He's the most honest person in town. A true inspiration he is to the Boy Scout troop he leads."

"No doubt about that," said Harry as he accepted his first piece of apple pie from Agatha. Gerry also had to agree Hank could be trusted with the large pot of money being bet.

Hank Grumley never finished tenth grade, but he had an uncanny memory and a sense for figures. He kept a running account in his head of whatever amounts people owed him. Nobody ever questioned his honesty or accuracy. When he needed to give any customer a verbatim list of every gasoline or car repair bill owed to him up to six past bills, he could do it at any time. This proved to be a good way of limiting long account extensions because he claimed he could not keep track of more than half a dozen bills per person for any longer than six months. Then the customer must pay up everything immediately before any more service could be rendered.

Hank being 6'6" and 288 pounds did not hurt his reputation either. He did his own bill collecting, and no one needed a second invitation to pay up. The one time Dexter had required repeated reminding, Grumley simply reached through Dexter's pickup truck driver's side window and confiscated his ignition keys. Dexter never forgot the truck's window had been closed tightly at the time. Even at age 48, Hank was not a man to provoke foolishly, as Dexter had finally and fully realized while be brushed the broken glass from his lap. It took three weeks wait to get a new pane of glass put in his truck, and Grumley charged him double to install it.

The next shocker illustrating the deep level of interest in the town-wide bet came during the Methodist Church services on the following Sunday morning. Located on the eastern edge of the town sat a small old, two-story, white-wooden church with high, square side windows and a freshly painted steeple. Fronting the north side of Main Street, the tree-shaded church yard, its new gray-shingled parish house, and an old adjoining cemetery took up the rest of the entire block. The original church built at that location had been constructed of logs and erected well over 130 years before. Graves in the cemetery attested to dead soldiers of five wars. Twelve soldiers of the town had succumbed to wounds received on various battlefields of the Civil War. Eight fought for the Union and four fell for the failed Confederacy. As a border-state town with southern sympathies, the village had seen brother fighting brother. Most of the headstones were chiseled of carved granite, the older ones were softened by the weather effects of wind and water. A few were of colored and polished marble. The neatly mowed parish lawn sported bright, fresh spring flowers growing up against the black wrought-iron fence bordering the graveyard at the front. The three other sides of the cemetery were demarcated by a waist-high stone wall, built over the course of many years when each family brought a large stone for the wall every Sunday.

The minister, Jon Martin Bishop, a tall and thin, 55-year old, raw-boned man, had a ruddy complexion and a serious nature. His face rarely smiled except when loudly singing long, Lutheran Church hymns. On this Sunday, soon after the opening hymn and the benediction of the service, he suddenly and solemnly announced his fear of a serious gambling epidemic in town. He reported the gambling fever concerned a wager on whether or not the Southern Pacific's Mainliner would stop approximately two-and-a-half weeks hence.

The minister declared gambling a bad and sinful habit, but he did like the idea of the small rural town finding renewed faith in itself. When the announcements were finished, more hymns were sung in typical, noisy Lutheran Church manner, more prayers were said, and the sermon commenced. Reverend Bishop wove a long sermon around the age-old question, "Does the end justify the means?" His conclusion appeared mixed and the congregation offered equally mixed reviews in later discussions depending on the side of the train tracks they had bet on, or how much they had already wagered. Few were neutral in their judgement.

The Southern Baptists had also gathered in serious force that warm spring Sunday, but they gathered to a deeper sounding bell in their red-brick church on the south side of Main Street. Their discussion on the wager was not for public consumption as most of them had already bet or were determined to do so in the immediate future come payday.

The Catholics did not discuss it in their gray stone church, also built on the south side of Main Street at the western border of town. They had bet considerably less money among the parishioners than is normally wagered during Monday night's Bingo games. This fully documented fact came from as trustworthy a person as Father Schaub himself at the Volunteer Fire Department's monthly meeting Tuesday evening.

Serious train betting had become rampant, even down to the local high school level. The odds were well known and thoroughly discussed by individual groups of students during recess and lunch periods throughout the week. Some decided to put the odds to work in their favor. None of them were old enough ever to have seen the famous train actually standing still.

The girls' varsity basketball team, which had finished first in its division in the county that year, wanted nice new uniforms in the high school's colors of green and gold. A difference of opinion existed between the blonds and the brunettes on the team as to whether the uniforms should be green with gold trim or gold with green trim. The single redhead who played center, demanded all green and no gold trim. By the following week, the girl's team had sold enough homemade cakes and cookies, and washed enough cars, pickup trucks, and tractors to collect over a $110. They bet this money on the line in three-to-one in favor of the Mainliner stopping in town.

The young athletes were loyal to the rural clinic and to their team physicians. They had good and continued reasons for their support. They all remembered how their redheaded teammate had almost died during her freshman year from complications from rheumatic fever with pneumonia. A young physician previously at the clinic saved her life. Through determination and good medical rehabilitation, as a junior she now became the team's most outstanding player and the cornerstone of their chances to make the regional playoffs the coming school year. Sharp new uniforms might help motivate them even more into the state playoffs.

With most of the town's 'good people' betting the young doctors could stop the fast train, you might wonder who had bet the train would not stop? Who were these villains of little faith? Who were these negative reactionaries? Well, every town has its self-appointed tough guys, its marginal sharpies, and those who avoid worthwhile risk while going all-out for an easy buck. The train stopping obviously was a remote chance for a big bet for the town. To bet the fast train would not stop wagered against the town making a comeback. Time would tell who was right and who was wrong.

Within the three bars in town, the vast majority of the regular drinking patrons bet against the train stopping. The more they drank, the more they bet. Little faith lives where hard liquor lurks. The chronic effect of alcohol on the minds and the livers of some of them had long since taken its toll. Strong drink had diminished all original thought.

Some of the townspeople commuted 30 to 35 miles a day over packed gravel and poorly paved county roads to and from jobs in Moberly. This special faction also almost exclusively bet against the fast train stopping. These were people who had partially given up on the old town and had found work elsewhere. Their fears for the future years of their lives were only further depressed by the thought others might actually be able to leave town faster and for distances and destinations even farther down the line. Since they could not afford to leave aging homes or dying farms around Essex, they resented the town's decline but refused to imagine it could make a comeback. They could not harvest hope sufficiently to see faith in the town itself, even if it started with just one train stopping, would be the key to actualizing their stunted dreams of bygone glory days.

Not until the last week before Train Day had Gerry discovered another faction betting against faith stopping the train, composed of a syndicate of three of the town's more prominent businessmen. On the surface they put up money claiming they were betting the train would stop. However, they had secretly arranged for someone else to hedge their bets by putting up much greater sums of money betting the train would not stop. When Gerry and Harry heard of these local titans hedging their bets, this infuriated the young doctors more than anything else about the train bet that this lack of faith demonstrated by the dastardly doubters.

Late Wednesday evening, two days before Train Day as it had come to be called, the young doctors finished up in the small red brick clinic when Harry approached the subject again. "You know, Gerry, this whole thing has gotten out of hand. Do you realize probably nine-tenths of the people in this part of the county have bet on whether that damn train will stop or not this Friday? I heard over $10,000 is already wagered on this. That's a large sum of money in any small town."

"That is an unbelievable sum, old friend," Gerry said with delight.

"Madge told me today during lunch, her husband, Hank, finally opened up a trust account at a Moberly Bank with all the money rather than keep it in a suitcase under their bed any longer.

She said she hadn't slept much in the last three nights worrying about it being right there under their bed."

Gerry thought about the magnitude for a minute, but before he could answer, Harry continued on with the conversation. His friend had seemed increasingly anxious lately. "What's more, if it doesn't stop, if the train doesn't stop, and we lose, not only are we out the pink slips on both of our cars, but we'll be the laughing stock of the county for years to come. They'll never forget us."

"Does that bother you?" Gerry asked.

"Sure, some. But it doesn't bother me half as much as the idea most of those good church folk, the women's sewing bee group, and even the Essex High School girl's basketball team may take a real bath. You know they can't afford to lose that kind of money. What will that do to their faith? I wanted to leave this town and its people in better shape than we found them. I wanted it to be a better place because of our having been physicians here."

"You worry too much, Harry. That's the problem with you and your faith. Look at yourself. Now is the time to get stronger in your own faith."

"What do you mean by that? What about my faith? Am I losing it?"

"Well I suspect maybe it's not quite as strong as you need it to be now. This is a good learning lesson for all of us. The two of us especially must keep faith the train will stop. It must stop."

"And if it doesn't? What will we do then? Have you staked out a fall back position?"

"In two days, we'll know. Stay calm. After all, I'm the damn fool who's going to be standing out there in my Sunday go-to-meeting suit with a packed Samsonite suitcase in my left hand with my right thumb stuck straight out in the breeze. If it doesn't stop, I'm the one who has to walk back the three blocks to the clinic.

You'll already be there seeing patients. Fact is, if the fast train doesn't stop, you'll probably end up seeing me as a patient. So, cheer up old friend, but maybe you should start back on your Maalox again."

"Okay, I'll try harder, but the worry does have me back up to a pack of cigarettes a day again." Harry tried to smile, but it looked more like a grimace than from happiness. He had even switched back to Camels.

Gerry finally realized the real dark depths of Harry's worry that evening at the Blue Bell Café. After eating his usual two hamburgers, fries and baked beans, Harry didn't even notice his missing favorite cherry pie, Madge had slipped a piece of rhubarb pie in front of him. He just started eating it without pause or comment.

"Friday is the big day you guys," she said as she shrugged her shoulders with forthright friendliness but a measure of semi-confusion. "I sure hope you all know what you're doin'. Sometimes I think I should have set the odds a little higher. Then you boys wouldn't have had to risk so much money. You know I'll give you enough food to make sure you both survive the rest of your rotation here, but I don't want my favorite doctors to end up the laughing stock of the county. If you lose your cars in the bet, you may even end up having to jump a freight train out of here. You could go out in a box car, though that's the one heading East." The sadness in her voice was heavy with concern. She had seriously considered the problem from many sides.

"See, Gerry. Now even Madge is worried about us."

"Damn it, Madge," said Gerry, "Don't tell me you're starting to lose faith, too. I'm the guy that's going to have to get out there in my black suit, shined shoes, one suitcase, and extend my thumb. I'm the one that's putting it all on the line Friday. Keep the faith everybody. Don't give up. Everything will be okay. The train will

438

stop."

"Are you really sure?" she asked. "Will the train stop?"

"Well, at least I hope so." Gerry's voice did not have the solid ring of comforting confidence it had demonstrated the previous week. Even his appetite had slipped, though certainly not to anorectic levels.

"Maybe we should all say a small prayer," said Madge. With sincere eloquence she invoked a blessing and asked for the Lord's help in stopping the train for the good doctor. Similar prayers echoed in many a humble home that week, including the Lutheran Church and its minister's rectory.

The Southern Baptists were still not revealing any attention to the wagers. However, as for the Catholics, rumors persisted that Father Schaub had been seen blessing the old railroad station after the eastbound freight went through Tuesday night, and again when the westbound freight went through Wednesday morning.

When Friday finally came, another sunny and unusually warm day for spring in Missouri, the tensions in town were like *High Noon* and Gary Cooper all over again. Gerry only had one suit so he had no trouble deciding what to wear. He put on the lightweight, nearly black, gray suit with a western yoke attached to the front and back shoulders. He wore the same suit to church every Sunday. He had bought it for his physician-sister's wedding the previous spring and hoped she would be proud of him.

The next decisions were more difficult. Should he wear his black Stetson hat or not? Should he wear his regular shoes or the dark cordovan brown cowboy boots? He decided it was indeed High Noon, and he really had to stop the 6,000 ton monster dead in its tracks in the town, so he had better wear the complete costume for such a confrontation. He pulled on the well-polished cowboy boots, balanced the Stetson low over his forehead, and then pushed it with a slight tilt to the right.

At 1:55 P.M., he opened the clinic's heavy oak front door and walked out into the bright Missouri sunlight. He stood still for a moment on the broad wooden sidewalk. Pale blue washed the sky with a few high streaky, white clouds. The wind blew steadily from the west and visibly bent the newly sprouting hedgerows dividing the farmlands on the hills behind the town. No one else appeared on Main Street. The heart of the small town looked deserted and nothing moved. Four of the stores had large signs in their front windows announcing, 'Closed for the Train'.

Harry insisted on carrying the small, tan Samsonite suitcase the three blocks to the railroad station. Both he and Gerry were quiet, each deeply into their own thoughts and prayers. They walked together the first block west on Main Street, on the weather-beaten wooden-board sidewalk. At the old red-brick post office and express building, they turned left, thereby heading south on Station Street. The next two blocks went downhill towards the old railroad depot platform. There was no turning back. The few large oaks and occasional elm tree lining the street rustled their new small spring branches seemingly in anticipation as the breeze continued from the west.

Neither of the young doctors were quite prepared for the sight suddenly visible ahead of them. They were stunned by the size of the crowd. There were cars and pickup trucks all over the place. Even a couple of well-worked and time-worn tractors - a red International Harvester and a green John Deere - parked along the street with fresh, damp mud from the fields still stuck to their large tread black wheels. The doctors had never before seen that much traffic in the small town. The seriousness of the situation suddenly hit them hard. There had never before been that many vehicles in the small town at one time. All the suppressed energy of the area suddenly focused in one spot - the platform in front of the small country station.

Cars lined up solidly on both sides of the railroad tracks. They were at least three to four deep for the distance of about a 100 yards both east and west of the station. It appeared as though half the county had showed up. Weren't any of these people supposed to be working?

"My God," Gerry said. His face showed the surprised look of sudden shock. "This is really out of hand." He wished his final choice of beverage before leaving lunch had been Maalox rather than a malt. He might get through the day without a peptic ulcer perforation, but his peristalsis had suddenly gone into overdrive. "You didn't by chance bring some antacid tablets with you?" he asked Harry quietly through suddenly clenched teeth.

"About your faith," said Harry with a feeling of deeply frozen fear reflected in his suddenly strained voice. "If that damn train doesn't stop, we're destroyed. Have you thought of that? I mean we're done in. We're finished for all time and forever too, at least in this county. Maybe even the whole state. All you have to do is throw yourself under the wheels of the locomotive. It will be easy for you. I'm the guy who has to walk the three blocks back to the clinic and start seeing patients again. I'm not sure I can do it. I'm really scared." The sweat on both his hands had increased, making it difficult to hold the handle of the small suitcase as he switched it from one hand to the other. Finally he put it down for a few seconds and dried his hands on the sides of his brown chino slacks.

There was nothing more to say that hadn't already been said. Gerry's knees were shaking, but in the best gunfighter tradition he could still summon up, he stopped to adjust his Stetson and pulled the brim even lower over his forehead. Suddenly he stepped down from the high, wooden sidewalk and out into the middle of the paved street. Harry followed and the two friends walked boldly downhill together towards the railroad station platform. Gerry knew the illusion of confidence is even more important than the actual confidence itself. It sets the scene in one's favor and gives a person increased standing in the eyes of others who may be dependent on them.

Halfway there, he stopped, turned to Harry, and quickly took the well-worn suitcase out of Harry's sweaty hand before speaking. "Maybe it's best you don't come any further, old friend." They shook hands firmly. They had been best friends and fellow students for four years. They knew in their hearts, no matter what happened, this one day would never be forgotten.

Harry slowly started back uphill towards the clinic. He could not handle staying and watching, and seeing the old LaSalle fire engine among the many vehicles parked along the railroad right-of-way had not helped him calm down. The tension was just too great, apart even from considering his half of the $1000 bet. Before last week he had never seen $500 in cash together at one time. Money had been scarce during his days of growing up in rural West Virginia. Now, in the next few minutes he might be losing that much money all at once. Was this maturity or damn foolishness? How had he reached this point in his life?

By now, both young doctors had been seen by the patiently awaiting town's people, many of whom had stepped out of their cars to wave at Gerry as he continued on down the hill towards them. Many hands were waving with nearly no sound. No one clapped. No one honked. No one yelled. The eerie silence seemed much like an old silent movie or a modern one where the sound track had suddenly been turned off.

Gerry saw the reverend touch the narrow, straight brim of his dark, black Homburg hat in recognition and then looked skyward as his lips moved in quiet prayer. His blessings were with the doctor. He had prayed in the old church at least three times that day. He tried to keep the faith, but sensed today they really needed

442

a miracle in Essex. But then the good Lord does work in mysterious ways, and this town surely needed His favor today. "God bless you, son," slowly a wistful expression appeared on his lean face, seemingly incongruous to his calling to the cloth.

Next Gerry gave a crisp recognition salute to the high school girls basketball team. They all stood on the sidewalk as a group with their coach. Three of the younger girls first broke the crowd's silence with a loud cheer for their doctor. The coach also served as the high school's Home Economics teacher and the mother of the red head who played center. She helped them unfurl a large green and gold banner saying, 'Hooray for our Doctor!' Her daughter held one end of the banner and served as the leader of the cheering section. Soon most of the crowd took up the loud chant and suddenly Gerry felt much better. The knot in his gut started to relax. Maybe the Maalox would not be needed. Now where is that train?

Sewing circle ladies could be seen dispersed throughout the large crowd. Some of them, including Agatha and Martha, sat quietly on the station platform eating lunch from a large picnic basket. As they looked up expectantly, the reflection of inner excitement could be seen on their caring, elderly faces etched with well-worn worry lines. The sisters' faith probably was the strongest of anyone in the assembled crowd. Never for a moment did they doubt their doctor would be able to stop the train. They did not come to see if it would stop. They came to see what it would look like when it *did* stop.

Out of his purple pickup truck, Weatherford suddenly appeared with Dexter at his side. Neither of them smiled. "Want me to carry your bag, Doc?" asked Dexter. He tried to laugh loudly, but he showed a sudden deep respect in his voice. He offered sincerely but Gerry graciously refused. Now they knew how high the stakes really were. Within minutes one of them would be a winner and the other one would be a loser. Which one would be broke and the laughing stock of the county? The coming train would soon tell.

"Doc, you're going' to be lookin' awful stupid standin' there by yourself on the platform as that there fast train passes you on by at 65 miles an hour," Weatherford said. "Sure' nuff, it probably won't even slow down. I wouldn't have missed this for three months wages at the rendering plant." No respect and only ridicule showed in his voice. Although he wore a new bright yellow cap advertising a recent change in fertilizer preferences, it did not appreciably improve his general body odor.

Cool to the end, the doctor's last words to Weatherford before steeping up on the high station platform made local history, "If you've gotta walk near me Weatherford, at least stand down wind."

The train's low pitched horn could be heard in the distance as the diesel engine came closer and closer up the gradual grade of the right-of-way between the green hills east of Essex. Soon the two, twelve-cylinder engines of the E9A diesel electric locomotive drowned out all the noise of the crowd as the sleek silver and red engine suddenly heaved into view. The breathtaking sight hurled itself straight toward the town with no sign of slowing down or loss of power. This monstrous thing of beauty had worked hard and put in overtime in the seven years since being built by the Electro-Motive division of General Motors in La Grange, Illinois.

Even after it had rounded the final big bend about 900 yards from the station, it still came on without any perceptible slowing. The doctor put his suitcase down and walked to stand tall at the edge of the platform. The time for action had come, and he stuck out his right arm with thumb extended, as he looked straight on down the line of parallel tracks. He felt he and the train were the only two things in the world. With its 2400 horse power engines and complete weight including the passenger cars of over 168 tons, the train was a formidable opponent.

The sudden ridiculousness of the situation seemed frighteningly apparent also to his many friends, loyal patients, and staunch supporters. Only a few hundred yards remained between the doctor and making a blooming idiot of himself as the train appeared poised to pass him on its fast way west. In spite of his bluster getting himself into this mess, it suddenly seemed impossible to him one man, dressed like an old western gunfighter, could ever stop a 168 ton train with his right thumb, extended or otherwise. How could any man have faith in that kind of miracle? The train engine's maintained a traction force reaching 56,500 pounds.

Suddenly Gerry knew this to be a moment of tremendous truth for him. It would be one moment which would stay with him until he reached his grave. This moment would live on in his family to be passed down to sons and daughters yet unborn. He and his progeny would tell the story at births, baptisms, weddings, wakes, and funerals not yet imagined. Whether or not he won or lost it would become part of the folklore not only of his family but also of that part of Macon County.

Many of his friends had to turn their heads at the last moments out of sincere embarrassment for him to mitigate the young doctor's damages. They admired his nobility of purpose but feared the futility of fact and fate. They felt sorry for him and thought by not looking his shame might somehow be less.

And then it happened much more suddenly than anybody had expected. Old Max, the train station dog, suddenly stood up and barked. He seemed to sense it first. Something was different. The train slowed. The train stopped. The noise of sudden air brakes and screeching steel on steel deafened the assembled crowd. History was about to be made that day in the small village of Essex, Missouri. The train pulled up just short of the station and stopped. Faith had won the day. The inner terror of failure suddenly converted to the outward tranquility of success. A smile from ear to ear spread over the young doctor's face.

The honking horns of the many parked cars joined in the symphony of sound of screeching breaks. Yet even louder arose the joyous sound of yelling and cheering of the large assembled crowd. Their cries and excited utterances were almost loud enough to drown out the siren of the old maroon LaSalle fire engine which had just joined in the cacophony of happy sound. Harry came back and sat atop the fire engine, cranking its klaxon handle with both hands, while Father Schaub sat behind steering wheel hitting the old horn.

Soon the clear strains of *Dixie* could be heard as the 38-piece high school marching band brass and drum corps struck up their theme song. They had never played it with more emotion. The factor of faith had finally won the day. All other noise stopped as the crowd sang the anthem of a rebellion long lost along with the band. Many of the townspeople had tears of happiness trailing from their eyes, and surprisingly, this included more than a few who had bet quite heavily against the fast train stopping. For the first time, even the hardened skeptics and dismal doubters felt some real faith in their small town's future. Nobody present would ever forget this day and they had all become believers.

Well, not quite all of them...not yet.

The purple pickup truck did not stay around long enough to see the final chapter finished. Dexter and Weatherford quickly disappeared in dismal defeat in a cloud of dust and exhaust racing back up the hill toward the local pool hall. It would be a long time before they made their next bet on anything. Their emotional depression lasted for weeks. Their financial depression would last for many months.

Not only did the fast train stop, but it stopped with the door to a large wide-windowed silver coach almost exactly opposite where Gerry stood tall. The broadly smiling, gray-haired conductor in his dark blue serge uniform jumped down with a portable yellow step to help Gerry up into the train. This miraculous moment for the young doctor lit up his life with the luster of pure gold.

Gerry waited until the last strains of *Dixie* echoed throughout the station, before he ascended the train's few metal steps. With all of the cheering and music and happily honking horns outside the train, the conductor's welcoming words were drowned out as the doctor walked forward into the half-filled coach to find a vacant chair. The passengers looked at him as if he must be some local celebrity.

He sat down next to a window facing the depot. The conductor reinstalled the portable step and followed carrying Gerry's small suitcase and then carefully placed it in the empty baggage rack above Gerry's head.

As the big train pulled out of the small country station, with great gusto, the high school band started to play *Amazing Grace*. They all knew by now this was the young doctor's favorite hymn. Gerry waved through the window at the smiling, singing crowd until they finally disappeared from sight in the distance. A feeling of welcoming warmth and sweet satisfaction flowed through him. For the first time in four weeks he felt a full sense of contentment and could finally relax. He headed home.

"I'm not sure you heard me with all the noise on the platform back there, but obviously Essex is one small town that really appreciates its doctor," said the old conductor readdressing himself to Gerry. Respect in his voice reflected his own competence and kindness. "Is there anything I can get you now? Supper won't be served in the dining car until after we cross the Big Sugar Creek River."

"How did you know I was a doctor? Am I actually starting to look like one?" Gerry asked the question with both hope and happiness in his voice. Maybe the suit and the Stetson made the difference. Or maybe he had finally started to look more mature, rather than as the skinny kid who had started his freshman year so very long ago. That would be great news.

"Oh, our main railroad office up in Chicago gave me a copy of your recent letter requesting the train to stop here in town today and a copy of our letter verifying we would stop. As the conductor on board, I am in charge of the train. Railroads are always sympathetic to rural health care needs in America, and if by stopping our train for a few minutes we can save any small town a full day of its doctor's valuable time, we are always pleased to do it. We will stop for physicians anytime and anywhere along the railroad right-of-way. I've heard it's been 26 years since we stopped here in Essex - not since the last days of the steam locomotives. I remember them well. This has been a bit of nostalgia for me today and an honor that I could order our engineer to stop here again." He had an authority to his voice ruling out any nonsense of action.

Okay, some may say there is a little more than just faith involved here, but the good Lord helps those who help themselves. Although it had not been just a question of faith, it also took hedging his bet and betting for a righteous purpose.

The two young doctors eventually financed their own trips to search for internships with portions of the money. Harry took an internship in east Texas, and Gerry took the one offered to him in Southern California, but they would continue to be best friends throughout their lives. The rest of their winnings were donated to the town's rural clinic. The clinic board spent the money to buy a good, used x-ray machine and three years of necessary clinic supplies. The subsequent new doctors used them to save the lives of at least 6,000 townspeople, four of whom had bet against the train stopping. If the train had not stopped, these lives could have ended in an untimely manner.

The high school varsity girls basketball team received their new green and gold uniforms. The uniforms ended up much more green than gold with the tie breaking vote being cast by the redhead who played center. She went on to play girls basketball at Northeast Missouri State College, where she majored in chemistry, won a scholarship to medical school, and became the first physician to come from Essex. Later, married to a surgeon, she and her husband established a modern medical office in a small rural town south of Jefferson City. She would always be a country doctor.

The sewing bee ladies renewed their faith and their treasury. They were still in the early stages of planning their big trip to St. Louis when the two young doctors finally left Essex forever, having finished their six-month internship rotation on May 31st. Only Agatha and Timmy knew what really happened when Agatha looked up her old soldier. However Martha later admitted to close friends her sister had stayed an extra week in St. Louis after the other '*girls*' had returned home. Not only that, but Agatha had planned to return again to see Timmy in August.

The purple pickup, local highway menace number one, was sold at public auction by the Moberly Bank. An unknown out-of-county resident bought the truck. Unconfirmed reports from trustworthy travelers to the east mentioned occasional sightings in and around Hannibal, Missouri, reportedly being driven by a teenage girl. The truck was hard to hide, and she kept it painted purple, but it never again clocked at over double-nickel miles per hour.

Chapter 15
Final Chapter
May 4, 1962

The fast diesel train picked up speed heading west and the young doctor finally relaxed. He sat back in his comfortable Pullman chair and surveyed the passing countryside through the large picture window to his right. The predominately green panorama of rural Missouri with its rich new foliage of fields and forests in full spring bloom flew by him. Shallow sloping valleys and gentle rounded hills extended to the horizon. A variety of hardwood trees concentrated in the larger wooded areas while soft woods grew in the hedge rows and in large strands of secondary growth. Sadly, Gerry realized these larger areas of hardwoods including oak, maple, walnut, osage, and poplar, were fast falling to the woodman's axe and the furniture industry at an accelerated rate. Within two generations, Missouri residents would have no idea the natural state the landscape formerly used to look. Grandparents would need old photos to describe the lush green landscape to future generations. Outcroppings of large rock formations periodically passed as silent testimony to the last great glacier's southern-most extension, thousands of years ago. The train quickly traversed many small creeks and streams, and trestle bridges spanned the occasional river of appreciable size. All the rivers' water flowed south toward the great Missouri River, which would then flow east to join the even greater Mississippi River before continuing south to the Gulf of Mexico.

Well kept farms, both big and small, with tractors in the fields and cattle and sheep in separate pastures, reminded Gerry of the great agricultural resources of this magnificent state. It had been a true privilege to start his medical career among these hard working people. He hoped he had served them well and would always be grateful for what they taught him. The lessons he learned were not always pleasant but they were always meaningful when marked with the mistakes he planned never to repeat.

Doctor Frank took off his western style suit coat, folded it neatly, and placed it on the seat beside him. Next he loosened his tie, unbuttoned his collar, and stretched out to rest his feet in his comfortable cowboy boots in front of him on the metal footrest he pulled out from the bottom of his seat. His Stetson and his suitcase were already stowed in the baggage rack overhead. Less than half full, the Pullman coach would stay that way all the way to Kansas City since there were no planned stops in the meantime. In Kansas City the stopover would only be 17 minutes according to the train's timetable Gerry had found in the seat pocket in front of him. The Express Mainliner of the Santa Fe Railroad traveled nonstop from Chicago to Kansas City.

The young doctor started to get hungry. Thank goodness he had listened to Madge when he had been too nervous to eat lunch earlier in the day at the Blue Bell Café. Madge thoughtfully made him a couple of thick sliced ham sandwiches and insisted he take them along in a small, tin biscuit box which he placed on top of the clothes in his suitcase. Standing up he reached for the suitcase, unlocked it and dug out the tin.

After sitting back down in the soft comfortable chair, he bent over and opened up the box. There were two sandwiches, some celery and a few sugar cookies all carefully wrapped separately in waxed paper. A true great friend, Madge knew the young doctor in ways he did not even know himself. He would always remember her kindness and generosity. Slowly he leaned back again and started to eat the first ham sandwich. She had even made it with cheese, no mayonnaise, and the exact amount of mustard Gerry liked. The rhythm of the train motion soon put the young doctor in a sleepy reflective mood.

The anticipation of the day and the excitement of the buildup of the last half hour leading to the train's arrival had been more tiring than he thought it would be. Victory was sweet but exhausting. He and his partner Harry had not lost their cars. Instead they won the big bet and had won more money than either of them had ever seen in one place before. To have faith is a wonderful thing, but to have good planning made it a lot easier to maintain good faith. The trip home to California would be a long way but it should be relaxing and provide him time to start studying for his medical boards. The examination would be two days long and had to be taken in less than a month. He planned to take the Missouri Boards the first week of June and then the California version a month later in early July. Already Gerry had researched the reciprocity each of these two states would provide and he knew if he passed both of these tests, he could then practice medicine anywhere in the country except for Florida. That state required its own separate exam, but he had no desire to move there. Florida had no surf like California's.

His dad had always reminded Gerry as he grew up that a man is the sum of his victories and his defeats. His dad hoped an understanding of the latter would better insure a predominance of the former. Today he certainly had a great victory, but Essex had also been the scene of the young doctor's worst defeat. The trauma of his breakup with his wonderful girlfriend, Sharon, would haunt him for years.

True enough, he gradually adjusted to losing her and certainly Sarah had tried her very best to make him happy. Yet deep inside, he knew there would always be a special place in his heart for Sharon, his first great love. He did not know if he would ever find or deserve another like her.

Without realizing it, he had finished eating his first sandwich and just reached for the second one when he suddenly spotted a folded note in the bottom of the tin, written carefully in ink on pink paper, signed by Madge. Obviously it had not been written quickly or with little thought.

Dear Doctor Frank,

By now you must have already eaten one of my sandwiches and hopefully feel better as you contemplate your great victory of faith. You and your partner, Dr. Thompson, have been a godsend and an inspiration to this entire village. We will never forget you and hope you will sometimes think of us.

Last night at home with my husband Bob, I prayed for you and Dr. Thompson, and I also prayed for you and Sharon. You know my big Bob is her godfather and has always taken that special responsibility most seriously. Forgive an aging lady for advice not requested, but in my prayers it came to me I must tell you two things:

(1) The love you and Sharon once shared may live on in ways you never considered before, but in ways that will be a blessing to you both.

(2) Get off you ass right now and walk through the train.

Love always,

Madge (and Big Bob)

Gerry could literally feel his heart skip a beat as he read and then slowly reread the neatly printed note. Folding up the pink paper, he carefully placed it in his pants pocket. What did she mean?

Quickly he stood up. That part was easy. Now to walk through the train. That should not be too hard. He knew the two baggage cars, one mail car, and the caboose were the only train coaches behind him. The other four passenger coaches and the dining car must all be up ahead.

The silver train swayed around a curve just as he stepped out into the aisle when it came into Brookfield. Without stopping there it slowed down slightly. Soon it flashed by the backyards of small homes both neat and cluttered, and passed by streets suddenly blockaded by fulcrum-lowered, black and white striped railroad gates with their flashing red lights and continuously ringing bells. Children waved and adults smiled. The doctor watched the landscape pass swiftly by and did not continue up the aisle until the train had passed completely through the town.

He thought how fascinating the doppler effect of the moving train going past the stationary bells made their noise so different when perceived by those who go and those who stay - similar to the differences life and circumstances for those who stay forever at home and those who move on to other places. He hoped his life would not always be a series of continually moving on. He put his suit coat back on as he walked. He felt he should be looking for something or someone. What exactly did Madge mean by her note? The message shook him and the mystery fostered a full circulation of his blood pumping through his body.

"Excuse me young man," said an older lady with white hair as she reached out and touched the doctor when he walked past her chair, "aren't you the young gentlemen the train stopped for back in that small town a while ago?"

"Yes ma'am, I'm afraid so," Gerry replied hoping to pass on forward but unable to move since she had tightened her grip on his right arm.

"Some of the banners those people held up back there said something about you being a doctor. Are you a doctor?" She asked with an expression of hope lighting up her face.

"Well only for that village ma'am," he reluctantly replied.

"Oh. That's wonderful. Now if you would sit down here with me for a while, I'd like to tell you all about the terrible gall bladder surgery I had last year. I know you would find it very interesting." Finally letting go of Dr. Frank's right arm, the elderly lady moved over to make room for him beside her.

"Maybe when I come back ma'am," he stammered, making sure he quickly stepped out of the range of her reach, "but right now I have to go pee." The shocked expression on her face gave him at least temporary confidence he might yet avoid hearing of her gall bladder surgery in the near future. He wondered why old people, especially much older people, think total strangers would be interested in their surgery stories even if the stranger is a physician. Hastening his footsteps, Gerry exited the coach and continued to walk forward through the noisy vestibule between cars into the next one.

Dr. Frank still couldn't figure out why he was supposed to take a stroll through the train, but if Madge had thought it important enough to leave him a note about it, he would not argue. Maybe, just maybe, it had something to do with Sharon. He knew she had left Essex in April, after quitting her job at the hospital and transferring from the teachers college to a school in Kansas City. Gerry still missed her, though he knew their romance could never continue with the real tragedy of her sterility. Having his own children was far too important to him. He had, however, thought of calling her on the phone from the Kansas City railroad depot.

The pros and cons of such a decision ran through his mind as he continued forward toward the dining car. Gerry figured it would be the train coach most forward. Though he realized it would not be open for supper this early, he thought he might have a look at the menu. He could afford to splurge a bit now with the expense money he had brought with him on the trip, knowing the bulk of the train bet's winnings were stored safely and soundly back in Essex awaiting his return. Nothing could be safer than to be in the custody or under the protection of Big Bob Grumley. The doctor wondered what would ever happen to anybody stupid enough to provoke physical retribution by that giant.

The cool breeze calmed Gerry as he passed through the semi-open vestibule between the last two passenger coaches and before entering into the last closed coach. He paused for a moment and carefully leaned over the open top half of the train's side door, first making sure the bottom half was well secured and tightly bolted. Looking outside, he waved at two schoolboys fishing in a creek along which the train traversed. One boy waved back while the other victoriously held up a string of three or four trout for quick inspection. Not much had changed in this back country since the days of Huckleberry Finn and Tom Sawyer. Soon the boys disappeared behind a grove of scrubby willows mixed with leafy alders growing along the creek bed.

Gerry still had no clue about the meaning of Madge's note, although he faithfully followed her directions as she knew he would. Opening the heavy steel door of the last coach, Gerry stepped inside the narrow hallway and walked past the women's rest room. The train lurched as it travelled around a gradual curve of track, and he grabbed the side railing and held on until the coaches forward motion continued in a straight line again. Carefully he took another four steps bringing him into the rear of the Pullman. All of its seats faced forward. Suddenly the unmistakable odor of vanilla hit him hard in the nose.

He could never mistake one of his favorite fragrances, and he knew only one woman who wore it as perfume. Sharon sat there by herself near the back of the most forward passenger coach. *Get off you ass right now and walk through the train*, Madge's note had said. Madge had always given him sound advice and good instructions.

He saw Sharon sitting on the left hand side, second row from the rear with her back toward him. She held a book in both hands but had not been reading it. Instead she looked out the large plate glass window beside her as if concentrating on the flickering images flashing by in the mid-afternoon sun.

Quickly Gerry slid into the empty seat next to her but did not speak as he turned toward her. She wore a short brown cotton jacket open over a pale green sweater. Her deeply pleated skirt matched her jacket. Her long legs were bare of stockings, but at her ankles were fluffy white bobby-socks, folded half-way down to her highly polished cordovan loafers. She did not turn toward him but continued looking out the large window at the passing countryside. "We will be crossing the Big River pretty soon," she said. "That's what life is - a series of crossings to unknown destinations and unpredicted fates."

Gerry realized then she must have known he sat next to her by seeing his reflection in the window as he sat down. His excitement at finding her made it impossible for him to coordinate his brain to his tongue for a few moments. "It's good to see you," he gasped, "and a big surprise I must admit. I can't believe you are actually here on the same train. Am I dreaming?"

"No, you're not dreaming," she responded quietly, trying to keep the excitement she felt out of her voice, "it's me."

"So, why are you here? This is not just a coincidence, is it?" he questioned.

"You don't want really to know, and it would take far too long for me to explain it to you. I don't think I could explain it in the time I have left. I get off in Kansas City," she replied sullenly, not yet daring to look directly at him.

"But Kansas City is almost two hours from here. That's a long way and a long time. Maybe your being here means you should stay on the train with me all of the way to Los Angeles." Gerry still stared at Sharon with amazement as he spoke. Then suddenly he smiled broadly with the fully open, toothy smile of joy that came so easily to his face whenever he was near Sharon.

Suddenly she turned away from the window and looked directly at him. Only then did he see a few tears running silently down her beautiful face. Neither of the two ex-lovers spoke momentarily. She reached for her purse, found fresh tissue, and slowly wiped away the tears. "Sorry, I certainly didn't mean to do that. I promised myself no matter what happened today I would not cry."

"Please understand, I never meant to cause you any sadness. It's just this children thing is an issue I can't compromise on," he said with conviction.

"Oh, I do understand," Sharon replied. "That's not my problem, and I promise you I'll never cry again about not being able to have children. I guess my tears are because I didn't know if I would ever see you again, and that thought bothered me. I purposely took a seat on this side of the coach so nobody could see me from the depot platform when the train stopped in Essex." She carefully brushed more tears from her face with a wrinkled pink tissue before continuing. "I figured if you found me after we were underway it would be fate and not my doing. You are such a big jerk I certainly wouldn't ever chase you again." She didn't smile as she spoke but leaned over and gently kissed the side of his face.

"But even when you loved me you always knew I was a bit of a jerk. I have never denied it, not even once." Gerry smiled again as he spoke trying to invoke humor into their strained conversation to hide both her embarrassment and his deep feelings.

"Yes, that's true, but it took me a long time to realize just how big of a jerk you are." Slowly a faint smile formed at the corners of her pretty, pouting mouth. Hesitantly she licked her lower lip before continuing. "You actually threw away the love of the finest women you may ever know. The real tragedy is you did it needlessly. Now we can only be friends. We can never again be lovers."

"Look Sharon, we have been all over this before and more than once. It's not your fault nor is it mine we broke up. It's nobody's fault. It's just one of those things. Fate dealt you a hand incompatible with my desires. Your chances of getting pregnant are minimal. Dr. Chase says your chances are less than five percent. I want my own children. For us to marry now and to spend the rest of our reproductive years hoping against overwhelming odds would be pretty stupid. Sure, we love each other very much right now but the frustration of your sterility would eventually destroy our love and the both of us along with it. It already has."

"It's funny how you could have so much faith the fast train would stop today, when it had never stopped in Essex in over 25 years, but you have no faith in my chances for children with you."

"That is different."

"What's so different?" she questioned with marked irritation in her voice. "I certainly don't see it as much different."

"I hedged my bet on the train stopping. The odds were much better on the train than a mere five percent or I would not have bet on it. You have to understand this Sharon," he replied with an obvious appeal for empathy in his voice.

"Actually, my dear Doctor, the odds were 100 percent on the train stopping but you did not know that. So I'm giving you the benefit of the doubt. You did stop the train with faith."

"No, not exactly," Gerry replied as he scratched his head in thought. "I have to admit there was a little more to it than fate."

"Is it anything you would like to tell an old girlfriend?"

"Maybe later, but first, what do you mean when you say the odds were 100 percent on the train's stopping? Rarely are any odds 100 percent sure on anything."

"These odds were, but you don't want to know about it. You really don't," she repeated with a sad smile floating across her face.

"Quit saying that. I do want to know. What is it you know about fast railroad trains that I apparently don't?" he asked, somewhat irritated.

"How to stop them suddenly in small towns of your choice," she softly replied looking down at her shoes as she recrossed her legs.

"Yes, by sticking out your right thumb," he added with a grin.

"No, not exactly."

"Then how?" Gerry asked with growing curiosity.

"By pulling one of the big emergency stop switches which is located between each of the passengers coaches. They're in the vestibule areas. You just grab the handle and pull it hard."

"Oh, my God," he exclaimed. "Now I understand. That's why you're here on the train. That's even why you're sitting at the rear of a coach. You were going to pull that damn switch if I could not stop the train first. You were, weren't you?" he questioned with final understanding. "How close did you come?"

"Four seconds," she whispered, still looking down at her feet. Her voice was so soft Gerry could not be sure he heard correctly.

"How close?"

"Four seconds," she repeated, this time considerably louder. "My dad and I both knew very well you and Harry could not afford to lose the bet. You got in over your head with those sharks, Dexter and his dumb sidekick Buntley."

"We did get into it a little heavier than we first intended," he agreed.

"You once saved my dad's hand, maybe even his life. We figured we owed you one, a big one. It was dad's plan."

"So tell me."

"Dad figured out the time and distance equations and calculated the speed of the train every day for a week as it approached and continued straight through Essex. Then he fashioned five separate high stakes, painted them bright yellow around their tops and hammered them deeply into the grassy ground along side the roadbed right-of-way. They were on the south side of the tracks and easily visible from the train if you knew where to look for them."

"And you knew where to look?"

"I sure did. Dad made me come back to town on my way to Chicago five days ago. He insisted I knew exactly where each of those stakes were located. We walked the rail bed there two evenings in a row to make sure I had them memorized and could even spot them in poor light." Sharon smiled as she remembered her dad's attention to detail.

"Why five stakes?" Gerry asked.

"One for each second of time left. If the train had not started to slow down in preparation to stop by the time my coach reached the fifth and last stake, I would know your test of faith had failed.

Then I would pull the big overhead emergency switch and stop it for sure. As it were, the train started to slow down just as we passed the second yellow stake. We had four seconds to spare."

"So relying on faith was futile and I worried for nothing?" he asked with resignation.

"No, certainly not. You really did stop the fast train completely on your own, and I'm still not sure how you did it."

"You don't want to know," he said laughingly. "You'd be disappointed."

"You're right for once. I don't. You have disappointed me enough for a lifetime. But even so, there is no way dad would let you lose the bet."

"Where was he? Now that I think of it, I didn't see Gustav at the station."

"He stood alongside the right-of-way east of town about 100 yards west of the fifth and last stake holding a red bandanna. He was afraid I might get confused and miss the last marker. If I saw him drop the red cloth, I would pull the emergency switch immediately. It might not provide enough time to stop the train exactly in the Essex Railroad Station next to the passenger depot platform, but it certainly would have stopped it somewhere in the village. That's all you and Harry promised you would do - stop it in Essex."

"What were you doing in Chicago?" Gerry asked.

"Where do you think I could get on this train, Doctor? The express leaves from Chicago every day with no stops until Kansas City."

"You and your dad sure went to a lot of trouble for Harry and me. What can I say but, thank you, sincerely?"

"And after all, you didn't even need any of our help. So forget it. No problem."

"No, I can't forget it. I never will. I owe you one," Gerry replied as he suddenly took Sharon's right hand between both of his own. He loved holding even a part of her closely again. He wanted to hold all of her next to him.

She started feeling a warmth she had not known for weeks and turned sideways on her seat to look at him better. "That feels nice, I have to admit it. I have missed you." She could feel her face flush as it frequently did when they first touched after any prolonged separation.

"So, you'll go with me now to California?" he asked with hopeful expectation.

Withdrawing her hand, she stood up, slipped off her jacket, and placed it over the back of the empty seat in front of her. When she sat back down she moved as close to him as she could and put her head on his shoulder. Her soft, curly auburn hair felt fine against his face. "No, it's too late for that. Much too late now, I'm afraid. Besides, I've made other plans for this Sunday. You'll still be on your way to California by then."

"Important plans, I suppose?" he asked with a quizzical expression on his face. "Is it something you could not put off for two weeks? What could possibly be that important?" Looking down at her sweater he saw the soft curve of her breast expand as she took in a big breath.

She let it out slowly as she spoke. "I'm getting married this Sunday in Kansas City in a small church wedding. Dad is driving down from Essex to give me away. I can't wait any longer. This is my last week of life as a single woman." There was a finality to her statement like a series of doors closing shut for the last time.

Neither spoke for moments. From the sound of her voice, Gerry realized the seriousness of Sharon's statement. She was not joking. Reaching out with both of her hands, she took his left hand between them and placed it in her lap. Gently she squeezed with increased pressure as the train went forward over another steel trestle above a large stream. The clickety-clack noise of the coaches' metal wheels on the open tracks became suddenly louder and offered another excuser for not talking.

Finally with much effort Gerry found his voice. "This does sound kind of sudden you have to admit. Is he anybody I know?"

"Yes," Sharon replied. "Yes, I'm afraid you do."

"Who is he? Who is this bold knight who has won the beautiful princess?" he asked, trying to keep some levity in his voice but failing miserably. Anxiety grabbed his gut and wrenched it into contortions. For a few seconds he again tasted the ham sandwich from Madge's lunch. He swallowed the gastronomic memory quickly.

"The handsome groom will be Dr. Herbert Huntley." Sharon stated the cold fact without any emotion. She had neither joy nor sadness in her voice. Again neither of them spoke for agonizing moments as the train rolled on in southwesterly direction through the Missouri afternoon.

Suddenly a long freight train passed on the track adjoining theirs, heading northeast in the opposite direction, temporarily cutting off the sunlight shining through Sharon's large window. After the freight's passage, Sharon moved her head from Gerry's shoulder and once again turned sideways in her seat. She looked directly at him before speaking. "I know Herbert is not your favorite person. He's not even my favorite person yet. But I do like him and I do respect him, both as a man and as a physician. With you doctors, it is difficult to separate the two entities. He and I have known each other ever since my surgery three years ago. We even dated for a while. If you remember, I was with him the night I saw you at that fraternity party so long ago."

"Yes, I know all about the surgery. He did the surgery with Dr. Cully because Dr. Chase was out of town that week at a medical seminar." Though Gerry did not have sufficient information and therefore no right to form a medical opinion, he could not help but think Sharon's chances for pregnancy might have been a lot better than five percent if Dr. Chase had been there to do her surgery.

As if she knew exactly what Gerry was thinking Sharon continued, "Don't go blaming Herbert for the way the surgery turned out. Even if he had made the first incision on my wrong side, he was new then, and I'm sure he did the very best he could do. I was acutely ill with an ectopic pregnancy and infection. Those surgeons saved my life that night, and actually it didn't turn out badly," she said smiling. Letting go of his hands, Sharon reached over and squeezed Gerry's thigh. "So don't look so mad or so sad. You should be very happy for me."

"I'll have to try harder. I just don't think he's the man to make you happy for the rest of your life."

"You hardly have a right to pass judgement on that," Sharon replied. "After all, you no longer wanted to marry me once you found out about my minimal chances for having children. Now you are finally free of me and not responsible for my future happiness or unhappiness in any shape or manner. Cheer up my friend."

"Look, I am trying. It just may take a while, though probably not more than a couple of years," he said with a forced laugh. "Seeing you on the train is a big surprise, but the news of your engagement to Herbert Huntley is overwhelming."

"Maybe Sarah Hall could help you forget," Sharon replied with a somewhat sly but noncommittal smile. "I understand she is more than willing to try."

"Where did you hear that?"

"It's a small city back there and rumors are hard to keep quiet around the hospital and clinics. Don't misunderstand me. She's a good person, and I consider her a friend. You could do a lot worse."

"I suppose you're right, but I think it will be a long while before I get serious again."

"So you are happy for me?" she questioned seriously. "Please be. I mean it most sincerely and with all my heart. My marriage to Huntley is the best thing for me in the long run. Think about it like I do now. Remember the evening at the pie auction when I told you what I wanted? Well I finally have my doctor," she said with laughing emphasis. "I was honest then and I still am now. Herbert is not you, but he is a good man and he really loves me just for me in spite of my gynecological and obstetrical status, which he certainly knows better than anyone else."

"Yes, Sharon, I do think you are correct about his love. He has probably loved you for years. I also have to grudgingly admit he has become a pretty good surgeon now within his residency. With his persistent academic interest he will become an even better one with more time and experience. You're right. I should be happy for you, and I will be if this is what you want."

"I do, so the matter is settled now once and for all," Sharon said with an emphasis not meant to tolerate further speculation.

"It is settled, if you're sure this is what you really want," Gerry promised. Silent response to his implied question permeated again for a few moments. She considered once again what she really did want. His silence was out of respect and concern for the complicated emotions he knew she must feel.

Finally she spoke. "Maybe it's not exactly what I want, but I'm smart enough to settle for it. I could not have married you no matter how much I loved you and always will love you."

"What do you mean? I thought you once did want to marry me," Gerry said as a statement of fact, not as a question.

"I did right up until April fourth when you fully realized and finally confessed you could never marry me or anyone else whose chances for pregnancy were less than five percent."

"I'm sorry."

"Don't be. At least we were always honest with each other, Gerry. I deserved to know. I had to know for sure. Some women might not have had to, but I needed to know before I could go on with my own life. Now I have gone on with it as have you. That's good for both of us."

"What do you mean you had to know then for sure?" There was something about the way Sharon had said it that troubled him.

The limitations of their love were overcome by the fact of life. He wanted children. The probability of her conceiving and carrying a pregnancy to term were less than five percent. He must face the fact the intense love they had shared for five months was the limit they would ever have together and it could never be better. This fact added to the unfairness of their total situation was at the heart of their troubles.

"Children are not forever, Gerry. Please listen carefully to me now because this may be the most important thought I can ever leave with you. I pray it will help you with the next good woman who loves you. Maybe it will help you with Sarah."

"I'm listening," he replied, now realizing how very serious was this very special woman. "I'm listening."

"Children are not even children for very long. They grow up way too fast, become adults, move away, and make separate lives for themselves. That is the good Lord's plan for us all, and it's how things should be. But marriage between a man and a woman is for life. Mine certainly will be. Maybe Latter Day Saints are right and marriage should be for the eternities. Your partner for life is the one you marry not your children. Parents are indeed responsible to and for their children, and that is only fair and reasonable and surely necessary for the continuation of the species. But of all human relationships, the most important involving mutual respect and dependable loyalty, must be the relationship between a husband and a wife. Never forget that." Letting go of his left hand, Sharon reached out with both of hers and held his face between them as she looked intently in his eyes. She now smiled broadly, without tears and with the special sparkle that in the past weeks had so frequently lit up her face.

Another few moments of silence hung in the air. Gerry soon realized Sharon's last statement had not been a question for which she waited for an answer. She deserved a response, but unlike her, his own thoughts and philosophy of life concerning man-woman relationships was neither distilled nor as clear as were hers.

"You may be right," he replied. "In fact you probably are right. Late in our relationship I realized how much more mature and grown up you are compared to me."

"Not really. Just in different ways. So don't start to foster disillusion to me about you at this late date."

"No, I really mean it. You are so much more mature than I am in some very important ways that it makes it scary. I guess my life has been so organized around school and education and motivation and the drive to become a physician for so long I never had time to sit down and think about what you are saying."

"You had the time but you probably used it to study," she said with regret in her voice.

"Okay, I admit it. I have spent a disproportionate amount of time in my life studying to prepare and to perfect my knowledge and skills as a physician. I have to. It's a compulsion. Please try to understand. My parents both sacrificed so much to put my sister and me through college and medical school. Their children were so important to them they did it willingly and happily. I know in my heart I can never make it up to them for all they did for me, so I feel I have to have my own children to make it up to them. That way, I hope each generation is better than the last."

"That is reasonable when you have the blessings of having children. But children are not necessarily the only goal in life. There are many other things in life that can be valuable and pleasurable in their own right."

"I know what you are saying, Sharon, and this is where we differ. Children are not the only goal in my life, but they certainly are the most important. I have wanted my own children ever since I was a child myself. Maybe it goes back to my dad, whose own father was killed when dad was only three. That father-child relationship was lost for an entire generation in our family. It makes me sad to think about it even now."

"Yes, that's where we differ. A child would be a wonderful blessing, but I want a husband who appreciates me for being me without reservations over my reproductive capacity. I have found that kind of person in Herbert and with the respect and loyalty we have already established, I know in time I will grow to love him very much. He will wear well."

"But will you love him as you loved me?" Gerry asked, unable to stop himself from asking such a stupid question. His ego often got in the way of good common sense. He regretted the question but he had to know.

"Yes," she replied after a short pause. "Yes, and maybe even more in a few years. Herbert is my choice now and for my lifetime. My love will grow knowing full well he loves me for who I am - including my limitations. That is where you failed me so miserably. You could never get past one limitation of my poor prognosis for pregnancy."

"I admit it. You're right. Don't rub it in." Suddenly the helplessness and hopelessness of their situation silenced the young doctor. He was too weary to talk about it any further. An expression of fatigue reflected in his eyes.

Sharon looked at him intently with studied concentration. "I don't mean to rub it in. I just want you to understand. I am grateful for this last chance to talk together. You know you will always have a very special place in my heart. You do know that, don't you?" she questioned as she reached out and brushed his hair back from his forehead. The touch of her hand now felt surprisingly cold.

"Yes. Yes, I do," Gerry replied in a voice so low, it was almost a whisper. "I am sorry I failed you, but I was honest. The idea of someday having my own children is too powerful for me to forego. I want at least four."

"I wish you luck. Now give me one last big hug while I'm still a single woman and then let's head for the dining car. All of a sudden I am very hungry," she continued with a forced smile. They were still holding on tightly to each other two minutes later when the Pullman porter in his stiffly starched, white jacket came through their coach, ringing the dinner chimes to announce the opening of the dining car.

Upon entering the dining car, the cheerful maître d' greeted the young couple and quickly gave them a table to themselves. The elegant pink and white china and heavy clear crystal table settings were complemented by freshly cut flowers. The service was superb and the scenery rushed past their window offering a continuous spectrum of color. As the shadows of the afternoon sun lengthened, the colors rapidly became more pastel in hue.

For a change Gerry didn't feel very hungry. He ordered a large bowl of New England clam chowder with a side order of Monterey Jack cheese and soda crackers which he slowly tried to finish.

To her surprise, Sharon found she was very hungry. She ordered the Kansas City Stockman cut of steak, medium rare, with a baked potato, carrots, salad, and a roll. She ate it all.

They kept their conversation purposely light and mostly about future plans rather than past history and recollections. Sharon told him Herbert would be transferring to Kansas City General Hospital at the end of the month to finish out his residency, while she attended college there in the big city. They had already found a small apartment near the hospital. After his residency is over, they would be moving back to Macon where Herbert had been offered a partnership in a small medical group that needed an OB/GYN specialist. "The clinic is only about 26 miles from my dad's farm, so it shouldn't be too far to commute."

"Will you both live on the farm with your dad?" Gerry asked. He tried to assimilate a mental picture of Dr. Huntley and Gustav Olson hunting or fishing together, but he could not put the idea in focus. He would miss old Gus. It would be hard to find a better father-in-law.

"No, not with my dad." We plan on building our own house close-by elsewhere on the farm. Dad is going to timber off some of the old trees on that high 50-acre parcel north of his house. To make it easier to get the logs out, he will extend the old dirt pasture road farther up the mountain. Then afterwards with the road already in, it will be easy to bring up the construction materials to build our house."

"Have you picked out a place for the house, an exact location?"

"Yes, I think so. Actually it's almost right there where my dad and Uncle Jim found that decaying body almost two years ago. I can talk about it now and not be bothered by it as it did before. Big Bob Grumley is going to help my dad do the timbering, and after they clear out some of the old growth trees, the place will be a perfect location for a home. I have the floor plans in my head already. The downstairs will be fieldstone built into the hill itself, with a southern and western exposure. The ceilings will have heavy, oak crossbeams, and there will be fireplaces in the living room and the library. The upstairs will be wood with large thermal windows and a view of over 180 degrees."

"It sounds great. I wish I could see it sometime."

"As a matter of fact, Herbert and I have already discussed the possibility in some detail. Also my dad and I talked about it. We do want you to see the house and to visit us when you can, but not for five years."

"That is a strange invitation. Why the five-year wait?" Gerry asked. The horn of the diesel engine ahead suddenly sounded loud and foreboding as it signaled its warning to a distant country crossing. Soon the doppler effect of the railroad crossing bells could be heard as the train crossed the highway intersection. Cars and trucks backed up for almost a 100 feet on both sides of the train.

"It will take five years for all the emotional wounds to heal," Sharon answered. "Unintentionally, we may both have inflicted a lot of trauma on each other. We need time apart to get on with our separate lives. Then in five years, we can probably be friends again, good friends with no danger of becoming lovers. Herbert and I will be an old married couple and you may even have a start on the family you want."

"Is that a real invitation?"

"It certainly is. We want you to come back to Missouri from wherever you are to help Herbert and I celebrate our fifth wedding anniversary in our new house and happy home."

"I will be there, I promise you." Gerry replied.

As the Mainliner slowed and pulled into the Kansas City Station at 7:05 P.M., Gerry and Sharon waited in the vestibule between Pullman coaches. He held her suitcase and makeup kit as she scanned the crowd for Herbert. Dr. Frank was not sure how he would feel upon meeting Dr. Huntley under the circumstances of Sharon's new engagement. Gerry and Sharon were engaged the last time the two doctors had spoken to each other. Things had taken a fast change. He promised himself he would try his best to be friendly. Huntley had been Sharon's choice after Gerry broke off their relationship. He had no cause to be sad and should be happy for her. Apparently he would have to try harder.

"Hey. There he is," she yelled as she waved at him from the half-open door. "Wave now. Let him see how everything is resolved and we are all good friends."

Dr. Huntley stood at the far edge of the crowd dressed in gray slacks, a white shirt with a red tie, and a light tweed jacket. His slacks were neatly pressed, but his jacket was limp and wrinkled as if he had slept in it. He smiled and shouted over the heads of the rest of the people standing between him and the train. A switching engine moving slowly on the track behind him drowned out his voice. Finally realizing the futility of speech, he raised his hands over his head and clenched them in fists as a fighter might in celebration of victory.

"Okay, okay," said Gerry in a feigned voice of sarcasm, "even if he did finally win you from me, that type of public display over his victory is in poor taste. Doesn't that guy have any class?"

Sharon looked back over her shoulder at Gerry to make sure he was smiling when he said that. She laughed in relief to see that he was. "No, dummy. He is congratulating you on your victory. By seeing you here he knows you stopped the train, or at least the train did stop."

Gerry had nearly forgotten about his victory in stopping the train with the surprise of seeing Sharon and hearing all of her news. "Did you tell him of your emergency switch plan?"

"No, and he never asked. I just told him I wanted to be on the train and would be going up to Chicago on a Greyhound bus to catch it. I'm positive he must have wondered why, but he never asked. There is a lot to Herbert you don't know yet or appreciate. He is a much better person than you give him credit for. Believe me Gerry. I know. Now please try to be friendly."

"Don't worry, I will be friendly," Gerry forcibly replied as the porter arrived and asked him and Sharon to please step back so he could open the bottom half of the outside door. The porter then pulled the floor plate up to provide access to the descending steps of the coach. A rush of people already bottlenecked the small vestibule and crowded into the narrow coach corridor behind them.

The crowd awaiting the fast train's arrival quickly thinned out as mutual emotional greetings were made. Soon the debarking passengers and most of those who came to meet them walked down the depot platform towards the stairs and main concourse of the station.

Dr. Huntley came over to Gerry and Sharon, hugged Sharon and kissed her passionately. Sharon returned the kiss to Huntley who held her tightly with both of his arms around her back. Gerry could not help but notice the emotions of pleasure Herbert and Sharon shared upon seeing each other again. Suddenly Gerry felt better and started feeling good for both of them. Sharon had finally found her doctor for life and obviously Huntley was crazy about her.

After Sharon let go of him, Herbert reached out and grasped Gerry's right hand in a sincere and firm handshake. "So you did it Doctor, you really stopped this huge train in that small town. I'm proud of you. You're a credit to your college and your profession.

They will be talking about this in Essex for years to come. Congratulations."

"I guess the real congratulations of the day go to you and Sharon," Gerry answered. "Congratulations on your engagement and coming wedding. I'm happy for the both of you."

"I do hope you mean that Gerry," Dr. Huntley replied in a friendly voice. This was the first time he had ever called Dr. Frank by his first name. "It will mean a lot to both Sharon and me if you do."

"I do. I really mean it," Gerry repeated in as sincere a tone as he could muster from the moment. He wanted to put all thoughts of personal hostility behind him once and for all. Silently he promised himself to try to like Huntley. It would be tough, but he would try.

"And what about Sharon?" Herbert asked with a small smile on his face. "After being on the fast train for the past five hours with this dashing, adventurous young doctor do you still want to marry old conservative me?" Huntley asked seriously. A little bit of an awkward silence hung in the air. The persistent noise of the switching engine seemed exceptionally loud as it coupled to a long string of empty passenger cars on the opposite track. "I do," Sharon replied, "you are about to be stuck with me for the rest of your life, Herbert."

"Well in that case, let's make it official." Taking his brown leather pipe tobacco pouch from his right jacket pocket, he routed around in it for a moment and pulled out a hidden box from which he produced a new diamond engagement ring. Firmly grasping Sharon's left hand he carefully placed carefully on her fourth finger, a beautiful ring with a three-fourths karat, blue-white diamond with brilliant cut, set in a high four-prong Tiffany setting of 18 karat white gold.